Brotherhood of Iron

Published by Mission Point Press
2554 Chandler Lake Rd.
Traverse City, MI 49686
(231) 421-9513
www.MissionPointPress.com

ISBN: 978-1-943995-10-3

Printed in the United States of America.

BROTHERHOOD
OF IRON

FRANK P. SLAUGHTER

Mission Point Press

This book is dedicated to

Paul Castor
1921 – 2015
and
Leo A. LaFond, miner.
1944 – 2016
Because of their passion,
the history of mining in
Michigan's Upper Peninsula
lives on in the imaginations
of old and young alike.

Chapter 1

Robert Castor sat slouched in his chair with his elbows propped on the armrests, glaring over his interlocked fingers at the two people across from him. Sitting in one of the straight-back chairs in front of his desk was his second son Jacob, and in the other was Rosemarie, a young lady he and Elizabeth had taken in as a little girl. Her father had been killed in a mine cave-in, and her mother, already an alcoholic before the accident, suffered a breakdown and quietly slipped out of town in the middle of the night.

"Will you build a house, or do you have one in town lined up to purchase?" he asked, knowing full well that his son had no savings.

Jacob shifted nervously in his chair and glanced sideways at Rosemarie before answering. "Well, sir, Mrs. Sibly over on Second is trying to rent out her upstairs, and we thought we'd set up there until we can save up enough for our own place."

"What about furnishings? Undoubtedly at some point you will want to sit down or perhaps even lie down—to sleep.

Will your current nest egg cover a table and chairs, a bed, or dishes and silverware?"

"Rose says that Mother has been putting a few things aside to help her get started," said Jacob.

Robert spun his chair around and regarded his son with a look of disbelief. "Does your mother know that it is *you*, her own son, that Rose plans to marry?"

Jacob let the question hang in the air for a moment as he gathered himself for the inevitable exchange that was at the core of the problem.

Before he opened his mouth, Rosemarie took up the cause. "Sir, Jake and I were meant for each other. You must see *that*," she said, as she arched her back and pointed her chin at Robert, affecting her best look of indignation.

Like the main battery of a battleship training around to settle on a target, Robert slowly turned his head in Rosemarie's direction. He was not a strict disciplinarian by any means, but the murderous look he gave her would have given pause to even one of his hardened miners.

"It does not surprise me terribly that Jacob here is oblivious to the social implications of all this, but you, Rose, surely you must know how this will look."

Jacob began to speak, but Robert held him in check with the palm of his hand and continued to address the young woman. "We took you into this family and raised you as one of our own children, the daughter Mother always wanted," he said, firing a quick glance at his son. "*I* think of you as my daughter, for Christ's sake."

Robert's uncharacteristic profanity in front of his two children shocked Rosemarie into momentary silence, and whatever argument Jacob had prepared to further their case and perhaps even secure some financial assistance began to fall apart as his father's anger rose.

In spite of his displeasure, Robert couldn't help but feel a little pride in his son. Of the four boys, Jacob had been the one who always seemed to be under his mother's thumb. Up to this point in his life, he had never really crossed her in any significant way, and now, witnessing this bloom of personal courage was a pleasant surprise. It also answered the question of why Jacob was somewhat less than anxious to join the army and march off to war like all the rest of the boys in town, including his two younger brothers. Robert decided he would work them both over a bit more, probably not enough to satisfy Elizabeth but hopefully enough to make sure they were serious. He was determined not to make the same mistake that he had made with his oldest boy Bill. That sad experience had pointed up to him how little influence he still had in the lives of his grown sons, and it was a hard lesson that had left them estranged. Bill had shipped out from Marquette on one of Cliff's ore boats three years before, and they had not heard from him since.

" ... said she was going to hire two new operators for the switchboard. It would mean working the night shift, but I'm sure I could do it."

Rosemarie's words pulled Robert back to the moment, and he scrambled briefly to collect the missing pieces of her sentence without revealing his temporary lapse. Her enthusiasm left him a little disarmed, so he simply nodded and said, "If this war drags on much longer, you two will need all the income you can muster to make ends meet." To Rosemarie and Jacob those off-hand words, "you two" shone a soft light of acceptance on their plans of starting a life together, and the strained atmosphere in the room began to ease. There was a long pause as they all sat looking down at their hands, each reluctant to stir the pot.

Finally Robert broke the silence. "OK, I need to do some thinking. For now, this is between the three of us, understand? Let me deal with your mother." He gave Jacob a stern look and continued, "You make damn sure that none of this affects the performance of your duties at the office. I expect to get an early start in the morning; be ready to walk down the hill at 6:30 sharp." To Rosemarie he said, "You lie low and don't go talking to all your girlfriends about this, or your mother will be reading about it in tomorrow's *Iron Ore,* and I don't even want to think about that."

Rosemarie stood and shot a sideways look at Jacob, bringing him promptly to his feet. She came around the corner of the desk, bent at the waist, and placed a light kiss in the center of the shiny bald area above Robert's temple. "Thank you, Daddy," she whispered a little self-consciously, even though she had thought of him as her father since she was six years old. Robert glanced up at her with a weak smile and an offhand wave and swiveled his chair around to face the bay window that dominated the back wall of his office, glad to be done with this conversation. As soon as he heard Jacob pull the heavy oak door to his office closed behind him, he fished a gold watch out of the pocket of his waistcoat and noted the time. He figured he had perhaps fifteen minutes' solitude to put a spin on what had just transpired before Elizabeth would present herself to see how things stood.

The land the Castor house stood on was unlike that of any of their neighbors. Upon his death, Henry Bolton, a wealthy lumberman and dear friend of Robert's father, had bequeathed to him the house, the adjacent ten acres of land, and the majority ownership in an iron ore mine just north of the town of Ishpeming in the upper peninsula of Michigan. When Henry, or Uncle Henry, as Robert had always known him, purchased the land, there was no town to speak of, but as the demand for steel increased and mills began calling for enormous amounts of iron ore, people came to work in the mines and the town grew. New city streets and neighborhoods were platted nearly every year until eventually the small, single-dwelling lots wrapped right around the eastern side of his acreage. The most notable feature of the Castor land that set it apart from all its neighbors was its forest of magnificent virgin oak and maple trees. All the surrounding land, in fact, as far as the eye could see, had been logged off over the years to supply charcoal for the smelters and shoring for the numerous iron mines that dotted the countryside. Once the trees were gone, a combination of dry, hot summers and raging brush fires had conspired to erase any evidence that they had ever been there. The townsfolk, the ones who considered themselves on Henry's "good" side, and there weren't many, always seemed to know when one of the trees was dead or dying and would offer their services to remove it. Uncle Henry was a crusty old coot, and no one dared cut so much as a stick of firewood off of his land without express permission. Robert smiled to himself as precious memories of his uncle and his adopted father Will Castor came welling up. He imagined Henry would be pleased to know how much he valued this gift of trees and the sweet images of his boyhood that lived there.

Robert swiveled his chair away from the window and pulled himself up to his desk in preparation for the arrival of his wife, Elizabeth. He knew she considered him something of a dreamer, and it wouldn't do to have her catch him gazing out the window when important family work was pending. His timing, at least on this day, was good, and just as he settled in, he heard a soft knock at the door. Robert didn't bother to respond, for he knew the door would open anyway before he could get a word out. George, his German Shorthair Pointer, who up until that moment had managed to sleep soundly through the family crisis, suddenly leapt to his feet barking wildly and lunged at the big window. Robert spun in his chair just in time to see an unconcerned black squirrel lope across the short area of open ground between the house and the woods.

"Damn it, George, you scared the crap out of me; now go lie down," said Robert under his breath. The dog ignored him for a moment and then cast a dirty look his way before lying back down beside the desk.

Elizabeth was not a striking beauty, but at forty-four she still commanded her share of second looks. Unlike most of the ladies in her social circle, she had maintained a trim feminine figure, although at the moment it was effectively disguised in a fashionable, nearly straight-up-and-down, high-waisted mauve walking dress. She was tall, always perfectly turned out, and she carried herself with an air of confidence that most men found a little disconcerting. She was also something of a contradiction. On the one hand, she was inflexible to a fault about breaking or even bending rules of any kind, be they the Ten Commandments or the list of household chores to be performed by each member of the family she kept posted on the kitchen wall next to the back door. When Rosemarie and the boys were youngsters and one of them expressed displeasure with any part of their meal, by household law they would be required to remain at the table until they had forced down a double portion. Over the years, the family dogs, having no problem with broccoli or carrots, had benefited the most from this practice. The other hand, the one Robert found most endearing, was her innate ability to find fun in places or situations that were invisible to the ordinary eye. She could invent games on the spur of the moment that would delight the children and her too, for that matter, sometimes using nothing more than buttons and matchsticks, and she loved to win. At such times it was not uncommon for her to bounce in her chair and clap her hands in unbridled glee, shameless in her self-satisfaction.

Robert looked up from his desk and the pretense of reading the newspaper, certain that *fun* was not in his immediate future. Elizabeth took the chair that had been occupied by Jacob just moments ago, carefully smoothing the back of her dress as she lowered herself onto the sculpted oak seat. Robert avoided looking directly at her as she dabbed at her nose with the linen handkerchief she kept tucked inside the cuff of her dress sleeve. Finally she dropped her hands in her lap with a sigh and said, "It's bad enough that you talk to that dog as if he understands every word you say, but then to top it all off you have to cuss in front of me. Well, was I right? Do they want to get married?"

Robert nodded almost imperceptibly and said, "Yes, dear, on both counts."

"And of course you put an end to this nonsense and made it clear that there would be no wedding?" said Elizabeth as she settled a look on Robert that made him clench his butt cheeks. The long silence between them said it all.

Finally, with the air of a man who knows he's already dead and has nothing to lose, Robert spoke. "I rattled their cage enough to see how serious they are, and I'm satisfied that they will do this no matter what we say. I think you should be very careful how you proceed—push too hard and you will only push them out the door, maybe even out of the state. The chances for your dream of rocking grandbabies in your arms will be cut by half." This last statement was a little harsh, but Robert was proud of himself for having put it together on the fly and for having the guts to speak it. Actually, it was more like reckless-ness, something he came by naturally.

"Perfect, Rob!" Elizabeth said as she abruptly stood up. "I see that once again you have gone soft on our children and you cannot be counted on to uphold proper decorum in this house-hold." She was mad and would have her pound of flesh, but Robert could tell he had given her pause with the comment about grandbabies.

Before she reached the door he said, "And Lizzie, Heddy Steiner is going to hire two girls to work nights on the phone company switchboard. I recommend you use your considerable influence to make sure that Rose gets one of those jobs. Perhaps a dose of real life will cool her off a bit."

Elizabeth paused for a moment with her hand on the doorknob but didn't turn around. Finally she jerked the door open and hurried out, pulling it gently closed behind her. Slamming a door for any reason in her domain was strictly against the rules.

Robert leaned over the left arm of his chair and retrieved a bottle of Johnnie Walker Black from the small bottom drawer of his desk. Not bothering with a glass, he tipped the bottle up and took a generous pull, the long satisfying burn having the desired effect of derailing his temper. His earlier comment to Elizabeth about losing touch with Rosemarie and Jacob came back to him, and he thought of his mother. In his mind's eye she stood, arms folded against her apron, on the front porch of the old Monroe Center farmhouse where he grew up. A pure and simple sadness showed through on her brave face as he backed out of the drive and waved goodbye. That was the last time he had seen her, the last time he had leaned in to kiss her lightly on the cheek, the last time he had breathed in her timeless fragrance, a fragrance that wound its way through all memories of his youth and held them together. He could smell it still.

Robert gently placed the whiskey bottle back in its drawer and slid it closed. He picked up the copy of the *Iron Ore* from the top of his desk and turned halfway to the great window for light. The headline read:

MAJOR HUN OFFENSIVE — PARIS THREATENED

The newsprint blurred as he tried to recall the date of the last letter from Johnny and Matt, posted just before they boarded the transport for France with the 5th Marines. As much as he wished it otherwise, he realized that his two youngest boys were most likely there already and quite possibly in harm's way. He

Great irregular patches of white chaux had fallen off the face of the house and the high walls that surrounded the courtyard, exposing courses of tan, flat rock beneath. In the center of the courtyard, there was a dried-up fountain with a bullet-pocked statue, the ubiquitous peeing fat boy, inextricably wrapped in creeping wild grape. Except for random clumps of black-eyed Susan, the gardens that lined the perimeter of the courtyard and front of the house were overgrown with wild mustard and cornflower.

John ducked through the narrow back door of the stable and immediately side-stepped with his back to the outside wall, skirting the large, round area of muck where the manure pile had stood when the Marines first took possession of the estate. Even though the manure had since been removed, water from the last rain had settled in the depression, reviving the offensive odor in spades and creating a disgusting trap for sleepy Marines making a midnight trip to the head. As John automatically looked down at his feet while moving along the wall, he noted the profusion of white cigarette butts that followed the foundation of the stable. Absentmindedly he patted his shirt pocket. Two rusty, ten-foot-high wrought-iron gates hung open in the archway, which was flanked on each side by a parade-ground-ready Marine from 3rd platoon. To relieve their boredom, they snapped to attention, bringing their immaculate Springfields crisply to order arms and moving their left hands smartly to their right side, palm-down, in salute.

John noted with professional interest that the first joint of their forefingers touched the barrel precisely between the stacking swivel and the bayonet lug. "As you were, assholes," he said, returning their salute with a little smile as if it were an everyday occurrence.

John walked down to the creek and picked up a well-worn cart path that would eventually take him to the edge of the small village to the west and his favorite place for solitude. It was a beautiful wooded spot just below the crest of the gradually sloping south bank of the stream, and this time of year it was covered with bluebells, dotted here and there with clumps of soft, yellow primrose. Sometimes when John was lost in thought, the afternoon sun would stream through holes in the treetops and splash the carpet of wildflowers with patches of brilliance, creating such a vision of beauty that everything else faded into the background. Behind him, just back from the brow of the riverbank, was the blanchisserie where the women of the village came to do their laundry.

John had discovered quite by accident that it was somehow deeply comforting to close his eyes and listen to the women talk as they went about their work. He knew only a few words of their language, mostly learned from the French veterans who had been instructing them in the art of war as practiced at the front: portez vos masque a gaz—put on your gas mask, or baïonnette au fusil—fix bayonets, but their phrases, the rhythms of their conversations intertwined with feminine laughter and set against the backdrop of the birds, the wind moving in the treetops, and the constant murmur of the river, touched a soothing chord deep inside him.

As he looked on, a young lady carrying a dented galvanized pail passed close by on her way to retrieve clean water from the river. She glanced his way briefly, as if feeling eyes upon her, but his forest green uniform blended so well with the spring groundcover that he went unnoticed. The girl was wearing a cream-colored, loose-fitting blouse and a full burgundy skirt cinched tight at the waist with a wide belt. Both garments carried wet places from splashed wash water. A few strands of loose auburn curls that had escaped her ponytail hung across her face, lending a slightly disheveled cast to her beauty. As she passed on the sloping, uneven ground, he could see the subtle side-to-side sway of her breasts beneath the gauzy fabric of her blouse, and moments later a hint of soap came to him on the light air. The girl set the bucket down on the bank of the creek, gathered her skirts around her pale thighs, and waded out into the water. She stood for a moment with her face uplifted and eyes closed, letting the sparkling stream cool her calves while sunbeams dodged around swaying branches and brushed moving patterns of shade and light across her face. John lay back and closed his eyes too, capturing the moment and listening to the stream as it bubbled over distant memories of long-ago days, only the texture rising now. He knew that soon his unit would move closer to the front and he would never see this place again, but today he embraced it, or perhaps it embraced him. It was a perfect moment, unexpected and rare, created by the confluence of ordinary things. In his mind he would return here many times in the days ahead.

Weighing heavily on John's mind these days, as indeed it was on all the Marines, was the prospect of going into battle. Their first months in France had been spent as stevedores unloading ships, moving mountains of American supplies around in warehouses and filling the role of military police in the port cities. Not exactly what they had signed on for, but eventually as the army had become resigned to having Marines in their midst, they had moved further east into the countryside and had begun to train in earnest. There was much for the Americans to learn. A recurring theme was long marches in full field packs and rifles in all kinds of weather. They dug practice trenches and filled them in again, bayonetted armies of burlap enemy soldiers, learned how to load and fire the different kinds of machine guns they were likely to encounter on the battlefield, and of course did all these things while wearing a gas mask.

A general order had been issued stating that gas masks would be worn in the "ready" position at all times; five seconds or less, they were told, is all they would have. The device was of British design and contained in a small canvas bag that was suspended from a neck strap to lie flat against the chest. When the alert was given, the soldier would rip off his helmet, open the bag, pull out the mask, and pull it over his head. Inside the mask was the end of a long rubber breathing tube that the wearer inserted in his mouth. The other end of the tube was connected to a canister of neutralizing agent that remained in the canvas bag. The last step and the one everyone hated most was placing the integral metal clip over the bridge of the nose, effectively forcing the wearer to breathe through the tube. On one of their road marches, they had passed a file of gassed French soldiers walking the other way, each one grasping the shoulder of the man in front of him. All wore dirty white bandages wrapped around their heads to cover their suppurating eyes, and their mouths gaped as they struggled to suck air through swollen tracheas. The smell of chlorine was so strong it burned in the noses of the Marines from across the road. No one complained after that.

"Where the hell have you been, Johnny?" said Matt as he stood up, brushing pieces of straw from his uniform pants. "Carter is blotto again and feeling generous. We all got liberty till midnight and I want to hit the Y. You in?"

John usually tagged along with Matt and his bunch when they went on liberty, but just to keep his younger brother out of trouble and to make sure he was available for morning roll-call. They generally hit the closest YMCA hut for whatever non-army food items and entertainment might be available, and, as Matt liked to put it, to sniff out the local talent. John was shy around women and usually content to sit back and watch his brother work, unless he was needed to entertain a tagalong girlfriend. Matt's first runner-up was generally flawed in one way or another, but John didn't mind. He had come to believe that he was just too self-conscious to attract beautiful young ladies out looking for a challenge. One time back at school in Minnesota, a girl had managed to sneak him into her dormitory room, and as the evening culminated in the act, he had asked her if she was all right so many times, especially during the critical moment when she became vocal, that she got in a huff and he had to climb back out the window in his drawers—and minus one shoe that he never saw again. Matt, on the other hand, had that smooth self-confidence that women found irresistible. He would spin incredible and sometimes wonderfully complex webs of bullshit that seemed to capture the imaginations of aspiring young women every time. While Matt and his lady-of-the-moment were off to parts unknown, John was content to indulge his two major weaknesses, billiards and chocolate. The first had become increasingly hard to satisfy as they got closer to the front, but the second seemed to be available, in one form or another, in most villages they passed through. Wartime shortages had affected the ingredients available to the French in many parts of the country but overall the quality was still superior to chocolate issued by the army.

"Shit, Matt, I just came from there."

"Awe, come on, Johnny, that little bird with the braids has got it bad for you, and besides, I heard they got some new records. It may be my last chance to shake a tail feather. If I get hit when we get to the front and can't—"

"Oh you dumbass, Matt, I'll go." John said, cutting him off. "If I get hit, you just remember how you tortured me my whole life."

The YMCA, at least in this little village, was not a hut at all but a former general merchandise shop that had closed shortly after the beginning of the war, its owner swept up by the vast French war machine and his wife, unable to manage alone with five young children, having moved the family west to her mother's house. The shelves that once held colorful tins, cardboard boxes, and bottles of all shapes and sizes, now held a respectable array of English language books in genres likely to attract young soldiers. The merchandise gondolas had been removed from the center of the store, and in their place were rows of benches and long, narrow tabletops arranged parallel to the front wall. On the end of each table was a shallow box containing stationery, envelopes, and sharpened pencils to encourage the soldiers to keep in touch with their families. A long counter spanned the width of the building, creating a back room that held a small kitchen and sleeping quarters for the YMCA workers. Next to the front door sat an open wooden crate that held stacks of dog-eared magazines, some dating back to the previous year.

Matt pushed through the door first, followed by John and two other members of their squad, Jim Donovan and Stan Zywicki. Mr. Feccelli, the hut secretary, waved over his shoulder in acknowledgment as he thumbed through a stand of records next to the gramophone by the front window. The on-duty canteen girl, who had been sitting on a bench across from the counter, stood up and brushed crumbs into her hand from the table before heading to her station. The homespun aroma of coffee and fresh baked chocolate-chip cookies filled the space, and to the Marines, a long time separated from home, the aura of women was also present. Except for two army ambulance drivers in the corner playing checkers and chain smoking, they were the only customers.

Matt went over to check the new records and help Mr. Feccelli make an appropriate music selection while John and the other two men stepped up to the counter.

"Hey, Teach, you got any tin you could spare? I'm down to my last smoke," said Jim.

"Yeah, just keep your shirt on a minute," said John, a little distracted by the radiant smile offered up by the girl behind the counter. She was indeed the one with the long, single braid of strawberry-blond hair that ended just above her waist. Short and of sturdy Scandinavian stock, she was wholesome but not overweight. Her fair, round face carried a perfect natural blush, and her smiling, pale blue eyes radiated a sincere kindness and attentiveness that struck John as something more than just regular fare.

"Good evening, miss. We'll take four coffees and four cookies, oh, and a couple packs of Luckys; better make that three," he said with a quick side glance at Jim.

"Four!" yelled Matt from across the room. John shrugged and grinned at the girl.

"The cigarettes are fifteen cents each," she said as she pushed the four packs across the counter at John. "You boys have a seat and I'll bring the coffee and cookies over to you."

"Don't charge 'em for the cookies, Mary Ann," said Feccelli over his shoulder. "Might as well use 'em up before we close."

"Thank you kindly, miss," said John. Then he added, "Mary Ann," setting the correct change on the counter. Mary Ann raked the coins over the edge and into her hand and then looked up at John with an openness that left little doubt as to her interest and said "Teach? I've never heard that name before."

"My name's John Castor—"

Just then, Matt walked up and cut in the conversation as he put his hand on John's shoulder. "We call him Teach because even though he's big and don't look particularly bright, he's the smartest fella any of us knows. Although that distinction is somewhat suspect since it has come to light that he joined the Marine Corps of his own free will."

"Mary Ann, meet my little brother Matt, black sheep of the Castor family," said John by way of introduction.

Mary Ann regarded Matt with a noncommittal look for a moment and then with a wan smile said, "Pleased to meet you, Matt."

The shot across his bow was plain, but he chose to ignore it, as John knew he would. "The pleasure is all mine, Mary Ann." As if on cue, Mr. Feccelli set the gramophone needle down on the surface of a record, and "The Darktown Strutters' Ball" filled the room. "I have a favor to ask. For all my big brother's wonderful qualities, he is, alas, a very poor dancer. If he will permit me, and if you will allow, I would love to have a dance."

Up until this moment, there had been two other conversations going on in the room, but they abruptly ceased to await the response from the young woman. Many of the hundreds of soldiers who came into the YMCA every week assumed that Mary Ann's fresh-faced naiveté marked her as an easy touch, but that was certainly not the reality. She had been in France working as a canteen girl for nearly nine months and in that time had heard every imaginable variation on a theme known to the A.E.F. Matt's approach was more direct than most, but still, she recognized the type and simply said, "I'm working," before turning away to fetch the coffee and a plate of cookies.

Matt shrugged and took a seat next to Jim, outwardly showing no more disappointment than if he had rolled boxcars coming out on a pass. John wasn't fooled. He sat across from his brother, shook a Lucky part way out of the pack, and offered it up. Matt stopped his subtle movements to the rhythm of the music and locked eyes with John as he dipped the end of the cigarette in the flare of a match. In that fleeting connection they savored the covenant of brotherhood, in their case enduring and pure, a bond born in chemistry but forged by their young lives.

In a low voice John said, "It's OK if I win once in a while." Matt grinned and blew smoke toward the ceiling. "How do you do that?" he said.

"Do what?"

"Always know what I'm thinking, even before I know it."

True to their ritual, John grinned and tapped his chest above the left breast pocket of his field coat.

Suddenly Matt looked up at the window and a moment later, without a word, bolted for the door. Once again, the room fell silent and all eyes followed Matt's hasty exit; even Mary Ann observed as she absentmindedly distributed the cookies and mugs of coffee to the three remaining Marines.

The music ended and the large dull brass horn of the gramophone began to issue hisses and pops at regular intervals as the needle settled into the locked groove. The door opened and in stepped two young ladies from the village followed by Matt. They stood there for a moment in awkward silence, scanning the room and searching their memories for what it used to look like before the war when their mothers brought them along on shopping trips to carry groceries. John's eyes steadied on the woman with the auburn hair, the woman from the stream. She was wearing the same maroon skirt and cream-colored blouse as earlier in the day, but she had added a black tatted shawl that accomplished its purpose of dressing up her look. Her shorter companion had bobbed blond hair with dark roots and wore a plain, straight, pale green dress, belted loose and low on her waist. Her dress, perhaps a size too large, gave her a shapeless look that seemed well suited to her rather uninteresting face.

Matt side-stepped from behind them and headed for the gramophone to start the record over.

Mr. Feccelli, who had taken a seat with the ambulance drivers and was no doubt feeling them out concerning the state of their spiritual lives, turned to the commotion at the door. "Whoa,

whoa there," he shouted as he jumped to his feet. "You can't bring them in here. YMCA rules—no local women allowed for any reason," he said, now holding up his hands palm out. "I'm warning you, Marine, associating with French women will get you trouble in heaps, in more ways than one."

Matt had his back turned as he tried to blow a clump of dust from the gramophone needle, and the only sign that he heard Feccelli's rant was a slight pause in his movements. He set the needle down on the record and turned the crank a few times, starting a flow of music that immediately began to erode the tense atmosphere of the room, and then he reached over the machine and threw open the casement windows. The two French women were already part way out the door by the time Matt reached them. He turned and flashed a big grin and a wink at his brother and then stepped out into the street.

Before the song ended everyone except Mr. Feccelli was crowded together at the window, watching the show. John found it surprising that a young lady from a sleepy little farming village in the French countryside would know the Grizzly Bear dance, but not only did the lady with auburn hair know the steps, she was easily a match for Matt's savoir-faire. They began by facing one another, each eyeing the other and circling slowly. Suddenly they reared up, raised their hands high and formed claws, and gave out their best "grrrrrrrrrrr," much as you would imagine real grizzlies fighting in the wild would do. From there the dance was on in earnest. When the record ended they were dancing chest to chest, arms upheld, hands making bear claws and hopping from one foot to another. Stan reached in front of the others and quickly set the needle down at the beginning of the record, anxious to keep the fun going. Everyone was grinning now, especially Matt, who was enjoying the French girl's ample bosom pressed against the front of his field coat.

John smiled and shook his head. Leaning out the window, he yelled, "Jesus, Matt, people will think you're retarded!"

His brother threw his head back and laughed without missing a move or disengaging. "I miss Mom too," Matt yelled back with a knowing look.

Chapter 3

T he Brill Interurban coach was not quite half full for the early morning run between Cleveland and Detroit, allowing the passengers to distance themselves from one another and claim sole occupancy of a bench seat, if so desired. The car had been elegantly appointed when it was built in 1912, but with the dramatic increase in working class traffic spurred on by factories feeding the nation's hunger for automobiles, and now by the war effort, it had been pressed into hard service. The seats were leather and still comfortable, although a bit lumpy and ripped in places, and the deep red, brocaded fabric of the headliner sagged away from the arched ceiling supports above the windows. Pages of newspaper, discarded food wrappers, and on this end of the coach, flattened white cigarette butts, littered the floor. Humid air warmed by steam radiators filled the interior and carried the sweet metallic smell of ozone from arcing electricity as the troller skipped over joints in the overhead line. Riding the Interurban had once been an experience in itself, but now it was just a way to get from one place to another, a ride to be endured. As the car sped west toward Detroit over the uneven roadbed, it swayed side to side in a leisurely motion that lulled its passengers as they stared out into the gloom.

In the second row of seats, on the right side next to the window, sat a disheveled, twenty-four-year-old deckhand from the steamer SS *Pontiac*, which at that very moment was up-bound in the west end of Lake Erie. Through half-open eyes, eyes that felt gritty and too big for their sockets, Bill Castor peered out at his immediate surroundings. A few feet ahead of him he could see the motorman and conductor through the open door in the rear bulkhead of the cab. Like actors in a silent movie, they shared coffee from a battered thermos bottle in the dim, flickering light. Both were unkempt by the early hour and turned out in shopworn, ill-fitting uniforms. Bill noted their stolen glances at the woman in the seat across the aisle and could have easily put words to the movements of their lips, but what ordinarily might have been amusing fell flat on his torpid mind. The woman, perhaps in her late twenties, sat straight-backed with her head canted forward and hands resting in her lap. She was dressed too warmly for the season in a black wool coat and close-fitting long dark skirt that gave away her skinny legs and made her seem frail. On her head she wore a gray cloche hat, stove in slightly in the back and pulled down so that it hid all but the upturned fringe of her bobbed hair. She had been riding in this position for hours, not reading or looking around, just darting quick, furtive glances out of the corner of her eyes. She made him uneasy, so he turned away and sagged against the window. Once again his thoughts turned to his current predicament and the hope that he could get back aboard his ship and still have a job.

From the depot at the corner of Jefferson and Woodward it was just a short walk down to the Detroit River front and the spot where he hoped to find the mail boat tied up. By now his youthful confidence was beginning to rebound, and he felt a little better about life. He checked his watch and then looked north toward Cadillac Square. From where he stood the whole world seemed to be in motion on the broad expanse of Woodward Avenue. Automobiles and trucks of every description swirled around him, and clanging streetcars rumbled along the sweeping, shiny, steel ribbons of inlay. Here and there, a tired looking draft horse hitched to a wagon stood like a rock in the swirling river of machines. In the midst but rising above all was a bright yellow cupola on a pedestal that contained a traffic officer. He alone held sway over the chaos by rotating the red and green stop/go sign on the roof of his perch. Cold air funneled up from the river through the maze of masonry canyons and held the raw exhaust fumes low and thick.

The young man stood there for several minutes watching the seemingly endless progression of vehicles when through the intersection and slightly east he spotted a tall, vertical, lighted sign with the words "Gaiety Theater" and underneath, just above a gaudy portico, a smaller sign that said "Burlesque." It was a legendary institution among Great Lakes seamen, and he instinctively patted his pants for his pocketbook before he remembered the grim nature of his current state of his affairs. The Midnight Maidens would have to wait for another time, he thought, referring to the billboard on the face of the building. With any luck, the cash he had left in his pocket after the extravagance of the night before would be enough to buy a ride out to the *Pontiac* when she passed by. That was the plan, but there were a lot of variables.

As he approached the rickety-looking dock, pushed up at irregular intervals by many winters of shifting ice, he surveyed the sleek motor vessel. She was wood, maybe sixty feet, he figured, and narrow of beam. Having seen her only from the deck of his ship, looking down from high above, he was surprised to find that she had more the look of a nimble yacht than that of a workboat. The stern carried the name *Betty M II*. Leaning on the back two legs of a dining room chair was a lanky, bearded, middle-aged man with a sun-faded Navy non-com's hat squashed down on the back of his head. He was holding a recently emptied can of Campbell's Pork and Beans in his lap and licking the back of a big silver spoon as he gazed off into the distance, deep in thought. Finally he tossed the spoon into the empty can and squinted up at his visitor.

"Howdy do" was all he said.

"Ahoy there, sir. Might you be the captain?"

The man he was talking to looked him up and down before responding. "That would be correct. Chief Boatswain's Mate David McKay, US Naval Reserve."

"Pleased to meet you. I'm Bill Castor off the *Pontiac*."

McKay was a quick study and smiled as he said, "Went on a little toot and missed your boat, did ya?"

All the clever reasons Bill had cooked up for why he needed a ride out to his ship went out the window, so he just shrugged and nodded his head. "Is it that obvious?" he said.

"I can smell the booze on ya all the way over here, and you don't look too perky, if you don't mind my saying so."

Bill's temper flared and that, too, was plainly visible on his face as he fought down the urge to speak.

"Oh, don't get all bent out of shape, son. I'm just giving ya a little shit. Been on your end of the stick a few times myself, truth be told, but don't take me wrong, I ain't touched a drop in over four years. Good God almighty, the old woman would have my nuts tacked up on the side of the barn."

Bill forced a smile and said, "I only got twelve bucks left after last night. Any way that might get me a ride out to my ship?"

"Uncle Sam is paying me to run the mail out there whether you're aboard or not, so yes, I'll give you a lift, and no, I don't want your money. You just make sure you don't get cold feet when we come alongside, 'cause I can't wait while you make up your mind. I 'spect your captain will hold off till he clears Port Huron before he takes on ballast, and that makes for a long climb from my deck to his. Just giving you a little warning. Come on aboard and make yourself comfortable. It'll be a little bit yet."

Bill looked down from the dock and decided he liked this man. With no more thought, he hesitated a moment to time the rocking of the boat and then jumped down to the deck and sprawled out on a stack of braided hemp fenders. He was below the bulkhead out of the chill river wind, and the sun warmed the dark wool of his pea coat, making him drowsy. He pulled down the bill of his cap and surrendered to the gentle motion of the *Betty M.*

It was a tricky business for the captain of the mail boat. He had to first match the speed of the big ship as it pounded away against the current of the river and then carefully sidle in, jockeying the throttle all the way to resist the suction of the huge ship's hull and make a soft landing. Once the mail boat was riding on her fenders up against the ship, a snap-line would be dropped down and the *Pontiac*'s mail would be hoisted up in a white pail that bore the label "US Post Office" in crude freehand letters.

Bill hung back on the port railing, watching events unfold, but he was ready to make himself useful if need be. This was a well-rehearsed and carefully choreographed endeavor but not a sure thing, by any means. As the *Betty M* closed the last few feet to the towering steel hull of the *Pontiac*, a long, rickety wood extension ladder was dropped over the side by Bill's crewmates and secured to the deck edge with the end of a heaving line. Bill knew the old man must have been watching with binoculars from the pilothouse and must have seen him riding out with the mail boat. He took the fact that the captain had ordered up the ladder as a positive sign. Maybe things would be OK after all.

Aboard the *Betty M*, tension continued to build as McKay closed with the *Pontiac*. Even a slight miscalculation or mechanical failure at this point meant almost certain death in the icy water from a swipe by the huge, partially exposed propeller. The sound from the *Betty M*'s big Gray Marine engines had been a deep exhilarating rumble when they started out, but now in close to the wall of steel, it was transformed into an overpowering, bellowing roar. Still gripping the wheel in his left hand and the throttle in his right, McKay leaned out over the deck as far as he could and looked up to judge the progress of the mail transfer. The white bucket, empty now, was just passing the halfway point in its descent and was sailing aft in the wind. He straightened up and looked over his left shoulder for the young deckhand.

Bill knew his moment was at hand and started for the narrow starboard deck as soon as McKay pointed to him. He was determined not to hesitate or show any outward signs of fear, even though he was having some serious misgivings as he stood gripping the bottom of the ladder and looking up at the small pale faces of his crewmates, who were watching him from high above. As the river water funneled into the tight space between the two hulls, it was churned into a fast-moving, wild torrent that dipped and careened over the railing of the mail boat, soaking Bill's pants from the knee down and chilling the bare skin of his face and hands. He turned and nodded a "thank you" to McKay and then stepped on the ladder and started up.

Bill lifted his leg over the lifeline and dropped down on the *Pontiac*'s deck, re-entering the world he was familiar with. His fellow deckhands, "Old Ray" and Charlie, were there to greet him, as was the third mate.

"Well, look who's here, Ray. I do believe it's Fuzzy, our long-lost drinking buddy, or should I say *ladies' man*," said Charlie. "No use trying to sneak a six- hundred-foot steamboat out of

Cleveland, I guess. He just keeps turning up like a bad penny no matter how hard we try to get rid of him."

"Looks like a dick without a head, if you ask me," said Ray as he turned away and headed forward. Bill started to help Charlie secure the ladder but stopped and turned sharply when he felt someone grip his upper arm. He was a little taken aback to find the gaunt, pinched face of the third mate just inches from his own.

"You get forward and clean yourself up and then get your ass up to the pilothouse. The captain would like to have a *word* with you concerning your immediate future," he said with a sneer.

Bill jerked his arm away without breaking eye contact and replied, "You ever put a hand on me again I'll break your arm and then I'll file a grievance on your skinny ass." The two men continued to stare at each other for a moment while Charlie made himself look busy, lashing the ladder to the rail.

"You better toe the line, Castor. I'm watching you," said the mate over his shoulder as he too started forward, no doubt to whine to the Old Man. Bill deliberately turned the other way and headed aft to the galley, hoping to find a leftover sandwich.

"Good Luck, my friend," Charlie called after him. Bill just waved his arm without turning around.

Chapter 4

THE ROOSEVELT
ISHPEMING, MI
JUNE 1, 1918

"What'll it be, Mr. Castor?" said the day barkeep of the Roosevelt.

"Damn it, Penny, how long have you known me? I been coming in here for over ten years, sitting on the same end of the bar and having the same thing for lunch every day, and you still ask me what I'm having. I'm starting to figure that maybe you aren't the sharpest tool in the shed, if you know what I mean. Here you go, Penny. I'll have my corned beef on sourdough instead of rye today. Now that'll give you something to talk about with the little woman over dinner tonight."

Penny looked over his shoulder at Robert as he finished drawing off a dark draft beer into a heavy, ceramic, German-style mug. He deftly flicked the head into the sink beneath the tap with a white bone foam scraper and walked down to the end of the bar where Robert sat, studying his own reflection in the massive mirror that hung behind the bar. Penny pulled the towel off his shoulder and wiped the bar in front of his cranky patron and then leaned in and in a low voice said, "Would you like that sandwich shoved up your ass sideways or will it be straight in for you today, Rob?"

Robert threw his head back and laughed hard. "Damn it, Penny, you're a good man! I don't give a doodlyshit what all the decent folks in town say about you."

"Hear anything from your boys?"

"Naw, I may never hear from the oldest again, at least not until he grows out of thinking I'm the dumbest son of a bitch that ever walked the face of the earth. I get my news about him from the Cliffs shipping office down in Cleveland. Johnny Johnson, skipper of the *Pontiac*, is keeping an eye on him for me. Johnny and Matt are somewhere in France now. Last letter we got had so many lines crossed out by the censors we couldn't make much out of it except that the weather was hot. They say those German spies are everywhere nowadays."

"I hear the miners in here grumbling about working with Germans. Some of those families been living around here for years and I never thought about them being any different," said Penny.

"To hear Elizabeth tell it, those *ooh la la* French ladies are the real threat. They bump uglies at the drop of a hat with every low-life that comes along and then turn around and give our boys the clap."

Penny chuckled and said, "Caught a dose myself down in Havana when I was in the Navy. Thought my dick was going to fall off."

Both men laughed. Robert got a faraway look on his face and said, "I had a case of the crabs once when I first moved up here. A trammer I was working with told me how to get rid of 'em with lighter fluid. Worked like a charm."

Penny's curiosity had been piqued, but he sniffed a joke coming. "So how does that work, Rob?" he said, taking the bait.

"Well, I'm glad you asked, my friend. You simply shave one side of your pubes, either the right or left side, don't make any difference which, but you only do one side. Then you squirt lighter fluid on the other side. Oh, and you gotta be real careful not to get any on your nuts or you'll be high-stepping all the way to Lake Superior." Robert tried hard but unsuccessfully to suppress a giggle. "The rest is simple. Just put a match to the lighter fluid and stab those little bastards with an ice pick when they run out!" With that, Robert burst out laughing and slapped the bar a couple of times with the flat of his hand. "Damn, that was a good one! Had ya going, Penny."

Penny rolled his eyes and headed back to the kitchen.

Robert heard the spring-loaded front screen door slam back against the door jamb and looked up in the mirror to see who the newcomer was. He wasn't surprised to see his son Jacob standing just inside the entranceway, blinking and waiting for his eyes to adjust to the dim interior of the room. When the young man could see well enough to recognize the form of his father leaning on the bar, he quickly crossed the worn plank floor, boards creaking with every footfall.

"Mr. Mather's assistant just phoned the office and left this message for you. Thought you'd want it right away," said Jacob.

Robert had been expecting a summons to "The Cottage" for the last several days and gave the note a cursory glance for day and time before handing it back to his son. "I think the home office is getting a little nervous about the Barnes-Hecker, maybe that strike over on the Keweenaw, too," he said as he turned back to the bar. "Want something to eat?"

Jacob thought about it for a minute before he remembered the food Rosemarie had packed for him sitting on his desk in an old miner's lunch pail that had once belonged to his father. He opened his mouth to turn the offer down, and then the thought of what he might find when he opened the pail flashed through his mind, and he quickly climbed up on a bar stool. Mrs. Palmer's little dog, who often slept on the sidewalk in front of the store next to the office, liked Rosemarie's cooking and was in line to have a pretty good afternoon.

With conscious effort Robert pulled his gaze down to the dark walnut tabletop yet again and tried to focus on the ink-smudged report on top of the stack of papers in front of him. This time, as with all previous attempts, his eyes were drawn into the pleasing deep current of wood grain that flowed through the table, and inexorably his thoughts were once again swept out through the window and over the rooftops of Ishpeming to the towering monolith of the Cliff Shafts mine, his mine. Across the table, Ed Puech, superintendent of the Salisbury mine, droned on and on about the unforeseeable obstacles that had prevented him from converting his operation from steam to electricity in a timely fashion. Robert thought to himself that surely he must be the most boring son of a bitch on the entire Marquette range. Even Mr. Mather was beginning to tire of the exercise, but preferring subtlety, his first attempts to stem the prodigious flow of bullshit had yielded mixed results.

The table this small gathering of mine bosses occupied was round to match the round porch-like room that hung over the bluff from the back of The Cottage, as it was called. The Cottage was the Mather summer home and sometimes company headquarters during its owner's numerous working vacations on the iron range. The nearly 360-degree view from the tall windows would have been truly spectacular before iron ore mining had transformed the countryside. Now the vista was dotted with rusty headframe towers, each attended by piles of red tailings and most issuing plumes of steam and dirty wood smoke. From this elevation the numerous railroad cuts in the hilly terrain appeared as random elliptical red scars in the dark green vegetation, and on the western horizon, a larger oblong wound marked an open pit mine where two steam shovels sent up puffs of white exhaust steam like Indian smoke signals every time they took purchase in the easy, low-grade ore.

For a decade or more, Cleveland Cliffs Iron Company had been engaged in acquiring not only the active mines but also the mineral-rich land holdings of these small companies that eventually would insure a path for its future growth. In 1913, Robert's mine, the Bolton, had been bought out, along with two others in the North Lake area. By 1918, Cleveland Cliffs dominated the entire Marquette range and had its center of operations in Ishpeming. With the takeover of his mine, Robert went from mine owner to mine superintendent of several mines for CCI. This arrangement was fine with Robert, who had precious little interest in the business side of things, but it was a real blow to Elizabeth's social standing in Ishpeming and Marquette. Even after several years, she wasted no opportunity to be heard on the subject.

William G. Mather, the man at the twelve o'clock position at the table, was Robert's boss and the man at the helm of CCI. During the negotiation for the purchase of Bolton Mine, Mather immediately recognized in Robert a resourceful natural leader, a man of integrity, a man all the miners knew by reputation and respected. He wasted no time getting Robert on the payroll and in charge of operations for his most important mines. Mr. Mather was a staid and quiet man, appearing almost timid to some. To regard him as such would have been a grave miscalculation. Mather wielded enormous power, but he did it with the delicate precision of a surgeon, never too much, never too little, and he did it with compassion, a rarity in early 20th-century industrial America. Leadership of CCI passed to him when his father, Samuel, died in the 1890s, not because of *who* he was, as many people suspected at the time, but because he was devoted entirely to the success of his father's company. He was a shrewd businessman, and he was a tireless worker. Robert, too, was a tireless worker and shrewd in his way, especially when it came to getting the best out of his miners, but two men could hardly have been more different. Perhaps it was for just that very reason that they had formed a deep and mutually satisfying friendship.

As Mr. Mather rose to dismiss the meeting, he shot a sideways look at Robert and quietly asked him to remain behind for a moment. The men filing out exchanged knowing glances and bowed their heads to avoid risking eye contact with their colleague. Mather turned away to the sideboard behind him and a moment later Robert heard the clink of ice cubes tumbling into rock glasses.

"Any word from your boys, Rob?" he said without turning around.

Robert took a seat again, this time one right next to his boss. "Well, yes and no. We had a letter a couple of weeks ago, but the Army only let a few lines come through. You'd think a kid asking for a tin of mink oil for his boots wouldn't jeopardize the war effort. At least we could see it was Johnny's hand and I guess that's something."

Mather fished in the wide side pocket of his fisherman's cardigan and set a small square envelope in front of Robert. There was no addressee, but on the reverse side in the center of the flap it was embossed with the lettering "SS *Pontiac*."

Robert looked up quickly and locked eyes with his boss.

"No cause for alarm, my friend," said Mather. "Johnny Johnson handed that to me last week when the *Pontiac* was tied up at Lower Republic. He's just a little concerned."

Robert looked down at the envelope for a moment as he struggled with the urge to rip it open. Finally he stuffed it in the inside pocket of his canvas work coat that was draped over the back of his chair.

"So talk to me about the Barnes-Hecker, Rob. Sinking that shaft seems to be going at a snail's pace. Rumor has it that Germany is just about out of steam, but for now, at least, the government wants all the steel they can get at any price. "

"I know, I know," said Robert shaking his head. "Every fifty feet or so, we have to stop and extend the shaft lining just so we can keep up with the flow of water coming in. That overburden must be just saturated. I don't know whether it's the swamp or if it's coming from North Lake. Either way, I don't like it."

Mr. Mather nodded while he considered the problem. Finally he said, "What do you want to do?"

"I guess I'd like to have some of your engineers look into draining North Lake. Might as well start there and eliminate that possibility. Maybe we'll get lucky."

Distracted by troubling thoughts about the Barnes-Hecker, it wasn't until Robert switched off the roadster's engine in front of his office that he remembered the letter from the *Pontiac's* captain.

CAPTAIN J. JOHNSON
ss *Pontiac*
CLEVELAND CLIFFS STEAMSHIP CO.

Dear Mr. Castor,

Just a quick note to report on the welfare of your son Bill, who serves as a deckhand on my ship. During fit-out this spring in Toledo on several occasions I observed Bill in a state of intoxication being helped back to the ship by his shipmates. To be sure, this occurred on his own time and is certainly not that uncommon in the world of the merchant seaman. For that reason I took no particular notice at the time. Unfortunately, for many men in this profession, these things tend to escalate over time until they are entirely unmanageable. I fear your son may fall into this category. In fact, several weeks ago in Cleveland he failed to return to the ship before we sailed and had to come out with the mail boat in Detroit as we passed up river.

During my years of sailing on the Lakes I have seen this pattern far too many times and thought it time to bring it to your attention in the event you are able to influence the situation.

Sincerely Yours,
Johnny Johnson

Robert slowly folded the note and placed it back in the envelope then tapped it on the steering wheel as he looked off into the distance and turned this new information over in his mind.

Chapter 5

The beginning of their journey to the front began in an organized fashion, late as usual but in good order. Once the fourteen-mile-long line of French trucks or camions, as they were called, finally began to move, darkness, fatigue, and the monumental confusion in the rear area caused by the rapidly advancing German Army conspired to throw the convoy into disarray. Sometimes they were stopped for an hour or so by snarled traffic, or occasionally they came to an open stretch of road and sped up, but for the most part they crept along at thirty miles per hour. Fortunately, the lion's share of traffic was headed in the other direction, away from the front. At first it was mostly civilians: young, sturdy women with children in tow, old men pushing two-wheeled carts or barrows piled high with household things, and old ladies hunched over under the weight of large wicker harvest baskets overflowing with everything they could carry away from their once-peaceful lives. There were small flocks of scruffy-looking sheep, terrified and tightly packed, chickens in slat crates riding the crest of someone's worldly possessions, and occasionally a cow or a goat following a lead. Just off the road dead horses and old people too exhausted or sick to go on lay on the trampled weeds—sometimes a couple, sometimes just a lone man or woman lying on a side, spooning pitiful little bundles of rags that contained their keepsakes. Most cast blank stares along the ground as if death had already come stealing. As the miles crept by, the Marines began to see a sprinkling of French soldiers mixed in with this pathetic human flotsam, and before long the trickle became a flood. They were gaunt and hollow-eyed men, haunted, arms hanging straight at their sides. They were not accoutered and they were unarmed, and like everything else on the Paris-Metz Highway, they were covered in fine gray dust.

John and Matt Castor sat shoulder-to-shoulder as far forward as possible on the plank bench that ran along the left side of the truck. The other ten Marines who shared their bench and the ones facing them on the opposite bench had hours earlier folded their bedrolls into flat squares and used them as cushions against the jarring ride over hard springs and solid rubber tires. Choking clouds of dust roiled up through the floorboards and came aboard over the tailgate to settle on every exposed surface. It stuck to the sweaty faces and necks of the men in their wool uniforms, eventually forming a disgusting crust that crinkled on their faces when they took a drink from their canteens or tugged at the hairs on the backs of their necks when they tried to doze. John had worked in his dad's mine the summer before college, and he thought he knew what it meant to be dirty. Nothing he had encountered there prepared him for this. He vowed that if he survived the war he would never be this filthy again.

"Shit, Johnny, this war is really starting to irritate me!" said Matt. "How long we been in this piece-of-shit French truck, anyway?"

John extended his arm to look at his watch and sheepishly realized that it was too dark to read the dial. "Too goddamn long," he said. Just then the camion lurched to the right and every Marine was instantly alert.

"Stan, that little son of a bitch is asleep! Grab him!" yelled John, referring to the small Annamite driver who had slumped sideways in the front seat and was about to tumble out.

Stan Zywicki turned quickly to his right and dove head first halfway over the rear bulkhead of the cab until he could get his arm around the man's neck and jerk him upright in the seat. All the drivers in the convoy had been on the road continuously for the last seventy-two hours and could not really be blamed, but the Marines had no desire to end their war early, pinned under an overturned camion in a ditch half full of stagnant water. Stan had the driver's undivided attention now, but the little man was too terrified to act. The Marine clamped his neck in the crook of his arm and pulled him up in the seat far enough to prevent him from suddenly slamming on the brakes and then reached around him and pulled the steering wheel to the left, guiding the truck back onto the road. A few tense moments passed before the driver finally reached up and gripped the steering wheel at ten and two and settled back in. Stan unholstered his government .45 and tapped the man's shoulder with the end of the barrel. The message was clear and successfully bridged the language barrier. John leaned back, closed his eyes, and tried to ignore the pain under his shoulder blades, where the sideboard cut across his back. He thought of the girl with the auburn hair.

It was a dark night, not stormy, but moonless and dark just the same. The area the Marines were entering now was close enough to the front that everyone was jittery about showing any kind of light, no matter how insignificant, for fear of attracting the attention of German artillery. In fact there had been an almost continuous buzz from enemy spotter aircraft fading in and out all night long. John simply stared at his brother's dusty field pack directly in front of him or sometimes the heels of his boots until he started to waver. What had begun as a route step had by now degenerated into an exhausted shuffle, and the clanking of various accouterments, noise that ordinarily wouldn't even be noticed, created a monotonous chorus that lulled the men into a semi-stupor. Mile after mile they walked, not knowing where they were or where they were going. They knew only that they were going to save Paris from the Hun and that the deep, dull thump of distant artillery was growing sharper with every mile.

The road curved sharply to the left for about fifty yards and then straightened out and started a gradual ascent. As John and Matt left the turn, they began to hear murmurs of clipped conversations travel back down the line of Marines toward them. John looked to his right, expecting to see the same dark impenetrable void that had been there all night and was startled by what he saw. Stretching down the road and rising above their heads was a field of hundreds of tiny glowing lights like motionless fireflies alternating between bright and dim. It was otherworldly and John could only stare in wonder.

"What outfit?" came a disembodied American voice from the darkness, seemingly much closer than it should have been.

"5th Marines. Who are you?" John heard the word "Gyrines" coming from the darkness, repeated in different voices and from the right and left.

"23rd Infantry, US Army" came a somewhat defiant reply. It was then that the smell of cigarette smoke reached John, and he realized the odd glowing lights were from hundreds of soldiers, resting and smoking cigarettes during a break from the march and sitting on an embankment where the road cut through a small hill.

"Don't worry, Army, we'll save some Boche for you fellas."

"Take ten, take ten, fall out, smoke 'em if you got 'em" was the cry from the sergeants up and down the long line of exhausted men. They had walked another mile or so after passing the 23rd Infantry, to the edge of a little village called Lucy-le-Bocage, and now the first order of business was to shed their sixty-pound field packs and rifles and drop down next to them on the edge of the road. They had been on the march, fifty minutes walking, ten minutes resting, hour after hour since the evening before, when they disembarked the convoy just outside Meaux. In addition to being tired and dirty, they were hungry as well. The field kitchens had not been able to keep up with the march and were strung out to the west somewhere on the Paris-Metz Highway. Those Marines who had thought it would be a good idea to fill their canteens with wine instead of water were the sorriest of the lot.

"Damn, Johnny, we been on the move for ages and it don't look any different here than what we left," said Matt. "Hey, Gunny, what's the name of this little burg, anyway?" he said to their Sergeant's back as he passed down the middle of the road, looking over men and equipment.

The older man didn't stop or turn around. "Lucy Birdcage," he said in a gruff, unnaturally loud voice that all Marine noncoms seem to possess. His words stood out even more in the unnatural silence that had fallen over the men as they quietly smoked or reread letters from home. Normally when the Marines had transitioned from the *hurry up* phase to the *wait* phase, there was an undercurrent of off-color jokes, good-natured ribbing that most often involved someone having an unusually small penis or perhaps the eternally ongoing discussion of female body parts and what might be done with them—but not this morning. Most of the men were struggling with the very things that were on John's mind—how would he behave in combat and would he live through it. The enormity of what they were about to do could no longer be denied. It was no longer "out there" as something that might happen someday. It was here now.

Matt was one of the few who seemed to have no reservations. He sat leaning back against his pack, carefully wiping the dust from his Springfield with an old sock saturated in gun oil and absentmindedly rolled a cigarette from one side of his mouth to the other with his lips. "What do you suppose Bill's doing about now?" he said.

John studied his watch for a moment and said, "Closing down some bar, I guess, or more likely holed up in some fleabag. Must be about one in the morning back home. Judging from the amount of mail we get from him, that asshole must have broken his arm."

The brothers fell silent as they watched the approach of a team of weary mules pulling an ammunition wagon. "I'll say one thing, Johnny, the Army doesn't generally know where it's going, but they sure got some damn fine equipment to get there in," said Matt, referring to the rugged construction of the heavy buckboard-type wagon piled high with wooden crates of ammunition.

In a few minutes they heard a sergeant farther up the line calling his men to draw ammunition. "Turn to, you beauties, fall in and draw ammo. Fill up your belts now, you're gonna need every round!"

Off to the northeast a gray German observation balloon began to emerge from behind a distant ridge. Several bright flashes emitted from its underside as the objective lens of searching field glasses caught the low sun. Matt nodded his head in that direction and said, "Speaking of mail, big brother, looks like we may have some on the way once that old Boche sausage gets up high enough to see us all sitting in the road like ducks in a shootin' gallery."

No sooner had Matt finished his sentence than they began to hear the dull thump of distant artillery. John cast a weary sideways glance at his little brother and then looked off across the landscape as if seeing it for the first time. Patches of reds and oranges had quietly crept into the soft grays of the dawn's half light as the slanting rays of the sun began to course through the new day. The tile roofs of Lucy-le-Bocage, the spatters of dew-heavy poppies in the young winter wheat, and the flaming tops of the tallest hardwood trees beckoned first to the yellows and golds and then finally the greens and the blue sky. Long thin wisps of ground fog floated just above the waking fields where they dipped into shallow ravines. The memory of a cackling rooster pheasant tugged at John's mind. He couldn't know it then, but of all the countless men who had looked out on this beautiful countryside down through the ages and taken solace, he would be one of the last. The innocent little village and the pastoral charm of the land around it were about to die.

Chapter 6

Bill Castor stood leaning forward with his head and shoulders sticking out through the foremost porthole on the port side of the windlass room, right next to the red-stenciled lettering on the bulkhead that read "DO NOT PUT HEAD OUT PORTHOLE." Even though his demeanor was casual, he was intently watching his counterpart far below on the fantail of a tugboat as it gingerly bled off speed to close the gap between the two vessels moving slowly upriver. In his left hand Bill held a heaving line at the ready, the end of which was tied to the bight of a thick wire mooring cable that poked out through the bullnose at his feet. In his right hand, pinched between his thumb and index finger, he cupped a cigarette against the wind, which was blowing hard from the south. Charlie held a similar stance, looking out the opposite porthole on the starboard side with both hands clutching the horizontal valve wheel that would feed steam to the huge mooring winch on the deck behind him and pay out the cable.

"Jesus, Fuzzy, are you going to throw that line or stand there picking your ass?"

"At least I do my own pickin', Charlie."

Bill straightened up and shot a wry look at his shipmate before leaning back out to keep an eye on the tug. He knew the old man must be starting to sputter up in the pilothouse, and the deckhand on the smaller vessel was staring up at him with a sense of urgency. "Oh, all right, Charlie, don't get in a yank." He took one last draw on his cigarette before flicking it away and watching briefly as it carried aft in the wind, glowing bright, and then he gave the carefully coiled heaving line an easy toss to the stern of the tug.

"OK, Charlie, he's got it, give him some slack," said Bill.

Charlie tugged hard on the valve wheel to break it loose and then slowly opened it until the massive winch linkage gave a mighty clunk and the pistons on each side began to issue little clouds of steam and slide slowly in opposing directions. The tug was very close aboard now, and Bill looked on with approval as the tugboatman, almost directly below him, deftly shackled a nine-inch manila hawser to the *Pontiac*'s cable and prepared to pay it out over the stern. The rhythmic chuffing of the tug's exhaust steam increased in tempo, and dirty water roiled up from under its counter as it surged ahead to take a strain. Thick, black smoke mixed with fly ash and hot steam issued from its stack, momentarily engulfing the *Pontiac*'s bow. It poured through the portholes, filling the windlass room with an evil fog that smelled like rotten eggs and stung the eyes and noses of the two deckhands.

"Son of a bitch!" exclaimed Charlie as he swung the port glass shut and started wiping his eyes with the back of his shirtsleeve. "Keep an eye on things a minute, Fuzzy," and with that he headed aft down the passageway toward the weather deck and fresh air.

All afternoon the *Pontiac* moved slowly up the malodorous and winding Cuyahoga on its way to the lower Republic dock, pulled this way and that around impossible bends by the powerful little tugs tethered to each end. Occasionally they would come to a complete stop as they waited for a bridge to swing open, but mostly it was hour after hour creeping along slower than a man would walk. Bill and Charlie stood side by side at the port rail, resting on their forearms and looking down through the open companionway at the brightly lit interior of the bumboat *Forest City*. She was sixty-five feet long with a small wheelhouse far forward in the bow and a four-foot-high boxy cabin lined with portholes that rose straight up from the gunnels all around. She was ugly, to be sure, but well suited to her purpose.

"I sure could use a few of those beers," said Bill, referring to the enameled tub of ice with just the tops of brown bottles sticking out.

"Is that all you ever think about, Fuzzy? I swear, giving you a few beers is like giving fire water to the Indians," replied Charlie. "Personally, I'd be happy with a couple of sticks of that jerky and a new pair of work gloves. I suppose a nudie magazine would be good, too."

"Damn, Charlie, would you look at that?" said Bill with an over-the-shoulder nod in the direction of the watertight door leading to their quarters one deck below. Old Ray had just emerged and started toward them with a stiff, self-conscious walk, no doubt a by-product of being dressed in his best "up the street" finery and new unbroken wingtips.

"Whoo doggy, he does look sweet, don't he?" replied Charlie with a broad smile.

Old Ray, the deckhand, was normally dressed in torn bib overalls and wool shirt, the same ones every day, both garments heavily stained orange from iron ore and stained darker where his ample belly crowned. His watery eyes were close-set above a permanently flushed golf ball nose, and his puckered mouth sank deep in gray stubble. Most days his teeth were in his pocket or perhaps buried under dirty clothes in his locker. On his head he generally wore a navy blue wool watch cap that had seen its share of moths. Old Ray returned their amused looks with a grimace that bared his snow-white dentures and revealed his uncharacteristic nervousness as he made his way to the ladder that hung over the side from the port rail, the same ladder used for the mail boat. Riding the bumboat to shore would give him an extra ten or eleven hours at home with his wife.

Just before his head disappeared below the deck edge, he paused and shot a serious look up at Charlie. "You keep an eye on Fuzzy. If he gets tossed in the tank and misses the boat again, we'll have to go through all kinds of shit breaking in someone new."

When the bumboat was ready to cast off, Bill and Charlie retrieved the mooring lines and hung them neatly coiled from hooks on the aft bulkhead of the forward cabins and then took a seat on the green slatted park bench that faced aft from the shade of the overhead.

"What's going on with Ray? He seemed as nervous as a whore in church," said Bill.

"His old lady is bunny thumping with the second mate on the *Schoonmaker*. Seems like everyone at Lake Carriers knows it except Ray, but he don't listen to anybody. He sends just about every penny of his check home to her, and she starts living high before we even clear the mouth of the river. Don't seem right, is all I'm saying." Charlie reached behind him and retrieved a worn old flyswatter from where it hung on the end of one of the bench slats. "She even threatened to divorce him a couple of years ago if he didn't go on the wagon. Guess she must have figured it cut into her spending money a little too much. Probably a good thing for Ray anyway; he can't stop once he takes that first drink." Without warning, Charlie lashed out at a large fly that had settled on the tip of his boot and did it with such force that the permanently curled business end of the swatter flattened out just long enough to do its work.

"Nice one, Charlie," said Bill. "Guess that explains why he never goes up the street with us. I was beginning to think he was some kind of teetotaler."

"You got to lead 'em just a little, my friend, about the width of the mesh, I'd say," said Charlie, holding up the swatter and admiring the fresh kill still stuck to it. "Naw, he just can't hold it anymore. I've carried his drunk ass back to the boat many a time."

The two men fell into a drowsy silence as they watched the dismal Cleveland Flats slip slowly by, buildings and factories just ghostly outlines in the permanent industrial haze. Bill's gaze was drawn to his left by movement, and he watched three little boys standing at the river's edge, chucking stones at the huge steel side of the ship. They were so filthy and ragged that they were nearly invisible against the tired, peeling grays and browns of their surroundings. The shortest of the three boys leaned forward as if he were "checking the sign" and then gave a nod to the imaginary catcher, wound up and delivered the pitch. Bill noted the splash well short of the ship, but the little boy threw up his arms and started bouncing up and down as if he had just struck out Babe Ruth in the bottom of the ninth with bases loaded. For this youngster with few prospects, where the stone landed was of no importance, really; it was the delivery, the moment of living outside himself that was everything.

Bill turned away as a wave of melancholy washed over him. He recalled long summer days with his brothers, tree forts and apple fights, campfires and crickets under stars so bright and close that it was easy to imagine the earth sailing through the dark infinity. He thought of Rosemarie and their secret swimming hole, a place that had been blasted from solid rock by early miners and then abandoned when a spring welled up. He closed his eyes and he could hear the buzz of cicadas and see the pale skin of her freckled face against cerulean water as she waited for him to jump. He wondered if she would ever forgive him.

"So what's it going to be, Fuzzy? I say we head over to Curly's and make a start. The ladies weren't too bad last trip, and I could sure use a little poon. You see that bulge in my sock?" Charlie pulled up his pant leg and then backhanded Bill's arm with a laugh.

"Yeah, yeah, that one you cut out of the herd last time we were there had marks all over her where folks had been poking her with twenty-foot poles."

Both men laughed and headed aft down the port side so they wouldn't have to pass under the huge walking beams of the Hulett unloading machines as their clam-shell buckets dropped into the holds of the *Pontiac* and scooped up tons of ore with each pass. The four legs of the Hulett's base ran on tracks parallel to the dock and were tall enough and wide enough to allow four trains to pass underneath it and be loaded simultaneously as quickly as the ore came up out of the ship. The machines stood about four stories tall, and from a distance several working together on one ore boat looked like prehistoric insects devouring the carcass of a giant worm.

Bill and Charlie headed for the front gate of the mill, carefully threading their way around mountains of iron ore, moving trains, and scores of laboring dump trucks with engines screaming in low range. Now and then they were able to see flashes of light and showers of sparks as they passed an open door. It was a little bit of an uphill hike to get to Curly's, and along the way they passed several taverns that bore no name signs and had their front doors propped open, allowing shrill feminine laughter and Celtic fiddle music to pour out into the street. Both men kept an eye on the places as they passed, partly out of curiosity but also because they knew this was not a friendly neighborhood. As they reached the top of the hill, they came abreast of a large two-story building that housed a bar on the first floor and rooms on the second that could be rented by the hour or by the night. It was clad in weathered, gray lap siding and was spanned across the entire front by an undulating porch that rested on uneven cement blocks. This establishment wore a large sign over the porch roof that said "The Short and Curly's" in big red script, and under that in smaller black letters, the sign said, "Where decent folks meet to eat!" The exclamation point was formed by what the sign artist must have thought resembled a coiled pubic hair. Like the other taverns, the front door of Curly's was held open with the back of a chair jammed under the door knob, and loud voices from inebriated patrons trying to be heard over the ragtime piano music spilled into the street.

The festive atmosphere in the tavern was contagious, and almost immediately Bill and Charlie fell under its spell. They shouldered their way onto the end of the bar and waited for one of the barmen to work his way down to them. Every time they spoke to one another, they had to lean in close to be heard over the din.

"Damn busy in here tonight," yelled Bill.

"Yeah, the *Pontiac* ain't the only boat that's got a crew in here. I recognize some of those fellas on the other end of the bar from the *Schoonmaker*." Both men realized the implications of what Charlie had just said at the same time and shared a look.

"Well shit the bed, look what we got here!" came a deep gravelly voice from behind them. Bill and Charlie leaned away from each other and looked over their shoulders to see who was talking.

"Curly, you asshole, damn if you ain't shorter than you were last time we was in here. You ain't any better looking neither, come to think of it," said Charlie.

Curly was short, as the name of his tavern implied, nearly as wide as he was tall, but "Curly" was something of a misnomer. If his head had ever seen curly hair, no one could remember it; in fact, his head was as smooth as a cue ball. Charlie was certainly right about one thing: Curly was definitely ugly. He had more warts than anyone Bill had ever seen. They were on every patch of skin exposed to public view: between his fingers, on his ears, cheeks, nose, and even one big one in the fold of his left eyelid that caused it to droop, something like the Hunchback of Notre Dame without the hunch. For a brief moment Bill flirted with thoughts of the parts of Curly that weren't visible, but he immediately abandoned the exercise as a shiver coursed through him. Whenever Curly detected even a hint of revulsion on someone's face, he would make a fist with each hand and hold them side by side out in front of him, palm down, as close to the face of the offending party as possible so they would have no trouble reading the letters tattooed on the four knuckles of each hand— "TRUE LOVE." As part of the routine, he would then give out a hearty laugh before turning away.

"Charlie, you know I love it when you talk bad to me," he said as he moved in closer. "I see you brought *young boy* with you again," he added, referring to Bill.

"Yeah, and he's my friend, so don't give him any shit," replied Charlie. "In fact, we both need to get our ashes hauled toot sweet. How's the talent look tonight?" Curly held his arm up over his head with just his index and middle finger extended to get the attention of one of his barmen and indicate two drinks for his friends. This effectively jumped Charlie and Bill to the head of the line, and two boilermakers quickly appeared on the bar in front of them.

"On me," said Curly. "I think Maria for *young boy* here, and you can catch as catch can. Busy tonight."

Charlie glanced back at Curly with a twinkle in his eye, but Bill was still surveying the room and missed the exchange. He reached over and dropped Bill's shot glass brimming with bar whiskey into his beer mug and watched it sink to the bottom and then did the same with his.

"Here's to you and here's to me, should ever we disagree, fuck you," said Charlie offering his mug. "Take my advice and drink up, mate." Bill shot him a quizzical look but needed no further encouragement.

Maria wisely delayed her grand entrance until later in the evening when alcohol had leveled the playing field. She was short and plump and carried herself with a confidence hardened off over the years by innumerable hits. Her dress was silver with a glittery quality and banded by two rows of long fringe, one hanging from the ample overhang of her breasts and the other from the short hem, fashionable for a woman half her age. The end effect was one of sparkle and perpetual movement. She wore a silver wig in the short bobbed style with a black headband trimmed in rhinestones and adorned on one side with a profusion of black millinery feathers. The fact that it rested on her head turned slightly to the left of center detracted somewhat from her credibility as a high-class hooker. In spite of all the things working against the aging prostitute, on this night her timing was impeccable. Charlie had just disappeared through the back door of the bar with an enthusiastic young girl in tow, headed for the stairs on the outside of the building that led to the second-floor rooms, and Bill was beginning to realize that it would likely be two weeks before he would get another chance if he didn't get lucky really soon. The big Huletts could unload a boat in eight hours, so time was precious.

"Honey, flag that bartender down and order me a Martini, will ya? " said Maria as she back-handed Bill's arm with a dollar. The young deckhand turned his head to the left and sized up the old hooker who stood close and slightly behind him. Out of all the other possibilities, the first thing that drew his attention was her big puffy lips, colored rather imprecisely with high-gloss red lipstick.

"Sure." He waited until the barman looked his way and then held the dollar over his head.

"You off the *Pontiac?*"

"Yeah," said Bill as he held out the drink. Maria cradled the body of the glass in her left palm and held out her right hand for the change. She took a long sip and studied her mark over the rim of the glass for clues that would determine her next move. The young man before her was pretty far along, perhaps even too far and obviously a novice, so she settled on the direct approach.

"Been upstairs yet?"

"Nope, not yet," said Bill without turning her way.

"Got five bucks?" This time the young man turned and took a better look. Maria could almost see the wheels turning in his head as he weighed his prospects against the sure thing that she represented. She knew time was on her side. She watched as he fished a five dollar bill out of the inside pocket of his coat, folded it in half lengthwise, and pointed it at her. Maria took the bill and stuffed it in her cleavage.

"Follow me," she said.

Maria led Bill to her living quarters instead of one of the filthy communal working rooms further down the hall. This was something of a special occasion, given her client's tender age, and she was determined to have some fun for a change. Her space was really a small apartment, a front room with a bed, wardrobe, and dry sink, and a smaller room adjoining with a chest of drawers and a counter that she used to prepare simple meals. There was also a wrought-iron wire ice cream parlor table and two chairs with the backrests bent in the shape of hearts. Both rooms had battered, dark oak wainscoting and pictures in heavy wood frames that leaned out from yellowing wallpaper on taut wires. Along the base of the wall across from the end of the bed was a tightly rolled up oriental rug, a prized possession. It was only used when Maria was alone and in for the night. Bill hung back as she crossed the floor to the dry sink and lit a beautiful, hand-painted oil lamp that cast a soft, yellow light and filled the room with the warm smell of scented lamp oil. The tiny flame flickered and danced on the burnished surface of a red satin bedspread.

From the outset, Maria took charge and wasted no time getting her young deckhand sorted out. She quickly changed out of her dress in the other room and came back wearing a long, dark blue silk robe adorned with two big, white hydrangea blooms, one over each breast, giving the flowers a 3D look with the stems and leaves trailing down each side to the hem. Bill was sitting on the edge of the bed, squinting to focus on what she guessed was his own reflection in the mirror hanging above the dry sink. He was droop-shouldered and wavering but overall he seemed more alert now than he was earlier.

"Well, there you are, Sweetie. Stand up here and let's get you more comfortable," she said. As soon as Bill was on his feet, she grabbed the front of his belt above his right leg, and with her left hand deftly worked the buckle and started pulling it out of the loops. When his pants were pooled around his feet, she put her hand on his chest and tipped him back so that he had no choice but to sit down on the bed again, and then she removed his boots. She stepped back, held her robe open with a fist on each hip, and looked Bill over with a critical eye that seemed to make him a little uneasy.

"You'll do," she said to herself.

Bill stared in slack-jawed wonder at the old prostitute standing before him in her underclothes. Beneath the robe she wore a long, heavy, hourglass-shaped corset. It was laced up the front with a complicated cross-hatch of cording, all the way from the bottom to the top, where it flared out into a balcony that supported her heavy, gelatinous breasts. A profusion of garters stretched from mid-thigh to the tops of her black silk stockings, six per leg. Maria watched Bill's eyes travel slowly down her form, his uncertainty spreading across his face. He need not have worried, though; she had been there before and knew exactly what to do.

For an overweight older woman, Maria turned out to be very agile indeed. With her coaching, Bill got on top of her, supporting himself on his outstretched arms and bent knees. Maria reached back over her head, grabbed the bent steel tubing of the bedstead, pulled her legs up and rested them on Bill's shoulders.

"OK, *now*," she exclaimed and Bill pushed forward, remarkably hitting the *sweet spot* the first time. All was well in the beginning, and her deckhand was able to establish a pretty respectable pace all things considered, but as the time passed without resolution, owing to Bill's heavy drinking earlier in the evening, Maria began to enjoy herself, perhaps even a little too much. Every unexpected move she made caused Bill's knees to lose traction and slide out from under him on the slippery satin sheets. To keep things going and regain lost ground, he was forced to adopt something resembling a fast knee walk followed quickly on by an awkward pelvic thrust. Just as she reached the moment of orgasm, Maria pinched Bill's head hard between her meaty thighs, let out a loud shriek, and abruptly straightened out her legs, shooting Bill feet-first off the end of the bed. One second he was there, and the next he was gone! The violent dismount was so sudden and unexpected that it never occurred to him to try and break his fall, and he landed on all fours, striking the bridge of his nose with such force on the steel frame of the bed that bright lights burst behind his eyes. The night was effectively over for Bill. He simply rolled over on the floor and surrendered to oblivion. When he awoke, he was sprawled on top of his bunk on the *Pontiac*, fully clothed, and Charlie was pushing a mug of coffee at him. He had a throbbing headache and his nose felt like it was broken.

"Come on, bird-dog, drink this; time to go to work." It was still the middle of the night, but unloading was nearly complete. The hollow sounds of the big clamshell buckets scraping on the steel plates of the empty holds echoed throughout the ship. Bill rolled out and hung onto the top bunk to steady himself as he tested his legs. He took two steps to the sink, splashed cold water on his face, and looked up in the mirror to see what was wrong with his nose. To his dismay, the person looking back at him had two perfectly symmetrical black eyes. It was going to be a long week ahead for the deckhand who went "upstairs" with an old whore, old enough to be his mother, and was carried back to the boat with two shiners.

Chapter 7

It took a moment, but eventually the red light on the switchboard, bright against the dim interior of the room, burned through the pre-dawn weariness that had closed around Rosemarie's mind.

"Central, number, please," she said.

"Rose? Can you hear me all right? Dr. Mudge here!"

"Yes, Doctor, no need to shout, I can hear you clearly."

"OK, then, write this down in case you get an emergency. I'm heading over to the Kloginhops' right now. Sounds like little Missy has this damn flu that's going around. Then I'm going to drop in on Mrs. Palomaki, be there about an hour, more if she feels like talking. Nothing wrong with her jaws... OK, after that I got to change a dressing for Max Halverson, and that should take me up till lunch time. I'll be at the hospital most of the afternoon. You got all that?"

"Yes, doctor, I'll ring you up if we need you."

"OK, Rose. What do you hear from Johnny and Matt?"

"Oh, I had the prettiest postcard all the way from Paris a couple of weeks ago! It was like a little picture frame around these tiny yellow flowers embroidered on a gauzy fabric... I think they were primrose. It was just beautiful!"

"And your brothers, Rosemarie, I presume they wrote something on the card—?"

"They're fine, doctor. Johnny said Matt was learning some new dances."

"OK, good. I'm going to ring off now and get the show on the road. Tell your dad I got a few nice browns over on Trout Falls Creek the other day." Rosemarie waited for the click in her headset that told her Dr. Mudge had hung up and then pulled the plugs out of the jacks and let the weighted cords fall back into the table. She glanced up at the school clock that hung above the switchboard and then quickly looked away as if to nullify the fact that the hands had barely moved since the last look. With a sigh, she picked up the April edition of *Woman's World* and started paging through the fashion sketches.

The phone company office was located on the second floor of the Miners Bank building in a sparsely furnished little room whose only positive quality was a single tall window that overlooked Main Street. There was a narrow cot for the night operator against the inside wall next to the switchboard, a curtained-off area in the dingy far end that they used as a privy, and a small potbellied stove and rickety crate to hold split firewood near the center of the room. There were steam radiators throughout the building, but on cold nights they just weren't enough. In addition to the switchboard, the girl on duty was expected to sweep the floor, tend the woodstove, and bring in firewood from the back alley. In spite of the long, boring night shift, it was a highly sought-after job for the young ladies of Ishpeming, and Rosemarie knew she was lucky to have it; in fact, she strongly suspected that her mother Elizabeth had pulled a few strings.

Some nights when it was perfectly still and the only sounds were the measured unerring tick of the big Regulator's escapement, the sudden clank of a steam pipe, or, more often than not, the scratching of mice feet on the tin ceiling, she would imagine a smoky wraith of her long-passed father floating in the dark corners of the room, watching, marking her progress through life. She even whispered things, important things, to him on occasion. It made her feel self-conscious, but the connection to her past, although thin, was still important. She thought about her birth mother too. The memory of her was faded, but the hurt was always there, just under the surface, touching her relationships, her choices, her dreams. She harbored a fantasy of one day meeting her face to face and saying *Remember me? I'm your daughter Rosemarie. Go to hell!*— or something like that, but she knew in her heart that she would not walk across the street to speak to her if she looked out the window one day and saw her mother standing there. How could a woman just pack up one day and walk away from her only child, with no intention of ever coming back? How could she leave her helpless baby who loved her unconditionally and depended on her for everything— leave her defenseless against the vagaries of life? Rosemarie knew she would succeed and make something of herself at any cost and never, never do that to one of her own children.

She gently closed the magazine and absentmindedly regarded the cover as it rested on her lap. The artwork depicted a tall, young cavalry officer in profile, standing very straight and looking down into the adoring eyes of his prospective bride. He was wearing the brown wool uniform of the American Expeditionary Force: over-the-calf tan riding boots, jodhpurs, Sam Brown belt and visor cap. The bride wore an ankle-length, layered white gown trimmed in white satin and belted at the waist with a white satin sash. Her sheer, lacy veil was turned back over her head in anticipation of a kiss, and it trailed down her back to the floor. The face of the young soldier reminded her of Matt, but the stature was Johnny through and through. In the unguarded moment she wondered what Bill would look like in uniform and then promptly rejected the notion as memories of him rushed in. She felt again the old familiar rejection that had so tainted her youth. First her mother, then Bill —and his leaving, as he did without a word, had cut deep. She vowed to never again risk it all.

Then there was Jake. Unlike his brothers, Jake was not exactly a man's man, but he was safe and controllable. She could discreetly guide him from behind to do her bidding. For now, at least, her adopted father, Robert, seemed to be grooming Jake for a good job with Cleveland Cliffs, but who knew what would happen when Johnny and Matt came back from the war, or if and when Bill finally returned? They had been keeping their distance from each other at home in an effort let things die down. Their father seemed content to let things ride, and their mother's initial stoniness was softening just a bit. As Rosemarie explained to Jake, it was important not to rock the boat so they could continue living at home and save their money for when they finally did get married. She was hedging her bet by setting aside part of her earnings for the wedding itself in case their parents refused to pick up the tab.

"Good morning, Mr. Castor. What can I do for you?"

"Morning, Vic. You seen this?" Robert laid a page of *The Mining Journal* on the counter between the two men. It was folded back on itself and then in half again so that just a big advertisement for a Ford Model T Snow Flyer was face up.

Vic Roland, owner of the Ford dealership, studied the ad in silence as he wiped his greasy hands on a shop rag. Finally he looked up and said, "I got a letter a couple of months ago from Detroit saying I could get one of these kits on spec so I could drive it around town and show it off. Been so busy it kind of slipped my mind."

"I gotta have one, Vic. I can make a case for needing it to get around to the mines when the snow is asshole-deep-to-a-tall-Indian. I think it would be the berries."

"They ain't cheap, and I'm not sure it would fit your Runabout, anyway. The one for a touring car is three hundred and fifty bucks, and I think they make one to fit a truck for two-fifty."

"I don't want it for my Runabout. This is going to be strictly for playing in the snow. You make me a good deal on a truck and I'll take one of these kits to go on it. I think since I'm going to be advertising for you every time I drive it, you should install it for free."

"Fair enough. I'll call down to Ford's and have some numbers for you tomorrow afternoon. Maybe you should sell that Franklin and get yourself a *real* car while you're at it," said Vic, feeling him out under the pretense of making a joke.

Robert rolled his eyes and said, "Shit, Vic, if it were up to me I'd give you that cold-blooded son of a bitch, but Elizabeth would skin me for sure. She's got to have prestige, even if it means freezing her ass and mine too. OK, I gotta get," he said, holding out his hand to shake on the deal. "Keep this under your hat, will ya, Vic?"

"You got it, Mr. Castor. I'll ring you at the office when I know something."

The Cliffs Shaft Mine was located right on the edge of town and was just a short walk from Robert's office on West Pearl. He and his son had taken this walk together many times since Jacob had started working in the office, sometimes stopping for a donut and cup of coffee at Star's or maybe to chat with the old miners who gathered to wet a line on the shore of Lake Bancroft across the road from the mine. Robert liked to use this time when it was just the two of them to recall one memorable family event or another from their shared past and spin it in Jacob's favor. It was his way of pointing up to his second son that he had indeed made a lasting impression, even though the truth was considerably less. The unwitting favoritism he had shown for Bill and Johnny, and Elizabeth for Matt, had cast a shadow too dark for anything Jacob did to shine through. This was another painful lesson learned that left Robert determined to redress the injustice and do it in such a way that his son would never suspect.

"You boys having the usual this morning?" said Star as she set a steaming mug of coffee in front of each man.

Robert blew across the top of his mug. "Morning, Sugar," he said. "Yeah, a couple of those big cinnamon rolls, please. Be a dear and toss mine on the grill for a sec with a little smear of butter." Star had already turned away from the table and gave her response by parroting Robert's instructions to the old lady in the back who was vigorously scraping the top of the griddle with an upside-down spatula.

"What are you thinking about, Pop?" said Jacob through a mouthful of gooey cinnamon roll. Robert looked up and refocused on the here and now in time to check his first impulse to answer his son with an off-hand wave and dismissive word or two.

"Remember that time we spent a week up near Lake Margaret hunting pats and camping on the Dead River? We sure hit 'em big, didn't we? I've never seen so many birds in one place before and I've been hunting 'em for thirty years. That was the year I bought all you boys a brand new Model 12."

Robert took a careful sip of steaming coffee and once again got that faraway look. In his mind's eye he saw his four boys moving slowly with him through a grove of yellow popple in the bottomland along the river. It was clear and cold that morning, the leaves on the ground rimmed with frost and crunchy underfoot. George was just a youngster back then and still working on his style, so his quartering was a little faster than Robert might have preferred as they advanced in line abreast with shotguns held close, barrel high.

Bill and Johnny were on the wings, strong and confident, natural hunters moving through thickets with their heads up, knowing that at any second a panicked grouse might explode off the ground with wild drumming wings from almost under foot. To his immediate right, Matt kept pace with his usual swagger, the butt of his shotgun held high on his hip with one hand, chewing gum and looking around as if out for a stroll in the park. Robert knew his casual manner was somewhat of a ruse. He was the best wing shot of the bunch, and if a pat did flush in front of him, it was more than likely he would snap shoot it before it was even four feet off the ground. Robert had once seen him take a brace of birds that way with an old cut-down side-by-side.

Most of Jacob's attention was devoted to simply keeping his footing and staying up with everyone else as he thrashed through the dense brush. Whenever he had to negotiate a fence or step over a log, Robert kept a close eye on him, ready to intervene at a moment's notice if the barrel of his gun should drop or swing in someone's direction. To his credit, Jacob generally got a shot off if a bird was lucky enough to flush in front of him and not one of his brothers, but Robert suspected that it was more a case of shooting in the general direction of the sound rather than a controlled aim. Whatever skills Jacob lacked as a sportsman he more than made up for as a scholar. He was a well-organized young man, a wizard with numbers, and a shrewd accountant. Robert had come to rely very heavily on his talents, even if he failed to appreciate them as much as his brothers' ability to fill a game pouch. Over the years, Jacob had endured countless verbal jabs from his siblings, who considered them harmless fun. Comments like *Even Jake could do that,* or *If Jake can do it,*

I can do it had become so commonplace that everyone assumed he didn't mind, but he did mind, and he had a long memory.

"Been a while since you were underground, Jake. You nervous?"

"Naw, I guess not," he answered, a little guardedly.

"When we get to the Dry, I'll talk to the men for a bit and go over the list we got from the head office, and then we'll ride down with them and have a look around a couple of the upper levels. Good for the miners to see us pencil-pushers getting our hands dirty."

The Dry was a long, two-room building next to the shaft house where the miners changed from their street clothes into their work clothes. One room had showers lining the perimeter walls and two long, galvanized waist-high troughs standing side by side, running through the center. A cold water line hung between them, serving faucets for the enameled metal basins that lay in racks down the entire length. Once a man was done washing up, it was an easy thing to just tip the basin up and empty the dirty water into the trough. The other room contained banks of lockers separated by benches. In front of each locker a set of chains dangled from pulleys high up in the rafters, near the peak of the roof. One was attached to a wire basket for boots, socks, and gloves, and the other terminated in an upside-down grappling hook, its four tines filed off flat to prevent them from poking through overalls or heavy coats. When the miners came to the surface after their shift, they would hang their wet clothes on the hooks, toss their smaller items in the basket, and hoist them up into the rafters where the air was hot and dry. Even though the day shift began at seven o'clock, it was customary for the miners to arrive a little before six, suit up for work, and then spend the remainder of the time swapping stories and sharing mostly mundane events from their hardscrabble daily lives—the kinds of things you would share with family. These were hard men who lived on the edge every day, in the mine and in their private lives. Underground, injury and death lurked in every drift, every dynamite blast, at the bottom of every raise. A crushed foot or hand could mean financial disaster for a whole family. There was no health insurance or workman's compensation to pay rent or keep food on the table; there was only the fiercely loyal brotherhood standing between them and the abyss. They were Scandinavian, Cornish, Italian, French Canadian, Irish and American, but more than any of these, they were miners.

By the time Robert and Jacob arrived, the heavy shelves on the front of the building next to the door were already crowded with the distinctive round Tiffen style lunch pails that all the miners carried. As they approached the front of the Dry, the jumbled sounds of conversation coming from within through the slightly open door died off sharply, indicating that their presence had been noted.

Just as Robert was about to push the door open the rest of the way, he suddenly pulled up short, causing an awkward moment for his startled son, who crashed into his back.

"Damn, Pop, what is it?" said Jacob as he tried to regain his dignity. His father looked at him over his shoulder and held his right index finger across his lips for silence. When he had his son's undivided attention he reached out with his left hand and gave the heavy door a good push. As soon as it began to swing inward there came a clunk followed by a cascade of water. Groans and cheering erupted simultaneously from the room full of miners, evidence that bets had been riding on the outcome. Had Robert not recognized the old tin-cup-of-water-balanced-on-top-of-the-door trick at the last moment, he would now be wet from head to toe.

"OK, listen up, men. Sorry to disappoint those of you who had money riding on me getting wet, but you sorry sons of bitches will need to get up a lot earlier than this to get the drop on my ass." Easy laughter rippled through the crowd of miners standing shoulder to shoulder between two banks of lockers. Robert was a big boss, their boss, but he was also one of them.

"The head office weenies sent me down here to tell you that it has come to their attention that some of you men are thoughtlessly getting yourselves killed on the job without first preparing a last will and testament. In case you didn't know it, that creates a lot more paperwork for the company, and besides, I'm sure you don't want your insurance payout going to your ex-wife. Next month Cliffs is sending some suits up here to help you men fill out the papers, and they strongly encourage you to take advantage of this opportunity."

There were a few groans from the back of the room and Robert held up his hands palm out. "They're making me do it, too, so no use bitching. The other thing, I just want to remind you, especially you men with big families, the company nurse is available on Tuesdays and Thursdays, and it don't cost you a dime. Those are benefits, my friends, but they don't do you any good if you don't use 'em."

Jacob stood slightly behind his father at the shaft collar, head bowed, staring at the high-top rubber boots he had borrowed from the locker labeled *GUEST*. Most of the miners were similarly attired, and he surmised correctly that the levels they were going to visit were wet. The miners were still talking amongst themselves but in lower voices, making it possible to hear the crackle of the steel cable as it passed by on its way to the huge spool in the hoist room. Within a few minutes, the far-off clanking of the approaching man car began to echo up the shaft, followed a minute or so later by the voices of miners from the night shift on their way to the surface. The pitch of the thrumming cable lowered slightly as it slowed to a stop with the upper compartment of the man car or cage, even with the shaft collar. The men, tired but happy to be off work, filed out and searched the faces of miners waiting to descend, looking for their counterparts to relay what supplies they would need or to warn them of any problems they might face. Once that final piece of business was complete, they quickly cleared the staging area and shuffled off toward the Dry.

Robert threw his arm out to stop Jacob, who was stepping around him to board the cage. "We'll get on last," he said. Jacob rolled his eyes impatiently but held in place as he was told. When the last miner had pushed his way in, there was just enough room for Robert and his son to get on, packed tight, shoulder to shoulder. Robert reached over and pulled the door closed and yelled for the bell signal that would start them going down.

There was a twelve-inch-high open space at the top of the cage walls, and Jacob set his gaze there as the speed of their descent continued to build, not because there was anything to see necessarily, but to keep from making eye contact with the miners who were pressed in close around him. Every time they sped past a level there was a brief flash of illumination from the primitive light bulbs that hung from bare wires above each landing. After a few minutes, Jacob became aware of a puzzling warm sensation on his right foot. He looked down as best he could in the tight space, half expecting to see some contraption transferring heat to the steel decking beneath his feet, but no plausible explanation presented itself. To avoid showing himself as a greenhorn, he decided to wait until he and his father were out of earshot of the men before he mentioned it.

Robert and Jacob were the first ones to exit the cage on the fourth level, and as they stood there waiting for the shift boss, the other miners filed past and began their long walk to their work areas. One man, tall and wearing an especially ragged canvas coat, paused and smiled at Jacob while squeezing his shoulder.

"I am Victor, I like dem boots." With that, he simply laughed and turned away to follow the other men down the long dark tunnel. Jacob followed Victor's retreating figure until there was nothing to be seen but a bobbing pinprick of light from the man's carbide lamp against a field of impenetrable darkness. How odd, he thought.

"Hey Pop, are these some kind of new boots? Seems like the longer you have them on, the warmer your feet get."

Robert turned and gave his son a quizzical look. "Both feet?" he said.

Jacob thought for a moment and replied, "Well, no, come to think of it, just the right one."

Robert threw back his head and laughed out loud and then reached out and pulled his son into a one-arm shoulder hug. "Well, I'll be damned! I'm going to go out on a limb here, son, but I believe someone peed in your boot during the ride down." He turned to Finn the shift boss, who was fidgeting in his struggle to remain silent and waved him forward. "Let's get after it. I gotta be back at the office by 11:00." Robert led the way, still chuckling to himself, and the three men flicked on their lights and headed deeper into the mine.

Every day at noon the miners came back to the surface to eat lunch and smoke a cigarette or two. Beneath the shelves that held the lunch pails was a long bench where they could sit and spread out the various courses of their noontime meal beside them on waxed paper.

"I gotta say, Vic, you may not be very bright, but you got seeds," said one of the men. "Not every man would have the brass to piss in the boot of the boss's son."

Victor sat on the bench, leaning forward with his elbows resting on his knees, taking deep draws on a cigarette. The lunch pail bearing his name rested on the ground between his feet. He smiled and grunted his acknowledgment and then casually turned up the soles of his boots one at a time and inspected them, thinking he might have stepped in dog shit on the walk up from the shaft. Finding nothing, he flicked his cigarette butt away and pulled the lid off his lunch pail.

"Oh my god!" someone yelled, "Who crapped their pants?" The men on each side of Victor jumped up and quickly moved away.

The confused miner looked down into his pail and there, draped across the top of his lunch and sagging at the ends under its own weight, was an enormous stink pickle, or what seemed enormous in context with the underlying pasty, shot through in places with an odd, pale marbling, reminiscent of a core sample.

"Maybe that boy, he ain't so dumb after all, Vic!"

Chapter 8

John rose up on his elbows and peeked over the little berm of dirt and dead tree limbs he and Matt had piled up in front of their long, shallow foxhole. They were on the line with their company, just inside a patch of woods facing a wheat field, green but already waist-high and headed out. Four hundred yards away on the far side of the field, the ground sloped upward into a dense, dark tangle of trees, brush, and vines, broken here and there by outcroppings of huge, gray rocks. Even to John's untrained eye, it seemed like a perfect defensive position. Something burning in the distance was sending clouds of black smoke billowing into the evening sky behind the enemy-held forest. As he looked on, an American, or possibly a French, heavy artillery shell burst in the air against the dark backdrop, sending bright shards of steel shrapnel wheeling in the afternoon sun like a shoal of herring.

They had been told that there were just a few Germans across the way and that they would likely fall back quickly once the Marines started forward, but no one really believed that. The rattle of machine gun fire had been relatively light but persistent since they had settled into this position several hours before, and the ground up and down the line of Marines was littered with fresh, green leaves and pieces of small branches that had been nipped off by bullets hissing through the trees. So far, at least, the Germans had mostly been shelling an area about a mile to their left toward Lucy-le-Bocage and had been content with tossing just a few whiz-bangs their way every so often to keep them honest.

Before settling back next to his brother, John once again studied what looked like four untidy bundles of light blue rags on the near edge of the wheat. No telling how long the French soldiers had been dead, but what killed them was an easier matter; there was a shell crater just a few feet away. Dying puffs of late afternoon wind sporadically lifted the hem of one soldier's coat at the back vent and then dropped it back in place. Once as a boy he had chanced upon a dead Blue Jay that had charged its own reflection and lay dead beneath the window of his father's office. Sharp autumn gusts had whipped around the corner of the house and passed over the aerodynamic shape of its broken wing, conjuring up the notion of life. It was not exactly sadness that he felt then, as now, but more in the way of fascination with the thin line between life and death. The image that troubled him most was of a dead German soldier they had seen that morning sitting propped up against a broken-off signpost at an intersection on the southern edge of Lucy-le-Bocage. The man had apparently died on his back with his right arm extended straight out from his side. Someone had bent his putrefying body into a sitting position with his stiff arm pointing toward Lucy, then hung a sign around his black, swollen neck that said *6th Marines PC 2 miles.*

"I don't know, little brother, it's a damn long walk across that wheat field. I sure hope the gunny's right about there being just a few chicken shit old Boche over there." After a long silence he added, "I got a bad feeling about this."

"Ah, Johnny, you always worry like an old lady, and it never comes to anything," replied Matt. "I just hope there's some Boche left so I can get me one. I haven't even seen one up close since we been here, unless you count those sad sack prisoners we passed on the road this morning. If that's all they got, we'll be fartin' in silk this time tomorrow." Matt lay on his back next to his brother with his arms folded across his midsection, looking up through the trees. He turned his head to the left without sitting up. "Ain't that right, Jimmy?" he yelled to their buddy six feet away in the next foxhole.

"What's the Teach say?" Jimmy shouted back, sounding far away because he, too, was below ground level.

"He thinks our ass is grass."

"Hey, you got any smokes?" said Jimmy.

Matt patted around on his tunic pockets for a moment, and then in a familiar routine, reached up and accepted a pack held out by his brother. After pulling one out with his mouth, he yelled over, "Heads-up, Donovan. Take a few and toss them back. Teach don't want you owing him a brand new pack of butts if you get your ass shot off." In a moment the pack came sailing back over and landed between the brothers. Matt picked it up, lifted the flap on the lower pocket of John's tunic, and stuffed it in.

"Fuck you, Matt," came a barely audible reply from Jimmy.

Around 5:00 in the afternoon, American artillery shells began landing on the German positions across the way with more frequency, but it was at best a half-hearted effort. The idea was to keep the heads of the German defenders down while the Marines advanced across the open ground, but in practice the spotty nature of the barrage only served to warn the enemy that an attack was imminent. Suddenly officers up and down the line began blowing their whistles and yelling at the sergeants to get the men formed up. John and Matt stood up and began squaring away their equipment just as their gunny was passing behind them. Most of the Marines, including John, had waited until the last possible moment to jettison all personal papers, mostly letters, according to standing orders, and now thousands of sheets of white stationery and ripped envelopes were scattered on the forest floor for a half mile in each direction.

"OK, Marines, lock and load. Fix bayonets. Turn to and fall in, squad formation, fall in!" the sergeant yelled at the top of his lungs. "Remember what you been taught and keep moving. Don't stop for your buddy if he gets hit. The best way to help him is to stick your bayonet in one of those Boche machine gunners over yonder. I don't know if we're putting gas on 'em or not, but make sure you put on your masks when you get to the tree line."

John and Matt lined up with their squad in the second rank. This part of the line was on a slight rise so they could look off down the formation when they "dressed right," and it was an impressive sight indeed: hundreds of battle-ready young Marines, confident and in top physical condition, the low sun casting their shadows along the ground in front of them in perfect alignment and flashing off the bright steel of their bayonets.

When movement in the ranks subsided, a portly old first sergeant stepped out in front of the men, looked to his right and then to his left, checking the formation as if they were getting ready to step off in review, then lofted his Springfield above his head to get everyone's attention. He had been in the Corps for nearly thirty years, and although it seemed unlikely by looking at him, he had received not one, but *two* of his nation's highest awards for bravery, the Congressional Medal of Honor. In his typical no-nonsense fashion, he pointed the rifle toward the enemy-held forest and simply started out across the wheat field. After a few steps he looked back over his shoulder impatiently and yelled at the top of his lungs, "Come on, you sons of bitches, do you want to live forever?" The Marines started forward, not in a desperate, glorious charge, but just walking, as if they were walking across a wheat field in Iowa on a pleasant early summer afternoon.

"Damn, Johnny, this reminds me of bird hunting back home."

John gave him a nervous nod and said, "We got to stick together, Matt. I don't care what the gunny says, if one of us gets hit, we got to stick together."

Matt seemed to finally lock onto what his brother was telling him and turned his head. "Don't worry, big brother, me and my trusty friend here won't let nothing happen to you." He hefted his rifle and nodded down at it. As he held John's eyes, he stumbled over a shallow furrow, but before he turned away, he let go of the grip on the butt stock and tapped the left side of his chest with his closed right fist. John hesitated for a moment, unwilling to accept the sense of finality the gesture represented, but then did likewise.

German long-range artillery had used the morning to zero in the Marine position, and now that they knew the expected attack had begun, it was just a matter of loading and firing as fast as they could. The "whiz-bangs," as they were called, were large-caliber, high-explosive shells that would come roaring in like a freight train and then for the last several seconds of flight would emit an unnerving scream before ending in a ground-shaking detonation. Most of the shells were landing in the woods they had just vacated, but without warning, three shorter rounds came in rapid succession and fell on the far right of the Marine formation. Fifteen men in the first rank literally disappeared amid tall plumes of dirt that seemed to erupt and blossom in slow motion, sending shockwaves racing across the tops of the wheat. Other Marines nearby were blown off their feet, some cut up by shrapnel, some merely stunned. Matt turned, and for the first time, John detected a flicker of uncertainty on his brother's face.

In the half-light of evening, the wild field poppies shone blood red against the green wheat as the Marines advanced slowly with steady precision across the field, dressing their lines on the move as if order was all that mattered. They were approaching the halfway point to the enemy-held forest when suddenly it erupted with hundreds of tongues of flame from clattering machine guns and rifles all along its length from both high in the rocks and low in the tangle of brush that bordered the open field. The air the Marines passed through came alive with thousands of hissing and snapping bullets, but they pressed on, bent forward as if walking against a driving rain. The first ranks went down almost as one, in a straight line in death as in life, the waist-high wheat effectively hiding the fallen from view. To the follow-on squads it seemed that they were there one moment, and the next it was as if the earth had swallowed them up.

John glanced to his right and yelled at his brother to hit the deck, but he quickly realized in that split second that he was apparently the only one of his squad that hadn't already done so. He immediately dove on the ground, and the wheat closed in around him. The vision he beheld in that fleeting moment before going to ground was so terrible it was seared in his mind for all time. The men who were slow to take cover died in place. Some fell straight down in a heap as if their legs had suddenly been pulled out from under them, some spun and reeled in a horrible dance as machine gun bullets struck them in rapid succession, stripping off pieces of their uniforms, equipment, and their bodies. He pressed his cheek into the dirt and called out to Matt.

"Matt, goddamn it, where are you?" he yelled. The sounds of battle were so overwhelming that he could barely hear his own voice. The measured clatter of a hundred or more heavy and light machine guns mixed with the truly angry sound of massed rifle fire, all blended together in an unearthly roar like a huge juggernaut whose only purpose was to devour American

Marines. John cradled his rifle in the crooks of his elbows and pushed himself along the ground on his belly, back the way he had come. The enemy machine gun rounds sweeping the field were clipping off the heads of the wheat above him, every bit as effectively as the mechanical wheat header the local farmer would have used during the harvest.

After a few minutes of inching along, keeping as low as possible, the top of a Marine helmet was suddenly right in front of his face. Its right edge was stuck in the top of a furrow, and the left edge was sticking up high enough that it had been chewed off in a horizontal line by a German machine gun traversing back and forth at its maximum depression. The dead Marine lay on his stomach with his head turned to the left. His right arm was thrown out to the side, hand still clutching his Springfield and left arm reaching over his head toward John. His haversack was still in place on his back, but the same pass that had sheared off the edge of his helmet had ripped through the heavy OD canvas and shredded a pair of long johns, sending clumps of white cotton fuzz downwind, where it clung to the sharp stems of the shorn wheat. John stared at the dirty hand in front of his face and he knew. It was his brother Matt.

The deafening noise and the raw fear of battle faded away for John as he inched closer. Matt's lips were still moving, almost imperceptibly, trying to share his last thought, but his eyes were still, fixed on the slender wheat stems in front of his face. John grabbed Matt's outstretched arm just below his elbow with the thought of turning him over but then thought better of it. Instead, he pressed his ear as close to his brother's mouth as he could, but it was no use. Matt was framing the words but there was no air in his lungs to deliver them. John rested his forehead on the back of his hand as the most intense emotion he had ever felt welled up in his chest with a tightness that stifled all but quick, shallow breaths. He thought his heart would stop, in fact willed it to stop, but in the end only part of it died there with his brother in the French wheat field.

"God help me, little brother, but I'm coming with you," he said softly as he patted Matt's shoulder, "but first there's something I gotta do."

John sobbed involuntarily and started to back away. As he put weight on his forearms, Matt's hand suddenly closed tightly around his left wrist, causing him to freeze and gape in astonishment. His brother's face was still frozen in death, but somehow a fleeting spark of life had caused his lungs to draw one more breath. John studied his brother closely for any other sign life, but there was none. When the air left Matt's body in one long final sigh, John was so close that he felt it on his eyes, and again he fought for control. He went through his brother's pockets, at least the ones he could reach without moving the body, and came up with a pocketbook and a pair of dice, which he shoved under the flap of the large side pocket of his tunic. He took one last look at Matt, let out a guttural scream, and stood up. He reached down, grabbed Matt's rifle and .45 from his holster, and then took off at a dead run for the dark forest and the stabs of fire coming from the Maxim machine gun that had cut down his brother.

By this time, the Marines had sorted themselves out and were advancing in squad rushes. One line of men would dash forward a few yards and then throw themselves on the ground and start firing at the enemy to cover the next squad's advance. The second squad would advance for a few yards and then lay down cover for the first squad. This leap-frog approach wasn't perfect, but at least it made more difficult targets for the Germans. It also made John's personal suicide attack a little more likely to succeed. He ran as fast as he could zigzagging right and left, jumping over startled Marines and passing through lines of others who also were running forward. Bullets filled the air, zipping close by like angry bees or plowing up the earth around his feet, but he kept going. Miraculously, aside from his canteen and one pouch on his cartridge belt getting shot off, he made it to the edge of the woods unharmed and dove behind a fallen tree. He had just one mission now: to drive Matt's bayonet through the heart of the man who had killed him.

John's mind was beginning to clear as he lay next to the tree, catching his breath and taking stock. The sound of the German machine guns was much deeper and louder now that he was in the forest only a few yards from where they were still pouring lead into his fellow Marines crossing the wheat field. The odor of rotten eggs from exploded artillery shells and the smell of crushed vegetation were powerful and offensive, but they reminded him of the gunny's warning to don gas masks when they reached the woods.

Just as he removed his helmet to pull on his mask, a bullet glanced off the top of the log next to his head, taking off the lobe of his left ear and grazing his cheek. John shouted a curse, toppled over sideways, and slapped his hand to the side of his head, reacting to the stinging pain. After a moment of working his mouth and swiveling his head, he determined that aside from a profusion of blood, nothing was seriously wrong. He moved down to the shattered end of the log and slowly eased his head out from behind its cover to search for the source of the shot. About twenty-five yards away, there was movement, and as he stared hard at the spot, the upper halves of several German helmets materialized above an outcropping of gray rock. They were almost invisible in the thick tangle of underbrush, but this was just about where he figured the machine gun was that had killed his brother. John pushed the barrel of Matt's rifle out in front of him, filled the sight with the helmet that was most exposed, and squeezed the trigger. There was an immediate metallic clank, loud enough to be heard over the sound of the rifle going off, and when he found the spot in the rocks again after recovering from the recoil, all the helmets had disappeared. John quickly finished putting on his gas mask and helmet and then made a dash for the place where he had last seen the German soldiers.

By now more Marines were moving into the forest and grappling with the German defenders in savage hand-to-hand combat. Desperate cursing, screams, and the Marines' own version of the rebel yell, punctuated by angry rifle fire, filled the shattered forest. The slaughter in the wheat field had taken a terrible toll, but the killing was just getting started. The Germans had been at this for four years and knew exactly how to utilize the thick underbrush and rock formations to their best advantage. The heavy Maxim machine guns were served by a crew of four men, and they were usually accompanied by a detachment of infantrymen. The machine gun positions were arranged in such a way that their fields of fire not only overlapped, but they could also cover one another when attacked. It was a favorite tactic of the Germans to have one machine gun emplacement hold its fire and remain concealed until its neighbor was overrun, and then suddenly to announce its presence by opening fire on the momentarily victorious Marines.

John thought he would have at most maybe a minute before the Germans recovered from the loss of their comrade. The difficult terrain would certainly have slowed him down even more if not for a small opening created by an earlier artillery shell, but even so, he knew it would be a close thing, and he still had several yards to go. Just as he was about to leap up on the rocks surrounding the German position, an enemy soldier popped up almost directly in front of him and tried desperately to bring his rifle around to get a shot at John. If not for his awkward gas mask getting in the way, he might have succeeded. John gripped his rifle in his left hand, pulled his brother's .45 from under the buckle of his cartridge belt and shot the German soldier in the face from no more than three feet away. The man reeled back with the force of the slug, bringing the barrel of his rifle up and involuntarily squeezing the trigger. The muzzle of the Mauser was so close to John's head that the blast burned the part of his face not protected by his gas mask and made him deaf in his already battered left ear.

For John, this had become more than just a battle between Germans and Americans for control of an obscure hunting preserve no bigger than a square mile in the French countryside. For him it had suddenly become a deeply personal matter. There was no past and there was no future, but only the brutal reality of the present: kill or be killed. John stepped on a small boulder with his left foot and launched himself to the top of the rocks that surrounded the enemy machine gun nest. Below him there were six German soldiers wearing long, gray-green coats, dirt-caked jackboots, and big, coal-scuttle-shaped helmets.

In that moment, two of the enemy soldiers were kneeling next to the man that John had just shot. The hands of the one on the right were red and shiny with blood. One man with his back to him was feeding an ammunition belt into the side of the machine gun, while yet another was busy linking belts from open ammo cans. The German soldier who held John's gaze the longest was the one hunched over and sighting down the barrel of the machine gun, spade grips jumping in his hands. All of their faces were concealed behind black gas masks with large, round, built-in goggles and canisters that hung down on their chests like some grotesque proboscis, making them look for all the world like giant insects scurrying around after being caught in the light.

Fortunately for John, the gas masks the Germans wore restricted their peripheral vision, and they didn't immediately see him standing on the rocks and looking down on them. The few extra seconds were all he needed to settle on a course of action. He fired two quick shots with his .45 at the man with the bloody hands, hitting him at least once in the neck, and then took a hurried shot at the other kneeling soldier as that man spun around to face him. He was wearing the tunic of an officer and also had a pistol in his hand. Just as he raised his arm to shoot, the slug from John's .45 struck the front of his helmet near the top, penetrating, but at an angle that caused the bullet to follow the inside curvature of the steel and exit behind his shoulders. The man was knocked backward off his feet but only stunned.

John stuck the .45 back in his cartridge belt and dropped down to the ground next to the enemy soldier who was bent over the ammo cans. He raised his rifle and brought it down butt-first on the back of the man's neck, sending him sprawling on his face amid a tangle of ammunition belts and spent shell casings. Before the German could recover, John changed his grip on his rifle and with a savage yell, drove the bayonet through his back. The German soldier firing the machine gun was intent on his job and hadn't yet noticed anything amiss, but the head of his comrade who was feeding belts into the gun turned and locked eyes, expressionless gas mask eyes, on the Marine.

John pulled hard on his rifle to free his bayonet from the German soldier at his feet, but it was stuck between the man's ribs and wouldn't budge. He once again pulled Matt's .45, aimed it at the loader's chest, and pulled the trigger twice. The gun fired once before the slide locked open on an empty clip. The single shot knocked the German off his feet, but he quickly regained his footing, pulled a trench knife from his boot, and lunged at John, knocking him to the ground and landing on top of him. John gripped the German's wrist with his left hand and pushed back as hard as he could to hold the tip of the knife away from his neck. Both men were grunting with exertion and snarling at one another, locked in a savage, primeval struggle that only one would survive. They were only inches apart now, and John could see the other man's eyes bulging behind the lenses of the gas mask. The German soldier was the smaller of the two, so even though he was able to add his weight to the downward thrust of the knife, John held it away as he used his other hand to pull his own .45 out of its holster. He jammed the barrel into the side of the German and pulled the trigger, just once this time, because he couldn't remember if he had chambered a round before they started across the wheat field. To his great relief, the gun bucked in his hand, even though the report was lost in the overwhelming background noise of battle.

John rolled to the left with considerable effort and let the German's body fall away to the ground beside him. He got up on all fours, dropping his head as he gasped for air. His arm muscles were quivering under the weight of his body, and he knew he was near the end of his endurance mentally and physically. It took almost everything he had, but he finally got to his feet and stepped over to retrieve his Springfield. This time he remembered his training and fired the rifle as he pulled, using the recoil to break the bayonet loose. He felt a sharp push on his left shoulder and a burning sensation, as if someone had touched the lit end of a cigarette to his bare skin. Then there was another push, more of a blow this time, as if he had been hit in the back with a hammer, and he stumbled forward. Suddenly it dawned on him that he had been shot. He always imagined there would be excruciating pain, but aside from the burning, he hardly felt it. He spun around to find the officer had regained his senses and was standing ten feet away with his arm outstretched, pointing a Luger at John's head.

John knew he was about to die. Time slowed down and for the first time he noticed a loud ringing in his ears. Just as everyone said, scenes started to roll through his mind, not his whole life flashing before him, but parts of it. There was a winter vision of his mother and father careening down High Street hill in an old flat-bottom fishing boat, screaming and waving their arms in delight as they sped toward the clear ice of Lake Bancroft. There was a summer vision of Rosemarie and his brothers sitting on the old swim raft, dangling their feet in the cool lake, droplets glistening on brown skin, giggling as schools of minnows nibbled at their toes. Finally there was a vision of a warm autumn afternoon, hunting squirrels with Matt near the old trapper shack in the woods behind their house. The crisp leaves of the great trees floated quietly down through soft light, and dark silhouettes scurried along high branches in the distance. Even old George was there, a ruffed grouse in his mouth, looking up for his due with pride in his eyes. He focused on the German officer's hand as it tightened and then closed his eyes to wait for the end.

Seconds passed and nothing happened. John opened his eyes and saw the German officer digging in a small leather pouch on his belt for another clip. Scarcely able to believe his luck, he pulled his rifle up level with his waist and worked the bolt to chamber a round. The German looked up, realized he was out of time, and simply threw his pistol at John before running for a space between the rocks that led into the forest. It was an easy shot for John, and the bullet struck the German in the back from only twenty feet away. The force of the powerful 30.06 cartridge flung the man hard against the rocks in front of him, and he slid to the ground, leaving a bright red smear on the face of the stone.

Suddenly remembering the last German, John racked a fresh round into his rifle and turned, half expecting to see the machine gun abandoned. The enemy soldier was still there and looking over his shoulder at John. He made no move to defend himself or to escape, even though he must have realized that the American, a terrifying visage in a gas mask, blood covering the side of his face and soaking through the green wool of his tunic, was going to kill him. In fact, he just slowly turned back and lowered his head to look down the barrel of the Maxim as it continued to spray lead across the wheat field. John closed the distance between them in two long steps and paused for the German gunner to look at him—but he didn't look.

John's blood lust was out of control now, and he planted his left boot on the man's shoulder and toppled him over away from the gun. The German landed hard on his back and lay still with his legs tangled in the tripod. In a blind rage, John raised his Springfield over his head like a spear and plunged the bayonet into the man's chest with all the hatred one man could possibly feel for another. Death quivers traveled up the cold steel of the rifle to John's hands. The enemy gunner slowly brought his right hand to his chest and carefully closed his fist around the few inches of exposed blade next to the pommel but made no attempt to pull the bayonet free. John tossed his helmet to the ground and peeled off his gas mask to ensure the last thing the German who had killed his brother would see in life would be *his* face. He then reached down and ripped the gas mask off the German gunner. He gasped in astonishment. Looking up at him was the cherub-like face of a young boy. The gas mask had kept his face clean and given his cheeks a soft pink blush; his eyes were amber, set in clear white. As John stared in horror, the boy gave him a sad half-smile and started to smack his lips. His mouth opened just a bit and a river of bright red blood flowed through his quivering lips and down each side of his face. John slowly backed away in shock. He had set free the ghost that would haunt him for the rest of his natural life.

As darkness closed over the shattered forest, John retrieved Matt's .45 and wiped it off as best he could on his tunic before slapping in a fresh clip and letting the slide pick up a round on its forward travel. He did the same with his own .45 and then sat on a boulder a few feet away from the German boy. The shock from his wounds was beginning to wear off, to be replaced by intense pain. Even so, it was nothing compared to the pain in his heart and the confusion deep in his mind. Sporadic enemy shells had begun to land close by, but he barely took notice. They were not the earth-shaking detonations of high explosives; they were the dull thuds of gas shells.

Chapter 9

B ill lay awake in his bunk, waiting for Old Ray to turn out his light and start snoring. His eyes were fixed on the bottom of the mattress above him, but he wasn't really looking at it. Stuck in between the ticking and the link-springs were several risqué photos the size of playing cards that a wiper had given him when he left the ship to take a shore job. His favorite lady had been captured in an artistic studio pose, holding up a fake parakeet to her pooched-out lips. The heavy sepia paper they were printed on was dog-eared with an occasional black smudge from an oily thumb, but fortunately, none of the important parts had been damaged.

Also stored in this fashion were two unfinished letters, one to Rosemarie and one to John and Matt. With a twinge of guilt, he pulled down the one to his brothers and held it out over the edge of his bunk to catch the light from the companionway behind him. Once he had gotten through the preliminaries (weather, health, women), he had stalled out and given up. It didn't seem much use recounting his exploits in Cleveland or Detroit, when they were probably walking down the Champs-Élysées with a couple of those French women you read about. Once again, he gave up and stuffed the letter in the sagging link-springs above him, causing Charlie to miss a beat with his snoring. Between him and Old Ray in the bunk on the opposite bulkhead, it was a miracle that he got any shut-eye at all. Eventually, even though his bunk light was still on, Ray finally took a long raspy breath, punctuated at the end with a sharp snort, and then settled into a steady rhythm. Bill reached over the side of his bunk and carefully eased the drawer beneath him out far enough to see the reassuring glint of the companionway light in the rolling, amber liquid.

After what seemed like five minutes but was actually several hours, the booming West Virginia drawl of Gary, the watchman on the mid watch, abruptly ended the peaceful repose of the three deckhands. "OK, gentlemen, every swinging dick hit the deck," he cried as he leaned in from the companionway. He paused briefly and waited for the deckhands to stir. "Captain wants all the hatch clamps snugged up as soon as you boys can grab a cup of joe and get your foul weather gear on. Better take the tunnel, no sense getting wet until you have to. Besides, I'm sure Fuzzy doesn't want to mess up those fancy boots. Ya know, most folks with a lick of sense wear boots like that to ride a motorsickle, not a steamboat," he said, referring to the new motorcycle boots that Bill had taken a fancy to when they were up the street last trip. There was a loud thump as Charlie landed on the deck from the top bunk.

"Come on, Fuzzy, let's get this over with. Old man must figure we got some weather coming." Bill rolled out, already fully dressed, and after taking a moment to admire his new footwear, began lacing up the boots. Across from him, Old Ray was also sitting on the edge of his bunk, but motionless, staring at the deck through his knees.

Charlie looked over at Bill as he pulled on his foul weather bibs. "That damn Ray don't look like he knows if he's afoot or horseback,"

"Fuck you," said Ray without looking up.

"Now Ray, that just ain't very neighborly like. Time to get your rubber pants on," said Charlie.

"Fuck you," again from Ray.

Charlie grinned at Bill and backhanded his arm. "He's not really a morning person. Let's go get some coffee."

Running along the port and starboard sides of the ship directly under the weather deck, between the cargo hold and the side of the hull, were narrow passageways called tunnels. The crew used them to get from one end of the ship to the other in bad weather when it would be too dangerous to be out on deck. They were especially important to the deck department officers and crew who lived in the bow of the ship, because they gave access to the galley located aft over the engineering spaces. Charlie slapped the battens up out of the way on the heavy watertight door leading to the starboard tunnel and stepped through after holding it open for Bill. They started aft, stepping through oval man-ways cut in the frames at fifteen-foot intervals, the hollow sound of their every footfall echoing off the cold steel. As they neared the halfway point, the slightly lower belly of the ship's hull hid either end of the tunnel from view and gave the impression of standing between two mirrors looking off into infinity, fore and aft. For Bill it was a creepy, disorienting feeling, even though he knew the tunnel was 450 feet long with a watertight door at each end. It always made him move just a little bit faster.

"Ray don't seem to be bouncing back very fast," said Bill. He and Charlie sat across from each other, sipping coffee in the crew's mess on short lunch-counter-style stools.

"Yeah, no shit. I liked it a lot better when he didn't know what his old lady was up to. At least he didn't get hammered before he come back aboard. Maybe he'll snap out of it before we're back in Cleveland next week. If he gets to drinkin' again, his sailing days are probably over."

There was a long silence between the two men, and when Bill looked up, he was surprised to find Charlie looking at him as if waiting for an answer to a missed question.

"What?" said Bill.

"Gotta be careful he don't get into your stash. Just keep it locked up, is all I'm saying." Bill thought about it for a moment but in the end just nodded, remembering the fifth of Jack Daniels and the one of blackberry brandy locked in the drawer under his bunk. The memory of two bottles of Jack he had hidden in his locker under some dirty laundry did not come to mind.

When Charlie and Bill came around the corner of the after-deck house, the wind struck them head on, making their jackets billow and prompting them to lean forward and slightly to port as they began the methodical task of checking the tension on every clamp on the twelve main hatchways. After about half an hour, a shout from Charlie, nearly lost on the wind, brought Bill out of the mind-numbing effects of repetition, and he followed the direction of his friend's arm to the bow. Far forward, silhouetted against the low deck lights, was the solitary figure of Old Ray, moving slowly, checking clamps, and working his way aft. Before turning back to his work, Bill glanced up at the pilothouse just in time to see the pale face of the third mate turn away and disappear forward into the darkened space.

The most severe storms on the Great Lakes usually occur late in the shipping season during the months of October and November, so this disturbance came as something of a surprise to the crews of the iron boats. Winds increased to forty-five knots during the night and swung around to come at them from the unlikely point of east-southeast, rolling up huge waves that boomed against the port bow and sent shivers through the hull—not the quick, sharp shivers from striking a dock, but long, deep tremors that traveled along the keel and up through the frames. The deckhand's cabin was one level below the weather deck on the port side, separated from the angry sea by the mere thickness of an iron hull plate. Every time the bow plunged into the face of an oncoming roller, submerging the cabin's only porthole, cold lake water forced its way past the brittle cork gasket under immense pressure and sprayed the outboard side of the compartment with the force of a fire hose.

"Damn, Charlie, I don't think we can save your bloomers," said Bill, referring to the voluminous white silk whorehouse souvenir that hung sopping, draped over the cabin light on the bulkhead next to the porthole. Over time, heat from the bulb had added a certain *character* to the garment, depending on one's point of view.

Charlie reached up, pulled them down, and squeezed the water out in his big fist. "These are my good luck charm. They'll dry," he said. Along with their wet bedding, they were hung over a steam pipe on the Orlop deck. The three deckhands spent the remainder of the night in their bunks fully dressed, boots and all, lying on bare mattresses. Somehow Old Ray was able to sleep through the crazy motion of the cabin and spraying water, but Charlie and Bill lay awake, mindful of every unfamiliar sound from the rivets and hull plates as they worked in the heavy seas.

Bill had eventually fallen asleep at some point, despite his discomfort, and now awoke with a start. The porthole that had nearly flooded them out the night before now framed cloudless, bright blue sky. The motion of the ship had eased considerably and become more predictable, but ranks of large waves still rolled up from the southeast, causing the *Pontiac* to hog amidships as they passed under the keel. Bill pulled his knees up to his chest and bounced the sagging form of his friend in the upper bunk off the bottoms of his boots, eliciting a predictable reaction.

"Come on, Charlie, drag your dead ass out. There must be an inch of water on the deck."

"Damn it, Fuzzy, I'm going to come down there and thump you good if you don't cut that out. Shit!" he exclaimed when he saw what Bill was talking about. "That damn scupper must be plugged up again. Go get a mop and a couple of buckets, and we'll scoop up as much as we can with a dust pan."

By the time the cabin was mopped dry, there was just enough time to head aft for breakfast before the work day started. When they stepped out on deck, they stopped and stared in disbelief. Every inch of the weather deck and all twelve hatches, an area slightly bigger than a football field, was covered with thousands of small silver fish. They were radiant in the clear air, sparkling as their flanks reflected the morning sun.

"Jesus, you ever see anything like that?"

"Alewives," said Ray. "Must have hit a patch of them last night when the deck was awash."

"Don't take a genius to figure out what we'll be doing after breakfast. The Old Man will want them gone before they start to stink," said Charlie.

"They're kinda pretty, but I can't say I blame him," replied Bill as they worked their way aft, shuffling their feet to avoid slipping.

"I'll be damned if I ever soogeed fish before," added Ray.

Joe the porter was a short stubby man, mostly bald and usually sporting a couple of days' worth of gray stubble on his sagging jowls. He wore a dirty white apron tied at the waist, topped by an equally dirty white porter's jacket with dried sweat stains around the pits from a warmer time. Joe was in his usual spot, perched on a stool to the left of the galley door with his arms crossed high on his chest and a soggy stub of an unlit cigar in the corner of his mouth, as the three deckhands stepped over the coaming and queued up at the coffee percolator to fill their mugs.

"Morning, Joe. Expecting company?" said Charlie, referring to the flyswatter that rose straight up from the crook of the old porter's left elbow. Joe grunted a response that could have meant anything, but it was just his way of buying time to scrutinize every sentence for verbal barbs that he had come to expect from the crew. Whatever the insult, his response always followed the same formula. He would select an appropriate keyword from the offensive verbiage, grab his crotch and say "I got your orange juice or fly swatter or whatever, right here." If it was a really grievous infraction, he had a habit of squatting just a little so his legs would part and then giving a little thrust with his pelvis to emphasize his retort.

"Bacon, scrambled eggs, and one of those bigass pecan rolls if you got any left," said Ray.

"Me too," said Charlie.

"Me three, only make mine a cinnamon roll," said Bill. Across the table from the deckhands, sat Harry the wiper and two oilers who had names Bill always had trouble remembering. It was easy to tell they were coming off watch from the smears of dirty oil on their faces and up both bare forearms below their rolled shirt sleeves. The creases in the skin of their hands and cuticles of their fingernails were permanently black.

"Any of you deck apes know when we're supposed to make the locks?" said one of the oilers in a way that seemed a little strained. Joe had returned from putting in their orders and jumped in ahead of everyone else.

"Second mate says five o'clock tonight, if we don't have to drop the hook and wait our turn." The oiler eyed Joe up for a moment, much as a lion would eye an antelope, but then just grunted and turned back to his plate, apparently concluding that he wasn't worth the effort.

"One of you boys willing to snag me a paper when we go through the lock?" said the oiler.

There was a bit of an awkward moment until Bill said, "Sure, I'll get you one."

"*Plain Dealer*, if he's got one. If not, The *Detroit News* will do." The oiler dug a dollar out of his wallet and tossed it on the table in front of Bill as he stood to leave. "Get yourself a titty magazine while you're at it."

When the three deckhands stepped out on the deck, the boatswain was leaning on the railing, smoking a cigarette and waiting for them.

"'Morning, Dizzy," said Charlie. "I guess you want us to get our foul weather gear on and soogee those damn little fish off the deck first thing."

"What fish?" said Dizzy with a smug little smirk.

The deckhands turned as one and again were brought up short in disbelief. The fish were gone and in their place were hundreds of ring-billed gulls. As with the fish, they covered nearly every square foot of the exposed weather deck. Each one stood facing into the wind, which happened to be from the south that morning. To the seamen who stood there gawking, facing north toward the bow, it seemed as if every single bird was staring at them.

Old Ray broke the spell first and started up the deck, waving his arms and shouting, but the birds held their ground as if they could sense the power of their numbers. Ray stopped before he reached the first hatch and stepped carefully backward until he once again stood with the other three men.

"Chicken out, Ray?" said the boatswain.

"No, goddamn it. I seen the first mate watching from the pilothouse. I figure he'd wait until I got halfway down the deck and then blow the horn to make all those birds light out at once. I just didn't want to get all shitted up." Everybody had a good laugh and then headed forward though the port tunnel.

"What's on our dance card for today, Dizzy?" said Charlie.

"Chipping and priming today, but we'll knock off early," replied the boatswain. "If we lock down without dropping the hook, it will be a late night for you boys."

The *Pontiac's* forward motion was just barely perceptible as she inched toward the concrete pier at a forty-five-degree angle. There were two down-bound boats ahead of them, so Captain John Johnson decided to put the deckhands ashore and tie up about half a mile north of the Poe Lock to wait his turn. The boatswain's chair dangled from the end of the landing boom next to Bill's hip as he stood on the corner of the number one hatch, waiting for the nod from the first mate. This part of his job always made him a little nervous, since even the slightest mishap here could land him in the cold water between the hull and the pier. There were big wooden blocks tethered to stanchions at intervals along the deck that could be kicked over the side to hold the ship off just enough to save a man from being crushed in such an emergency. That was the theory, anyway.

"OK, Castor, saddle up," shouted the mate. Bill pulled himself up, swung his legs onto the seat of the boatswain's chair, and nodded to signal his readiness.

"Swing him out!" Dizzy was tending the line that controlled the boom, and at the mate's command gave it a hard pull to send it swinging out over the water.

"OK, mate, over the dock," shouted Bill. Immediately the first mate eased his grip on the line attached to the boatswain's chair and let it slip through his hand, dropping the deckhand to the pier. As soon as he was out of the chair, Bill waved and the boom swung back into the ship to pick up Charlie.

Just as Dizzy said, it was a long night of shifting the heavy steel cables from one bollard to the next so the mates could use the ship's steam winches to pull her along the pier toward the lock. It was one in the morning by the time the mammoth gates of the Poe Lock closed behind the *Pontiac*. Even though it was the middle of the night, the locks were brilliantly lit for the line handlers who hustled back and forth under the watchful eyes of the mates to keep the ship properly positioned as she began her descent to the level of the St. Mary's River. Charlie was standing by the stern line, engaged in a long-distance shouted conversation with an old friend on the Steinbrenner that was upbound in the next lock over, and Bill stood by the forward spring line, quietly smoking and looking forward to the moment when he could pull off his boots and have a nightcap before falling into his bunk to rest his aching muscles. He sensed movement out of the corner of his eye and turned to see the stooped old vendor approach with his wooden cart loaded with stacks of newspapers, cartons of cigarettes, pouches of Red Man and pipe tobacco, as well as a few worn books that he circulated between ships as a courtesy. Bill suddenly remembered his promise to the oiler and fished for the dollar bill as he fell in behind the old man.

"You carry the *Plain Dealer*?" he said. The old man didn't reply but bent over, with effort, and pulled a paper out from under a brick on top of one of the stacks.

"That'll be seven cents, sonny."

"You got any girlie magazines?"

The old man froze from fussing with his merchandise, cocked his head toward Bill, and regarded him up and down with a sour look. "I don't engage in such nonsense, thank you very much," he spat.

The deckhand offered up the oiler's dollar and said, "OK, OK, sorry, just give me the paper, then." The man grabbed the bill and turned back to his cart.

"I sell health magazines," he said holding one out. Bill took it and tilted it to deflect the glare from the overhead light. *Nude Living* was the title. The cover showed three pleasant-looking ladies wearing big floppy-brimmed straw hats and sandals, nothing else. One was bent over at the waist, facing the camera and preparing to swing a crochet mallet between her legs while the other two looked on with big, toothy smiles.

"Don't be thumbing through it, sonny. If you want it, it's seventy-five cents."

"Yeah, I'll take it." The old man pulled a wad of bills out of his pants pocket and added the oiler's dollar. He deftly pressed the push levers on the four-barrel coin changer that hung on his belt and held his cupped hand out to Bill.

"Paper's seven cents, so that makes it eighty-two cents all together."

Bill nodded absentmindedly as he turned away with the newspaper under his arm. After a few more minutes of studying the three nudists, he folded the magazine in half length-wise, reached around behind him, and tucked it in the waistband of his trousers. When he looked up, the *Pontiac*'s main deck was even with the top of the lock, so he simply stepped aboard. When he turned to head aft and find the oiler, he saw Old Ray, leaning on the rail back by the galley and talking to a lock worker. The old man quickly looked to his left and right, then leaned out and exchanged money for something that glinted in the harsh lights.

Chapter 10

The savage and confused fighting of the day before had decimated the ranks of the 5th Marines and left small groups of men isolated and scattered throughout the southern third of Belleau Wood. All night long the darkness had been ripped by machine gun tracers and the unnatural illumination from star shells that rendered the surreal landscape of shattered forest in photographic negative. The ceaseless moans and incoherent ramblings of wounded men from both sides were bad enough, but the primal screams of agony that echoed through the night unnerved even the strongest men. The land still reeked of spent high explosives, but added to it now was the smell of death.

Light from the new day did little to clarify the situation. Sergeant Lindsey and Corporal Benedict were, as far as they knew, the only survivors of their platoon. Just before nightfall, they had joined up with remnants of other units and now were moving cautiously through the underbrush, attempting to locate more Marines to fortify their tenuous position against counterattack. There was no line of communication to a higher authority that might be counted on for orders, and they had no idea where they were or even which direction the German line was. The only things they were sure of were that they were Marines and they were there to kill the Boche any way they could. If they had to do that on their own hook, so be it.

"I don't know, Benny, judging by the sun, my ass is turned completely around. I would have sworn north was that way," said the sergeant, nodding his head to indicate the direction back over his shoulder.

"You still got a compass?" The corporal slid his hand under the gas mask bag that lay against his chest and dug around in the upper pocket of his tunic. He pulled out a crushed pack of Camels and tossed them away with a little curse under his breath and then went back in and this time came out with a standard-issue compass, slightly the worse for wear. He scrutinized it for a moment to make sure the needle still moved and then handed it to Sergeant Lindsey.

"Sure enough," said the sergeant, "that damn sun is right on the money." Benny rolled his eyes and leaned back against the smooth, gray boulder they had taken cover next to.

"Butt me, Sarge," he said. Lindsey shook up a couple of cigarettes and held the pack out to the corporal. A moment later, Benny closed his eyes as he drew comforting smoke deep into his lungs.

"We'll move southeast for another thirty minutes or so and then head back if we don't turn up any more men." Lindsey picked at a piece of tobacco that had stuck to his lip and then spat around the tip of his tongue. Just then there was a pop, pop, pop in rapid succession. The two men brought their rifles around and rolled on their bellies.

"That's close!" said the sergeant.

"Yeah, and it's a .45." Lindsey and Benny moved carefully in the direction of the sound until they came to an area that was slightly raised and crowned by an outcropping of large rocks. Lindsey carefully eased himself up from a crouch and was just about able to peek over the top when the edge of his helmet scraped against the rock. There was an immediate POP, much louder now, and small chunks of soft rock rained down on the tops of their helmets. Lindsey turned his head and locked eyes with Benny.

"Marine! This is Sergeant Lindsey and Corporal Benedict, Company D, third platoon. Don't shoot, we're coming in!" There was no answer. Lindsey held his hand out palm down so that Benny would stay put and then rose up slowly until he could see over the rocks. It took a few moments for him to make sense of what he saw. Directly across from him, there was a narrow opening in the rocks that surrounded what once appeared to have been a German machine gun nest. In front of the opening were the bodies of four or five enemy soldiers, hard to tell exactly because they were literally piled on top of one another as if they had come into the open area one at a time and had been shot down in turn. Just to the left of this, another German was draped over the top of the rocks on his belly in such a way that his wounds had caused him to bleed out down the inside face of the rock, creating a pool of dark coagulated blood at its base. Large black flies were already beginning to light on the filmy surface. There were bodies everywhere, including one near an overturned Maxim machine gun that had a bayonet, still attached to a Springfield rifle, sticking out of his chest. It was then that he saw the lone American Marine sitting on a flat rock facing the pile of bodies, each hand resting in his lap and clutching a .45. He wore no helmet and his gas mask dangled at the end of its air tubing from its canvas bag. The side of his head and front of his tunic were caked with dried blood, and his suppurating eyes were swollen and crusted shut.

"What's your name, Marine?" said Sergeant Lindsey. The man turned his head to the sound but kept his silence and made no move to fire his pistols. By now Benny was looking over the rocks and taking in the gruesome sight. Horrifying sights were everywhere in Belleau Wood, but this was something different. The sergeant and corporal slid off the top of the rocks and landed on the ground in front of the solitary Marine.

"How bad you hit? Can you talk?"

Once again the man turned slightly to face the sound of the sergeant's voice, but he made no attempt to speak. Even though the man's eyes were closed, the pain etched on his face was plain to see. Lindsey looked down and noticed the slide on the .45 in the wounded man's left hand was open on an empty magazine, and the one in his right was cocked and ready to fire. The sergeant took a step forward, but as he did, the man calmly brought the loaded .45 up to his temple. Almost too late, Sergeant Lindsey realized what was happening and lunged, batting the barrel down with the palm of his hand. POP, the pistol went off a split second later, the slug ripping through the side of the Marine's right foot. He didn't even flinch; in fact, the sergeant didn't realize the Marine had been hit until he noticed the blood pooling beside his boot.

"Jesus, Sarge, this fella's off his rocker!"

"Shut up, Benny," Lindsey gasped as he twisted the gun out of the man's hand. "Make yourself useful and see if you can come up with his dog tags."

The sergeant fished a pack of cigarettes out of his pocket, lit one, and stuck it between the man's lips. It stayed put, but it brought no noticeable reaction, and the man made no attempt to take a puff.

"John Castor," said Benny. "I remember this fella. I used to play poker with his brother on the ship coming over here."

Lindsey pulled a small notepad and a pencil stub from his breast pocket and jotted down the information. "OK, take a quick look around and grab the dog tags from any dead Marines you find while I figure out what we're going to do... can't leave him here."

Benny sidestepped around the bodies by the opening in the rocks and cautiously slipped through. Sergeant Lindsey gently pulled the other .45 from under John's hand, put in a fresh magazine from his own pouch, and chambered a round before tucking it in his cartridge belt. He had already used the tourniquet and several of the gauze pads out of his first aid kit but was able to find a bandage roll and set about wrapping it around John's head to cover his eyes. He looked up as Benny stepped through the opening in the rocks.

"There aren't any," he said.

"There aren't any what? What the hell you talking about?"

"There aren't any dead Marines out there."

Suddenly it dawned on Lindsey what Benny was getting at. He tied the gauze bandage off with a granny knot and slowly looked around, once again taking in the horrific scene and trying to imagine how it had unfolded.

"This kid is one hell of a Marine," he said, partly to Benny and partly to himself, "one hell of a Marine." He didn't say it out loud, but he wondered how any of them would ever come out of this war with their sanity.

"This damn Gyrine sure isn't getting any lighter," said Chauncy, at the head of the stretcher as they picked their way along the rubble-strewn road on the outskirts of Lucy-le-Bocage.

"Yeah, I hear ya. He's a big one all right, they all are. Let's take five and grab a smoke when we get up by that barn," replied Tom on the other end of the stretcher.

The thatch-roofed barn he referred to was much larger than the others in the area. The long north wall formed one side of a courtyard that lay in front of a rambling, two-story chateau. A six-foot high stucco wall enclosed all and reflected pale pink in the afternoon sunlight. The high, ornate, wrought-iron gates of the compound stood open to the road. The army stretcher bearers set their charge down on a little strip of grass that bordered the road and sank to the ground next to him, close enough to the end wall of the barn to lean against it. From their vantage point they had a good view of the sleepy little farming village of Lucy-le-Bocage. Had it not been for the dead German cavalry horses and their riders lying bloated to impossible proportions in the fallow field across the road from them, they might have imagined the war had not touched this place.

"Mighty fine get-up on those Boche across the way," said Tom, after he'd taken a couple of drags. "Hey, chum, want me to fix you up with a fag?" he said as he nudged the stretcher with the tip of his boot. The Marine made no sign that he had heard the offer.

"Hey, Shit-for-Brains, can't you see he's been gassed? Hell, it's all he can do to suck in enough—" Just then a large-caliber German artillery shell rumbled in and exploded on a little hill on the other side of the village. Both men rose as one and watched intently. Thirty seconds later, another shell burst next to the road on the near side of the village.

"Lucy's going to catch hell. Let's get out of here!" shouted Chauncy. With an efficiency born of much practice, the men quickly took their stations at either end of the stretcher and lifted together.

Before they could get turned around to move away from the village, a tall woman with sandy blonde hair and wearing an ankle-length forest green cloak stepped quickly into the middle of the road in front of the iron gates. Even though she was turned away from them, watching the shells that were beginning to rain down on Lucy-le-Bocage, her apprehension was clear in her subtle movements. The shells were falling so rapidly now that the detonations overlapped, creating a single earthshattering roar. Clouds of gray masonry dust from collapsing buildings blossomed above the rooftops, and black, oily smoke from structure fires came from all points of the village until pulled into one ugly pall by heated air. The woman turned suddenly and looked right at them as if they had called her name, but even if they had, she would never have heard it. They were perhaps forty feet away and could not see her face clearly, but they felt transfixed nevertheless. As if coming to a decision, she simply raised her arm and pointed to the gate and then turned away.

"Got any better ideas?" yelled Chauncy over his shoulder. "Go! Go!"

When they reached the gate, they halted and waited for the woman to notice them. Beyond her they could see a small procession of old people coming up the road from the village. When the woman turned, Chauncy and Tom momentarily forgot the shelling, or why they were even there, for that matter. The last thing they expected to encounter that day, especially amidst a bombardment, was a stunningly beautiful woman. They simply stood there with their mouths open. Never in their young lives had these farm boys seen such a vision of loveliness in the flesh and up close. She wore her hair elegantly high on the back of her head, tucked and pinned in a neat and precise manner, despite the circumstances. Against each cheek lay a tight cluster of pin curls. Her bangs fell below a blue and black silk headband, sweeping right and left of center over her forehead to just above her eyes, eyes of the palest blue, the color of clear ice under a blue winter sky. There was little patience in those eyes for the looks from the American soldiers. She had seen it all before and knew the power she had over men, but she was not amused. She glanced down at the man on the stretcher with a softer look and lightly touched the dirty white bandage that covered his eyes.

Chauncy thought he knew what she was thinking and said, "We was taking him to a dressing station in Lucy ... I mean Lucy-le-Bocage, before the shelling started."

She did not speak but again pointed until the stretcher bearers snapped out of their trance and headed for the small, open door on the side of the house. When Tom looked back over his shoulder, she had already dismissed the encounter and was waving the first old couple of the ragtag procession off the road and through the gate.

On the far right of the courtyard near an overgrown, crescent-shaped rock garden, lay another cavalry horse, jet black and regal-looking, even in death. The tack was well-oiled black leather with bright brass rings and buckles befitting such an animal. Its breastplate carried a gold metal coat of arms trimmed in yellow and black enamel. Unlike the other horses in the field across the road, this one had not been dead long. A few feet away, next to a shaded portion of the courtyard wall, was the moist, mounded-up dirt of a fresh grave. As they drew near, Chauncy and Tom could see where machine gun bullets had pocked the front of the chateau and shattered most of the tall windows.

The wine cellar beneath the front corner of the main house had been part of the much smaller original house dating back to the seventeenth century. The only way in or out was from a single steep stone stairway that led from the back end of the long room to a heavy door at the top and then to the courtyard. The old stone walls and arched ceiling were covered with a thick layer of chaux, built up from countless repairs over the years, giving it the feeling of adobe. The extensive collection of fine wines that once occupied the diagonal cross-hatch of cubbyholes in better times had long since been looted by the soldiers of various armies as they passed on the road. By design, the cellar was dark and cool in spite of the warm days. The centerpiece of the room was a long, heavy, oak wine-tasting table. All but one chair had gone the way of the wine, and the table's only purpose now was to hold the body of the wounded Marine. The flame from a single candle, quivering from the explosions, burned in a rusty wall sconce, not giving enough light to completely penetrate the darkness, but enough to give the frightened old people sitting along the base of the walls something to cling to.

The intensity of the shelling ebbed and flowed. It would move away and it would come near, but it never stopped. One especially violent detonation from what was probably a short round brought down a large piece of chaux from the ceiling and filled the air with ancient dust.

Arielle Landers, the only remaining member of her family that lived at the chateau, sat on the cold floor, apart from the others. Her legs were drawn up under her skirts and cloak, and she supported herself upright by leaning her left shoulder against the wall. Several times during the last few hours she had gotten up and checked the condition of the wounded American, but there was no noticeable change. Whatever was going through his mind was tearing him apart. Since the shelling began, his legs were in constant motion, as if trying to run, and occasionally his arms would flail and his head would whip from side to side. It was as if he were reliving some terrible moment, but he never uttered a sound or attempted to sit up. Most of the time his mouth was open and he struggled for breath. Arielle got to her feet and took a seat in the chair next to the table. She studied the American for a moment in the dim, wavering light and then reached down into her bodice and retrieved the linen handkerchief that had once belonged to her mother. She dabbed at the man's glistening face to remove white plaster dust, and then unfolded the handkerchief and placed it lightly over his mouth to keep him from inhaling the foul-tasting debris. She gently laid the back of her hand against the American's temple to judge his fever and found that it, too, was unchanged. With a sigh, she closed her eyes and rested her head on her folded arms, trying not to think.

A loud crash and violent shaking brought Arielle awake with a start. It was the closest one yet. More pieces of the ceiling came down, and even a few bricks from the walls worked loose and fell on the backs of the old people huddled in the dark. Every shell that landed nearby brought groans and ardent prayers. During a brief break in the noise, Arielle overheard one of the stretcher-bearers say that the Boche were shelling the road. When she looked over at them, all she could see was their white Red Cross armbands, the weak light of the candle giving them an eerie disembodied glow. For the first time since the war began, she stopped struggling and let herself sink in the sea of despair that swirled around her. Her mother had died when she was still a little girl, and her father had been in Belgium when it was invaded by the Germans. It had been almost four years and there still was no word. Both of her older brothers had died on the same day at Verdun. At last she felt her own death was at hand, and she was mildly surprised to learn that she really didn't have a strong opinion about it one way or the other. Perhaps it was for the best after all, she thought. Certain sacrifices had been made to save her father's house and land, even the village, and now it didn't matter. The people she had known all her life despised her, and the chateau was in ruins.

Arielle slid forward on the chair and laid her head on the wounded American's chest. The coarse wool tunic scratched the side of her face, but she could feel his heart beating, and somehow it made dying not such a lonely business. She closed her eyes and started to recite the Lord's Prayer: "Notre Père, qui est aux cieux, que ton nom soit sanctifié, que ton règne vienne, que ta volonté soit faite sur la terre comme au ciel. Donne-nous aujourd'hui notre pain de ce jour."

Arielle felt the American go still and looked up. Her mother's handkerchief had fallen away, and his head was raised as if he were looking at her through his bandage.

"Please don't stop," he said in a voice so soft and hoarse that she might have missed it if she hadn't seen his lips move. Arielle's grasp of the English language was poor, but she remembered enough from her early school days to understand what he wanted. She stared at him for a moment, feeling spontaneous anger rise from the unabashed appraisal she was accustomed to receiving from men, but she quickly rejected the anger when she remembered that he could not see her. As soon as she spoke, he smiled and lay back.

Arielle took his hand and continued: "Pardonne nous nos offensés comme nous pardonnons aussi à ceux qui nous ont offensés. Et ne nous soumets pas à la tentation, mais délivre-nous du mal, car c'est à toi qu'appartiennent le règne, la puissance et la gloire, aux siècles des siècles. Amen."

The more Arielle thought about it, the more astonished she became. At first she thought the American understood her language and was taking comfort from the familiar words. Then she considered that perhaps the prayer itself had something to do with his dramatic change. As she became more convinced that he hadn't understood a word, she began to focus on the latter possibility. At that moment, in spite of herself, she felt the spark of a connection to him, to something she had turned away from long ago. To test her theory, when she was sure he was awake she said, "Je vais vous donner une médaille pour bravoure."

There was no reaction at first, and then he turned his head to the sound of her voice, his upper lip quivered, and he nodded in the affirmative. He turned away and brought his closed right hand up to rest on his chest over his heart.

She thought it a little odd, but there were many things she didn't understand about Americans. She took his left hand in both of hers and whispered,"C'est sur OK. Vous serez mon Sammy." It was just a popular French nickname for American soldiers, but it would do for now.

Chapter 11

Elizabeth leaned on the polished wood of the armrest next to the window, thumb under her chin, and pursed lips against her curled index finger, watching the alternating landscapes of forest and clear cuttings as the steam locomotive labored up the long grade between Marquette and Ishpeming. There were iron red rocks, too, some in outcroppings or cuts, some solitary. She had traveled these rails many times in her life and knew the land well, but it was the rocks that harkened back to her childhood; a Galapagos tortoise here, an old man's face there—the images formed so many years ago came back easily. The train slowed and crossed a trestle over a deep cut where a fast-moving stream widened out into a small lake. Her gaze was drawn to a little cove covered with lily pads on the north shore, where she always promised herself she would fish one day. It made her think of those cherished summers long ago, tent camping with her father and younger brothers, lazy days when they would sit quietly in Uncle Louie's dilapidated fishing boat, squinting at bobbers afloat on the flat water of a lee shore, water spiders skittering here and there ahead of fleeting wakes.

Her mother never took part in these outings; in fact, Elizabeth couldn't even imagine her there, her countenance stern enough to change the rhythms of their lives even on the shores of a pristine lake deep in the woods. She carried the day anyway, eventually, when her only daughter began to fill out, and overalls and bare feet gave way to hair ribbons and white muslin dresses with leg-of-mutton sleeves. As the forests and rocks and lakes passed her window, her thoughts came near, but only close to the point of realizing parallels between mother and daughter, then and now.

The young man in the seat in front of her had the upper half of his window down, presumably for fresh air, but the air that was rustling the plumage of her expensive hat smelled of coal smoke, and she imagined black soot settling on her person. Her annoyance increased with each passing mile. You would think the woman sitting with him would have the good grace to keep him sorted out, she thought. She just didn't understand young people these days, least of all her own grown children. Finally she grasped the top of the seat back in front of her and said, "Young man, would you be so kind as to raise your window? I'm afraid this awful smoke is making me ill."

When the man turned to look at her, he wasn't at all sure whether he would comply or not. Sensing his indecision, Elizabeth covered her mouth with the palm of her hand and blew out her cheeks. She was pleased to note the speed with which the young man raised his window and helped his companion move further back in the coach.

With that bit of unpleasant business out of the way, she sat back and picked up the trail of her unfinished thoughts. Maybe Robert was right about Rosemarie and Jacob. He had told her she needed to back off and start treating them as adults or she might lose them completely. It was easy to read her son's mind, but Rosemarie was another matter entirely. She couldn't put her finger on it exactly, but she sensed the young woman had a plan that she wasn't sharing with anyone. She had floated the idea of Rosemarie and Jacob getting married with her most trusted friend Elsa at the Peter White Library board meeting earlier in the day, and Elsa hadn't seemed scandalized in the least. "You can only raise them so far, and then you must simply get out of the way," she had said. Word would get around to the other ladies in her social circle, sooner rather than later, judging by the potential juiciness of the information. That would be the real test. She was sure there must be something worse than being scorned by one's peers, but she could not think of an example at the moment.

A long blast of the train's steam whistle focused her attention back in the present, and she watched the late afternoon life of Negaunee slide slowly past her window. With a long exhale of steam and the clank of car linkage that traversed the length of the train, they eased to a stop next to the long low red brick Union Station. This train was made up of combination cars that carried both passengers and freight, and as soon as it stopped moving, several teams pulling high-wheeled flatbed wagons pulled alongside each car next to the freight door. When the couple who had been sitting in the seat in front of her walked past on their way to the exit, the young man shot her the "stink eye," but he quickly realized he was out-gunned when Elizabeth looked up. The woman in tow simply smiled and giggled.

The purpose of the meeting she had attended at the library was to organize a drive for books to send to the boys overseas. Naturally, the talk around the table centered on the war, and everyone, it seemed, knew someone who had lost a son. One lady in their own group, who wasn't present at this morning's meeting, had received a telegram from the War Department expressing sympathy, etc., etc., for the loss of a son. Elizabeth shivered involuntarily, not able to imagine herself in that circumstance.

Some of the talk had been about an article in this month's *McCall's* concerning French war brides coming to this country and the problems they faced trying to adapt to the American way of life. She didn't worry about Johnny getting some French floozy in the "family way," but Matt often let the wrong part of his anatomy do the thinking.

The train loped along for a few minutes on the short run between Negaunee and Ishpeming, until finally the engineer blew the whistle and closed the throttle, letting momentum carry them into the First Street Depot. Parked a few feet away by the portico on the end of the station was a shiny Model T Runabout with the top down. Her husband Robert sat in the driver's seat, and next to him on the passenger side sat George, looking around as if he owned the world. Elizabeth made a mental note to check for dog hair before she got in. She kept her seat while the other passengers filled the aisle, waiting their turn to exit the coach, not to avoid the press of humanity, but to take the opportunity to observe her husband surreptitiously. It was hard to tell how long he had been waiting. He could sit there all day and still not look bored. Robert was curious about everything, so he never seemed to lack for amusement. She smiled in spite of herself when he bit off a piece of the jerky he was working on and offered it to George, who seemed to treat it as a common occurrence. Robert was a man's man, but he was also a kind and generous man; Elizabeth knew well the two didn't always go together. Although he was frustrating and juvenile at times, the mere sight of him still warmed her heart. He turned to look at the dog, and she saw his lips moving as if they were deep in conversation. She smiled again when George turned and looked at him briefly as if offering his own opinion before a distraction got the better of him.

"Rob, I saw you talking to that dog. You know, people are going to think you're retarded," she said in way of greeting.

"Well, good day to you, dear. I hope you had a pleasant journey."

Robert held the door for her as George jumped back into the belly of the folded-down top. Before getting in, Elizabeth paused on the running board and swiped her gloved hand across the seat a couple of times, more to make a point than because she noticed anything objectionable. Robert turned to speak to her as they headed up First Street toward home, but before he could get a word out, he saw George casually press forward from behind her to sniff the trio of long thin pheasant feathers protruding fashionably from the side of her hat. George had the good sense to tread lightly, but unfortunately, at that same moment, a long string of slobber escaped his impressive lips and attached itself to the back of Elizabeth's wrap. Robert didn't trust himself to speak, even if he could have remembered what he was going to say. Elizabeth caught him looking at her out of the corner of her eye.

"What?" she said, with a trace of irritation in her voice.

"Oh, nothing, dear, just wanted to admire the prettiest girl in the U.P., is all," he replied with a big grin. She blushed and gave him a dismissive wave of her hand.

"OK, Jacob, let's get this over with so I can read the paper before supper," said Robert with a nod to the *Iron Ore* that lay on the corner of his desk. Jacob sat across from him, turning an expensive looking fountain pen between his index finger and thumb, the same one he had carried every day since graduating from college. A short stack of papers rested on the desk in front of him. The attorneys sent by Cleveland Cliffs to help the miners prepare their wills had reviewed Robert's as well. It had been drawn up soon after Matt was born and now was very much in need of review. The business at hand was to review the proposed changes indicated by handwritten notes in the margins of the document, initial them if he agreed, or strike them if he did not. True to character, Robert wasn't especially interested in the exercise.

"What's first on the list, son?"

Jacob slid a thick periodical out from under a pile of cast-off mail to use as a writing surface and then crossed his legs and prepared to get down to business. "OK, the first thing to decide is whether or not you want Rose included, and if so, the wording should be changed to *natural and adopted* instead of just *natural.*"

"Well, of course she should be in there." To himself he thought he better give this some more thought if she and Jacob got married; it wouldn't be fair to let them double dip.

"They want you to initial all changes, Pop," said Jacob.

Robert didn't turn away from the big bay window but simply waved him off. "You initial it for me, and let's get on with it."

The rest of the modifications were pretty straightforward, mostly involving tracts of forest land that Robert had acquired in recent years, including the hunting cabin up on Lake Margaret, so it didn't take long to finish up. Robert spun around in his chair and slid the newspaper over in front of him while Jacob was jotting down the last few notes.

"I suppose you will be on your way early tomorrow to have a few words with Rose at the telephone office before work, so perhaps you can drop that off for me," said Robert. Jacob looked up quickly, unaware until just now that his daily rendezvous with Rosemarie just before her shift ended was common knowledge.

Robert fought down the urge to smile and said, "Thanks for helping me with this, son. Tell your mother I'll be in here until supper is ready."

When Jacob had closed the door behind him, Robert tilted back in his chair and studied the front page of the *Iron Ore*. The headline was in bigger type than normal: *U.S. MARINES SAVE PARIS*. The details were sketchy, but if the war correspondent could be believed, the Marines had almost singlehandedly routed the entire German army near some little town named Lucy-le-Bocage. There was no word on American casualties, but the article reported that the enemy had suffered dearly. The hair on the back of Robert's neck bristled as he read between the lines. He slowly turned his chair around to face the big window so he could lose himself for a moment in the gathering darkness of Henry's forest.

For the second time, Jacob pounded on the phone company door at the top of the long stairway that doubled as a fire escape in the alley behind Miner's Bank. He folded his arms across his chest and shivered, cursing himself for not wearing a jacket. Finally he saw the heavy curtains stir over the little window next to the door, and then he heard the bolts slide open. (There were three, mostly for the peace of mind of the night operators.)

Rosemarie stuck her head out and looked up and down the alley like a conspirator. "Hurry up, get in here," she said impatiently. "I don't want to lose my job."

Once inside, Jacob leaned forward and kissed her lightly on the lips. It was not much, but even if the meeting had come to an end right then and there, to him it would have been worth every step out of his way in the chilly, pre-dawn air. Rosemarie turned and quickly crossed the room to the switchboard, grateful that no call light was flashing. She sat down and slipped her head through the neck strap of the heavy breastplate transmitter, letting it rest on her chest with the mouthpiece curved up like an inverted powder horn. Next, she set the headset in place, careful not to disturb her hair.

Jacob sat on the edge of the cot next to the switchboard and watched her every move, still a little incredulous that someone this good-looking would want to marry him.

"What's in the satchel?" she said, referring to the leather bag Jacob carried.

It didn't register with him at first, and then he suddenly remembered why he was there. "I have to deliver Pop's will to the attorneys this morning as soon as I leave here. I thought you'd like to know that he changed it to include you in an equal share with the rest of us."

He had Rosemarie's undivided attention now. "Oh, my, that is wonderful news!" she said. "Can you show me?"

A little tug from his conscience made Jacob hesitate a moment, but then he pulled the little bundle of papers out of the leather bag and handed them to her. There was a long silence filled by the crisp tick-tock of the clock hanging above the switchboard and the occasional muffled *pop* from burning pine wood in the parlor stove.

Finally she looked up and said, "What do you suppose would happen if, God forbid, something happened and no one could find Bill? It seems to me since he ran off of his own free will, he really shouldn't be included here at all."

Jacob was silent. This was an unexpected turn of events, and he rocked from one butt cheek to the other as he tried to sort things out on the fly. On the one hand, he didn't want Rosemarie to think he was a coward, but on the other, he knew what she was suggesting was wrong. In the end, a mental image of Rosemarie and Bill swimming buck naked together in the water-filled, open-pit mine deep in the forest won out. He took the papers back, fished his fountain pen out of his pocket, and crossed out Bill's name in two places then placed his father's initials next to the changes. When he stood to leave, Rosemarie pulled on the

front of his shirt until he bent at the waist and pressed his lips
to hers for what seemed to him a truly heartfelt kiss.

Chapter 12

THE CHATEAU

LUCY-LE-BOCAGE, FRANCE

JUNE 8, 1918

John lay on his back just below the blue flower tops of the ground cover, looking up through the trees at the mackerel clouds. They reminded him of his grandfather. "We got some weather moving in. Don't get too far from the house, or Grandma 'll skin ya," he would say. The ground trembled under his spine almost continuously, but there were no smells or telltale black smoke from the shelling. John's shoulder and upper arm were stiff, and any movement or even just the thought of movement sent shooting pains up his neck. When he touched the front of his tunic there, it felt wet. His crotch and underarms were on fire where his sweat reacted with the gas, but it was the pain that encompassed his eyes and forehead that bothered him most. He started to investigate, but the fear of what he might find caused him to drop his arm back at his side. He had seen men with half their heads missing, talking and smoking with their buddies. They would die, of course, but they didn't seem to know it yet, and it was easier for everyone else to simply let it go at that.

The sound of footsteps approaching from back over his head broke into his thoughts. They were purposeful but light, coming straight to him; whoever it was stopped just out of his field of view. Fear gripped John and he turned his head from side to side, trying to see who was there. Finally the footsteps resumed and a muddy jackboot passed inches from his nose. At first he thought the bare-headed German soldier might keep walking, but then he stopped next to John's feet, facing away. He seemed uncertain. A rifle hung from the back of his shoulder by its sling. The arms of his ragged gray coat draped down over his hands, and his head seemed small without a helmet. John looked on in horror as the German turned slowly to face him. It was the boy! He would never forget those eyes—sad eyes, eyes that had seen too much. He smiled at John as he un-shouldered his rifle, and then he reached down and gripped the handle of Matt's bayonet that protruded from his chest. He pulled it out in one steady move, wiped it on the sleeve of his coat, and attached it to the barrel. John was gasping for breath. He knew what was coming, but this time he was determined to embrace it with open eyes. He owed the boy that much.

At that moment, he began to hear the voice of the French lady from the *blanchisserie,* "Donne-nous aujourd'hui notre pain de ce jour." John lifted his head to the sound, but there was only darkness. When the woman took his hand, he said, "Please don't stop," and then he lay back to let the soft melody of her words settle over him. "Pardonnec nous nos offences comme nous par-donnons aussi à ceux qui nous ont offensés. Et ne nous soumets pas à la tentation, mais délivre-nous du mal, car c'est à toi qu'ap-partiennent le règne, la puissance et la gloire, aux siècles des siècles. Amen."

In spite of the constant crashing of German artillery shells, John floated in a layer of calm that stayed with him even when she stopped speaking. He could feel her there, close, her fingers touching the skin of his palm, touching something deep in his brain. She spoke again and he heard the word *brother.* She was asking about Matt. He lifted his face to the sound of her voice again but didn't try to speak. He placed his closed fist over his heart in the boyhood gesture of loyalty he and Matt had always shared, and then he lay back in the darkness, fully awake now and feeling not so alone.

About two hours before sunup the next day, the shelling stopped, leaving the young and old alike dazed and exhausted. Chauncy stirred first, climbing the stairs and pulling the heavy door open just enough to poke his head out. It was a new moon, so there was nothing out there but darkness and the smell of fresh dirt. No sense leaving the wine cellar until it was light out, he thought. He put a brick between the door and the jamb to hold it open for fresh air, and then he took up his spot on the floor next to Tom. "Black as the ace of spades out there," he said. "What time you got?"

Tom tilted his wrist this way and that to catch what light there was to be had from Chauncy's trench lighter. "Quarter to five," he replied. "Once we can see what we're doing, should be able to flag down an ambulance for our friend there," he said, pointing his chin at the Marine and the French woman.

"Wake me up after you get him up those stairs," said Tom as he leaned forward and rested his folded arms and head on his bent knees.

When he opened his eyes again, light was streaming through the open door at the top of the stairs, and the old people were getting ready for the exodus away from the fighting. Anxious to be on their way and hopefully rid of the Marine, Chauncy and Tom wrestled the stretcher up the stone steps and out into the courtyard. Even though it was overcast and still early morning, their eyes ached from the light. At some point during the night, a platoon-size unit of French soldiers had taken refuge

in the courtyard and was going about the business of burying
the dead, both men and animals, in the fresh shell craters. One
of the shells had landed conveniently close to the dead cavalry
horse by the opposite wall, and two soldiers were busy sawing off
its legs so it could be easily rolled into the hole.

"Well don't that beat all?" said Tom. "I got to remember that
next time Pa wants help burying one of his horses. Makes 'em fit
in a lot smaller hole, too."

Chauncy just nodded without turning away from the ugly
sight. The old people from Lucy-le-Bocage who had stayed behind,
trusting that their village would be spared, were filing past, bent
over under the weight of harvest baskets and canvas sacks filled
with their belongings. The beautiful French lady stood by the
gate with a leather suitcase at her feet, watching them leave;
none of them spoke or even looked at her. Finally, one of the
last old ladies stopped in front of her and unleashed a tirade in
rapid-fire French, punctuated by hammering her clenched right
fist into the palm of her left hand. When she had said her piece,
she spat at the woman and marched over to speak to one of the
Frenchmen working on the horse.

"I wonder what that was all about," said Chauncy. "That
French lady ain't too popular around here, I guess."

"Looks like she's getting snitched on, too," replied Tom.

John had been lying quietly on the stretcher a few feet away,
but this talk of the woman who had looked after him in the
wine cellar prompted him to break his silence. "What are you
... talking about, what's ... going on?" he asked in a raspy voice
between gasps.

"I think your lady friend is in some kind of trouble. One of the
grand-mères is over there talking to the Frenchies, and they're
doing a lot of finger-pointing, mostly at her."

"Please ... would you ask ... her to come over ... here?"

"Sure, chum, I was going to walk out to the road to see if I could snag an ambulance to take you to a field hospital, anyway. Come on, Tom," said Chauncy.

In a few minutes, John heard her approach and then felt her fingers tugging on the dirty bandages covering his eyes. She recoiled slightly when he reached up unexpectedly and grasped her wrist. "Comprenez vous ... English?" he said.

"Very ... small," she replied after she had thought about it for a moment.

"Is there trouble ... with the ... French soldiers?"

There was a long pause as Arielle looked around to assess the situation. The old woman and one of the soldiers who were trying to dispose of the dead horse had left the courtyard.

Before she could turn back to John, a French lieutenant appeared at the gate and looked around. "Oui, very bad. I go."

She started to stand up, but John tightened his grip on her wrist and held her in place. "No, stay! My name is ... John Castor," he said as he pointed to himself with his left index finger and waited.

"Arielle Landers," she replied.

"You must ... trust me, Arielle ... and agree ... with every-thing ... I say. Comprenez-vous?"

Out of the corner of her eye she could see the lieutenant approaching, and fear gripped her. She nodded her head in the affirmative and then remembered that John was blind. "Oui," she replied softly, giving in to the strange American.

The French officer walked up and stopped behind Arielle, who was still kneeling next to John. "Êtes-vous Mlle Landers?" he said.

Arielle turned her head and looked up at him for a moment before answering, noting as she did a slight widening of his eyes.

"Oui, c'est exact," she replied with a confidence she didn't feel. "et vous êtes?"

"Je suis Lieutenant Dupuis à votre service. I'm afraid I must ask you to come with me," he said.

Once again Arielle started to stand, but John gripped her wrist even tighter and held her down. "Do you ... speak any English ... Lieutenant?" said John between painful gasps.

"Oui, I mean yes, my English is passable. What uniform is that?" he said, referring to John's forest green tunic.

"I am ... a ... United States Marine."

It was clear to Arielle that John had the lieutenant's undivided attention now, even though she had no idea why.

"Ah!" he said, as if someone had switched on a light. "You American Marines are in all the papers. In Paris you are famous, monsieur, and I see you are well acquainted with the Boche," he said referring to John's wounds. Had John been able to look the Frenchman over, his pristine uniform and polished boots would have marked him as a greenhorn. Fortunately, that distinction between the two men was not lost on the lieutenant. "How may I assist you, comrade?"

John could scarcely believe this favorable turn of events, and his brain was working hard to stay ahead of things. In the end, he decided to press ahead with his original idea and hope for the best. "I am engaged ... to marry Mademoiselle ... Landers, and I would ... like her to stay ... by my side ... until we can ... reach an American ... field hospital. If you ... would get us on ... an ambulance ... headed in that direction ... I would be grateful." John had the uneasy feeling that he had gone too far, but it was too late to turn back now, and he was nearly at the end of his endurance. He hoped that if Arielle understood what he had said, she was able to avoid showing astonishment.

There was a long silence as Lieutenant Dupuis weighed all the elements of the situation. Finally, his face took on a decidedly stony veneer as he spoke. "It is the least I can do to repay the sacrifice you have made for my country."

John faced toward the sound of the lieutenant's voice, missing a little to the right because he still had not regained full hearing in one ear, and raised his right hand to his temple in salute. As soon as the French officer spoke, he dropped his arm.

"I wish you and your ... fiancée ... good luck, comrade." He spun on his heel and started for the gate and then abruptly stopped and turned back. In French he said, "You must never return here, Mademoiselle Landers. The American has given you a great gift. Use it well." With that, he turned away again, shouting for his sergeant.

Field Hospital Number One at Bezu-le-Guery was a collection of small buildings, including a church and a one-room school that had been pressed into service because it was close to the front and straddled an important crossroad. Once the wounded had received initial treatment to stabilize their wounds, they were transported to larger facilities near Paris for more comprehensive care. The jarring ride in the Canadian ambulance, although mercifully short, had taken a toll on John, and he lapsed in and out of consciousness.

The woman driver had supplied Arielle with an empty crate to sit on behind the passenger seat, and from there she was able to cradle his head in her lap to soften the jolts as the vehicle bounced over the broken surface of the road. When they arrived at the hospital, orderlies and nurses descended on the convoy and whisked the wounded men away to different areas with an efficiency that surprised Arielle. She was even more surprised when she stepped down from the back of the ambulance and realized that the church she had been christened in had been turned into a hospital. She tried to follow along, lugging her suitcase, when two orderlies moved John to a tent that had been set up with portable showers for gas victims, but a tall, thin, pinched-faced Red Cross woman held up her hand and pointed to the front of the church. The look of disdain she received was hard to miss. While she stood waiting, she saw a nurse emerge from a fly on the back side of the tent and dump an armload of clothes on top of an already large pile. She recognized John's Marine tunic.

The 13th-century Catholic church had survived the war remarkably well so far, suffering only minor indignities in the way of looting, and now, from the removal of the pews so that stretchers laden with wounded men could be placed side by side on the floor. The tall, arched, stained glass windows that lined each side wall were covered with canvas tarps and blankets to prevent light from attracting German artillery. Arielle sat next to John's stretcher in the vestibule, trying to reconstruct in her mind what the interior had looked like the last time she attended mass here. The contrast was so disturbing that she quickly dropped that train of thought. Halfway down the same wall she was leaning against, there was a chancel of ornately carved dark wood hanging out over the main floor of the sanctuary. It was filled with wounded German prisoners. The only things she recognized from the past were the pulpit and two brass candelabra on floor stands by the altar. The candelabra on stands, as well as a large one of black wrought iron suspended from the ceiling on heavy chains, supplied light to a makeshift operating table. A doctor wearing a long, white, bloodstained apron and attended on either side by a nurse was bent over a patient. An orderly stood behind them, holding a hissing gas lantern over their heads. If not for flashes of glistening crimson and occasional sharp screams from patients not fully under, she might have imagined an otherworldly bubble of pure light amidst a sea of suffering.

Arielle looked down at John and was pleased to see him resting quietly for a change. She thought it must be something they had given him while he was on the table. The fresh bandage that covered his eyes and left ear was stark white and stood out in high relief against his weathered skin. She carefully lifted the blanket off his chest and saw that after they had bathed him and treated his shoulder wounds, they had dressed him in pajamas. Around his neck, where the high collar of his uniform had rubbed, there was an angry, red band of blisters from the mustard gas. Now that his face and hair were clean, aside from the letter "T" someone had painted on his forehead with iodine, she could see that he was actually quite handsome.

Arielle closed her tired eyes and listened to someone nearby receiving last rites from an old priest. She realized now that the low murmur she had been hearing for the last hour from different parts of the church was the priest going about his sad business. She began to retrace the chain of events that had completely upended her world, a very fragile world, as it turned out. Even more amazing, her life had somehow become linked to this perfect stranger, an American, who lay next to her. She thought again about the last thing the lieutenant had said to her. She vowed to herself she would help him recover, or failing that, ease his dying.

"Sorry to make you jump, mademoiselle; I have a chair for you," said an old stoop-shouldered priest. "I was making my rounds and you looked so uncomfortable, my dear." The old man extended a hand to help her rise.

"Hello, Father Douglas. Do you not recognize me?" said Arielle as she stood and brushed the back of her skirt.

The priest gripped Arielle's forearm and leaned in to study her face in the poor light. "Ari, Ari Landers?" he said with a note of disbelief in his tone. "Oh my, what a lovely young woman you've become. So much like your mother!"

Arielle gave him a wan smile and looked down.

"I was so sorry to hear about Peter and François, oh, and your dear father. What a terrible tragedy." The old man saw tears begin to well up in Arielle's eyes and fell silent. He darted a quick look behind her at the suitcase sitting beside the wounded man on the stretcher but didn't remark on it.

There was an awkward silence as they both searched their memories for common ground. Finally, to break the silence, Arielle said, "It has been a long time since I've been to confession, Father. Would you have a few minutes for me now?"

"Of course, my dear, follow me. We had to move the confessional to the opposite wall." The priest turned and moved off with short, shuffling steps, picking his way carefully around the wounded soldiers.

Arielle knelt and crossed herself in front of the screen that separated her from the priest. "Forgive me, Father, for I have sinned. It has been ... three years since my last confession."

She paused for a moment as she struggled with how to begin. Finally she decided against speaking in general terms and launched into the telling of her story, leaving nothing out. Father Douglas had heard things from some of the other parishioners, but not until now was he able to fit all the pieces together. In spite of all the suffering he had seen since the war began, he was still appalled that such a lovely, prosperous family could be reduced to a sole survivor, a sad, beautiful young woman with everything that remained of her past life in a single suitcase.

Arielle took a minute to dry her eyes and collect herself before stepping out of the confessional. When she did, Father Douglas was waiting for her. "You must walk the path, Ari, no matter where it leads, no matter what happens. It is your journey and the only guiding light is the faith that shines inside you—faith, my child. There is a plan, even though you cannot see it. One day you will look over your shoulder and my words will come back to you."

Arielle nodded and looked down at her dirty shoes. They were once so beautiful.

"I would like to meet your American soldier, Ari."

She nodded, still avoiding his eyes, and started for the other side of the church.

John was awake now and taking breaths in short, ragged draws. When Arielle and the priest drew near, he turned to the sound of their feet on the ancient stone floor.

Father Douglas knelt next to John's stretcher and leaned in for what little privacy there was to be had. "I am Father Douglas, young man, and you are lying on the floor of my church," he said in English.

The old man saw alarm in John's reaction. "No need to worry, my son, I'm only here to see if they are treating you well."

John's reply was barely more than a whisper. "The gas has ... burned my throat ... and eyes. They said ... I will be moved to a hospital ... near Paris soon. There is a woman ... with me. We are ... to be married when ... I can walk ... and see again," said John, keeping up the charade. He shivered and turned his head away.

Father Douglas picked up the edge of his blanket and started to pull it up under his chin when he noticed the dull aluminum dog tags resting on the bandage that crisscrossed John's chest. He studied the inscription carefully for a moment and then tucked the edges of the heavy wool blanket around John's shoulders. "May I say a prayer for you, son?"

John turned to the priest and rolled up on his elbow so suddenly that they almost bumped heads. "One for my mother ... and father ... and for Matt, my brother Matt," he said, with an intensity that startled the old man.

At first light the next morning, a convoy of ambulances, American this time, lined the side of the road in front of the church. They were splattered and caked so completely with mud that the big, red crosses on white circles adorning the canvas sides were nearly invisible. A crisp-looking Army captain with dark brass caduceus collar disks on his tunic stood on the flagstone walk in front of the church, checking the dog tags of each wounded soldier before he was loaded into the back of an ambulance. As the stretcher-bearers paused in front of him, he would look the man over and dictate a brief assessment of his wounds to a burly sergeant who stood a short distance away, writing furiously in a leather-bound ledger. This procedure also effectively weeded out malingerers. There were three men on stretchers ahead of John, but already Arielle was aware of the fleeting sideways glances the officer directed at her.

John lay quietly, taking a little comfort in the morning sun on his bare arms and face. It was the first time in several days that he could take a breath, albeit a shallow one, without bracing for the pain. He was covered up to his armpits with a heavy, wool army blanket, and a cloth drawstring sack containing his personal effects rested on the stretcher between his legs.

Several times as they waited, soldiers had tried to engage Arielle in idle conversation, a few even in her own language, but her clipped responses left little doubt about her accessibility. At the moment, she was struggling to check her irritation with the medical corps captain, knowing it was in her best interest to appear helpless and confused. An unexpected hand on her shoulder made her jump. She spun around, preparing to unleash a verbal broadside on whoever it was that had the audacity to put a hand on her, when she was brought up short by the sight of Father Douglas.

"Oh, my, my, it seems I am always frightening you, Ari," he said softly. Before she could voice her apology, he took her hand and curled her fingers around a heavy envelope with a wax seal. "Your faith will see you through, my dear, but you will need this, too. May the good Lord forgive me, but I think the Americans call it stacking the deck." When the old priest was gone, Arielle looked down at the envelope. On the back flap above the seal was the name of the church, Saint-Rufin et Saint-Valère. Slowly she turned the envelope over and read the words:

CERTIFICATE OF MARRIAGE
JOHN CASTOR AND ARIELLE LANDERS

Chapter 13

"Hey, Charlie, you ever tried one of those marijuana cigarettes?"

"Na, I seen Crazy George smoke that shit once. That dumb son of a bitch thought he could fly. The mate had to tackle his ass and we brought him back aboard in the galley's cargo net," replied Charlie.

Ray collapsed the section of Sunday's *Plain Dealer* he was working on and peered over the top edge at Bill, who lay in his bunk across from him. "You wanna give it a try, just go on up to the windlass room and smoke a piece of heaving line: same shit."

Charlie laughed and said, "Don't give him any ideas, Ray. We get to Duluth, we won't be able to tie up 'cause there won't be any heaving lines left."

Even Bill chuckled this time. Ray shook out his newspaper and held it up to search for the place where he left off. "You better stick to Jack Daniels, Fuzzy. For sure don't go smoking it when you're up the street. Unless you're close enough to see the stack above the rooftops, you'll never find your way back to the boat," said Charlie after a long silence.

Ray chimed in from behind his newspaper, "If these damn teetotalers have their way, we may all be smoking hemp."

"Check the want ads, Ray, and see if anybody's got a couple hundred feet of three-inch hawser for sale," said Charlie. "Better safe than sorry, is what I always say."

Ray chuckled and looked over at Bill again. "I seen George sitting out on number nine hatch in the middle of the night smoking that shit. Guess he figures if he's amidships he can see somebody coming from a long ways off."

Just then there came a knock on the door frame of their cabin, and the three deckhands craned their necks to see who their visitor was.

"Hey Finus, what brings you all the way up to the sharp end?" said Bill.

"Well, boys, we was having a little nip back aft to celebrate my leaving the ship when we get up above, and I thought damn, maybe I should do something nice for my less fortunate deckie shipmates; so I brung y'all a few beers," said Finus. He swung a canvas gunnysack off his shoulder and set it on the deck with a clink. "You boys have a good life." With that, he turned to leave.

"Hey Finus, how come you're getting off?" said Charlie.

Finus turned around and leaned back in from the doorway. "Got a job doing the same thing I'm doing now, only the engine I'll be working on don't move around all over the lakes like it does on this big ass boat. Electrical generating plant. You can catch me at Fitger's Tap Room if you ever get over that way."

"Might just surprise you one of these days, Finus. Thanks for the beer," said Bill.

Old Ray reached down and fished a bottle out of the bag and held it up to catch the light as if he were reading the label on a bottle of fine wine. "Well, Stroh's ain't exactly my first choice, but that's right neighborly of him just the same. I think we better get this cold, Fuzzy. Would you do the honors?" he said.

Bill swung out of his bunk and walked over to the porthole. He picked up a galvanized pail from the deck at his feet, attached a snap line to the bail, and then pushed the bucket through the porthole and followed it with his head and left arm. He paid out the line until the bucket was just skimming the surface of the water, and then in one swift movement, he dunked it and let it fill just enough to give it some weight. He pushed on the rope with his left hand to swing the bucket forward, let it swing back, and then pushed again until it was swinging in a long arc. Finally, as the pail reached the end of its forward trajectory, he gave it some slack and let it hit the water just behind the swell of the bow wave. The trick was to quickly pull the bucket up full of water just as the forward travel of the ship brought it directly beneath the porthole. Wait a few seconds too long and it would become a sea anchor and pull the rope right through the hands. They had lost several buckets before perfecting the maneuver, and Bill had a diagonal scar across his right palm from a bad rope burn, but all went well this time, and nine bottles of beer were soon chilling in ice cold Lake Superior water.

At a little over two thousand feet in length, dock number five was the second longest of six iron ore loading facilities in Duluth harbor. It towered one hundred fifty feet above the water and dwarfed the *Pontiac* as she lay alongside. Ore trains from the mines on the Mesabi Iron Range would run out on the dock and drop their loads through the open space between the rails from hopper cars, filling enormous storage areas called pockets. When the ship was in position, forty-foot chutes would be lowered into the holds, and the pockets would empty by gravity. It was a very efficient system, and turn-around time for the ore boats was a matter of hours, rather than days as in earlier times. The bad news for the ship's crew was that there was no time to go up the street, especially not for the deckhands, who spent the entire time handling lines on the dock when the ship was shifted back and forth to balance the load.

Charlie and Bill sat on the posts of a mooring bitt across from the fantail, smoking cigarettes and killing time until they were needed again. Even though only a couple of feet separated the two men, mile-long ore trains clanging and screeching overhead and hundreds of tons of raw iron ore roaring down the chutes into the cavernous holds of the ship made conversation nearly impossible. For the first few hours, Old Ray had hung around the aft winches, resting his forearms on the railing, chain smoking and watching the ashes he flicked off the ends of his cigarettes float slowly down to the water between the side of the ship and the dock. It wasn't until late in the afternoon when loading was nearly complete that Charlie realized he hadn't seen his friend's scowling face at the rail since lunchtime.

Dizzy, the boatswain, met them at the top of the ladder as soon as the two deckhands came back aboard. "Head up forward to the windlass room and get ready to take in the bowline, Charlie. The kid and I will handle things back here," he said. "As soon as we clear the dock and everything is stowed, you boys grab some chow and then we'll soogee the deck, if it's still light enough."

Charlie started up the deck toward the bow and Dizzy called after him, "If you see Ray, give him the word."

Charlie waved his understanding without stopping or looking back. "Where is that damn Ray, anyway?" he said.

Bill took the opportunity to lay a little ground work for Ray's defense, just in case. "He's probably in the head. Last I seen him he was feeling kinda puny," he said. The boatswain, not especially quick-witted, mulled that information over for a moment and then finally just nodded and turned away to look for the second mate.

Charlie stepped over the hatch coaming into the companionway, leading up forward to the windlass room and then thought better of it and backtracked to the weather deck and took the ladder down to the dunnage room. He pushed the door to their cabin open and said, "Ray, damn it, you're gonna get your ass in a crack if you ... "

He stopped short when he realized he was alone. He started to turn around and then froze. One end of Bill's mattress was pulled off the springs, the corner dangling limp over the side rail of the bunk and the bedding pulled back, exposing the striped ticking. A jumble of clothes was spilled out onto the floor from Bill's open locker. Charlie reached down and tried the drawer under his friend's bunk and found it still locked. In all the years he had been on the boats, he had never seen anything like it. Shipmates just didn't steal from one another. He debated about what to do, knowing he had only a few minutes before he would be missed. Finally, he pushed the mattress back on its springs, tossed the pile of clothes into the locker, and headed for the weather deck, hoping the old man hadn't already ordered the lines singled up.

Old Ray didn't show up for dinner, and he didn't show up to help his shipmates soogee the deck. Charlie was becoming more and more concerned with each passing minute, and now he was beginning to get troubled looks from Bill. The scene in their cabin earlier in the day kept nagging at him. It had to be connected to this strange turn of events with Ray, but it just didn't add up. He hadn't told Bill about someone going through his things while they were on the dock, and now, enough time had passed that he would have to appear shocked when they both went below after knocking off for the day.

Bill started at the forward end of the main deck with a mop and a bucket full of kerosene, while Charlie and Dizzy unspooled a fire hose and connected it to one of the deck hydrants. The Hulett unloading machines in Cleveland had left the deck spattered with thick black blobs of grease, and chunks of ore left behind by the loading dock made it hazardous to walk from one end of the ship to the other. Dizzy figured they would kill two birds with one stone. The boatswain and Charlie gave Bill a head start with softening the grease with kerosene and then followed up pushing the piles of iron ore aft with high-pressure water. Dizzy was no heavyweight and always seemed about to lose control of the fire hose nozzle, so Charlie kept a close eye on him as he followed behind pulling the heavy hose.

"Damn, Charlie, what the hell happened here?" said Bill with a puzzled look on his face. "Looks like someone's been going through my shit."

"How do you figure?"

"Well, my bunk is messed up, for one thing, and my locker isn't like I left it," he replied.

Charlie tried to play it down so Bill wouldn't run up to the pilothouse and blow the lid off things. "You ain't exactly the tidiest person I ever met."

"I'm telling ya, someone's been rooting around in my stuff. I'll bet it's that damn third mate looking for whiskey. That son of a bitch is trying to get something on me, Charlie, I know it."

The words *looking for whiskey* tripped a switch in Charlie's mind, and instantly everything fell into place. "I'll be right back, Fuzzy." said Charlie, as he squeezed past Bill on his way out the door.

When Charlie reached the top of the ladder to the port door of the pilothouse, he was relieved to see that the second mate and wheelsman were the only two present.

"Hi, Charlie, looking for a little wheel time?" said the mate.

Charlie stepped forward, gripped the brass handrail that surrounded the raised steering station, and looked down at the deck, collecting his thoughts. Finally he looked up at the mate and said, "We can't find Ray, Steve." His words hung in the silence of the pilothouse while Steve processed the information.

"What do you mean you can't find him? Did he go up the street and miss the boat?"

"No, Fuzzy and I were on the dock the whole time, and there's no way he could have gotten past us. Last time I saw him was in the galley when we broke for lunch."

The second mate swiveled his chair around and stared out over the bow at the gathering gloom of evening. Without looking down, he dug in his chest pocket for a cigarette, buying a little time. "He been hitting the sauce again, Charlie?" he said at last.

"Naw, he's been pretty good," he replied, the thought of Finus's beer crossing his mind. "In fact, I expected him to fall off the wagon when he found out about his old lady shacking with the mate on the *Schoonmaker*. He took it better than I thought, but it's been eating at him."

"OK, here's the deal, Charlie. You got until the end of my watch to find him. Wake up Gary to help you and search from the aft end of the tunnels forward. Check all the compartments down to the bilge. If he don't turn up, I'll have to tell the Old Man and put it in the log."

An hour into the search, Charlie and Bill stood at the top of the ladder leading to the lower dunnage room. When they opened the hatch in the deck and peered down into the space below, there was nothing but total darkness.

"He can't be down there," said Bill.

"Yeah, seems like he would have turned the light on." Charlie reached over to the bulkhead and turned the switch for the compartment's small overhead light. "Let's get this over with. The second mate said to check every compartment down to the bilge."

The lower dunnage room was used to store things that weren't needed very often, wire mooring cables, fat coils of manila line, hawsers, that sort of thing; in fact, this was the first time Bill had ever been in this compartment. The port side was lined from the deck to within a few feet of the overhead with lockers filled with buckets of paint, enough to give everything from the waterline up a fresh coat. As soon as their eyes were adjusted to the dimly lit space, the two men began picking around the jumble of supplies for any clues as to Ray's whereabouts.

"You see that?" said Charlie, pointing to a hurricane lantern sitting on the deck in front of the paint lockers. Bill followed Charlie's finger and nodded his head, not sure what to make of it. Charlie looked up to the space between the top of the lockers and the overhead, then down to a stepladder leaning against the bulkhead. He turned his head to make sure he still had Bill's attention and then rolled his eyes up to the top of the lockers again.

"Ray! I know you're up there. Come on, don't make me come up there, damn it! We been looking all over this fucking boat for you."

Charlie looked over at Bill. "I'm going up." A few minutes later, with Bill steadying the stepladder against the motion of the ship, he peered over the top edge of the lockers. Ray lay passed out on his side with his knees drawn up, his left hand still clutching an empty bottle of Jack Daniels. There was another empty bottle of Jack and one of blackberry brandy near his feet.

"He's here and out cold. Go see if you can find Gary while I try to figure out how to get him down without breaking all our necks." It took the three men the better part of two hours to get Ray down from the top of the lockers and up the steep ladder to the deck above. Charlie had carried Ray back to the boat a few times after a night of drinking, but he had never seen him like this before. He knew it would mean the end of Ray's sailing days with Cleveland Cliffs, but he was becoming more and more worried about his friend's condition and had decided to fetch the second mate down to their cabin.

"You're right, he don't look too good," said Steve. "He's no spring chicken either. We're about six hours from the Soo, and we'll put him ashore when we lock down so they can get him to a hospital. You boys get his belongings together and watch him real close until then. Turn him on his side if he starts to puke; seen a man drown that way once."

When Gary and the mate were gone, Bill and Charlie sat side by side on Bill's bunk, elbows resting on their knees and staring at the deck between their feet. "I had a bad feeling the other night when Ray helped us drink those beers, but I gotta tell ya, I never saw this coming," said Charlie.

Bill didn't reply but got up and walked over to his locker. He opened the door and stood silently for a long time, looking at the pile of dirty clothes. He gently closed the door and leaned his head against it with his eyes closed.

Charlie watched his friend for a few minutes, trying to settle on something to say, but nothing seemed right. Finally he said, "Come on, Fuzzy, let's pack up his shit."

It was early morning and still dark when they handed Ray over at the Soo. They loaded his unconscious body and his duffle bag onto a flatbed cart and hauled him to the main gate, where an ambulance waited to take him to War Memorial Hospital.

That was the last time they ever saw Old Ray. He never regained consciousness and two days later his heart finally stopped.

Chapter 14

Robert looked over at George, ready to grab his collar should he decide to bolt when he killed the engine of his Model T Runabout. Always the optimist, no matter where they were when the engine stopped, George was certain they were going hunting. This time he made no such move, perhaps distracted by the commotion taking place a short distance away. A small group of men were gathered around a team of mules next to the shaft house, preparing to lower them down into the mine. The main shaft was too narrow to use a conventional horizontal sling, so a special harness was used that held the animal's legs folded close to its body and allowed it to be lowered vertically, rump first, to a level far below, where it would pull trams full of ore for the rest of its life. The mules would be blind in about two weeks from existing in total darkness, and most lived only seven years. Robert felt a pang of guilt, knowing these animals would never again see the light of day. It made him think of G.D., the family mule when he was growing up on the farm in Monroe Center.

As they looked on, one of the men broke away from the group and started walking toward them. Robert recognized him as the captain, but try as he might, he could not recall his name. This mine was one of the last remaining independent operations on the Marquette range, and his boss, Mr. Mather, had suggested several times that maybe they should consider buying out its current owners. Robert had always managed to talk him out of it. It had been run on a shoestring for many years; still using mules to pull trams was evidence of that, and now the quality of the ore coming up was very low-grade. Because these miners were treated poorly and paid less than men working for Cleveland Cliffs, the union had made substantial inroads here. Once established, unrest could quickly spread to other mines on the range. Robert was here today to casually look things over and get a feel for the mood of the miners under the pretense of dropping off paperwork.

"Morning, Cap, how the hell are ya? Haven't seen you since our boys played ball a couple of summers ago."

"Good morning, Mr. Castor. Yeah, they had a pretty good season that year. Whipped Negaunee bad both times they played 'em, as I recall. Worth the price of admission, *that* was. So what brings you around this fine day?"

"The pencil pushers down in Cleveland wanted me to give you this renewal contract to pass on to your boss. Nice and sunny today, so I thought I'd take a ride and deliver it myself." Robert reached under the seat, produced a large envelope, and handed it over to the mine captain. "How's things going out here? Word is you boys are going union."

Cap turned around and with a sigh leaned back against the front fender of Robert's car while he searched for words. "I guess the big union mucky mucks figure this war ain't going to last forever, so they'll get what they can while Uncle Sam is still buying steel. I don't mind telling you, Mr. Castor, I'm getting too old for this shit. There was a day I could put a good man to work with a lazy man and end up with an average miner—ten foot of drift per shift out of them. Not anymore. The good ones are all following the money over to your outfit." He turned and looked at Robert, and his disillusionment was plain to see in his face.

"Your bosses decide to throw in the towel, come and see me and we'll work something out," said Robert. He turned the key and moved to get out and crank start the car, but the mine captain held up his hand.

"I'll get it, Mr. Castor, stay put." He walked around to the front bumper, reached down, and with one swift turn the engine fired to life and settled quickly into a satisfying rumble. Robert nodded his thanks and got a weary farewell wave from the mine captain.

Rather than go back the same way he came in, Robert decided to take the long way to town down an old, overgrown tote-road left over from the early logging days. About halfway between the mine and the state highway, they came to a crude bridge made of two large logs spanned with heavy oak planks laid side by side. The planks were dark with creosote but still warped enough to jump and clatter as they took the weight of the Model T. The icy water of the little creek that ran under it had etched a deep meandering path in the spongy loam of the cedar forest. Robert stopped the car halfway across and ducked just in time to avoid George's powerful back legs as he disappeared over the trunk. By the time he was out of the car he could already hear the beating wings of a startled grouse.

Robert put his hands in his pockets and leaned back against the passenger door as an inexplicable wave of melancholy washed over him. Below, the backs of shadowy fingerlings holding in the fast water were silhouetted against a patch of clean sand. Following the water to where it disappeared under a toppled cedar drew his eyes to a sunlit clearing, a beckoning oasis in the subdued light under the trees. Without further thought, he reached behind the passenger seat, pulled out the blanket he carried there to cover Elizabeth's legs on cold days, and headed into the forest.

Warmed by the sun and lulled by the sound of bubbling water as it swept through a tangle of smooth roots a few feet away, Robert closed his eyes and listened to the sounds of the forest return as its creatures gradually accepted his presence. He thought of picking raspberries with his mother near a creek much like this one. She was a well-educated woman, maybe even the smartest person he knew when it came to book learning, but still she loved to pick things: raspberries, blueberries, wildflowers in the meadow behind the house. He had an image in his mind as clear as a photo of her holding out her hand with an especially large berry for him to marvel at. Her fingers were long and slender, and he remembered the feminine ways they did everyday things. In the fall they picked apples. He, his mother, and Peep could pick down their thirty trees in a couple of long days, a little more if it was a good year. Some they traded with the neighbors, some his mother made into apple butter, but most were pressed for cider. Robert licked his lips unconsciously as he recalled the wonderful taste of fresh-squeezed Snow Apples. Peep was Robert's adopted father. Peep and Robert's mother had married when he was five, about two years after a tree had fallen on his birth father as he was putting up wood. Even after all these years of spotty communication, Robert still felt close to Peep. As he looked back on his life now, he could see the faint impression of Peep's loving hand, gently nudging this way or that, every step of the way. Sometimes in the middle of the day he would look at his watch and picture what Peep would be doing. The cadence of his father's life was bound to the land, and to the seasons. Everything else was secondary, especially since his mother had passed. There was no one Robert respected more than Peep. He still, after all this time, subconsciously weighed life's big decisions against what his father would do. Robert made a mental note to call him up Sunday night and smiled at the vision of him standing straight and stiff in front of the phone hanging on the wall in the parlor, as if the ringing was somehow an affront to his dignity.

The sound of a twig breaking interrupted Robert's train of thought, and a few moments later George came loping up and dropped unceremoniously on the blanket next to him, panting hard with the tip of his long tongue curled back on itself. All four of his legs were caked with black swamp muck. He shot a sideways "where the hell were you" look at his master that made Robert smile and reach for the spot behind his right ear. He closed his eyes again and thought of Jack, his childhood dog, of exploring the dark, mysterious, virgin forests near the farm, and of his favorite climbing tree with thick horizontal branches spaced just right. His mind's eye could see Peep through a hole in the treetops, following a walking plow across a distant meadow. The long-ago image of his father still shimmered in midday heat. Mostly, though, it was the creek, the sound of the fast water bubbling over smooth rocks that made this moment feel like home.

A sudden sharp bark from George brought Robert awake with a start. As he sat there looking around and trying to orient himself, the vaguely familiar persistent car horn in the distance began to burn through his mental fog, and at last he knew it was the family car, the Franklin. Jacob was the only other member of the family still at home that could drive, and that thought quickly brought him to his feet.

"Come on, Bud, let's move out; must be trouble at the mine..."

Elizabeth eyed the conductor until he looked away and then gathered up her skirt and stepped off the train. Robert's car was not parked in the usual place, but then it wouldn't be the first time he had become distracted with one thing or another and failed to show up at the appointed hour. She was returning from her weekly luncheon in Marquette, so there was no need to wait for luggage. By the time she reached the station lobby, she had made up her mind to walk home and give him a dressing down later when he finally showed up. It was uphill but thankfully only a few blocks, since the shoes she chose that morning matched her dress but not necessarily her feet. As she passed the Dutch door of the Western Union office, she had a momentary uneasy feeling, as if people were turning away to avoid eye contact.

Elizabeth turned on High Street, still imagining different scenarios that could explain Robert's thoughtless disregard for her needs, but when she looked up and saw his car parked in the street next to the house, all that was forgotten and alarm gripped her. Something was very wrong.

"Rob ... Rob, where are you!" she shouted as she pushed through the side door into the kitchen. "Is everything all right?"

There was no answer. Her heart pounding now, Elizabeth hurried down the main hallway and threw open the door to her husband's office. Robert was sitting at his desk, turned away, looking out the window. Elizabeth opened her mouth to vent her rising anger but froze when he swiveled in his chair and she saw the look on his face.

"What is it?" she cried. He did not speak but glanced sideways at the surface of his desk. For perhaps the first time since they had turned this room into an office, it was not littered with a jumble of papers and coffee-stained mugs. In fact, it was completely bare except for a single piece of paper. Everything that had been on the desk was now scattered about on the floor as if by a great wind. Elizabeth started across the room, but Robert jumped up and met her halfway to the desk. He wrapped his powerful arms around her and held her close, even though she struggled to break away.

"Damn it, Rob, let me go! Tell me this instant what is going on!" When she felt the slight tremor in his embrace and realized he was not going to do as she asked, she rose up on her tiptoes and looked over his shoulder at the top of the desk. The document was a Western Union telegram. In a flash she knew.

"Which one," she said softly into his ear, the sound of her own voice strange as if coming from somewhere else.

"Matt," said Robert.

"And Johnny?"

"Nothing." Shock and grief gripped Elizabeth so tightly, so completely, that she could not take a breath. Her field of view narrowed to a small circle of failing light, and she slumped against her husband. Robert knew he should do something, but he couldn't move. Elizabeth's raw emotions had started his own. He held her limp body close to his, her arms dangling and swaying side to side as he shifted his weight from one foot to the other. Robert pressed his face into her hair and wept with the anguish only a parent who has lost a child knows.

Chapter 15

BANQUE DE PARIS
3 RUE D'ANTIN, PARIS, FRANCE
JUNE 27, 1918

Deep cold from the polished granite bench beneath Arielle Landers passed easily through the thin material of her summer dress, sending a shiver up her spine. From where she sat, just outside a suite of offices to the left of the main entrance, she could observe the comings and goings of the bank's diverse clientele and for a while passed the time trying to guess each person's story. Fluted stone columns topped with Corinthian capitals rose twenty-five feet high above the marble floor and supported the overhang of the second story. The center of the building was open from the lobby to the fifth story and capped by a dome of black cast iron and leaded glass panes that shed interesting patterns of light down across the stone balusters on each floor. It occurred to her that if the intent of the bank's owners was to construct a building that would impart a feeling of security and permanence to its customers, they had succeeded in grand style. The effect, however, was somewhat diminished by the wartime shortage of manpower that had left the building's elaborate appointments dirty and looking shopworn.

She had been here before as a little girl, those times when she accompanied her father to the big city on his monthly business errands. After visiting the banker who handled his financial affairs, the very man she hoped to see today, there would be a visit to the Parc des Buttes-Chaumont to see the waterfall and of course a stop at Fouquet's for candy before boarding the train for home. Her father had seized on the idea that the white water cascading over the cliff and the rainbow it created above the huge boulders below held a special fascination for her, but in truth, after her mother died, it was where her father came to remember happier days.

"Excuse me, Mademoiselle, Monsieur Bouchard will see you now."

Arielle stood and smoothed the back of her dress before falling in behind the aging but still trim receptionist. As she was ushered into Bouchard's office she steeled herself for the moment of recognition, but for some reason it never came. The man behind the desk was much heavier now and his face sagged below the line of his jaws, but she could see traces of the younger man she remembered. Bouchard pinched the bridge of his nose and nodded to one of the empty client chairs. He leaned sideways and tugged an overworked handkerchief from the back pocket of his trousers, buried his nose in a fold, and gave a mighty blow. It was so loud that Arielle flinched. He took a couple of swipes under his nose and then opened the handkerchief for a cursory inspection of the outcome before wadding it up and stuffing it back in his pocket. Arielle fought down her revulsion as he lifted his dull, watery eyes to her.

"What brings you here today, Mademoiselle ...?

"Landers, Arielle Landers," she said, finishing his sentence.

Bouchard looked up quickly and retrieved his glasses from the top of his desk. "Why yes ... yes, it is you. You were just a little girl the last time you were here with your father," he said as he extended his hand across the desk in greeting. Arielle took it in hers and swallowed hard, the horrendous nose blow still fresh in her mind.

"It is very gracious of you to see me on such short notice, Monsieur Bouchard. I know you are busy, so I will state my business quickly. I am here to replace my father's name with mine on all of his accounts. He has not been seen or heard from since the Germans overran Belgium four years ago. I must accept that he is dead. Both of my brothers were killed at Verdun, so that leaves me as the sole survivor. The chateau is in ruins after the recent fighting, so I have nowhere to go. Eventually I will want to sell the land."

"I see, I see. I remember seeing your brothers' names in the paper, but I didn't know about your father. Such a shame, my dear. I'm very sorry to hear it. Your father's holdings at our bank are considerable, but under the circumstances, it will take time to confirm his death. It may not even be possible until the war is over. I have the authority to withdraw five thousand francs from your father's accounts for emergencies, and I think that will help you get settled somewhere until we can straighten all this out. Perhaps I can even help with disposing of your land as well when the time comes. I will have my assistant prepare the papers for you to sign so I can set things in motion. I am so sorry, Arielle. This is all such a terrible tragedy. Even if we win this war, what will become of us?"

John's bed was the last one at the end of a long room filled with wounded American soldiers. Like an army barracks, which in fact it had been at one time, the room had a row of beds set perpendicular against each side-wall with an open space up the middle wide enough to allow moving the beds and equipment in and out. Like all military hospitals in France, it smelled of ether, chlorine, and rotten cabbage, the last from gas gangrene. Some of the men in this ward were suffering from exposure to mustard gas, but most had far more grievous wounds: limbs missing, guts lacerated by shrapnel, faces horribly disfigured. A few men had to be fed by the orderlies so they wouldn't stab themselves with the silverware to end their own suffering. Even though John and some of the men in the other beds around him were blind from the gas, they always knew what time of day or night it was. They knew the sounds. The night was the worst. In the small hours they lay awake and clung like drowning men to the tick tock and gong of the clock above the door at the far end of the room; it was the only thing that separated the darkness in their injured eyes and the darkness of death. Every night they lost a few men.

The man in the bed next to John was not blind, but he fell in and out of consciousness several times a day and didn't seem to remember anything from one lucid spell to the next. "Hey fella, what time is it?" he said.

John thought for a second, recalling the last time he heard the clock strike the hour. "Two something," he replied without offering any encouragement in the way of conversation. He knew his neighbor was going to keep talking anyway, at least until his pain medication waned. John was propped up in bed with a rolled blanket and a couple of pillows behind him, intent on deciphering some new sounds in the room and was a little annoyed by the interruption.

"I'm Pete Olson ... from Flagstaff. You ever been there?"

"Nope."

"Shell landed right on top of our dugout while we was sleeping, buried every last one of us." He was quiet for a moment and then said, "I could hear 'em, talking—or praying—something. They were so far away, I couldn't do nothing. My legs was hit, ya know. What time is it?"

"Two something," replied John. He had heard this story, word-for-word several times before. "You might as well put a sock in it and save your strength, chum. You ain't getting any more 'monkey' until rounds at 3:00."

This apparently had the desired effect, for the man fell silent. John once again focused on the sounds coming from the other end of the room. Someone was opening and closing drawers and what sounded like clanging a broom or mop handle against the metal tubing of a bed frame. The sounds were constant and coming closer.

"Y'all awake, Marine?" came a deep pleasant voice from right at his bedside. It was so close and unexpected that it caused John to take a sharp breath into his burned windpipe, setting off a coughing fit.

"Whoa, fella, didn't mean to make you jump," said the man. "I'm Colonel T.J. Meyer, Chief of Medical hereabouts."

Not only was John taken by surprise by his visitor, he was amazed that someone was addressing him as "Marine" instead of "Soldier." No one had done that since they had taken his uniform at the first aid dressing station. "Nice to meet you, Colonel." John heard the clipboard holding his medical information being lifted off the hook at the foot of the bed.

"How are they treating you, Castor?"

John thought for a moment. "I only got one complaint, sir; no one will tell me if I'm going to be able to see again or not." John had never spoken to a colonel before, so he was careful not to be too pushy. He felt a stab of cold on his chest.

"Breathe in, big one now; go slow. OK, I heard worse." Colonel Meyers tugged on the thick gauze bandages over his eyes and shoulder wounds and then pulled up the wooden folding chair from where it rested against the wall.

"Well, it's that damn mustard gas, hard to predict. Damnedest shit I ever seen, pardon my French." The Colonel paused for a moment to savor his own joke.

"Some men get their full sight back and some are just plum blind. Too early to say in your case; give it a month. One way or the other, y'all's war is over. You're gonna be shipped home as soon as y'all can show me a little Two-step."

"Yes, sir. Thank you, sir," replied John in a decidedly unenthusiastic tone. He heard the chair scrape across the plank floor but knew the Colonel was still standing there. He felt a soft touch on his shoulder.

"Cheer up, cowboy. I'd say your chances are real good for a full recovery. From what I hear, y'all don't let much git in your way. I also heard there's a perty lady coming around to see y'all every day."

There was a slight hesitation while John's thoughts caught up. "Oh, yes, Colonel, my wife. I hope to find passage for her to the States when I get out of here."

"Well, there ya go, then. Damn good reason to look on the bright side." John heard the floor creak as Colonel Meyer turned to go.

"Sir, may I ask you a question?"

"Sure, cowboy. What is it?"

"Is some kind of search going on down the way?" said John as he nodded his head toward the unusual sounds he had been trying to identify.

The Colonel chuckled. "Nah, nothing like that. We're pulling out all the stops to make sure we're squared away for General Pershing's visit this afternoon."

It was Arielle's routine to arrive at the 85th American Base Hospital shortly before noon so she could help John, or "Sammy," as she called him, with the noon meal and then hopefully, if he wasn't needed elsewhere, the staff interpreter would join them for a short English lesson. No one seemed to mind since it freed someone up to tend one of the other patients, and the men, orderlies and patients alike, welcomed her presence as the high point of their day. She had also started supplementing the dreadful Army hospital food with pastries from the little bakery near the l'Hotel Pavillion, where she had a room. Many eyes followed her as she crossed the ward, but absent for once was her usual discomfort. In fact, she even smiled and made eye contact with some of the soldiers. She slowed as soon as she had a clear line of sight to John's bed and was warmed to see his face already turned in her direction, his mouth carrying just the hint of a smile, enough so that she knew he was aware of her presence.

"Ahllo, Sammee," she said softly in her heavily accented English as she slid the folding chair closer to the side of the bed.

"Bonjour, Mademoiselle," he replied in his best imitation of a Frenchman.

A soft giggle escaped Arielle, and she briefly covered her mouth with a gloved hand before resting it on John's forearm. He fought down the urge to reach for it.

"I am...ah...to you ...the wife. I am *Madame*."

John blushed and took another stab at it. "Bonjour, Madame, comment allez-vous?"

Arielle was amused but pleased that he was attempting to learn her language, and maybe a little guilty, too, for being able to scrutinize him without his knowing. Even though only a couple of weeks ago he had been a complete stranger taking refuge in her father's wine cellar, she could see changes in his face, the skin pallid and tight over the bone. It was the kind of slow wasting away that comes from deep within. She couldn't see his eyes, of course, but there were other signs: the way he pursed his lips when he remembered something that happened at the Front, or when he started to speak of his brother Matt and then thought better of it. Without realizing it yet, perhaps because it seemed so unlikely, Arielle was drawn to John. Not to his world or social standing as might have been the case in peacetime, but to him. At first he was her only avenue of escape, her way into the U.S. without a visa, but as they spent more time together, the lines of reason blurred and a more heartfelt purpose emerged. Time and again, as pieces of John's character were revealed to her through their interactions, she had to remind herself that physical attraction had no part to play here. They were both out of their element, adrift on a sea of human suffering and turmoil, where even the slightest touch of tenderness or soft words of understanding were everything.

"I am ... well, merci ... I mean *thank you*," said Arielle after studying the ceiling for a moment while she framed her response.

The mid-day meal was a rushed affair on this day as preparations continued for the arrival of the commanding general of the American Expeditionary Force in France. The ubiquitous metal food trays, stamped *U.S.* to discourage other foreign powers from pinching them, and conveniently sectioned to prevent the comingling of the meal's few unpalatable elements, had been cleared away, along with the objectionable smell of slumgullion stew. Arielle was taken aback by the small portions allotted to each patient but even more shocked by the terrible quality of the food itself. Sometimes horsemeat or salt pork, an inferior grade of canned salmon that the men referred to as *gold fish*, or perhaps potatoes boiled in their skins and served with a sprinkling of the soil in which they had been grown. She had always thought of America as the "land of plenty," but there was no evidence of that here.

She was rummaging in her handbag for a day-old scone and a pat of butter folded in a sheet of wax paper she had picked up that morning when a sudden commotion at the far end of the ward near the door made her look up. The hospital staff had crowded into the open area between the rows of beds, so it was hard to get a good look at what was going on. Abruptly the activity ceased, and there was silence in the ward except for a single deep voice, the words indistinguishable, almost musical at that distance. Pretty soon there was a shuffling of feet, and the mass of people moved to the next bed. The routine was repeated over and over again until finally Arielle and John could hear what was going on.

"What outfit, son?" the deep voice would say, or sometimes, "Where you from, private? Anything I can do for you?" The general stopped at every bed and chatted with every man who was conscious. Twice along the way he awarded a medal, simply pinning it on the soldier's pillow.

When the general reached the bed next to John he said, "Well now, who do we have here?"

"I'm Pete Olson...from Flagstaff. Ever been there?"

John smiled as he listened to the same story he had heard countless times delivered now to General Pershing and his audience. Ever since learning of the general's visit earlier in the day, he had been working an idea that he hoped might come to fruition if he should get a chance to meet the man. Arielle's presence was part of the plan, so he had decided not to share it with her for fear she would bolt. So far, it seemed, everything was falling into place nicely.

Arielle knew from pictures in the newspapers who the man was, now that she could get a good look. Through an opening between two nurses with their backs to her, she could see him, tall, dignified, and impeccable in his mustard-brown tunic, cavalry riding pants, over-the-calf boots with spit-shined toes and peaked hat. His face was strong and permanently tan from years in the saddle, crisscrossing the American West and parts of Mexico. Arielle wasn't fond of facial hair, but his brush moustache made him look very dashing indeed. Just under the visor of his hat were the eyes of a man who had ordered men to their deaths. At each bedside he stood parade-ground-straight with his hands clasped behind his back, listening intently to each soldier's responses to his questions. From time to time, he would turn and give instructions to his aide-de-camp, a dour captain with wire-rimmed glasses, but never once did he address the hospital staff or correspondents who crowded around with notepads at the ready.

The visit with the man in the next bed began to wrap up, and John went over in his mind again how he would answer the stock questions being asked of every man. He felt confident that he could steer the conversation in the direction he wanted it to go. He heard the shuffling of feet and Arielle tightened her grip on his hand. John's plan was completely forgotten as soon as the general delivered his first words.

"I've spoken with every man in this ward but you, son, so I think you must be John Castor, 5th Marines. Am I right?" said the general, darting a quick glance and nod at Arielle.

"Yes sir, I'm John Castor and this is my wife, Arielle."

General Pershing bent at the waist, holding her eyes and gently shook her slender hand with just his fingers. "Je suis enchanté. Parlez-vous anglais?" he said in very good French.

"Oui, un petit peu," she replied, feeling a blush rise in her cheeks.

The General was rumored to have an eye for the ladies, but the intense look he focused on Arielle was not of that variety. He straightened up and addressed John. "I would like to visit with you for a few minutes, son, if you're up to it."

"Yes, of course, sir. Please have a seat."

The General turned toward his aide-de-camp and a folding chair magically appeared. To the war correspondents pressing in he said, "Please give us a little privacy. I will speak to you outside in a few minutes." General Pershing crossed his legs and reached under the flap of his right lower tunic pocket to retrieve a short, dark cigar. He hesitated a moment with second thoughts, then dropped it back in his pocket. "Probably not a good idea," he said to himself under his breath. "So tell me, Marine, how were you wounded?"

John hesitated while he collected his thoughts. He was still off his guard by being singled out by the general, and he had a bad feeling in the pit of his stomach that he was in trouble for something he did at Belleau Wood. "My outfit attacked across a wheat field near the town of Lucy-le-Bocage. We got about half-way across when Boche machine guns opened up all along our front."

At this point, John's upper lip began to tremble and he stopped talking as he struggled with the images from that day. He knew he would have to steel himself and get the story out quickly or he never would. Arielle squeezed his hand, not understanding everything he said but recognizing his struggle. "We caught hell, General. We caught holy hell, but nobody stopped. My brother was right next to me when he was hit ... killed. After that I just wanted to get the Boche who killed my brother ... and I did kill him. I killed 'em all. One of them shot me in the shoulder, I guess. There were a lot of gas shells coming in after that."

General Pershing arched his brow when John told about Matt getting killed, and he held up his hand to stop him from going on before he remembered that John was blind. By then it was over and no one spoke. Arielle looked alarmed. Finally the General reached out and patted John's leg under the blanket.

"I'm sorry about your brother, son. I know a little bit about losing family. It's damn hard." After a moment of staring off into the past, he dug in the breast pocket of his tunic and pulled out a folded piece of paper.

"Do you know a Sergeant Lindsey?"

"The name sounds familiar, sir, but no, I guess not."

"I have here a report he submitted to his company commander dated June 10th. I'll just read the part that concerns you:

'At roughly 0900 on June 7th my corporal Avery Benedict and I were attempting to consolidate our position by making contact with pockets of men who had become scattered and isolated by the difficult terrain and heavy fighting of the previous day. During that endeavor we stumbled across a single Marine, Pvt. John Castor, sitting on a rock inside what had been a German machine gun nest. We counted eighteen (18) dead enemy soldiers. A few had been bayonetted but most were shot at close range. In spite of being blinded by gas and having difficulty breathing, the Marine in question held this position through the night, thus denying its retaking by the enemy. During a brief reconnoiter of the immediate area in the event there were other wounded men needing assistance, it became obvious that Castor acted alone against this formidable enemy position. It is my recommendation that he be formally recognized for his initiative and valor in the face of overwhelming odds.

"Is that about what happened, son?" the general said quietly as he folded the paper and stuffed it back into his pocket.

John was greatly relieved to learn that he hadn't done something so bad that a general had come looking for him. "Yes sir, I suppose so. I was mad and just wanted revenge. I wanted to kill the man with his finger on the trigger of that machine gun."

The General nodded and stood up to take his leave. "Be that as it may, I happen to agree with Sergeant Lindsey's recommendation. Is there anything I can do for you before I leave, Marine?"

John was struggling to stay ahead of things and almost missed his cue. "Oh, yes sir, there is one thing if it wouldn't be too much to ask. I very much want to secure passage for my wife to the States as soon as possible, but I'm not sure how to go about that. Might you know who I need to speak to, sir?"

The General smiled and said, "I will have my staff look into it and contact you in a few days." Again he bowed at the waist to Arielle. "Au revoir, Mme Castor. Je vous souhaite une bonne vie en Amérique," he said.

Arielle did not stand but offered her hand. "Merci Général Pershing. Vous êtes très gentil."

After giving the hospital staff a little pep talk, General Pershing paused on the steps outside the ward and motioned for his aide-de-camp. "Private Castor is the one, he's the real McCoy. Cut the paper work when we get back and have it ready for me to sign first thing in the morning. You can use the wording of Sergeant Lindsey's report. Also get in touch with the YWCA in Bordeaux. Have them make a spot for Mrs. Castor in their hostess house and make sure they get her on the next transport to the States."

AMERICAN EXPEDITIONARY FORCES
OFFICE OF THE COMMANDER-IN-CHIEF

FRANCE, JULY 17, 1918

Dear Mr. and Mrs. Castor,

I am directed by the Commanding General of the American Expeditionary Forces in France, to inform you that the Congress of the United States has authorized the award of the Medal of Honor to your son, Private John P. Castor, U.S. Marine Corp for extraordinary heroism above and beyond the call of duty in action against a German machine gun nest at Belleau Wood, France on June 6th, 1918.

The decoration and citation will be presented by General John J. Pershing in a ceremony at Chaumont, France on August 12th, 1918. Enclosed please find a copy of the citation for your information.

Sincerely Yours,

Col. L. Hevelhorst

Chapter 16

Crazy George wasn't much of a talker, but he seemed to know where he was going, and that was good enough for now. Bill hadn't felt very sociable since they got the word about Ray, so it was just as well. It was almost two in the morning, and the worn street bricks glistened in pools of dim light beneath the gaslights along the way. It had rained hard earlier in the evening while Bill and Charlie were shooting pool for shots in Curly's, waiting for George to get off watch, and lazy puffs of steam swirled briefly above the storm sewer grates before dissipating into the cool night air. The windows of all the shops and houses on each side of the street were long dark. They had made so many seemingly random turns onto unfamiliar streets and alleyways that Bill had no idea where they were.

George stopped and pointed to his left. "It's down there. Follow me and stay close."

Bill didn't answer but did as he was told. Just off the sidewalk, a short flight of steps led to the below-grade landing of a basement apartment. The word "Mootas" was written on the heavy door in crude, hand-painted, red letters that diminished in size and curved downward as they approached the jamb. Just above that was a square wrought-iron grate covering a viewing door.

George knocked once and the viewing door slammed open immediately, revealing a man's head in profile from the nose up. "Who sent ya?" the man said.

"Lurella," replied Crazy George.

There was the metallic sound of a deadbolt, and the door swung inward, hiding the shadowy doorman from view and giving the two men the first impression that no one was there. George went first, followed closely by Bill. There were five battered, restaurant-style tables and chairs in the middle of the room, all occupied, and along one wall, end-to-end, several retired church pews, one of which held a patron sleeping in the fetal position. Tacked to the crumbling plaster along the top one third of all four walls were stylized charcoal drawings of nudes engaged in various bizarre sex acts. Layers of marijuana smoke laced with incense drifted through an eerie blue light that enveloped everything in the room.

The doorman fished three marijuana cigarettes out of a tattered cigar box and dropped them into George's hand and then turned up his palm for payment. George stepped out of the way and nodded to Bill, who ponied up the seventy-five cents. On George's recommendation, they decided to share the first one until Bill got the hang of it. They took a seat next to each other against the wall, and George lit one up, leaning back and closing his eyes as he sucked the smoke deep into his lungs. He passed it to Bill, who also took a long pull, trying to emulate his shipmate but blowing the smoke out right away, having overlooked the part about holding it in as long as possible. He didn't know what to expect, or when to expect it, but by the time they were halfway through the first reefer, he could see a change in Crazy George. His hat was tipped forward from leaning his head against the back of the pew, with eyes half closed and an amused smile that seemed to be frozen on his face.

"Some good shit, eh?" he said, casting a sideways glance at Bill.

Bill took a hit and replied through a grimace as he held his breath this time. "Yeah, kinda making me lightheaded. Don't see what all the fuss is about."

George smiled big, showing a mouth full of yellow teeth. "Enjoy the journey, fella."

Feeling more relaxed now, Bill began looking around the room, noticing things that had escaped him when they first arrived. Directly across from them, on the other side wall, was a Wurlitzer Nickelodeon that resembled an upright piano. A middle-aged black man sat on a stool in front of it. His folded arms lay on the ledge above the keyboard, creating a cradle for his head—resting or passed out, it was hard to say. As Bill looked on, a customer walked up and dropped a nickel into one of the slots on the front of the machine next to the sleeping man and brought it to life with a roaring ragtime number. The man didn't even twitch when the music started up right below his head. Bill's newfound ability to find a deeper meaning in almost everything he saw picked up instantly, or what seemed like instantly, on the incongruity of a comatose man playing a spirited ragtime song to a room full of people fried on marijuana.

Bill backhanded George's arm and pointed his chin at the nickelodeon. George nodded and said, "Yeah, he's good."

Bill had always considered himself "the quiet type" in most social settings. He found it gave him an air of mystery that the ladies found irresistible, and it served him well in many a waterfront saloon packed with inebriated sailors, where the wrong word carelessly uttered in the highly charged atmosphere could earn a man a broken head. After smoking the second reefer, much to his amazement, he found he could not stop talking. Free of the usual prerequisite of making an observation, deciding how he felt about it, and framing an appropriate response, he discovered that it was really quite easy to talk endlessly if he simply put his every conscious thought into words. At Mootas there was certainly no danger of causing a brawl; in fact, it would have been hard to imagine a more docile gathering. People moved around from table to table, dropping in on conversations and expounding at length on any number of subjects. Many times the "wisdom" or "sage advice" they had to offer up to the world at large far outstripped their God-given intellect.

At the table with Bill was a couple, perhaps in their thirties, dressed in clean but threadbare attire and a late-middle-aged man in an expensive-looking shiny black suit and bow tie. The man and woman seemed friendly (although preoccupied with newly-professed love), but the man in the suit was a classic example of what it meant to be stoned. He sat bolt upright in his chair with hands in his lap, his unblinking eyes fixed on the table top in front of him. His expressionless face was topped with sandy colored hair, glossy with tonic and combed straight back. Bill made a couple of attempts to get a rise out of him, but to no avail. The couple had either given up before Bill sat down or were so wrapped up in themselves that they didn't care one way or the other.

"How long has he been that way?" said Bill.

The man and woman turned to him, each waiting for the other to speak. Finally the man cleared his throat for what seemed like an eternity and said, "He's like that all the time. Don't know what he does for a living that calls for him to be dressed up like that this late at night, but every time we see him in here it's the same thing."

"Divorce. I say it's a divorce," said the woman. Their speculation was interrupted when the doorman stopped at their table with the cigar box. The woman watched her man anxiously as he dug in his trouser pockets for a quarter, eventually coming up empty-handed.

Bill slid a dollar across the table and redirected a reefer to the couple when the doorman dropped four in front of him.

"Oh, sir—" The woman began to gush before she was cut off. "Bill."

"Oh, Bill, thank you so much!" she said. "I'm Marissa, and this is my fiancé, Donald."

Bill smiled and nodded, but the couple had already moved on and focused their undivided attention on striking a match. He briefly examined his purchases and then promptly dropped them as he fumbled putting them in his shirt pocket. When he bent down to retrieve them from the floor, he pulled back with a start. The stoned man was wearing hornback crocodile skin brogues… with eyes! At first glance, in his altered state, the shoes looked like two live reptiles preparing to strike. The man had big feet, so the threat seemed considerable.

Bill's heart was pounding. "Sweet Jesus, you see this fella's shoes?" said Bill.

"Yeah, pretty wild, huh? Takes some real scratch to own a pair of those," replied Donald with a chuckle.

Surprising everyone, the stoned man suddenly pushed his chair back and stood up. "If you'll excuse me, I must go iron my shoelaces," he said. With that, he turned, showing few ill effects from smoking marijuana for several hours, and headed straight for the establishment's only restroom.

Bill turned back from following the man's shoes and glanced over Marissa's shoulder toward the entrance, noticing as he did the doorman watching the stoned man's movements very carefully. Probably going to get bounced when he gets back from the can, Bill thought.

"Hey Fuzzy, so what do ya think? A lot different than Curly's, eh?" said Crazy George as he grabbed an unused chair from an adjacent table and joined them. He still had that perpetual grin on his face, but surprisingly he looked more alert now than when they first got there.

"I don't know, George, not sure I'd give up beer for this shit. I like my beer and Jack pretty much—getting laid, too. Not much of that going on here."

George just nodded and looked up as the stoned man returned to the table.

"Take a gander at that fella's shoes will ya? Ever seen anything like that?" said Bill.

"Yeah, he was ankling around in those last time I was here; with a real looker, too. Lordy, that little bearcat had some jugs on her, I tell ya. Those babies would just sit up and bark at ya. They sat right over there in the corner, necking the whole time."

Bill nodded as he pictured the scene. "So what time is it, anyway? Seems like we oughta be heading back," he said.

Crazy George reached inside his jacket and pulled up on the silver chain clipped to his belt until a smallish pocket watch emerged. "Almost three thirty. If we leave here by five it'll give us plenty of time. They won't be finished unloading until around nine, so we can grab something to eat before we get called out. Besides, it'll be getting light by then. Better to wait till then."

Bill nodded but was having a little trouble processing all the information. The stoned man, much more animated since returning from the restroom, produced the stub of a previously smoked reefer, carefully lit one end with a small, onyx, lift-arm lighter, and sucked the smoke through his teeth with a sharp intake of breath. Bill watched him out of the corner of his eye, partly to observe his technique and partly to see if he would burn his thumb and finger.

The man looked over at Bill, evidently sensing his interest, but made no attempt to engage in conversation. In fact, there was nothing at all to read in his facial expression, and it made Bill a little uneasy.

"Castor … Castor! Wake up, time to go," said Crazy George.

Bill slowly dropped his feet to the floor and rolled up on his butt as he struggled to place himself in time and space. To say his mind was foggy would have been a colossal understatement. He sat there for a few minutes, looking around the room and working his tongue around the inside of his mouth in an attempt to relieve his cotton mouth.

Crazy George laughed and said, "Looks like Herbie paid you a visit."

"What the hell you talking about?"

"He's the little man who shits in your mouth while you're sleeping off a night of drinking and smoking. Kind a like the Tooth Fairy, only not as nice."

"You really are crazy," said Bill with a note of irritation.

When Bill and George finally stepped out of Mootas, it was already getting light. There was no sun, or for that matter, no way to tell if it was overcast or clear, thanks to the choking layer of smog that had settled in the Cuyahoga River valley during the night. There was just a dirty half-light. Only the milkman seemed to be stirring at this hour; the clip-clop of his horse's hooves on the wet street bricks a block over sounded unusually loud and hollow. Just before they reached the end of the block, they came abreast of an empty lot where a house had once stood. Remnants of the stone foundation were still visible in places through the thick undergrowth, and two huge lilac bushes stood on either side of a cement walk where it passed through a gray, weathered picket fence.

"Hey George, hold up a minute. I gotta pee," said Bill as he ducked off the sidewalk and got behind one of the lilacs. As he stood relieving himself, his mind started to replay snippets of his time at Mootas until something in the tall grass to his left caught his eye.

"Come on Fuzzy, stop playing with yourself; we still got a long walk ahead of us."

"George, come over here a minute and look at this," replied Bill with a tone in his voice that piqued George's curiosity. In the grass at Bill's feet was a single, hornback, crocodile-skin brogue. The two men looked at each other for a moment and then without a word, quickly retreated back through the opening in the fence and resumed their trek back to the boat.

When Bill and Crazy George reached the dock behind the mill, the *Pontiac* was riding high in the water, but the Hulett unloaders were still methodically groaning and rumbling as they worked to bring up the last of the iron ore. Between each machine and the side of the ship sat a small bulldozer attached to a steel cable-lifting harness waiting for the clamshell bucket to pick it up and deposit it in the hold. They would be used to push whatever ore was left into the center of the hold directly beneath the hatch, where the Hulett's bucket could pick it up. The extension ladder the crew used to come and go from the ship was in its usual place at the aft end of the weather deck, and beside it on the dock, looking fragile and out of place, was a new, deep blue, Type 57 Cadillac. High above, the second mate was leaning on the railing, watching them come aboard.

"Morning, Steve," said Bill as he stepped down on the deck. He had the visor of his hat pulled down as far as he thought he could get away with, without calling attention to it. He was counting on the shadow to disguise his bloodshot eyes.

"Morning, men," he said. "Castor, you have an important visitor in the guest stateroom up on the Texas Deck. Go splash some water on your face and get on up there." It was clear to Bill that this was not a request. A few minutes later, as he stood in front of the mirror over the sink in the cabin only he and Charlie shared now, pieces of the puzzle regarding his visitor began to fall into place. William Mather, the man who owned this ship and several others like her, as well as the town he was raised in and hundreds of square miles of Upper Michigan, was the only man with enough clout to drive his car though the steel mill yard and out onto the dock while unloading was in progress. He became more certain with each passing moment that his father had asked Mr. Mather to check up on his "wayward" son. This line of thinking brought to an abrupt halt any effort to make himself presentable. He even went so far as to pull one side of his shirttail out from the front of his pants to appear more unkempt than he actually was, if that were possible.

In spite of his anger and self-righteous bravado, Bill was still a little nervous at the thought of meeting one-on-one with the big man himself. He knocked twice and pushed the stateroom door open when he heard the expected summons from somewhere within. Mr. Mather had been sitting under a porthole in an overstuffed chair, reading from an expensive-looking, leather-bound book trimmed with gold filigree, but stood and offered his hand when Bill entered, never batting an eye at the deckhand's appearance.

"Nice to see you, Bill. It's been a good long while. Please have a seat," he said, gesturing to a matching couch across from his chair. "Your father asked me to find you and deliver a message in person." Bill felt a resurgence of anger and started to fidget, but the response was short-lived.

"There's no good way to say this, so I'll get right to it. I know you're anxious to get back to your duties." Mr. Mather looked up sharply to gauge Bill's reaction and saw the dawning of alarm breaking through Bill's surly exterior. "I'm afraid I have some very bad news for you. Your brother Matt was killed in France early last month. I'm sorry, son, sorry for your whole family."

Bill leaned forward, rested his elbows on his knees, and hung his head as he processed the news. When he finally looked up, Mather could see a young face transformed in an instant by the kind of sorrow that runs close to the bone. "Anything about Johnny?"

"He's in the hospital over there and expected to make a full recovery."

Bill hung his head again and struggled for control. Mr. Mather stood and placed a small card on the side table next to the couch. "If there's anything I can do, call this number and tell my assistant how I can reach you." He placed his hand on Bill's shoulder and felt a slight tremor. "Stay here as long as you need to," he said and then walked out and closed the door behind him.

Chapter 17

"Thank you, Anna. That was excellent. If you'll fix a plate for Mrs. Castor, I'll take it up to her," said Robert as the young woman began clearing the table.

"Yes sir, I've been keeping things warm. I'll bring it right out. Would Mrs. Castor like tea with her supper tonight?"

"Yes, that would be fine. Make sure you get enough to eat before you put everything away."

Rosemarie quietly backhanded her bread plate containing an uneaten roll smeared with butter to her left so it fell under Anna's gaze. She flashed a quick glance at Robert, and then Jacob to reassure herself that her subtle move had gone unnoticed by everyone except the new housekeeper.

"So Rose, have you and Anna had a chance to compare notes on your shared cultural heritage? The Cornish are a proud people, sure enough, and that was especially true of your father, God rest him. If he were still here, he would be very proud of what a lovely young woman you've become. Anyway, you two have a lot in common, I expect."

Rosemarie shot him a hateful look, but Robert pretended he didn't notice. It certainly didn't faze him in the least; it was only proof that he had hit the mark. He had been married to Elizabeth for twenty-six years, and Rose wasn't even close to her level of orneriness. He was quite sure that if Anna's family even *had* enough rolls to serve each person at the table, there would never be one buttered and uneaten. Rosemarie dabbed at the corner of her mouth with her linen napkin and then stood and shuffled sideways out from between the table and her chair. She paused briefly while she waited for her "look" to burn through Jacob's state of oblivion and bring him to his feet.

"You two may be excused. I hope your shift is uneventful, Rose, and Jake, I'll see you first thing in the morning. Plan on a busy day tomorrow."

Since receiving the news about Matt and Johnny, Elizabeth had not only withdrawn from society, but from her family as well, scarcely leaving her room on the second floor. When she wasn't lying in bed, propped up by a stack of pillows, re-reading old letters from the boys or poring over photos, she sat in a small armless rocking chair next to her window that overlooked the town. From her vantage point, she could see the diamond where the boys and their friends had spent nearly every summer of their young lives playing baseball, choosing up sides and squaring off against one another. When she closed her eyes, she could hear the repetitious *pop* of a hardball striking oiled leather over and over again as the boys played catch behind the carriage house. In her mind she could visualize them with perfect clarity careening along the snow-covered street below on their one-man, one-dog sleds as they raced to the finish line at the bottom of the hill. Every year, the whole town turned out and lined both sides of the street to cheer on their sons. Day after day, she looked out at the town and remembered her sons in it. She saw the miners make the same footfalls on the same sidewalks as the shifts changed at the Cliffs Shaft Mine. She saw their wives hanging out the laundry on the clotheslines behind their company houses; every husband's underclothes, like the skin of their hands, were permanently stained orange by the iron ore that meant everything. Neighbor dogs announced the arrival of the postman or the milkman, and on Tuesdays, Earl the egg man. So many of these long-forgotten simple events, once an important part of her daily life when the boys were little, had quietly slipped away.

Elizabeth blamed the stuffed-shirt politicians for Matt's death, for sending American boys overseas to help a sinful and morally bankrupt country, but she also blamed herself. How could she have been so naïve to think that her boys would don a uniform and march off to save the world from tyranny without the slightest notion that they might not come back? Of course she had wept that day when the train pulled out of the station, but it was more for the finality of their leaving home rather than the fact that they were going to the greatest killing field the world had ever known. She should have done everything in her power to stop them from going. She could have pushed Robert to call in a few of the favors it seemed everyone in the Upper Peninsula owed him, or she could even have contacted Bill Mather, who routinely dined with some of the most powerful men in the country. She knew in her heart of hearts she could have stopped them somehow, would have stopped them, if only she had looked on events leading up to the tragedy with a clear eye. Every day, sometimes every hour, in her mind she walked to the edge of the cliff and looked down.

There was a knock at the door and Robert opened it, juggling on one arm a tray containing her dinner. "Brought you a little supper, Lizzy. Would you like it over there or on the desk?"

Elizabeth slowly turned away from the window and regarded him stone-faced. Even the slightest facial expression seemed like too much interaction. "On the desk, Rob, thank you."

"You really should try to eat something, dear. You might find this more to your liking—the new housekeeper is a very good cook," said Robert, thinking that last bit was sure to get a reaction. Elizabeth simply nodded and turned back to her vigil.

"Her name is Anna and I've asked her to check on you and bring you whatever you need while I'm gone." Again there was no response.

Robert was often exasperated by his wife's feisty and frequently overbearing ways, but this behavior was unnerving. He would gladly endure the worst harangue she could dish out if only he could have the old Elizabeth back. With a resigned sigh, he said, "Tomorrow afternoon I'm going down to Peep's to break the news to him in person. I'll stay a couple of days and be back late Thursday." His announcement was met with more silence.

Following an impulse, he moved to Elizabeth's side and gently caressed her cheek with the back of his fingers. The spark was still there after all these years. "I love you, Lizzy," he said softly. He squeezed her shoulder and turned away. Not waiting for a reply, he closed the door behind him.

Elizabeth felt a sudden surge of despair well up and closed her eyes as tight as she could to keep the dam inside her from breaking and washing away what was left of her sanity.

Walking Rose down to the telephone office for her overnight shift was usually Jacob's favorite part of the day. It was a short walk, only four blocks, but they were alone together and it was dark. They held hands, of course, and if Rose was amenable, they might even stop and kiss when they came to a dark patch of sidewalk between the streetlights. The walk wasn't long enough for a very involved conversation, the kind he craved, so he had started writing letters to her while he ate his lunch in the little town square by the statue of *Old Ish* the Indian.

"Father makes me so angry sometimes!" said Rosemarie, more to blow off steam than a statement of fact. She was walking so fast that Jacob was having a little trouble keeping up.

"Why are you so upset about Anna?" Just then he stubbed his toe on a section of sidewalk that had heaved up, and he stumbled forward. "Damn it!" he cried as he fought to stay on his feet and regain his dignity.

Rosemarie didn't break stride or act as if she even noticed. "I certainly know more about running our household than that little hayseed from Cowshit Bluff, and I don't need or want any help." Jacob didn't respond. Even he could see the holes in that line of reasoning. They walked the rest of the way in silence until finally they stood facing each other at the bottom of the steel stairs that hung on the back of the bank building in the alley.

Rosemarie sighed and finally regarded him with her arms folded under her bosom. "I'm sorry for spoiling our walk, Jake. Mother will be back to her old self again soon and we can make good on our plan." Jacob hesitated for a moment, looking down at the ground between them, and then he fished the folded-up letter from his pants pocket and handed it to her. Without a word he turned and walked away, leaving Rosemarie staring at his retreating form with her mouth open.

Jacob was angry, so rather than head right home and risk running into his father or the new housekeeper, he decided to go sit by the lake for a little solitude. There was a strip of sand at the foot of High Street that served as a public beach for the residents who lived on Strawberry Hill, and as a boy he sometimes went there to be alone, sometimes to cool off if he was mad at one of his siblings, but more often than not, to lick his wounds. He pulled off his shoes and socks and then stepped off the sidewalk and walked to the edge of the water. The sand still held warmth from the afternoon, and it felt good against the cool evening air.

The moon was just touching the dark tree line on the far shore, but it still had enough in it to cast a mystical glow on the sun-bleached deck planks of the old community swim raft. It lay perfectly still on the calm water but seemed to drift through the universe where the brilliant stars in the night sky met their own reflection in the black mirror of the lake's surface. Jacob saw Matt sitting out there dangling his feet in the cool lake water. He seemed so lost and alone, something he never was in life. Just for a moment, the vision cleared away all petty feelings of endured injustices and left a brother's love. It had always been there, just forgotten, buried under the debris of life's everyday struggles. Pain welled up in Jacob's chest, and he let out an involuntary sob before looking away.

Most of the male passengers seated near Robert were slouched in various creative postures with their eyes closed, doing whatever they could to eke out a little comfort. Many of the women had their eyes closed as well, but for the most part, they were still sitting decently upright. Since its arrival at the St. Ignace ferry dock a little over an hour before, the Michigan Central train had been moving first one way, then the other in fits and stops amid the clanks of car linkage and the drawn-out screeches of brakes on steel wheels. The ferry could hold all twenty passenger cars, but first the train had to be disassembled and loaded piecemeal in order for it to fit in the Chief Wawatam's 320-foot hull. Using long rail spurs and switches, the railroad men had turned the train completely around and were now backing the cars into the hold, placing five cars in each of the four parallel sections of track on the ship's deck. The train had approached the dock from a sweeping right-hand curve, giving Robert, who was seated on that side with his head out the window, an excellent view of the men as they scurried around, coupling and uncoupling cars. The "Chief" was tied to the dock bows-on with her massive beak-like sea-gate raised and billows of dirty black coal smoke streaming away down-wind over her starboard side, leaving a mile-long blemish drifting low over the blue water. The sight reminded Robert of a giant bird eating a worm.

The weather was good, so the run across the Straits of Mackinac to the Lower Peninsula took about forty-five minutes, with another half hour to couple a fresh engine and reassemble the train. By one o'clock they were rolling along south once again. The landscape that slid past Robert's window seemed to be of one extreme or the other, exceptionally beautiful or exceptionally ugly. Sometimes there would be mile after mile of cut-over land where logging companies had reduced great forests to nothing more than a waist-high jumble of brown pine branches and treetops, and other times there were beautiful farms with painted barns surrounded by a picturesque patchwork of cultivated fields. Here and there were large orchards with row after row of apple and cherry trees, lush with green fruit. All the memories of Robert's youth were set in country just like this, and watching it roll by deepened his melancholy. Occasionally the tracks would swing out to the west and follow a bluff overlooking Lake Michigan. The dark smudges of coal smoke from distant ore boats on the horizon made him think of Bill. Perhaps he was out there, looking back at a similar dark smudge from the train, drifting above the hazy green hills.

It was four-thirty in the afternoon by the time the train started to bleed off speed for a whistle-stop at the Grawn station. Pushing his leather satchel in front of him, Robert bent at the waist and looked from side to side out the windows, searching for his father as he moved down the aisle toward the door. In spite of his gloomy mood, he couldn't resist taking a closer look at the engine as he walked across the ballast stones toward the station. Though the train was stopped, its brass bell ringing slowly with mechanical precision, the engine was like a restless brute. A tight, quick pillar of exhaust steam and black smoke roiled skyward from the stack, and all along each side just above the wheels, small relief valves hissed jets of horizontal steam that blossomed into white clouds and engulfed the first few cars as they carried on the wind. With two mournful slurs of the train's whistle and a blast of steam from somewhere near the pilot wheels, the engine began a slow chuffing that sent a burst of soot and sparks skyward with every pulse. Robert turned away and headed for the station. Just as he was about to step across the siding, he caught a glimpse of Peep through the open space between two flatcars piled high with logs. His father stood in the shade of a huge spreading maple tree, checking the bit on one of the draft horses harnessed to his buckboard wagon. Robert looked on, feeling the love he had for this man flow though his veins. After a few moments Peep looked over and met his son's gaze with an intensity that would have intimidated anyone but Robert. He tipped his wide-brimmed hat in his old familiar manner, and Robert nodded in return as he stepped over the rails of the siding and closed the distance between them.

They shared a quick embrace, but there were no smiles or pleasantries exchanged, both men feeling the heaviness of the moment, even though only one knew the exact nature of their business. Robert tossed his satchel under the seat and climbed aboard. Peep offered the reins to Robert.

"I'm sure Max and Belle won't hold it against you that you prefer automobiles nowadays." He shot a quick sideways glance at his son.

Robert forced a smile and looked down at the worn floorboards between his feet. "I just want to watch and enjoy the ride. In a few minutes they were passing the first farm on the edge of town and the Newaygo to Northport Road stretched out in front of them, straight south in a long, tan ribbon until it disappeared through a notch in the tree line of a distant ridge.

They rode for a while in silence until finally Peep said, "Which one?"

Robert turned and looked at his father to make sure he understood correctly, then leaned forward and rested his elbows on his knees. "Matt," he said. "It was Matt." Maybe it was speaking his son's name, or maybe it was sitting next to his father behind a team of horses as he had so many times as a boy, safe in the unconditional love that radiated around him, but Robert just stopped fighting the horrible emptiness inside him and wept.

Peep swallowed hard, shifted the reins to his left hand and put his arm around his son.

They stopped several more times to rest the horses before cresting the high ridge and entering the tiny village of Monroe Center. Robert was surprised at how much the sugar maple trees that lined each side of the road had grown. A few more years and their tops would meet over the road. On the left was a two-story building that housed a general store on the first floor and a meeting room on the second. On Saturday nights, the upstairs room doubled as a dancehall. Across the road from the store was a small hotel with a stable for the stagecoach horses, and next to that, the one-room schoolhouse where Robert's mother had taught years earlier. Further up the road, just before the cemetery, stood a picturesque little church with open belfry and tall, slender steeple. Its clapboards were soft white in the waning light, but the slanting rays of sun had infused with a spiritual luminosity the three arched, stained-glass windows on the south side of the building. Fifty years ago in front of this church is where their lives had converged: a beautiful widowed school-teacher, her four-year-old little boy, and a hard-bitten Civil War veteran trying to make a new life.

"Seems like forever ago," said Robert.

Peep looked over at his son and gave him a sad smile. "Seems like yesterday to me."

Once the horses were fed and put away, they walked single-file up to the house in silence, following a hard-packed path through the tall weeds. The generally overgrown appearance of things surprised Robert and seemed a little at odds with the neat, freshly painted yellow lap siding and window sashes of the old farmhouse. Directly behind the house was the forty-acre meadow that Robert remembered so well from his childhood. It was covered in knee-high quack grass and green prairie gold-enrod, broken here and there with large patches of wild daisies. Close in, just on the other side of the orchard, there were a couple of oddly shaped areas of broken ground that looked like someone had started to plow and then thought better of it. The house and the original log cabin that Peep had turned into a smokehouse appeared to be afloat on a sea of Queen Anne's Lace and purple knapweed; they were everywhere, solid all the way out to the orchard, even thrusting out through the narrow band of weathered latticework that closed off the crawl space under the porch. As they approached the kitchen door, Robert could hear the low hum of honeybees working the knapweed on what he thought was probably their last sortie of the day. Long tree shadows reached far out into the meadow from the fence line on the west side. It was beautiful here this time of day. The smells, the sounds of the birds, the peepers by the pond, the soft warm light of evening: these things would always haunt the sweet memories of Robert's boyhood.

"Has Johnny written to you yet? As close as those boys were, he's got to be hurting real bad." Robert sighed and retrieved a battered envelope from his coat where it hung on the back of his chair and passed it across the kitchen table to Peep. There was a long silence while he waited for his father to finish the letter. Finally Peep carefully re-folded it, tucked it into the envelope and set it on the table between them.

"That's a lot to chew on. How did Elizabeth take it?"

"She doesn't know yet. I needed to think it through before all hell breaks loose."

Peep gave him a wan smile and nodded his understanding. He leaned forward, placed his elbows on the table, and rested his chin on the backs of his hands. Robert started to speak, but when he looked up, Peep's eyes were closed.

His father's face was leathery and deeply etched from countless hours of walking in the sun behind a team. Chickamauga had left him with a pale, diagonal scar from just above his right eyebrow, across the bridge of his nose to his left jaw, giving him a somewhat fearsome look. If ever a man's countenance belied what lay beneath, it was his—that is, if you were on his good side. He mustered out of the army in 1864, as the result of an improperly set broken leg, and returned home a disillusioned and guilt-ridden man with a permanent limp. Peep's best friend had died in his arms and he had seen and done things in the heat of battle that he couldn't put behind him. In those days he was sober only just enough to hold down a job. Hoping to make a fresh start, he went to Saginaw and landed a job as a land looker for a lumber company, surveying and mapping out stands of virgin white pine trees in the northern Michigan wilderness. Along the way, he used his earnings to buy up stands of timber that had been passed over by the lumber companies as being too far away from major rivers and tributaries to make harvesting it a profitable endeavor. Following the Great Chicago Fire in 1871, the demand for lumber skyrocketed and Peep became a wealthy man almost overnight.

Finally he sighed and dropped his hands on the table. "There's a censor's stamp on the letter but I don't see that they crossed out anything."

"Well ... yeah, they censor everything. Most of his letters have everything struck but "Dear Mother and Father" and "Love, John." At least until now we could take some comfort from just seeing his familiar hand. I'm grateful to the Red Cross lady who took down his words, but it's just not the same; I mean it just don't seem real. They say there's spies everywhere these days, so I guess we should be thankful for what we get."

"Johnny's got a good head on his shoulders, always has. I think you should trust him and do what he asks; I'm guessing there's a lot more to this story than shows in his letter. He was mighty careful not to get it censored; that ought to tell us something." Robert idly tapped the bottom edge of the envelope on the table as he absorbed what Peep had said.

The older man pushed his chair back and stood. "Let's sleep on it and have another go tomorrow. I had my housekeeper open up your old room and fix the bed." Peep chuckled and crouched down to bank the embers in the cook stove for a quick start at breakfast.

"What's so funny?" said Robert.

"She found a dead black squirrel in your bed when she peeled back the covers—thought it was a big rat. I'm telling ya, I never heard a woman cuss like that; I thought she was going to shit her drawers!"

Robert laughed softly and shook his head and then turned and started through the dark parlor for the stairs on the far side of the room.

Peep called after him, "There's a hole in the ceiling that I haven't gotten around to patching yet, so don't be surprised if you have company in the morning; I figure that's how they're getting in."

Robert didn't respond but stopped halfway across the room, sensing something out of place. To his right, a few feet away in the space under the staircase, was a narrow bed with rumpled bedclothes. Next to it, a shaded oil lamp and short stack of books rested on the stool to his mother's pump organ. Robert closed his eyes and felt the loneliness of the room wash over him.

Following a restless night of lying awake, listening to the old house contract in the cool night air and the grandfather clock downstairs striking the hours in relentless succession, Robert finally decided to cut his losses and get up. He could hear Peep moving around in the kitchen and the smell of coffee was in the air.

"Good morning, Peep. Can you spare a cup of that coffee?" said Robert as he stood in the doorway between the kitchen and dining room, rubbing his eyes. He walked over to the sink, worked the handle of the pitcher pump a few times, bringing up a gush of clear, ice-cold water and captured enough in his hands to splash on his face. "Damn, that's cold!" he said.

His father glanced away from stirring scrambled eggs in a cast-iron skillet. "You aren't going soft on me now, are ya? You know where the mugs are. I make it strong, so don't hurt yourself."

Robert smiled as he reached up in the cupboard. He was glad he had decided to spend a couple of days with his father. It was exactly what he needed right now. As they ate breakfast, the two men sat at the kitchen table and made small talk about things going on in their lives, and both were content to delay talking about Johnny's letter.

"That's real beautiful workmanship, Peep," said Robert, referring to the wooden box with shiny brass hinges that sat between them on the side of the table against the wall. He ran his hand lightly back and forth across the lid to judge its smoothness.

"Old man Bancroft made it for me. You remember him—wanted to have something nice to put a few important things in, keepsakes and such. A copy of my will is in there, too, and a few notes about what to do with things when I'm gone." Just then Peep straightened up in his chair and looked over Robert's shoulder at something out back. Without a word, he stood and retrieved a beat-up old lever- action Winchester from behind the door, carefully rested it against the door frame, and squeezed off a round. The report was deafening in the small room.

"Jesus Christ, Peep, what the hell you shooting at this early in the morning?"

"Chickens. I can't get around fast enough to catch 'em anymore, but I'm still a fair shot. That one won't go far without a head, not that he was having a lot of deep thoughts. I'll pick off another one in a few minutes and we'll have enough for a nice supper."

Robert shook his head and laughed out loud for the first time since getting the news about Matt. Peep stayed by the door waiting for another hapless chicken to present itself in the area of bare hardpan between the house and barn, but there were no immediate takers. "I think those damn chickens have finally tumbled to what I'm doing. Have to put some scratch out there to sweeten the deal, I guess."

"I didn't know you had a pistol," said Robert as he fished an old Colt Army revolver out of the wooden box. Peep turned away from his vigil and watched his son in silence. "Damn, this is a real antique! If only it could talk, I bet there'd be some real stories to tell. Souvenir from your Army days?"

"Don't drop that thing. It's loaded."

Robert didn't take the warning seriously, thinking his father would never keep a pistol around the house with a round in the chamber. He looked up and was taken aback by the stricken look on Peep's face. Obviously something about the gun had touched a dark chord. In truth, it wasn't so much that, but more the opening of a long-ago locked door to his father's distant past, a door to things he hoped would never again see the light of day.

"What is it, Peep? What's the matter?"

Peep stood the rifle in the corner and then turned back to his son, looking uncharacteristically frail and uncertain. "Let's get some fresh air," he said.

The old orchard was situated on a little knoll, maybe seventy-five yards from the house. It was actually the highest point of land on Peep's acreage, so even sitting on the ground, one had a nice overlook of things. There were thirty apple trees, give or take, in three rows with a Redhaven peach on the eastern end of each row that Peep had put in as a birthday gift for Emma. One especially wet spring, fire blight had created a few gaps, but the tops of the survivors had eventually spread out and intertwined so the dead trees weren't greatly missed. The branches of the old trees were permanently gnarled and arched downward by heavy crops over the years. On the eastern slope of the high ground, there was a large patch where low-growing wild strawberries had choked out the tall weeds, leaving a pleasant place to stretch out. Robert and Peep had come here often back in the day. They would lie on their backs side by side, discussing this and that and watch the billowing, white summer clouds sail low across their land.

"I'm sorry, Peep. I didn't mean to upset you." Robert shot a concerned look over at his father, who was sitting up with his folded arms and chin resting on his bent knees, obviously struggling with something.

"It's nothing you did. It's something I've kept bottled up for a long, long time—some things I'm not especially proud of."

Peep knew this was the moment, the moment to break his silence about what happened back in 1863 that changed his life forever. He was certain at the outset that there were no words that would imbue the telling with the raw ugliness it deserved, and there was simply nothing even remotely comparable in Robert's life that would allow him to properly understand. Nevertheless, he had to try. Peep looked straight ahead while he spoke, as if he could see below him on the plain the long, slowly undulating ranks of butternut tipped with bright steel advancing across open ground. Thousands of men had died that day, many of them by *his* hand every time he pulled the lanyard, but there was one that still came to him in the darkness, night after night, year after year, his image clear and always the same. His gaunt, wild-eyed face would materialize out of the smoke a few feet in front of the gun, only to be ripped apart and swept into oblivion by the fiery blast of double canister. One moment he was someone's husband or father or brother, and the next, nothing more than scattered bits of smoldering flesh and cotton. Seeing friends die stayed with a man forever; seeing enemies die did, too.

"That old Colt Army does have stories to tell, and I'm sorry to say I know most of them. I was in a light artillery unit during the war. At Chickamauga we got overrun by Longstreet's division, lost all the guns save one. An enemy shell burst right overhead, and a piece of it sliced open the belly of my Sergeant. That's a bad way to go, a slow, painful way to go. I tried to help him, but there just wasn't anything to do. He was going to die; he knew it and I knew it. He handed me his service revolver and asked me to end it quick, so that's what I did. Later that night, after I'd broken my leg, my best friend Jimmy and I were hiding underneath a big pine tree, waiting for dawn so we could find our way back north. There were Secesh all around us, some looking for their wounded and some stripping the dead for anything of value, mostly coats and shoes, I guess. Winter was coming on, you know. I wasn't thinking very clearly by then; in fact, I was asleep when one of them tried to help himself to my shoes—thought we were just two more dead Yankees. I killed him with the sergeant's pistol, the one down there in the box, and then I killed another one that was with him."

There was a long pause before Peep continued. "Turned out, in the light of day, they were just a half-starved farmer and his boy. There was one more, the asshole that give me this scar. I don't feel bad about that one. He had it coming." Peep's chin dropped down on his chest and he looked sideways at his son.

"Everyone who knows this story is dead except you and me, and the only reason I'm telling you is I want you to understand what can happen to a man in war. Johnny's going to need your help when he comes home. Don't ask him about it. Just let him talk if he wants to. He may look all right on the outside, but don't you be fooled. That business with this French woman doesn't mean doodlyshit next to what he's seen … and probably done."

After another long pause, Peep looked at Robert and continued. "You know why that old pistol still has one round in it?"

Robert just looked at his father and shook his head.

"That's the one I saved for myself. I come that close to using it," he said holding up his right hand with his thumb and forefinger close together. The two men were silent as the unasked question hung in the air between them.

"What stopped you, Peep?" said Robert, the words barely audible.

The old man squinted at something off in the distance, something only he could see. "You'll probably think I'm a crazy old coot, but I guess I'll risk it anyways; hell, I *am* a crazy old coot. You can take this or leave it as suits you." Talking about things deeply personal was not an easy fit for Peep, so he took a deep breath and gathered himself before going on.

"Back in the winter of '69, I was on my way to stake a claim on a nice stand of cork pine on the Manistee River south of Sherman, and I got caught out in a real bad snowstorm. I set up camp out of the wind in a deep draw to ride it out. It was just me and that ugly old mule, G.D." Peep stopped and looked over at Robert with a sad smile at the shared memory.

"I'd been sitting by the fire underneath a canvas lean-to, hitting the pop-skull pretty hard, when I see a deer step out into a clearing a short ways off. Seemed like a good idea at the time to have a nice venison steak for supper, so I took a quick shot at it with my Winchester. Well, I was so squirrely from drinking all afternoon that I hit too low and just it knocked down. I grabbed that old Colt Army and waded through the snow to finish it off, but when I put the barrel to its head something just snapped inside me and I couldn't do it ... and I knew then and there that I wanted to die with that deer, right there in the middle of nowhere. After the war, it seemed pretty clear to me that there was no such thing as God, nobody calling the shots, if you will. It seemed living or dying was just the luck of the draw. I sat down next to that deer, put the barrel up to my head and for some reason, maybe just to cover my ass in case I figured wrong, I asked God to forgive me for all the terrible things I'd done in the war. That's when it happened. I felt a warmth rush through my body, not a warm feeling, mind you, but a warmth like I never felt before. You can draw your own conclusions, but I knew then, and I know now what it was. Someone was telling me not to do it, that everything would be OK. For the first time since the War, I felt like my friends who died were in a better place, and maybe I'd see 'em again. You've known me most of your life, Robert, and you know I'm not one to preach. Truth be told, if it wasn't for your mother pushing me, I would have been pretty scarce at Sunday services. I wish now I would have had the courage to stand up and bear witness. Anyway, if you never believed anything else I've told you over the years, you believe this. I was holding your mother's hand when she died, and I could see in her eyes that she believed it." Peep started to say something else, but thoughts of Emma made it catch in his throat. Instead, he just hung his head as if telling his story had taken his last ounce of energy.

Robert sat there stunned, trying desperately to process everything his father had said. He had never heard him say this much in one sitting before, and he had a way of boiling things down on the fly that made you listen closely. Once when Robert was five years old, he saw Peep shoot the ear off the man that had killed G.D., but he would never have guessed that his father had it in him to kill another human being, never mind *four*. Even stranger was the thought of his committing suicide. If he didn't know Peep as well as he did, the part about the "warmth" would have seemed contrived, but he could not take it lightly. If Peep said that's the way it was, then that's the way it was. In any case, he would have a lot to think about on the train ride home.

Chapter 18

Ten American Army MPs, in crisp uniforms and spotless puttees, stood at parade-rest in line, abreast at precise intervals across the open door of the dockside warehouse. Their mission was to block curious stevedores from getting in, and to block curious French ladies waiting to board a transport from getting out. Arielle and thirty-five other young women who had been staying at the Bordeaux YWCA hostess house had arrived at the dock just after daylight and since then had been waiting in an open bay of the huge building across from a mile-long line of ships. As the morning wore on, they were joined by other groups of women from YWCA halfway houses all over southwestern France. The shouts of dock workers and the straining engines of trucks and tractors from adjacent sections of the building echoed off the high ceiling. Coupled with the low hum of hundreds of nervous female voices and almost an equal number of crying babies, all about a year old, the press of humanity was nearly overwhelming. Arielle sat on her suitcase apart from everyone else near the big door that faced the dock, trying to get as much fresh air as possible in hopes of shaking the dull headache she'd had all morning. Her tongue felt fuzzy and tasted sweet from the heavy exhaust fumes that hung in the air.

"The Americans are a strange bunch."

Arielle snapped her head around quickly, startled out of her thoughts by the voice behind her. "Oh, Claire, you frightened me," she said.

The young woman who had just joined her set her suitcase down and took a seat following her friend's example. Like Arielle, she was one of the few women not holding an infant swaddled in blue or pink blankets. "Why in heaven's name do they paint their ships in such an odd manner?"

Arielle looked over at Claire and then followed her gaze out past the MPs. Every ship up and down the dock was painted in bold geometric shapes that followed no discernible design. Most were painted in varying shades of gray and blue, broken up into absurd patterns by bands of stark white. Arielle had been absentmindedly watching the boom of an elevated crane move slowly back and forth and dangling a cargo net. It pulled something in white sacks out of the ship's hold and swung it over the dock to a waiting rail car. Now, when she focused on the gaudy, dazzle-camouflaged ships in the background, they brought to mind some giant naval version of cubist art. Not feeling especially chatty, she simply shrugged her shoulders and looked at her wristwatch again.

Claire laid her hand on Arielle's forearm. "Don't be so anxious. Life in America will be wonderful—you'll see."

Arielle looked at her friend again as if she were about to say something but then just turned back to stare out at the ships. Finally, feeling a little guilty, she said, "Is someone meeting you in New York?"

"My husband is already there; well, not *there*, but in the States. He said he will come to New York to get me and promised to be waiting when we dock. His family lives in Oklahoma, wherever that is."

Arielle sensed a slight uncertainty in Claire's tone. "How did you meet your husband?"

"I taught English before the war; when the Americans began arriving last year they needed translators. It was perfect. I had a lot of men to pick from," she said with a self-conscious smile. "Dean was the best dancer, and he always brought Mama food in cans from the mess hall when he came for dinner. He called it 'monkey meat' or something strange like that. I still don't know what he meant, but Mama thought it was something exotic from America."

"Do you love him?"

Claire hesitated while she framed her response. "I think he's a good man, at least he's good to me and that's enough for now, I guess." There was a long pause before she continued. "There's nothing left for me here. I'm tired of being hungry and wearing the same dress day after day. I'm getting out."

Arielle nodded her understanding. "I'm going to northern Michigan, a place called Ishpeming. My ... husband is still in the hospital here, so I'll stay with his parents until he comes." Arielle thought to herself how much easier it would be if Mr. Bouchard at the bank had been able to give her an advance before she sailed. She could have just stepped off the ship and disappeared into the vast interior of the United States to start a new life. She looked down at her hands resting on her lap and thought back to the last time she saw John.

The Army doctor who was in charge of the hospital, accompanied by a nurse, had come by shortly after she arrived and removed John's bandages. The area around his eyes was covered with large, angry red patches of skin, something like a bad poison ivy rash, and it was generously smeared with a white ointment. His eyelids were glued shut by dried seepage. Arielle stood at the foot of the bed and said a little prayer under her breath while the nurse sponged his eyelids with warm water. When she had finished and stepped back out of the way, Arielle held her breath and brought her hand up to her mouth, trying not to overreact. This was the first time she had seen him without the bandages and it took her by surprise, almost as if she was meeting him for the first time. What surprised her most were his eyes. The whites were amazingly clear, given the damage to the surrounding skin, and the irises were the deepest sapphire blue she had ever seen.

After several moments of tense silence, the doctor leaned over John and waved his hand up and down at varying distances from his face. She heard John tell him he was able to see dim shadows, but that was all. The doctor straightened up and dropped his hands into the big side pockets of his lab coat. "Don't be discouraged, young man. This is a good start."

Even though John tried to downplay it, she knew him well enough by now to see through his bravado to the deep disappointment beneath. When they were finally alone again he seemed hesitant, even a little distant. She helped him with lunch, mostly in silence, but all the while waiting for him to say what was on his mind.

As her appointed time to leave for the train station drew near, he finally opened up. He produced an envelope from underneath his pillow containing two months' pay in American currency, and then he felt around on the blanket until he found her hand. In a halting voice he said, "I know you may decide to go your own way when you get to New York, Ari. I hope you don't, but I won't blame you if you do." After a short pause, he turned to face her. "I dearly hope you will go to my parents' home in Michigan and wait, at least until I get there."

While he was speaking, she had been staring down at her hand resting in his. It wasn't the gentle momentary pressure of "thank you and farewell" that they customarily shared before she left each day; it was different, it felt a lot like hope. When she looked up at him again, his poor face and his emotion-filled words made her heart ache. His eyes, although sightless, drew her in and held her transfixed. Finally, with a slight shake of her head, she forced herself to look down.

"Puis-je toucher votre visage?" he asked.

Arielle did not answer but looked up quickly, grateful that the nurses had left the privacy partition in place after working on John's eyes. She scooted her chair closer to the side of the bed, leaned forward, and closed her eyes, slowly bringing John's hand to her face and pressing it against her cheek. He was a big man with the rough hands of a combat Marine, a man who had killed other men with those same hands, but the touch of his fingers as he traced her lips, the slope of her nose, the tips of her eyelashes, was so tender, so compelling, that tears began to run down her cheeks, drawn by a powerful emotional connection, emotion that had nothing to do with loss or with the war. When his fingers passed through the dampness on her cheek, he brought his other hand up and gently cradled her face. The pieces of the puzzle they had both been avoiding began to fall into place of their own accord. She knew then that she *would* go to Michigan; she promised him she would wait.

"Arielle, Arielle, are you OK?" said Claire, trying to break into her friend's thoughts.

"Oh! I'm sorry, Claire, I'm just not feeling very well. What did you say?"

"How did you meet?" said Claire with a tone of exasperation.

Arielle quickly refocused her attention but was still caught off guard by the simple question.

"He and some other soldiers came to our chateau to escape the shelling. We all took shelter in the wine cellar until it was over, almost two days down there in the dark." She stopped there, suddenly realizing where her explanation was leading. She never wanted to go back there in thought, or in deed.

"I'm worried about you, Arielle. We've known each other for what—two weeks now, and I haven't seen you smile even once in all that time. You're too serious. It could be a lot worse, you know. If I had *your* looks, I'd be strolling along the Rue de Passy on some pretty rich man's arm. Maybe what you need is something to eat." Claire reached down into her handbag and produced a crumpled white bakery bag with transparent grease blotches. She fished out a flattened jelly filled donut, a little the worse for wear, tore it in half, and offered up a piece.

Arielle took one look at it and felt bile rise in her throat. She swallowed hard. "No, thank you. That's very kind, but I can't. It must be the thought of an ocean voyage that's upsetting my stomach."

Claire shrugged her shoulders and somewhat indelicately stuffed the rejected half in her mouth along with the rest, making her cheeks bulge.

What started as a faint sound of unknown origin grew steadily louder until the voices of men singing emerged from the sound of army boots landing in step. The words were indistinguishable, but the rhythm was timed perfectly with the footfalls of the soldiers stepping sharply and the droning cadence of their sergeant. Thankfully for Arielle, the sounds presented a timely diversion from the conversation between her and Claire. Eventually the source of the sounds came into view and halted a short distance from the two women, between the warehouse and a long, fifteen-foot-high stack of wooden crates. The soldier who had been marching beside the group shouted a command, and as one, every man did a crisp left face. Most of the women paid no attention to the newcomers, but Arielle and Claire were so close to the door that it was hard not to be drawn in.

"My, my, will you look at that," said Claire. "I didn't think the American Army had any black soldiers."

"Other than their hats, and the way they march, they don't look much like soldiers," replied Arielle. Each man sported a regulation campaign hat rather than the more convenient foldable overseas model, and most wore straight-legged Army pants, but that's where the uniformity ended. Some had coats, some bibbed overalls, some wore boots with their pant legs rolled up, and some had shoes. To a man, though, they all seemed happy and strangely proud for such a ragtag-looking bunch.

As the two women watched, more commands were shouted and the men broke ranks and set to work loading the heavy wooden crates on a train of flatbed carts pulled by a small tractor resembling a metal box with a steering wheel sticking out of the top. The white sergeant paced up and down nervously but offered nothing in the way of direction or admonishment; in fact, he paid little attention to the soldier-stevedores. They seemed to know what they were doing and were happy to get on with it.

"That must be what slavery in America looked like," said Claire.

"Oh, I don't know. They look like they're enjoying their work, I think."

As if to confirm her observation, the sergeant blew his whistle and yelled, "OK, men, take five, smoke 'em if you got 'em." He then walked over and monkey-jumped a cigarette with the help of one of the black soldiers who was already taking deep drags. Occasional outbursts of laughter were carried to the two women on the heavy air off the Gironde Estuary.

A shrill blast from a pea whistle effectively focused everyone's attention toward the open door of the warehouse. "Ladies, attention ladies," shouted a YWCA secretary, struggling to be heard over the noise of the dock. "We will be going aboard the *Mercury* in a few minutes, so please listen carefully. I would like all the mothers traveling with children as well as all the mothers-to-be, to form a line starting right here." She swung her arm in an exaggerated underhand arc to pinpoint the area she was referring to, then took several side steps and repeated the signal. "I want all the ladies traveling alone to line up here." As soon as her last words died away, hundreds of anxious conversations broke out all at once and the scene inside the warehouse looked as though someone had kicked over an anthill.

"Let's go so we can get our pick of staterooms," said Claire, leaning in close.

Arielle simply nodded and fell in behind her friend. When everyone was finally sorted out, the line of women with children and those in the "family way" was easily three times longer than the one Claire and Arielle stood in.

"I'm glad we're not queued up over there," said Claire, nodding toward the other line. "Maybe we can get a stateroom for just the two of us. That would be the berries, just like one of those holiday cruises you see in the back of magazines."

Once again, the lady with the whistle let loose a piercing blast, bringing all conversation to a halt.

"As soon you're on board and have your cabin assignments, you should stow your luggage and proceed immediately to the main salon, where the first officer will go over the rules of the ship. He asked me to tell you that our convoy will be steaming through submarine infested waters, so a strict blackout will be enforced. There will be classes on what to expect when you get to America, and there will be mandatory English language instruction; in fact, while on board we expect you to speak only English unless it's an emergency. When we leave the building, keep your little ones close and watch your step."

Claire once again sat on her suitcase and dug a pack of cigarettes out of her oversized handbag. She shook one up and pulled it out with her lips and then held out the pack to Arielle. When her friend waved off the offer, she shrugged and dropped the crumpled pack back in her bag. "You should try smoking, Arielle. This American tobacco is fabulous—might even calm you down."

Arielle was only half paying attention. She was watching intently as two Red Cross nurses with clipboards started working down the line of women, pausing to ask questions of each person. Her eyes darted from the nurses to the open door, to the other line across the way and then back to the nurses.

By now Claire was becoming concerned by her friend's odd behavior. "Dear, what in the world is the matter? This isn't the end of the world. If you don't like it over there, just get on another ship and come back, for pity's sake."

Arielle reached down and picked up her suitcase. "I'm sorry, Claire." Without waiting for a response, she turned away, walked across the hard packed dirt floor of the warehouse, and took a place at the end of the other line.

Chapter 19

Bill looked across at the battered storm lantern sitting on a makeshift shelf with a wavy box of kitchen matches that had seen moisture. He had studied it many times, mostly because there was nothing much else to look at. The only thing that ever changed was the spider web that spanned the space between the globe and the rough sawn wood of the wall.

Suddenly the door flew open and his brother Jake stood there in his red drawers. "I hope you fall in!" he screamed and then slammed the door shut with such force that old dust filled the air, transforming the morning light into rays where it streamed in from the louvers over the door. Inexplicably he did feel himself falling, slowly tumbling toward the disgusting brown morass below.

When Bill opened his eyes in the fog between dream and reality, his chin was resting on his chest and immediately before him was the front of his white "up-the-street shirt," dirty and bloodstained. The next thing that registered was an obnoxious and overpowering smell. In fact, it was so terrible and close that he started to think maybe the nightmare about his grandfather's outhouse wasn't a dream after all. Gingerly he brought his elbows back until he could use his bent arms to lift his head away from the wall and straighten his neck. As soon as he moved, before he even had a chance to lift his head, he was sick. Without leaning one way or the other, he simply opened his mouth and vomited up what seemed like an endless stream of foul liquid all down his front. The Boilermakers from the previous evening were far less pleasant as they worked their way out the same way they had gone in. The aftertaste was strong enough to set off even more spasms of nausea that persisted until he re-lapsed into oblivion.

The next time Bill opened his eyes he was being pummeled by a jet of water from a large-diameter hose. A chorus of low moans arose from the wretches sprawled on the concrete floor of the holding cell as the unsympathetic jailer methodically worked the night's accumulation of various ejecta toward the grated floor drain in the center of the room.

"Al-key, al-key-hol-ic," he said in a sarcastic, "yoo hoo" manner. "Time to rise and shine, boys." The man with the hose caught the movement when Bill sat up and immediately directed the high pressure stream at his head. Bill got his crossed arms in front of his face just in time to avoid a direct hit, but the force still slammed him back against the wall. Not fully appreciating his situation but in the mood to lash out at anything, he flailed around, trying to get his feet under him.

"You son of a bitch! It's not going to be so funny when I shove that hose up your ass," he screamed.

"Oh no, looks like I missed a spot," replied the guard. He then brought the jet of water back and directed it at Bill's crotch, again knocking him down. The deckhand made one more attempt to stand, but this time his wet stocking feet slipped out from under him in a pool of someone else's vomit.

The guard laughed and said, "OK, boys, I want you to be real, real careful when you stand up. That nasty old puke is slippery as greased owl shit." With that, he turned the water off and disappeared down the hallway.

Bill leaned back against the cold, and now wet, wall and tried to reconstruct the events of the previous night. He surveyed the other occupants of the cell for clues but didn't recognize any of the faces, at least of the ones he could see. Most were older men dressed in a hodgepodge of dirty garments and with several days' growth of gray stubble, the skin around their mouths puckered and sunken over toothless gums. One man near the floor drain lay on his back with his fingers interlocked over his stomach as if taking a leisurely nap. The corners of his mouth were turned up slightly but his eyes were cloudy and fixed under droopy lids.

A spontaneous shiver coursed through Bill's body, and he squeezed his eyes shut as tight as he could. For the first time in his life, Bill began to take a hard look at himself. It was not lost on him that he was by far the youngest person in this group of drunken derelicts and that apart from the obvious age difference, he was no standout. Down-and-out men like these were not uncommon in the Flats; every street corner seemed to have its regulars, sometimes passed out in the vestibule of a shop or maybe panhandling to pay for a few ounces of grain alcohol. He always looked away whenever he encountered one of these men, never once thinking that there might be a story behind the man's decline with parallels to his own.

Bill had never been arrested, although he and his brothers came close one time when they stole the family cow from the back yard of a Finnish family and painted every cuss word they could think of in big white letters on its flanks before turning it loose in town. The possibility of being thrown in jail never even occurred to him. His mind was still dull from the residual effects of marijuana and whiskey, but at least a part of it was seeing things more clearly than ever before. Suddenly missing from his persona was the nearly ironclad self-confidence that had propelled him forward in life up to this point, and only now did he realize it had also made his journey untenable. This was just not the way things were supposed to turn out.

"Come on, you sorry asses, on your feet. This ain't the Ritz." There was a jangle of keys and a heavy clunk when the bolt of the cell door released. The jailer pulled the door open as he stepped back to make way for the exodus. Bill had been standing against the back wall, waiting to see what was going to happen next and started forward immediately.

"Not you, Castor. I'll get to you in a minute. Just have a seat," said the guard, motioning to a bench of sorts made from two courses of cinderblock stacked on their sides.

"Where's my boots?" shot back Bill, a little louder than was probably good for him.

The jailer waited until everyone had filed past him and then walked into the cell and kicked at the man lying by the floor drain. "We got a stiff here," he shouted to someone down the hall.

The guard stepped over the body and crowded Bill backward face-to-face until he was pressing him up against the wall with his thrust-out chest. "You're in deep shit, boy. Those fancy boots are the least of your troubles." The jailer stared Bill in the eye for a moment longer and then shoved him sideways toward the bench. "Like I said, have a seat." He walked out and slammed the cell door shut behind him. At the last second before disappearing down the hallway, he stopped and turned back. "Those boots of yours are being held as evidence, sonny boy. I just might bid on 'em myself when you get the chair." Finally he chuckled to himself and went on his way.

Mr. Mather had turned his chair toward the west facing window of his office, hoping to find inspiration in a change of scenery but instead had become distracted by the forest of tall factory chimneys out across the river, billowing dirty smoke into the atmosphere. It wasn't the unnatural ugliness of the scene that captured his attention but rather the volume and sometimes the color of the smoke that he used as quick indicators of productivity of not only his steel mills, but those of his competitors as well.

Two soft knocks on the door frame behind him and quiet steps approaching his desk across deep pile carpeting pulled him back to the moment and Greg Ward, head of the Cleveland Cliffs legal department. Ward was a short, spare man with thick glasses that made his penetrating gaze seem larger than life. Aside from that, he was attired in a precise and businesslike style, though somewhat lacking in imagination. The man's "holier than thou" manner made Mather uneasy, so private, impromptu meetings like this one were rare.

"Thanks for popping up on such short notice, Greg. Please have a seat," said Mather as he motioned toward a brown leather Queen Anne-style chair in front of his desk.

Ward settled in and crossed one leg over the other. "Thank you, sir. How may I be of assistance?"

"We're both busy today, so I'll cut right to the chase." Mr. Mather opened the upper right-hand drawer of his desk, produced a note-sized envelope with a tear along the top edge, and slid it across the desk to Ward. "SS *Pontiac*" was embossed on the flap of the envelope.

When he had read the note, Ward carefully returned it to the envelope and slid it back across the desk. Boring though he was, he was also a smart man used to thinking on his feet, and he quickly pulled together all the important elements of the message, some that were spelled out and some that were less direct. After a silence long enough to appear like hesitation, Ward said,

"May I presume your interest in this deckhand stems from the fact that he is the son of Robert Castor up on the iron range in Ishpeming?"

This response touched off an immediate flash of anger in Mr. Mather, but there was no outward sign that might have foreshadowed the comeuppance that Ward was about to receive. Mr. Mather slouched a little to the right in his chair with his elbow on the armrest and his chin on his fist as he regarded Ward. "Before we get to the specifics of this issue, let me ask you a question, Mr. Ward."

The formal title before his surname raised a red flag for the lawyer and garnered his undivided attention.

"Let's say, for the sake of argument, that I had no previous knowledge of the subject in question, other than that he was a seaman employed on one of my ships. How would your response to a directive from me regarding this case differ from one, if as you say, this person was the son of a personal friend of mine?" Mather was pleased to note that the other man's smugness had vanished, replaced now with uncertainty. Thanks to his endless hours presiding over meetings since taking over the company from his father, Mr. Mather could spot a mile away, even in a polished attorney like Ward, someone buying time while he worked up a positive spin.

"Well, Mr. Mather, I won't bore you with—"

Mather raised his hand palm out, cutting Ward off. "Please don't insult me with generalizations. I called you in here today to hear your ideas and see what my options are. Now that it's obvious you can satisfy neither without including a substantial load of horseshit, I will tell *you* how this will go. I want you to assign the best and brightest legal apprentice in your department to poke around and gather all the information he can about this case without raising any eyebrows. I want this handled in a very thorough but unobtrusive manner. Is what I've said very clear?"

This time Ward's instinct served him well and he simply nodded in response. "Whoever you choose will report directly to me starting tomorrow morning. See to it that there is not the slightest misstep. That's all for now."

"Yes, sir, I'll get on it right away." Ward stood and quickly headed for the door, anxious to be gone before his cranky boss thought of something else.

The periphery of Sergeant Kingrey's desktop was covered with untidy stacks of "in process" papers, leaving the center area clear for one or two "decoy" documents that he counted on to demonstrate that he was actively engaged in important police work. Nearly all exposed surfaces, paper or wood, carried brown coffee mug circles. Right now, though, elements of his lunch wrapped in wax paper were spread out on his desk along with a steaming wide-mouth Thermos bottle containing stringy raccoon stew. His back was to the stationhouse entrance as he hovered over an open file drawer, covertly pouring a shot of Canadian Mist into a mug of coffee. When he turned back around, as if by magic, there was a young man in a tight-fitting black suit and smallish derby hat standing in front of his desk. He reminded Kingrey of the leprechaun on a beer sign down at Bun Brady's.

The smirk on his stealthy visitor's face confirmed that his lunchtime ritual had been observed. The Sergeant decided to fight his first inclination to send the young man packing.

"Good afternoon, Sergeant. I understand you're holding a fellow by the name of Bill Castor."

"Who wants to know?"

"I'm sorry, my name is Harrison McGilvery from the head office of Cleveland Cliffs. Castor is missing from one of our ships, and we're trying to track him down."

The old Sergeant regarded the young man for a moment and then started pawing through one of the fresher stacks of reports on his desk. "OK, here it is. Well, he was here but they moved him over to county lockup. Just missed him by a few hours."

"I guess that explains why he wasn't on board when his ship sailed. Don't you usually just hold the sailors until they sober up and then take them back to their ship?"

"Yep, that's the procedure. Says here your boy came in as a "drunk and disorderly and left as a murder suspect."

There was a long silence while McGilvery stood with his hands behind his back staring at his feet. "Well, that does change things a bit, doesn't it?"

"I guess you read about those headless bodies showing up over in Kinsbury Run? We picked Castor up over that way not too far from a dope house called Mootas. Couple weeks back a vaudeville front man turned up dead about a block from there." The Sergeant made a soft clicking sound with his mouth as he studied the report. He flipped the first page over the second and continued reading. Finally he looked up. "Looks like Castor's boot print was found at the scene."

Mr. Mather had been poring over the balance sheets for Cleveland Cliffs Iron Company most of the morning, but uncharacteristically was having trouble staying on task. Unlike many CEOs of large companies, he shunned the summary reports in favor of detail. The practice had worked well over the years but it *could* be mind-numbing at times, even for him. The war in Europe wasn't exactly winding down, but the Germans were clearly "on the ropes." He knew that within days of the surrender, when it came, the government would cancel contracts en masse and the market price for American steel would go into free fall. The only question, and the one that kept him up at night, was: Who would be left holding the bag when the dust settled?

It was a welcome distraction when his secretary stuck her head in the door and announced a visitor. "Harrison McGilvery to see you, sir."

Mather opened the shallow center drawer of his desk and swept his paperwork out of sight. "Send him in, Sally."

"Good morning, Mr. Mather," said Harrison. Mather simply nodded and motioned him to a chair. His first impression had been favorable earlier in the week when he had given the young man his marching orders, so he decided to use this as a teaching moment.

"So what have you learned since our last meeting, Harrison? What I expect from you now and in the future are the facts, only the facts. If I decide I want your assessment when everything is on the table, I'll ask for it. Understood?"

"Yes, sir. On the evening of September 9th, Mr. Castor was involved in a bar brawl at a place called ..." There was a pause while Harrison looked down to check his notes. "'Short and Curlies.'"

When the young man raised his head with a confused look on his face, Mather covered his mouth with his fist and cleared his throat to cover a laugh. "Please go on," he said, recovering quickly.

"Somehow he avoided being picked up by the police when they arrived to put down the disturbance and made it all the way over to Kingsbury Run, where he was later found passed out, unconscious, that is, near a dope house called Mootas. He was arrested as "drunk and disorderly" and detained at the Second District Police Station. Evidently there have been several murders in that area, possibly connected to those 'Torso Murders' that are in the papers. When they were processing him, someone recognized the unusual tread pattern on the bottom of Mr. Castor's boots, and eventually it was confirmed that they matched impressions taken at the scene of one of the earlier murders. I went over to the County Jail and was allowed to speak with him for a few minutes. He doesn't deny being at Mootas that night but says he and a shipmate, uh, George Evans, left and walked back to the ship early the next morning. He said when he got back to the ship he met with you and received word about his brother being killed in the war. A public defender has been appointed to his case, but I don't know who it is yet. That's what I have so far, Mr. Mather."

The older man looked at his folded hands resting on his desk and nodded. Finally he said, "How was he, as far as you could judge?"

"I didn't notice anything in particular. He's in a cell by himself, so I suppose that's a good thing— you always hear a lot of stories. I guess he seemed ... resigned, maybe. Not like he's guilty and finally got caught, but just in general, I mean."

There were a few moments of silence and then Mather said, "Do you think he did it?"

"I have some things to follow up on, like talking to the shipmate and visiting the crime scene, but no, so far I don't think so. It's a little premature, but I do have a theory about what's going on here if you'd like to hear it."

Once again Mather just nodded his blessing. "This is an election year for the sheriff, and the election is coming up pretty soon. If I were him, I'd keep Mr. Castor on ice, no matter how flimsy the evidence, and if the real Torso murderer isn't apprehended by, say, a week before election day, I'd charge him with it and make sure every reporter in the city was on hand when the announcement was made. It would be front page news in every paper. So what if there's no conviction, or if the real killer is captured after the election?

Mr. Mather had known the Cuyahoga County Sheriff for quite a few years, and something like this would be no surprise. He was also very impressed with Harrison McGilvery. "I think you may be onto something there. I want you to keep digging for anything that will help our case in the event Mr. Castor is charged. Did he say if he needed anything?"

"The only thing he mentioned was he'd like a chance to call his father. They don't let prisoners make phone calls, you know."

Mr. Mather thought about that for a minute and then spun his chair around to his credenza and produced a wooden box just the right size to hold a single tall bottle of whiskey. The arched logo, "Macallan Anniversary Malt," was burned into the top. He scribbled a note on a sheet of his personal letterhead, folded it in half, and tucked it under the lid in such a way that part of it was sticking out. "Find out when the night shift begins over at the jail and see that the desk sergeant gets this."

Chapter 20

"You speak very good English, Anna. You must have come to this country when you were very young."

The hand holding Anna's silver polishing rag shot up, and she covered her spontaneous giggle with the back of her wrist. "Oh, yes, ma'am, my mother was pregnant with me on the ship coming over.

She always says she made me wait so I would be an American citizen."

"Do you speak Finn?"

"Mother taught me when I was a little girl so I could keep my grandmother company. I'm out of practice since she passed. She taught me recipes from the old country."

"Oh, I loved that Pulla you made last week! I've had it a few times but never with cinnamon and sugar. Maybe it's the rationing that makes me notice the sugar more. Anyway, you must write down the recipe for me when you have a chance." Elizabeth was sharing the kitchen worktable with Anna, paging through her favorite cookbook for ideas. She glanced up when the housekeeper didn't respond.

"I was just thinking the other day that I'm hungry for Italian." She left the cookbook open and stepped over to the walk-in pantry. "Anna, would you read off the ingredients for that lasagna recipe?" she called back.

After a few moments with still no response, Elizabeth leaned back and peeked around the doorframe to see Anna bent over the cookbook, desperately trying to sound out the words. When Elizabeth came up behind her and laid a hand on the young woman's shoulder, she jumped in surprise then collapsed on the stool as if the life force had suddenly rushed out of her.

"Oh please don't fire me, Mrs. Castor!" she begged. "My mother will disown me. I had to quit school to help support the family after Papa's accident. Mama says it's more important for my brothers to get an education." Anna covered her eyes with the palms of her hands and began to sob. A black smudge on her cheek made her seem even more pathetic.

Elizabeth moved in closer and wrapped her arm around Anna's shoulder, pulling her in. The soft scent of pine tar soap reminded her of her mother.

"Nobody's going to fire you, dear; we can fix this. We will set aside one hour every day, just you and me. All those expensive schoolbooks we had to buy for the boys are still up in the attic. I'll have Jacob get them down tonight after dinner."

Elizabeth patted Anna softly on the back and moved over to the window that faced the lake. In the winter when the trees were bare, she could see the skaters circling on clean ice, sometimes couples, sometimes children trying to outdo one another. Now, floating in the space where a dead tree had been removed, only the swim raft was visible, framed by mottled greens and flecks of sparkling blue. She could not shake the guilt from outliving one of her children, or the grief that gripped her so completely, but having a mission, however slight, gave the thought of tomorrow just a hint of promise. Before she could turn away from the window, she saw her husband pull up in his Runabout and park by the sidewalk across from her. She was surprised to see he had the convertible top up on such beautiful warm day. He didn't get out right away, nor did George, somehow knowing he should wait. As she watched, Robert leaned forward and rested his forehead on the steering wheel. In that moment, her own anguish caught in her throat and threatened to overwhelm her. That crazy dog is more attuned to my husband than I am, she thought. Without a word she turned and took a step toward the staircase and then stopped, turned again, and rushed out the kitchen door to the street.

The moment Robert had been dreading was finally at hand. It had been years, or at least it seemed like years, since Elizabeth had allowed herself such an open display of concern and affection toward him, especially in broad daylight where the neighbors might see. He savored the moment, even though he knew she was misinterpreting his purpose in coming home early and the cause of his despair. The very last thing he wanted to do now was hand her Johnny's letter. He watched her for a moment as she moved along the floor-to-ceiling bookcase on the wall across from his desk, stopping now and then and cocking her head to read the spine of a book. The contrast between her state of mind now and her state of mind two weeks ago was so great it almost seemed impossible. Her face had regained its radiance and not a hair was out of place. Even her gestures showed confidence.

"If I knew what you were looking for, dear, I might be able to help."

"I thought you had a couple old dictionaries in your office, but I don't see them. I need to get Anna in here to dust," she said, brushing her hands together. Elizabeth finally gave up and took a seat in the chair in front of Robert's desk. "What did you need to speak to me about, Rob?"

Robert looked at her for moment, almost losing his resolve, then reached into the inside pocket of his jacket that lay on the floor next to his chair and retrieved the letter. He took it out of its envelope and passed the folded pages across the desk to her. Elizabeth locked eyes with him for a moment and then looked down and studied the letter. Finally she rested her hands in her lap and silently regarded her husband, causing him to shift uncomfortably in his chair. She re-folded the letter and extended her upturned hand across the desk for the envelope. When she turned it over and looked at the postmark the suspense got the better of Robert.

"Lizzy, please don't be mad at me. I just couldn't drop this on you so soon after getting the word about Matt. I wasn't—"

Elizabeth cut him off with a wave of her hand and allowed a tense silence, at least for Robert, to linger in the air between them. At first he thought she was just getting up a head of steam, as was her practice, but when she spoke, he was surprised, still wary, but pleasantly surprised.

"What do you think we should do?" she said. Robert had rehearsed his pitch many times over the last few days so he was able to launch into it without delay.

"As hard as this whole thing has been on us, Johnny was there when it happened. He's a strong boy, but nobody could go through that and come away unscathed. When I showed the letter to Peep, he told me about the battle he was in during the Civil War, and it really opened my eyes, I can tell you that. I think we should trust Johnny's judgment. I'm sure he can imagine what we must be thinking and I'm sure he wouldn't do this without a damn good reason. When he comes home, we can sort it all out then."

"Who else have you discussed this with?" Robert's plan of bringing Elizabeth's motherly instincts into play was a good one, but he knew he wouldn't get off scot-free.

"No one, Lizzy. My father has been there; I'd be a fool not to seek his advice." Elizabeth looked down for a long time, absent-mindedly smoothing the battered envelope on her lap. Either unwilling or unable, she decided not to argue the point. Past conversations within her social circle about the shameless gold-digging French whores kept running through her mind.

"Whatever we do, it *will not* include having a two-bit French floozy living under our roof, no matter how temporary." She looked up at her husband to make sure there was no misunderstanding. "Is that clear, Rob?" Robert nodded in the affirmative but didn't follow it up with a verbal promise. He knew this wasn't the end of it, but he thought things had gone pretty well, all in all. He felt like a heavy load had been lifted off his shoulders and now he had some time to work something out.

The dining room at the Castor house had always seemed a little small to Robert, even though by the standards of the day, most would have considered it spacious. Now, with three fewer people and two table leaves stored in the pantry, it felt too big.

"My compliments to the chef, Anna. That was excellent," said Robert. The young housekeeper blushed and did a slight dip before continuing to clear away the dishes.

"I loved those green beans with little pieces of bacon in them. What do you call that?" said Jacob.

Rosemarie glared at him and said, "Green beans with bacon, silly." She was anxious to steer the conversation away from the housekeeper's praises.

Elizabeth shot the "look" at her. "Smothered Green Beans," she corrected. "Thank you, Anna. Mr. Castor and I will have coffee tonight. How about you two?" Jacob held up his hand palm out and Rosemarie shook her head without making eye contact.

"I know you must get ready for work, Rose, but if you and Jacob will stay at the table for a few minutes longer, your father has some news about Johnny to share."

Robert finished chewing his last bite and wiped his mouth with his napkin before tossing it on the table next to his plate. "This concerns you too, Anna, so please stay," he said. "We don't have any details about how all this came about, but the upshot is that your brother is engaged to a woman he met in France before he and Matt ... were sent to the front, before Johnny was wounded."

Robert paused and looked around the table. Elizabeth was composed but looking down, Rosemarie had a faraway look on her face, and Jacob, with his mouth agape, could only be described as incredulous. "The only things we know are that her name is Arielle, and she is on her way here."

Jacob hadn't moved or changed his expression, but Rosemarie's head snapped around as if he had just announced the family was moving to China.

At last Jacob regained his senses. "Here, as in the U.S., or here as in 'this house'?" he said. Now all three people at the table were staring at Robert.

"Here, as in Ishpeming. We're not sure where she'll stay yet. Your mother and I have to work that out."

"This woman is French?" said Rosemarie, looking at Elizabeth instead of Robert. Her mother returned a barely perceptible nod.

"I think we should all withhold judgment until she arrives and we can find out first-hand what's going on," said Robert.

"You two may be excused," said Elizabeth.

Jacob stood and carried his dirty dessert plate and fork to the kitchen, and Rosemarie simply tossed her cloth napkin on the table and headed for her room without even pushing her chair back in.

As Jacob passed through on his way upstairs, Robert called out to him, "I'm going over to the Barnes-Hecker first thing tomorrow morning. You're welcome to ride along... ."

Jacob paused and considered the offer a moment. "I don't mind walking to the office, Pop. I'll see you when you get back."

There was a soft knock on her bedroom door, and even though Rosemarie knew who it was, she still answered it with a "yes" in the form of a question.

"It's me, Jake."

Rosemarie had just finished changing to get ready for work and was brushing out her hair in front of the mirror over her vanity. Her shift spanned the nighttime hours, but old Mrs. Steiner insisted on her operators showing up dressed as if they were working at a bank.

"It's not locked," she replied, consciously making sure her tone of voice was more inviting than was her natural inclination. Since that day they received the news about Matt, Jacob had seemed a little less of a sure thing. She watched the reflection of the door in her mirror as both hands worked behind her head, winding and pinning her hair into a neat bun.

When Jacob's face appeared, he looked quickly around the room as if he were going to see something indecent, and then he let his eyes settle on her back rather than her face reflected in the mirror.

"I'll be downstairs when you're ready to go," he said.

"I'll be down shortly, dear," she replied, watching closely for his reaction to her use of "dear." His eyes darted to her face in the mirror and matched her smile before quietly pulling the door closed behind him.

It was a warm night and they were a little early, so Jacob and Rosemarie sat for a few minutes on the park bench in front of Gately's. The days seemed to be getting shorter, although in this case that perception was helped considerably by the darkening sky of an approaching storm. They could already hear distant thunder.

"Don't be so nice to that damned Anna. She's a sly one, and I know she's up to something, but I just can't put my finger on it. Being friendly just encourages her, and that will only lead to trouble. Look at me, Jake. Do you promise?"

Jacob was silent but nodded his head in response. "What do you think of Johnny getting engaged? You could have knocked me over with a feather," he said.

"I know. Surprised me, too. At first I was mad because they seem to have accepted it without batting an eye, but the more I think about it, this might actually help us. If there is a wedding, Mother and Father will have to treat us equally, and if this French lady turns out to be a tramp, then it will just make us look good. Either way, we have to keep our eyes open and be ready to seize an opportunity."

Jacob thought he knew what she meant, but he wasn't about to ask for clarification and look stupid. Rosemarie sensed his uncertainty and took his hand in hers. "I love you, Jake, and I want us to be happy. I want us to raise a beautiful family and have our own house."

Jacob looked at her and thought his heart was going to burst. As soon as she spoke the words, "I love you, Jake," he stopped listening. He had no idea what else she said.

Rosemarie paused at the top of the stairs on the back of the Miners Bank building and dug through her handbag for the key to the telephone office. There were bolts on the inside of the door that would prevent someone getting in even with a key, but the common practice was to slide them open just before the operator coming on duty was expected to arrive.

"Oh, thank heavens, Rose. I'm sure glad to see you! It was so hot up here today, I was sweating like a long-tailed cat in a room full of rocking chairs—my granddad used to say that. When I get home, the first thing I'm going to do is strip right down buck naked and have a nice cool sponge bath." Geneva had her patchwork tote over her shoulder, the ends of two knitting needles sticking out, and a library book in the crook of her arm, ready to dash out the door. In response to the funny indentation in Geneva's hair from the headset, Rosemarie unconsciously reached up and felt above her ear for the new silk headscarf, like the ones in the magazines. The discoloration on the front of the other girl's blouse where the heavy mouthpiece had caused perspiration to bleed through just seemed typical of someone from that part of town.

"It's cooled off now, so you'll feel better by the time you get home," said Rosemarie.

"Gotta dash, Rose. I got a hike ahead of me. Everything's ducky with the board, log is up to date. I'm off tomorrow, good thing, too—I think I'm coming down with something. Toodles!" As if to prove the point, she broke out in a fit of coughing, covering her mouth with her hand. When she finally had it under control, she waved and stepped out onto the landing and pulled the heavy door shut behind her. Rosemarie turned away from the door after sliding all the bolts closed and saw the red light

BROTHERHOOD OF IRON

above the switchboard begin to flash. I hate it when the lines get busy before I even get settled in, she thought.

As it turned out, except for a few calls routed through the Marquette office and a shouting match on a party line between two old biddies (who, in anger, could only speak in their native tongues, which were different), things quieted down shortly after ten o'clock. Rosemarie pulled the gooseneck lamp that was attached to the switchboard down so the light was easier on her eyes and then opened the magazine she had pinched from her mother's mail and commenced her nightly fantasy about decorating the house she and Jacob hoped to have someday. She was so engrossed that the buzzer signaling an incoming call caused her to gasp in surprise. Quickly recovering before the third buzz, she flipped the toggle switch on the trunk line from Marquette.

"Ishpeming Central, this is Rose speaking," she said.

"It's me again, Rose. I'm patching a call through from Cleveland. Here they are." Rosemarie heard a few clicks and then the Cleveland operator came on the line.

"Ishpeming, this is Cleveland long distance. I have a call for you." There was a pause and Rosemarie could hear bursts of static on the lines from the electrical storm that had passed through the area earlier.

"Ishpeming Central, I'm ready to connect you now. Go ahead."

"Hello, operator? I'm trying to reach Robert Castor," said Bill. Rosemarie was stunned and was just barely able to check her first reaction to respond with "Bill?" In the long silence her mind raced, trying to decide what to do.

"Hello, are you there, operator?"

"One minute, please," she said. Rosemarie fumbled through the ranks of shiny brass patch cord plugs sticking up from the switchboard and pulled up the one that would connect the call through to the phone on her father's desk. Her hand trembled as she hesitated, poised to push the plug into the jack. Suddenly,

– 228 –

an especially loud crackling on the line spurred her to action and she opened her fingers, letting the cord fall back into the board. She slid the earpiece forward off her ear but she could still hear Bill's faint voice saying "hello, hello" over and over. Rosemarie closed her eyes and toggled the trunk line switch, breaking the connection to Cleveland.

Chapter 21

Arielle lingered in her seat, collecting herself for the next and final step of her journey. As the other passengers filed past her toward the exit at the end of the coach, she gazed out her window and began looking over the people standing on the station platform, hoping to match someone with the mental image of John's father formed weeks before at the base hospital. Her search was cut short when the conductor came up the aisle behind her, cleared his throat, and nodded to indicate that she had reached her destination. Arielle glanced around and saw that she was the only one left in the train car. She stood and out of habit rather than need, smoothed the back of her tight skirt before side-stepping into the aisle and falling in behind the old man. The Red Cross lady in New York who was charged with making sure she boarded the right train and had all the transfers she would need to reach Ishpeming had graciously allowed her enough time to purchase a new dress and a pair of stylish shoes with ankle straps and curved heels. The new outfit made her a little more confident about meeting John's family, but it did little to take her mind off the dire situation she was in. She was alone in a country where she knew no one and she was with child, a child whose father lay in an unmarked grave in front of the rubble that once was her family's home. The good news, if you could call it that, was she considered her circumstances so hopeless that she had little fear of whatever the future held. Her one regret was John. Against all reason, she had felt the spark and for a moment dared to hope. She prayed only that he would come before her pregnancy became obvious and people started to draw the wrong conclusion. If only she could be gone by then ...

The locomotive had come to a stop directly across from the park bench where Robert sat, just off the west end of the platform. It was a good place from which to study the mechanical intricacies of the engine and still be able to keep an eye on the people milling about, waiting for their luggage. It was a warm morning and George lay at his feet, pressing his belly to the cool cement sidewalk and rolling his eyes back and forth following the activity. This was their second day of meeting each train coming through from downstate. He watched the last passenger in the procession step off the train car and was just starting to turn back to his preoccupation with the locomotive when he saw the old conductor swing onto the platform and immediately turn to hand down a young lady. The conductor moved with such uncharacteristic animation that Robert had to look twice to make sure it really was him.

"Damn, George, would you look at her? Good thing Elizabeth isn't here or I'd be in the shithouse for sure," said Robert under his breath, feeling a little guilty for staring. The woman was tall and slender in a fashionably short, mid-calf and close-fitting, mustard-color dress. It was cinched in at the waist with a black belt and had a double vertical row of black buttons down the front. She wore black heels and a wide brimmed black hat set at a rakish angle low over her eyes. She carried herself with grace and sophistication that was easy to recognize, even from a distance. He had watched so many people come and go over the last two days that it didn't dawn on him immediately that she might actually be the very person he was waiting for. Had she jumped off the train doing the cancan in black stockings and garters, she would have more closely fit the image that came to his mind when he thought of French ladies. Robert shook his head and forced himself to turn back to the now less interesting steam engine, but still he couldn't resist taking a quick peek now and then to monitor her movements. Several minutes passed and when he looked over again, the crowd on the platform had dispersed and the woman stood alone with a large suitcase beside her. Suddenly, she turned her head and looked right at him. Robert was taken aback at being caught out and amazed that she seemed to be able to read his mind. He turned and glanced over his shoulder to see if she was looking at something or someone else beyond him, but there was only a swayback old horse tied to a lamppost. When he turned back, she was walking toward him.

"Crap, I think I've stepped in it now," he said under his breath, bracing himself for a dressing down. When she reached the edge of the platform, she stopped and put her hand, palm down against her brow to shade her eyes from the sun.

"Monsieur Castor?" Robert just looked up at her slack-jawed. The fact that she was a stunning beauty and that she was speaking to him with such a lovely, exotic accent, rendered him temporarily unable to string a coherent response together. Finally the lights came on in his head and he knew who she was. He jumped up and removed his fedora, barely avoiding being knocked ass-over-applecart by George, who was reacting to the stranger at the same moment.

"Arielle?" he said, regaining his composure. After days of being surrounded by strangers in an unfamiliar land, the relief of hearing her name spoken in welcome was clearly evident on the young woman's face.

"Oui," she said with a deep sigh. "I mean yes, yes, I am Arielle." Robert wasn't sure if he should hug her, or maybe kiss her cheeks as he'd seen some French Canadian miners do once, but he knew something was called for. He decided to steer the safest course and reached up to shake hands. Arielle misinterpreted the gesture and used his hand to steady herself as she negotiated the worn wooden steps in her heels. Suddenly remembering her luggage, she turned and started back up, but Robert held on to her hand.

"Please sit," he said, nodding at the bench. "I'll get it." When he returned, he set her suitcase on the end of the bench and took a seat beside her, not sure where to begin. Unfortunately, George was feeling no uncertainty and picked that moment of awkward silence to introduce himself. He sat in front of her knees with his drop ears tilted forward and an intense look in his eyes that was hard to ignore.

"This is George. He can be a little forward sometimes, especially if he likes you." Robert curled his fingers under his collar and gave a tug. "Come on, boy, leave this poor woman alone."

"Oh, he is very wise, I think," said Arielle with a little smile. She reached out with both hands and scratched George behind his ears in just the right way to make him close his eyes and groan. Robert was touched and felt a wave of relief. George, now in a state of rapture, rested his head on her lap where capillary attraction immediately transferred a splotch of slobber from his big lips to the fabric of her dress.

"Oh, no, I'm sorry, dear. I should have seen that coming!" This time, with some serious effort, he succeeded in dragging George away.

"It's OK," she said, taking a couple of perfunctory brushes at the spot.

"My wife Elizabeth and I naturally have a lot of questions, and we can talk later, but what can you tell me about my son?" Arielle looked down at her hands while she collected her thoughts. When she looked up into Robert's eyes, he thought she was going to cry; in fact; he had never seen such unfathomable sadness on such a pretty, young face. Fear for his son seized him with such force that he forgot to breathe. Arielle saw instant alarm transform his face and reached out for his hand.

"Non, non, he is OK. He is ... strong, better," she said in a rush, searching for the right words. When she saw his face soften she went on, choosing her words more deliberately. "He was burned with the gas." She put her hand first to the corner of her eye to indicate where, then around her neck and armpit. She knew from spending time at John's bedside that mustard gas attacked moist areas of the body and that he was burned in his groin area, but she chose not to mention that. "He was blinded. All is dark shadows with him. Le docteur says he will see ... again, and he will come home very soon."

Robert nodded in response as he digested the information. Finally he stood, helped Arielle to her feet, and then picked up her suitcase. "Before we go up to the house, I'd like to give you the nickel tour of our little town and tell you about our family, just so you'll know what you're getting into. I'm over there," he said pointing to the Runabout.

The evening meal was tense, but Robert knew it could have been much worse. Rose had been called in early to take over for the girl on the day shift who had suddenly taken ill, so Elizabeth's stoniness was at least partially counterbalanced by him and Jacob. The other neutralizing factor was Arielle herself. Her poise, intelligence, and refined beauty were so far removed from the popular American misconception of French women that

Elizabeth was forced to abandon those grounds for rejecting her and go in search of a suitable replacement. Early on, Robert noticed that every time Elizabeth would reach for something on the table, she would lean in and take a deep breath. At first he thought perhaps his wife was coming down with a cold but then with great amusement, he realized that she was trying to determine if their guest had body odor—evidently her backup French stereotype.

It was good that Rose was not there to witness Jacob's reaction. Predictable and superficial though it was, Robert was thankful for the ally at the table nonetheless. Anna seemed to be maintaining her neutrality, but she must have connected with Arielle at some point during the afternoon, since the slobber spot on Arielle's dress was gone and it had been pressed.

"Anna, if you will put together a meal for Rose, perhaps we can twist Jacob's arm to carry it down to the telephone office," said Robert with a wink. "Will you be having coffee, dear?" he said to Elizabeth. Anna paused with an armload of dirty dishes to wait for her answer.

"No thank you, Anna," she said.

"And how about you, Arielle? Would you care for a cup?" said Robert.

"Non, merci." Arielle started to correct herself with the English version but instead darted an almost imperceptible glance at Elizabeth and kept her silence.

In a corner of Robert's office opposite his desk were two rarely-used, forest-green leather loveseats arranged at a ninety-degree angle to one another. Elizabeth and Robert occupied one, and Arielle had tucked herself into the far end of the other angled toward them. The young woman pulled a handkerchief out of her purse, dabbed at her nose for a moment, and then dropped her hands in her lap and looked up with a sigh of resignation, first at Elizabeth and then at Robert. Elizabeth had seen enough to know that Arielle was not some foolish young woman looking for a meal ticket, so she softened her approach. Her only miscalculation was assuming the tension evident on Arielle's face stemmed from the prospect of parental scrutiny, when in fact, it wasn't sharing her story that she feared, it was remembering.

When it was clear that Robert was not going to speak first, Elizabeth reluctantly opened the conversation. "How did you and Johnny meet?" she said.

Arielle returned her look in silence for a moment, thinking perhaps that she had missed something in the translation. At last she realized that John's parents had nothing whatsoever in their experience to draw on that might help them understand the story she was about to relate.

"Sometime during the first week of June, soldiers came from the front with a wounded man on a … stretcher. The front was just one or two kilometers from our land then. As they were passing on their way into the village, the Germans began shelling the road. I gave the Americans shelter in our wine cellar. There were old people from my village down there too. They put the wounded man, John, on the table, and I tried to comfort him, but it was no good; we had little water and only one candle, and the bombs were landing very close in the yard above us. It went on all day and all night. John was very bad with fever. His shoulder was bleeding and he had breathed the gas. It was choking him. I did what I could, but it seemed that we would all die anyway." Arielle paused there and dabbed at her nose again.

"Was our youngest son, Matt, there?" asked Elizabeth.

"Non, he was not there." By now the color had drained from Arielle's face and her hands were trembling. Elizabeth also had a handkerchief under her nose, and she too looked pale.

Robert held up his hand to stop the narrative. "Maybe we should call it a night and try again tomorrow when you're rested," he said.

"Non, I must finish. I can't do this again," she replied.

"OK, but we can stop anytime. So you and Johnny had never set eyes on one another before he was wounded?"

"No, our part of the country was under German control," she replied.

"You said yesterday that before you boarded the ship, his vision was starting to improve but he still could only see shadows?"

"Yes, that is correct."

Robert slumped back in the couch and stared at his hands while he processed that information.

Elizabeth was finally starting to see that perhaps she and Robert were not the only injured parties in all this. "What about your family, your mother and father? Did they think it was OK that you left home and moved so far away?" she said.

Arielle turned her gaze on Elizabeth and hoped her fight for patience didn't show. "My mother died when I was a girl. My father was in Belgium on business when the Germans invaded, and we never saw him again after that. My brothers ... my brothers were killed at Verdun two years ago. It is only me now. My home and my village are nothing ... just piles of stones." Arielle could go no further. For just a moment she stopped struggling against the darkness that was always pressing in from just an arm's length away. She put her hands over her eyes and began to sob. For a brief instant, Elizabeth's motherly instincts almost got the better of her self-righteous indignation over being forced to host a French woman in her home. Robert, however, *did* follow his instincts and collected Arielle's hands together in his as he knelt on the floor next to her. Something that Peep had said to him when they talked in the orchard tugged at the back of his mind: *he may look all right on the outside, but don't you be fooled.* Until just now, he never imagined it might apply to this young woman as well.

Chapter 22

"**M**om, Mom!" said Jacob as he pounded on the door. Having heard the telephone ring directly below her room in Robert's office, Elizabeth was already awake and sitting on the edge of her bed, fumbling for the pull chain on her reading lamp. Any call coming at this hour could not bring welcome news and her son's desperation only confirmed it.

"OK, OK, Jacob, hold your horses," she replied as she shrugged into her robe. When she pulled open the door, her son was already rushing down the stairs, tucking his pajama shirt-tails into his pants.

"Jacob, wait! What is it ... who called?"

"It was Mrs. Steiner. She said Rose has taken sick and needs to go to the hospital." Without waiting for an answer, he turned and continued on down the stairs.

"Wait, I said!"

Jacob turned once more and looked up at her with a horrified look on his face. "Take the Franklin and drive her over there. Put her in the back. My blanket is under the seat. I'll come as soon as I'm dressed."

She heard the jangle of keys as Jacob pulled them off the nail by the back door and a few minutes later, the distinctive sound of the car's air-cooled engine starting up. Robert had left for Cleveland the day before on unexpected business, and when the phone rang, she was certain it must be some dire news involving him. She was still upset but just thankful that the emergency was within her sphere of influence.

Elizabeth had just stepped back into the same dress she'd had on earlier in the day when there was a soft knock at her door. "Come in," she called.

Arielle walked into the room, already fully dressed. She had come across one of John's old English textbooks and fallen asleep in the chair in his room trying to decipher the sketches he had made in the margins. When she saw Elizabeth struggling over her shoulder with the top buttons of her dress she moved behind her and made short work of the task. "How can I help?" she said.

Just then they heard the Franklin pull up and stop in the street below. Elizabeth hurried over to the window and pushed the drape aside.

"Damn! Follow me!" By the time they reached the sidewalk, Jacob had wrapped Rose's limp body in the car blanket and was cradling her in his arms. "Jacob! What did I tell you?"

When Jacob passed through the headlight beams of the still running car, they could see the stark anguish on his face.

"Old la—Mrs. Steiner said the hospital has no more beds and are turning people away. She told me to bring Rose here and said she would send Dr. Mudge."

OK, let's get her in the house before we make matters worse."

Elizabeth and Arielle both looked up when the doctor stepped on a creaky step as he descended the staircase from the second floor. They had been sitting in the parlor waiting for the verdict for over an hour.

"She has this damn flu that's been going around; very nasty stuff. Damn near every available space at the hospital, including the hallways, is filled with patients. The only ones we're letting in are ladies with a 'bun in the oven,' if you know what I mean; almost one hundred percent fatal for them." Jacob's distress over Rose's illness seemed to confirm some of the rumors he had heard recently, so Dr. Mudge watched Elizabeth's reaction closely. "I guess it's probably just as well you didn't take her there, since they couldn't do anything more than what you can do here. The next forty-eight hours are critical. Do whatever you can to keep her fever down, and make sure she drinks lots of water. Oh, and make sure everyone wears one of these until the danger is over. This strain is contagious as hell." Dr. Mudge pulled a little stack of folded white muslin facemasks from his coat pocket and handed them to Elizabeth. "I'll check in tomorrow when I get a chance and see how things are going."

As soon as the doctor was gone, the two women went upstairs to check on Rosemarie. Elizabeth had thought she looked a little peaked at dinner, but she was shocked at the remarkably swift transformation. Her hair was as wet as if she had just taken a swim, and her skin was bluish and pasty looking, glistening with beads of sweat. Her labored breathing, coming in short raspy breaths, was painful to listen to. Elizabeth looked around the room for Jacob and found him sitting on the floor in a corner by the head of the bed. The look on his face was heart-wrenching and made her annoyance with Rosemarie and him over their marriage plans seem petty in light of this recent development. She knelt next to him and draped one of the masks over his nose and mouth. When she reached behind his head to secure the ties, he looked up at her with such unbridled fear, it reminded her of times when she held him in the middle of the night after he'd had a bad dream.

"Stand up, Jacob. I need your help. If you two are going to make a life together, you have to be able to deal with a few setbacks without going all to pieces. Please show Arielle where the linens are kept, and then go down to the kitchen and fill the largest bowl you can find with ice-cold water and bring it here. Rose is burning up."

"Excuse me, Mr. Mather, your ten o'clock is here a little early. Shall I show him in?" Mather held up his hand, palm out, to stop in mid-sentence the person occupying his client chair.

"Yes, send him in." When the door to Mather's office opened again, Bill followed the older man's cue and came to his feet. He turned, prepared to shake hands with someone he had never met, and instead found himself face to face with his father. Both men froze, too shocked to react, but love and regret flowed between them in that instant. Even though Bill had come to the realization late, this was the man he respected above all others in the world. For Robert, who was determined to avoid letting bygones taint the moment, all that mattered was getting his son back. He slowly reached out and offered his hand without breaking eye contact. Bill reached back and took a strong grip, feeling the crushing weight of fear and helplessness, two things he had precious little experience with, lifted from his shoulders. Without letting go, Robert pulled Bill forward into an emotional bear hug.

"Damn, I've missed you, Billy," said Robert into his son's ear.

"I've missed you too, Pop, I've missed everyone."

Robert pushed Bill out to arm's length and looked him up and down. He thought his son looked gaunt and the clothes he was wearing seemed a little out of character. He had changed, but then after all it had been three years, he thought. Robert turned to Mr. Mather and said, "I don't know how you arranged this, but I'm truly grateful." Mather returned his smile and looked at his watch, thankful that he had Sally clear his schedule for the rest of the day. He sat down and motioned for Robert and Bill to do the same.

"Sorry to spring this on you, Rob; this whole situation has been a little unpredictable right from the start. I'll let Bill fill you in and then I'll tell you where we stand and what needs to be done."

Bill squirmed nervously in his chair for a moment, clenching and unclenching his hands, and then launched into his story. All in all, it was a surprisingly candid recounting of events, sparing none of the self-deprecating details. From time to time he glanced over to gauge his father's reaction, but even though Robert was fighting down his kneejerk reactions, his outward appearance gave nothing away. When Bill was finished, there was a long silence as he and Mather waited for his father to speak.

"I wish you would have called me, son. I would have been on the next train out," he said.

"I tried, but the call was cut off. I only had one chance and Mr. Mather had to pull strings even for that."

"As it turned out, it was probably better this way, Rob. I had the legal department quietly look into the matter, and it's their opinion that Bill was just in the wrong place at the wrong time," said Mr. Mather.

The confused look on Robert's face prompted more explanation. "You've probably read about what the newspapers here are calling 'The Torso Murders.'" Robert nodded that he had. "A vaudeville front man was found dead in a vacant lot over near the Lower Republic dock. Just so happened that this took place near a ... shall we say, shady establishment frequented by Bill here and some of his shipmates. To make a long story short, or at least shorter, when Bill was picked up by the police and tossed into a holding cell to sober up, one of the officers recognized the odd tread pattern of his boots and matched them to an impression taken near the crime scene. The Cuyahoga County Sheriff is up for reelection in November, and he would be a shoe-in if he could announce the capture of the serial killer that's been cutting up people over in the Flats. I know the man personally and he would have no qualms about pinning the murders on an innocent man to win an election. When he heard about Bill, I imagine he thought it was manna from Heaven."

Robert was finally starting to see why his boss had become so involved without letting him know what was going on. "So how were you able to get Bill released?"

Mr. Mather leaned back in his chair and allowed himself a rare smug grin. "Well, I reasoned with him ... then I bought him a steak dinner and appealed directly to his sense of self-preservation. Men like him always have skeletons, and I happened to know where several of them are buried."

"I don't know what I could ever do to repay you, sir," said Robert.

Mather waved him off. "The important thing is to get Bill back on Michigan soil as soon as possible to make sure there are no further attempts to pin something on him. The convoluted extradition laws between Ohio and Michigan should serve as a suitable deterrent."

Bill hung his head and started to fidget in his chair again.

"I know you want to get back to your ship, but you'd be looking over your shoulder every time you were in Cleveland. In fact, no matter what company you sailed for, sooner or later you'd end up back here."

"Mr. Mather is right, son. Come back with me and let the dust settle on all this."

"If you still want that kind of life later on, you can always try saltwater sailing or maybe a tow boat on the Mississippi. I've got a lot of connections and could help you with that," said Mather.

Bill nodded his head in resignation but didn't speak.

"Don't worry about Mom and the rest of the family; this is just between the three of us."

Mr. Mather leaned back, opened the center drawer of his desk, and retrieved two train tickets. "Forgive me for taking the liberty," he said as he slid them across the desk. Just then his office door opened, and before he could voice his displeasure at the interruption, the look on his receptionist's face captured his attention.

"Sorry to barge in, sir, but I have an urgent call for Mr. Castor, and I didn't think it could wait."

Chapter 23

As the steam locomotive settled into its traveling pace north of Saginaw on a long unbending stretch of track, Bill sat with his eyes closed, pressing his spine into the seatback just enough to dampen the gentle swaying motion of the coach. The way his body naturally counterbalanced the movement felt familiar and comforting. The hypnotic clicking of steel wheels on the rail joints gradually drew his thoughts into a dreamy, black void, where images from his past jumped out at him like some crazy funhouse ride.

Looking back on his life aboard ship from his current vantage point, especially when he compared it to what his brothers had experienced in France, just made him feel all the more guilty. In fact, when he added that to the guilt he felt for Ray's undoing, there just didn't seem to be a way out, or even a reason to look for one. As time passed, his "social drinking" gradually morphed into a deadly cycle of drinking to forget, followed by depression and ever-increasing remorse.

Like the measured wink of a lighthouse from a dark shore, one memory had beckoned from across the water as he endured the endless, humiliating hours and days locked up in the county jail. It always came to him the same way as he lay awake in the dark. In his mind's eye he stood before an arched door made of heavy, gray-weathered planks and set in a high wall covered completely with English ivy. When he opened the door and stepped through, he was in the old log trapper's shack deep in the forest behind his family's house. He was different there, unencumbered by past transgressions. He felt unspoiled, and he felt promise. During his youth, it had sometimes been a pirate ship, sometimes a fort where he and his brothers had fought off Indians. He smiled inwardly when he recalled how sick they all had become smoking a peace pipe loaded with real tobacco pinched from their father's desk. The memory that played over and over in his mind, however, was one from later years when he and Rose used the old shack as a hideaway. It was there on a rickety cot under the cabin's only window that they had made love for the first time. It was a perfect moment. The afternoon sun had shone through the dusty pane and tattered yellow curtains to cast a beautiful, warm light on their contentment. They lay there facing each other in silence, heads resting on their rolled-up clothing. He remembered the fragrance of her hair, still damp from swimming, the taste of her kiss, the soft beauty of her freckled face against a background of rough-hewn logs. He remembered her look of innocent wonder as her eyes roamed slowly over his face, mapping every detail. Even he had fallen under the spell of the moment. Back then, he believed moments like those would always be out there for the taking, but no woman had looked at him that way since. More than anything, he wanted that moment back.

Robert glanced over at his son across the aisle and wondered what thought was behind the contented smile on his face. More than that, he wished he had a little of that same calm. Elizabeth, he was sure, had the situation with Rose well in hand, but he could clearly hear the fear in her voice when they talked on the telephone in Mr. Mather's office. With a sigh, he turned back to the window and the autumn fields sweeping past. Troubled as he was, he couldn't resist mentally hunting the golden groves of Aspen along the rivers they crossed. Unconsciously he put his hand palm down on the seat beside him, missing George. He glanced over at Bill again and hoped he had done the right thing by downplaying Rose's illness. He didn't want anything to interfere with getting his son back to Ishpeming.

Elizabeth awoke with a start when she felt herself begin to topple forward out of her chair. She had been at Rose's bedside for most of the previous thirty-six hours, doing what she could to keep the young woman's fever under control. Her directive to Arielle to stay away had gone completely unheeded, and Elizabeth was not accustomed to going unheeded in her own household. When all was said and done, though, she had to admit, if only to herself, that the timely cups of tea and warm pastries were the only things that had kept her going. Elizabeth had also insisted Arielle wear one of Dr. Mudge's face masks during her visits to the room to assist with changing the bed linen, but she had ignored that demand as well. At first Elizabeth had passed it off as that innate notion of immortality all young people seem to possess, but she realized now that Arielle harbored no illusions about death and was comfortable with the possible consequences.

Rosemarie stirred and brought Elizabeth back to the moment. Elizabeth stood and stepped over to the dresser, where she dipped a hand towel in a pan of tepid water and wrung it out. When she turned back to begin sponging the young woman's face, she was surprised to see Rosemarie watching her. She still looked very sick, but this was the first time since coming down with the flu that she was fully conscious.

"Well, well, well, look who's awake." said Elizabeth. She leaned over the bed and held the back of her wrist against Rose's temple. "Thank heaven," she said, more to herself than to Rose.

The young woman opened her mouth to say something but instead broke out into a rattling cough. Finally she said, "What day is it?"

"It's Tuesday, dear." Elizabeth folded the hand towel over on itself lengthwise a couple of times and then draped it across Rose's forehead. Suddenly feeling a wave of relief and fatigue, she turned her chair to face the side of the bed and then leaned forward and rested her head on her crossed forearms. The next thing she knew, Jacob was gently shaking her shoulder.

"Mom, Mom ... Are you OK? Wake up." Elizabeth slowly lifted her head and rubbed at her eyes to clear away the sleepy dust. She was surprised by the fading evening light in the room, and something left undone nagged at the back of her mind. Suddenly remembering, she jumped up and spun around, almost knocking Jacob down. She picked up the enamel bowl from the dresser and stuck it in his midsection.

"Fetch some cold water and a fresh face-cloth: one of the brown ones from the linen closet downstairs. Keep an eye on Rose and try to get her to drink. Sponge her face and neck with the cold water once in a while. Your father and brother Bill will be home tonight, and I've got a lot to do. Jacob nodded his understanding a little prematurely and was just turning to leave when his mother's words sank in. Instinctively he looked over at Rose, expecting her to be asleep, but not only was she awake, she was looking back at him.

Bill held his mother in a long emotional embrace as they stood in the kitchen with Robert and Jacob looking on. Elizabeth wasn't quite ready to forgive the three years of silence, but having her first born back under her roof again gave her a satisfying sense of closure. Jacob's welcome, at best, was stony. Over the intervening years since Bill's big split with the family, which he took for granted would be irreversible, Jacob had been keeping a mental checklist of abandoned entitlements that he now considered rightfully his.

"Long time no see, Jake," said Bill as he extended his hand. There was just the slightest hesitation before Jacob reached back. The man who stood before him was clearly not the older brother he remembered. There was no smirk, no arrogant disdain. He was tempted to let down his guard, but he had been burned so many times in the past.

"Been a while," he said.

"Jacob, why don't you go check on Rose and see if she's up for some company; I'm sure Bill would like to say *hello*," said Elizabeth.

Jacob nodded uneasily and then turned away and headed for the stairs. When he was gone, Elizabeth led the way into the dining room and motioned for Robert and Bill to have a seat at the table.

"I think we're going to need to put a leaf back in, Rob," she said. She turned to Bill. "Has your father told you about the big changes on the horizon for our family?"

"Well, he told me about Johnny's French lady."

"Her name is Arielle. You will meet her when she comes down for supper. The other change involves Rose and Jacob. They plan to marry next spring."

Elizabeth paused and watched Bill closely as her words sank in. She could almost hear the smart-ass remark the "old" Bill would have delivered now, but there was only silence as an emotion couldn't read crossed his face. Long ago she had suspected there was something between him and Rose, but back then she

had passed it off as nothing more than the "coming of age" exper-
imentation most teenagers go through.

Bill looked down at his hands. "That is big news. You and
Pop OK with that?"

"At first, no." Elizabeth looked over at Robert. "Back in our
day something like this would never have been allowed, but
times are changing. Your father and I are convinced that they
love each other and have decided not to stand in their way. Our
family has been through enough."

"I think what your mother—"

Elizabeth suspected her husband was going to whitewash
the situation and cut him off.

"What I'm saying, son, is stay out of it."

During all the years Bill was on the boats, when he thought of
his family, if he thought of them at all, they were frozen in time,
just as he remembered them the day he left. Looking around
the table now, he was struck by the fact that the only thing that
was the same was the table itself. Rose was still not feeling well
enough to come down for supper, Jake was a little more friendly
but still guarded, his mother was quiet, and his father was
doing his best to sound lighthearted and keep the conversation
going. The French lady was the real shocker. Not only was she
strikingly beautiful with perfectly coiffed hair and just a hint of
expertly applied makeup, but she moved with such grace that
several times he had become mesmerized and had to make himself look away. When she responded to his polite questioning,
her direct look was a little disconcerting but more than that,
there was a mysterious sadness about her that seemed to run
deep.

"When is Johnny coming home?" said Bill. He directed the
question at Arielle, but she seemed a little nonplussed, and

Robert answered before she could sort out the English words for a response.

"The last letter we got from him said sometime this month but not to worry if it was later than that. He said the Marine Corps does things in its own sweet time."

Bill nodded and renewed his attack on his second helping of his mother's famous pot roast dinner. He was touched that she remembered it was his favorite. Bill was dying to know what circumstances had brought such a beautiful and sophisticated woman and his painfully shy small town brother together, but his father had pulled him aside before sitting down for dinner and asked him to steer clear of any conversation that would remind her of the war.

"How long you home for, Bill?" said Jacob.

Bill was glad for the extra time afforded him by a mouth full of food to consider his answer. "Not sure exactly, been thinking about making a career change. Hard to spend money out in the middle of the lake, so I got some savings; thought maybe Pop could put me onto something."

Robert met his gaze and nodded. "You thinking about something at the mine?"

"Well, maybe. I've heard working for the state is a pretty good deal too," replied Bill.

"OK, I'll sniff around. Whatever I come up with might not pay as much as you're used to, might need to tighten your belt a little," said Robert.

Bill nodded and washed down a bite of potato with the last of his wine.

"I don't know if Jacob has already told you, Bill, but Rose has a real good job with the telephone company," said Elizabeth. Bill looked up at her while still chewing, so she went on. "Those switchboards are a wonder to behold. I swear I don't know how that girl remembers where all those wires go. The only thing your father and I don't like is her being in that building all by herself at night. God knows who's lurking around in town after the taverns close."

Bill had turned back and was staring down at his plate in thought. "That seems a little risky. What time does she go in?" he asked.

"I walk her down there at 8:30 and she goes on duty at 9:00. She locks herself in and it's against the rules for her to open the door for any reason until she's relieved," said Jacob. Bill nodded without looking up.

As usual, most of the family declined Robert's offer of coffee when he got up to take his dishes in and fetch a cup for himself. Anna was staying home to help her mother with her two younger brothers who had come down with the Spanish flu, and Elizabeth was being extra cautious about having her back in the house until she was absolutely sure the danger of spreading the disease was past. Elizabeth and Arielle stood and began the kitchen cleanup by clearing the dishes from the table. Bill gave Jacob a ten-minute head start when he left the kitchen with a tray for Rose, then excused himself to his father.

Through the partially open door Bill could see Jacob sitting in the bedside chair leaning in close to Rose in hushed conversation. When he knocked on the doorjamb, his brother leaned back and turned, unmasking Rose's face in the process. Bill had the uneasy feeling they had been discussing him.

"Hello there, Doll. Mind if I interrupt for a minute?"

A friendly, disarming smile spread over Rose's face. "Oh Billy, I didn't believe it when I heard you were really here in the flesh! We had given up hope that you would ever come back," said Rose in an upbeat voice. Bill thought she looked a little ashen and her eye sockets were dark against her pallid skin, but three years had given her face a mature angularity that he knew must serve her well when she was healthy.

"You know what they say about bad pennies," he replied. Bill didn't look at Jacob directly,, but his peripheral vision told him using his old nickname for Rose had had the desired effect.

"Oh, I must look a fright," said Rose. "I've been so sick, Billy. Everyone thought I was going to die. I haven't been out of bed in over a week, but Jake has taken good care of me, thank heaven." With that, she patted the top of Jacob's hand that lay next to her on the bed.

"Well, I just wanted to pop in and say hello; I'll leave you to your meal. It was good to hear your sweet voice again; I'd surely recognize it anywhere...even over a bad phone line. I'll drop in again when you're feeling better and we can talk over old times."

Bill turned slightly and gave Jacob a wicked smile. "She's all yours, little brother."

Chapter 24

Arielle's stomach gave a loud growl, and without giving herself away by moving her head, she checked her peripheral vision to see if anyone had noticed. Satisfied that all was well, she sighed, thankful she chose this remote spot in the bustling station to await the arrival of the next train west to Ishpeming. Before returning her attention to the pamphlet she had picked up from the rack near the main entrance, a pamphlet espousing the wonders of life in San Francisco, she glanced up once more at the station clock high above her on the wall between the arrival and departure boards. Even though she had spent more time shopping for a new traveling outfit than she planned, she still had forty minutes to kill. None of the dresses she had tried on that morning were especially appealing and tended to be a little more practical than the edgy fashions she had seen in New York. Something roomier but discreet was her main consideration now. The real reason for this shopping trip was to supply a plausible cover for a doctor visit and a chance to open a bank account with the long-awaited advance funds from her father's banker in Paris.

Arielle had started planning her move the previous week. She knew she was running out of time, and the unexpected arrival of John's older brother, along with all the related family inter- actions, made her feel even more like an outsider, if that were possible. As the days and long nights passed, her fantasy of John returning and making everything right began to be pushed aside by the reality of becoming a mother and raising a child on her own. The plan was to get a temporary room in Marquette and do some research at the library so she could make an informed deci- sion on a more permanent destination. The Red Cross lady in New York had told her that some of the larger cities had exclu- sive support organizations whose members were all French war brides. The camaraderie she had witnessed aboard ship on the way over sounded especially appealing in light of her pregnancy. The owner of one of the dress shops she visited that morning had been intrigued by her accent and eventually, after a long chat, had offered her a job if she would also agree to model some of the merchandise at the local spring fashion show. She was thrilled, but for only a moment, before the reality of her circumstances closed in around her.

Arielle heard heavy boots running across the floor behind her and looked around just in time to see a young soldier reach- ing wildly with a baseball to tag out a boy no more than five years old. The soldier looked fresh-faced and spotless in his new uniform tunic that still carried the deep fold marks from the manufacturer. The soldier froze and gave Arielle a sheepish grin when he realized the spectacle he was causing. A deep voice from slightly behind her said, "Don't pay him no mind miss— just burning off a little energy."

Arielle turned and looked over the newly arrived sergeant in a glance. He was a little pudgy but wore his uniform with metic- ulous precision; shined brass, spit-shined shoes, and campaign hat tilted forward at a rakish angle. "No trouble, Sergeant. Are you and your men headed for France?"

After regarding her for a moment and weighing the significance of her accent, he touched the brim of his hat and said, "Don't trouble your pretty little head about that, miss." Anger flared in her eyes at the condescending patriarchal response, but before she could properly skin him out with a few choice words, he was gone. She wondered how he would act when he finally realized how little his silly preconceived notions resembled the real war at the front. How would he act when he realized it was too late to turn back?

She looked down at the San Francisco pamphlet, and her hand was trembling.

"ALL ABOOAAAAAARRRRRRD for Negaunee, Ishpeming, Champion, and Michigamme," cried the conductor.

Arielle was still shifting her packages around in her arms as she fell in on the end of the line of passengers filing out the door onto the platform. For some inexplicable reason, she was apprehensive about getting on the train. It was still early afternoon and Ishpeming was but a few miles to the west, so she would be home long before dark; it just didn't make any sense. Nevertheless, when the railroad men added a freight car to the end of the train, sending a squealing clank back up through the line of cars, she strained on tiptoes to see what was happening, thinking she might get left behind. As she looked over the shoulder of the man in front of her, a movement on the steps of the next coach to the right caught her eye. A boy in a radiant, white porter's jacket hopped down on the platform and trotted over to her. Without preamble he took the packages from her and said, "This way, please." Arielle was a little taken aback by this sudden turn, but quickly set her misgivings aside in favor of getting on the train before it pulled out of the station. The boy moved out ahead of her and had her packages and hatbox stowed inside the coach by the time she reached the steps. A worn, wooden stepstool magically appeared, and he handed her up with a poise that seemed unlikely in one so young. Arielle paused just inside the door and dug down to the bottom of her purse for a loose quarter, but when she turned, the boy was gone.

This car was quite full, and most of the passengers looked as if they had been riding for a long time. A quick survey revealed several empty seats about halfway up the aisle. She set her sights on the one that faced the rear, thinking she could keep an eye on her packages from there. As she drew near, she saw that a soldier occupied the forward-facing seat across from the one she planned to take. When she stopped next to him, he snapped out of his preoccupation with the world outside his window and jumped up to move his duffle bag and make room for her.

"Sorry, ma'am," he said.

Arielle didn't respond or even look at the soldier, assuming he was the one she had seen in the depot playing with the little boy. As a defense against small talk, she kept her eyes averted and started digging through her purse under the pretense of reorganizing its contents. Several minutes passed and she was beginning to feel a little foolish, since the soldier hadn't made any attempt to engage her in conversation. Finally, out of curiosity she glanced up at him. Her sharp intake of breath was so sudden and loud that the soldier looked over at her in alarm. She was thunderstruck. Across from her, not three feet away, sat John! Arielle covered her mouth and tried desperately to pull herself together, but to no avail. John slowly raised his hand to his face and touched his fingertips to the pale scar tissue around his right eye, thinking that the disfiguring burns from mustard gas had put her off. He didn't think his face was so bad that it justified that kind of response, and he wasn't sure what to do about it anyway, so he just turned back to the window and tried to ignore her.

By now it had dawned on Arielle that John simply didn't recognize her. That, coupled with the fact that she was seeing him in a completely different context, was almost too much to take in all at once. She was off balance, and as the silence stretched out, the situation became more and more awkward. Perhaps it was respite after all the days and months of uncertainty while her unborn child grew inside her, or maybe it was the feeling of rejection from the one man whose gaze she welcomed. She closed her eyes and tears started to roll down her cheeks. She hated to cry in public, but in the end, it was the relief she needed to steady herself. She reached into her handbag and produced the scented linen handkerchief that she always carried to remind her of her mother and started dabbing at the corners of her eyes. Finally she dropped her hands in her lap with a sigh and looked over at John. He was staring at the hanky with a puzzled look on his face. Slowly, as Arielle looked on, the light of understanding spread through his expression and he quickly looked up.

"Ahllo, Sammee," she said.

The day was cold, but the sun, even though low in the sky, made it seem warmer than it really was. It was one of those beautiful, late autumn afternoons when the air is clear and rich with the smells of fall. Brown, yellow, and red leaves rustled along the ground before puffs of wind and collected in the vestibules of stores and offices in town and covered the streets and yards of the neighborhoods. Even their burning was a pleasant reminder of the changing seasons. The ladies who worked at the depot had assembled dried corn stalks into decorative shocks around the posts that supported the roof over the platform, and with the help of a switchman, placed big, bright orange pumpkins on either side of the depot doors.

Robert stood waiting in his usual spot, leaning back against the driver side door of his Model T, watching the train slow to a stop against a backdrop of blue sky and sunlit hardwood trees in all their fall glory on the hills to the northeast. He knew full well that this might be the last day to have the top down, so before checking the progress at the Barnes-Hecker mine that morning, he and George had taken a long, open-air ride, stopping once to hunt grouse along the south rim of the wetlands that not long ago had been North Lake. The sleeves of his red flannel shirt were rolled back to just below his elbows, and the legs of his tan duck pants were still dark with moisture below his knees. He wore a mouse-colored fedora pushed back on his head, and his powerful forearms were folded across his chest. George sat by his side, alert for someone he expected to recognize getting off the train.

Arielle had insisted on purchasing her own ticket for her shopping excursion to Marquette, reasoning with Robert that she needed to learn how to do things for herself in her new country. Robert had given in, but that left him not knowing when she was coming back. He had sensed a change in Arielle's demeanor over the last few weeks, and he feared one day he would come home from work and find she was gone. He had the uneasy feeling he was missing something, but of course Elizabeth was quick to point out that what he didn't understand about the female mind could easily fill a set of encyclopedias. Most evenings, as the family sat around the dinner table, she would engage in light-hearted conversation and respond amicably to ribbing about a mispronounced word here and there, but her eyes were haunted. After much soul-searching, Robert had finally decided that today was the day he would come right out and ask her when he picked her up from the station. The last thing he wanted was for her to slip away before Johnny came home. As luck would have it, the stationmaster in Marquette used to work for him in the mine, so he knew which train she would be on for the return trip.

There were only three passenger cars in this train, and almost immediately people on the car farthest back started to file down the steps to the platform. Robert was already at work, or at least on his way to work taking the long way around, by the time Arielle left for the station, so he didn't know what color of dress to look for. The few women on this car were easy to eliminate by age and stature. A flash of color caught his eye at the top of the steps of the next car to the left, and in another moment the tall graceful form of Arielle stepped down on the platform and turned back to speak to someone still on the train. With a slight smile Robert realized that no matter how many women got off the train, he would have had no trouble spotting the beautiful but sad young woman. The military cut of her outfit reminded him a little of the Cossack acrobats who had come through town with the traveling circus a couple of years back. She was wearing a long-sleeved gabardine tunic of deep teal blue over a matching form-fitting skirt that was just short enough to reveal black pumps and a glimpse of her shins in black silk stockings. The long collar and wide belt were black velvet. He recognized the black, wide-brimmed cloche hat from other outfits, but somehow she managed to make it look a little different each time.

Robert looked down at George. "OK, let's go, boy. Now damn it, don't jump on her this time." He looked up and started to take a step and then froze. Standing with her and holding an armload of packages was a tall soldier in tan over-the-calf riding boots, breeches, and overseas hat.

"Well, would you look at that? Where in the hell did he come from?" said Robert to himself, feeling a little betrayed. The tall soldier turned and looked toward the cab stand where Robert was parked, and instantly they recognized each other. John set Arielle's packages down next to his duffle bag and headed toward his father, walking as fast as he could while favoring his injured foot. Robert and George met him halfway, where they hugged each other so tight it would have been painful under ordinary circumstances.

John spoke softly into his father's ear, but the desperation and pain in his voice were clear.

"I couldn't keep him safe, Pop, I couldn't keep him safe, I couldn't... ."

Robert grabbed a fist full of John's tunic above each shoulder and pushed him out to arm's length. "Stop it, son, stop it! Look at me, Johnny!" said Robert as he bent his knees a little to bring his face under John's downcast eyes. "There was nothing, nothing you could have done. When you're ready, we'll talk about it, and that will be the end of it. I love you, son. We all love you. I just thank God in Heaven, I'll always thank God until my dying day, for bringing you home to us."

John looked into his father's eyes and gave a nearly imperceptible nod. His conscious mind was starting to win the battle over his emotions, and he backed up a step and turned to look for Arielle.

Word had spread fast, and now everyone inside the depot was pouring out onto the platform, applauding their returning native son as they gathered around. Arielle's heart ached watching John and Robert, but if ever there was doubt about her leaving, there was no question now. Her presence would only complicate things, and she never, ever wanted to do something that would jeopardize the loving family bonds she was witness to.

She had lost sight of them in the throng and was about to make a try for the depot lobby when the stationmaster stepped out of the crowd in front of her. "Don't worry about your packages, miss. I'll have a boy bring them up to the house with Johnny's bag. Follow me." With that he turned and started yelling, "Excuse me, make way, make way, please."

John held the passenger door of the Runabout open for Arielle, but before she could get in, George seemed to come out of nowhere and hopped up on the seat ahead of her. Johnny reached for the dog's collar, but she waved him off and pushed George over with a slightly indelicate nudge of her hip as she swung up on the seat. Johnny turned the crank to bring the engine to life and then with a slight grimace stepped up on the running board next to Arielle and clung to the seatback with one hand and the top of the windshield with the other as Robert turned out onto First Street.

Someone must have called ahead to warn Elizabeth they were coming, for when they turned the corner and headed up High Street, John couldn't believe his eyes. Running toward them down the middle of the road was his mother, holding her skirt up to keep from tripping and waving a dishtowel over her head! Robert was so taken aback by the sight of his wife careening toward them that he inadvertently hit the brakes without disengaging clutch, bringing the car to a sudden, shuddering halt. Out of instinct honed long ago to keep the kids from hurting themselves in a quick stop, he threw his arm out in front of Arielle, just in time to cup her right breast as she pitched forward. At that same moment, George spun on the seat between them and vaulted over their shoulders to exit out over the back of the car, in the process digging the nails of a back paw into Arielle's thigh. Her loud shriek shook Robert to his core, and he jerked his hand back as if he had touched a hot coal. Arielle turned to Robert to reassure him that no harm had been done, but when she saw the stricken look on his face, the words caught in her throat. She quickly turned away, bent forward, and vigorously brushed at the paw print George had left on her skirt. Arielle's perceived reaction to the simple faux pas kicked Robert's guilt reflex into high gear, and he threw his head back to consider the feasibility of getting out of the car and just walking away. After quickly rejecting the notion, he looked over at the young woman and found her bent over in the seat shaking and gasping for breath, confirming to him beyond any doubt that he was in deep shit.

Arielle, unable to control herself, looked up at him again and this time burst into hysterical laughter. All of the emotions she had bravely fought down over the last three years began to flow unchecked. She picked up Robert's right hand then let herself fall sideways in the seat to lay her head on his shoulder. The good news for Robert in all this, other than belatedly learning that he would not be accused of intentionally ravaging Arielle's bosom, was that even before they had come to a stop, John had stepped off the running board and grabbed his mother around the waist in an emotional embrace that lifted her off her feet and effectively shielded her from the drama unfolding in the car.

John carried Arielle's packages and followed at a discreet distance as they ascended the staircase to his old room. Once inside, she walked over to the mirror above the dresser and started making repairs to the few areas of her hair that had dislodged when she removed her hat, all the while darting quick glances at John's reflection through the crook of her arm. He piled her packages on the floor next to the reading chair and then sat on the edge of the bed and fell back with a sigh, flinging his arms straight out to either side. He lay still, apparently in thought, but the similarity of his position with that of the men she had seen in the field across from her family's chateau sent a tremor though her spine.

John was thinking at that moment how thankful he was that he had decided not to call ahead. After witnessing the spontaneous welcome at the train station, he could well imagine the uproar if they knew he was coming. He sighed and felt himself settle a little deeper into bed. The familiar patterns in the ceiling plaster made him feel like he was finally home. John turned his head and met Arielle's gaze in the mirror. "Thank you for waiting; I know it was a lot to ask," he said.

The young woman carefully set her comb down and turned to face him. "Why was it important to you?" she said softly.

He wasn't expecting such a direct question and took a moment to answer. "Well, I thought ... I guess I thought we had a ... connection. I know we both figured we owed each other something, but I thought it was more than that."

"We must talk very soon, John."

He sat up quickly and raised his hand to stop her. "I understand, Ari. I won't try to stop you and you really don't owe me anything."

Arielle felt a wave of despair wash over her and looked down. "Is that what you want?" she said.

"I want you to be happy is all. You're so beautiful, Ari, even the old men on the train were craning their necks to get a look. You could have any man you want, anywhere in this country and parts of Canada too, I expect," he said with a sad smile.

Arielle opened her mouth to say *"And what about you?"* but instead held her tongue. A conversation she had overheard between two Red Cross ladies on the ship came back to her: *"... they all looked so pitiful standing on the dock, waiting for their soldiers who never came. I guess those boys had a change of heart, once their feet were back on American soil."* Maybe it was better to just let it drop, she thought ... but she couldn't. "You didn't know what I looked like until today."

John held her eyes a moment longer and then looked away without responding.

"It can be a curse, too," she said.

He still didn't say anything, but it was clear to her that he didn't fully grasp that angle. Finally he broke the silence. "I suppose it would be easier for everyone if we kept up appearances until you have to leave. I can sleep over there on the floor under the window and be up and out of your hair early, give you as much privacy as possible."

Arielle just nodded, feeling more lost and alone than at any time in her life.

Chapter 25

"Still a lot of water out there," said Robert, partly to himself and partly to John.

"What's that, Pop?"

"Oh, just thinking out loud. Sinking a shaft out here this close to the lake has been a real trial, right from the start. Up until last month, we had to stop every other day and extend the lining just to keep up with the water coming in. What'd they teach you in college about that?"

John looked away from Robert and focused on the rusty headframe of the Barnes-Hecker rising above the trees while his mind switched gears to search for a suitable answer. "Well, you'd need to use smaller charges when you're blasting so you didn't damage the cement shaft lining, and of course that would slow down your progress even more."

"Exactly. What they probably didn't teach you is that stockholders don't give a rip how much water you got coming in or what you have to do to get rid of it. They want the shaft to go down, the drifts to go out, and the ore to come up, and as fast as possible so they can turn a profit on their investment."

Robert and John stood silently side by side, looking out at the vast swamp before them for a while longer.

"Three thousand gallons ..."

"Huh?"

"Three thousand gallons a minute we were pumping out of the shaft until we drained North Lake."

"Damn, Pop, you ever see anything like that before?" said John.

Robert just gave his son a sideways knowing glance. "OK, let's saddle up and get on over to the shaft so we'll be waiting when the men come up for dinner. Shit, I don't know why I always stop here. This place gives me the heebie-jeebies."

Robert pulled up between two fifteen-foot-high stacks of shoring timbers next to the railroad tracks that ran past the Barnes-Hecker headframe. As soon as he killed the engine, John started to get out but hesitated a moment and then pulled his leg back in and quietly closed the door, when he saw that his father still had something on his mind.

"Tell me about you and Arielle, son." John took a deep breath and slumped back in the seat.

"I guess you know how we met ... taking shelter in her wine cellar while the Boche, the German artillery, flattened her town and her farm. We both thought we were going to die. In fact, at that point I didn't ... well ... her family had been wiped out and she had no place to go. Being married to an American was her only hope to get passage to the States; I owed her that much. She came to the hospital every day and helped me with meals, and I guess along the way I kinda got attached. I think she felt the same way at first. Anyway, she's going to leave soon. When I ran into her on the train and saw how beautiful she is ... I can understand."

"What's that supposed to mean?"

"Oh come on, Pop, she's way out of my league."

"Don't sell yourself short, Johnny," replied Robert with a trace of irritation in his voice. "You're smart, you've got a good education and a solid family behind you; I'd say your prospects are pretty damn good. Did you at least tell her how you feel?"

"She's leaving, Pop. Just let it be, and please, please don't you and Mom stick your nose in and try to talk her out of it."

Before Robert could respond, there came three measured rumbles, like distant thunder, from deep underground, prompting him to look down at his watch. "That'll be the last blasting before dinner. Let's get over to the shaft."

Father and son stood back a short distance from the shaft collar, looking on as the man-car emerged from the shaft and came to a halt with a little bounce. The good-natured banter and ribbing among the miners ceased as soon as the first men out of the cage became aware of Robert's presence, and even though many of them had known John since he was a boy, the uniform and the fact that Matt wasn't at his side rendered him unrecognizable at first.

"How the hell are ya, Bill?" said Robert as he extended his hand to the mine captain. "Johnny, you remember Mr. Tippet, don't you?"

John stepped up and also shook the captain's hand, but it seemed a little ludicrous to call him "Mr. Tippet" when they had played baseball together before the war. "Howdy, Bill."

"Damn, Johnny, I didn't recognize you. Just a sec ... Hey fellas, it's Johnny!" Almost as one, the small group of miners turned around and came back to stand around the young man. All of their faces carried a perpetual weariness that seemed to be ubiquitous among the miners on the iron range. Most of the men already had cigarettes going, so John retrieved a pack of Luckys from his tunic, pulled one out with his mouth, and bent forward to touch the tip in the wavering flame between cupped orange hands.

Bill Castor turned and glanced back over his shoulder, noting with a little surprise the quickly waning autumn light through the big windows that looked out on the street from either side of the vestibule. The clock above the transom over the door told him that if he was going to have one more beer, it would have to be a quick one, or he would risk his mother's wrath for being late for supper. So far he had managed to *walk the straight and narrow*, or at least as far as anyone in his family knew, and he wanted to keep it that way. It had been good to have a night to himself in Marquette after taking the Civil Service exam, but he was still feeling a little rough around the edges. Penny finally looked his way from the other end of the bar and nodded when Bill held up his index finger.

The momentary distraction caused him to miss the entrance of a newcomer, and when the plank floor creaked behind him, his head snapped up to check the mirror. "Hello there, Billy. Mind if I join you?" said John.

Bill spun around on his stool, but all he could manage was a slack-jawed stare. The man before him was so different from the brother he remembered, he could have easily passed him on the street and not recognized him. He had aged far beyond the three years that had passed since they had last seen each other. Daily walks and the strict regimen of exercise forced on all the ambulatory patients at the army hospital had put meat back on his bones and given him a little color, almost as if nothing too terribly bad had happened to him in France, but to those who knew him before the war, his face told a different story. His skin was leathery from long marches and endless days exposed to the elements, and there were deep creases in the corners of his eyes. Gone was the big, quiet kid who always seemed to have a book in his hands and a shy half-smile on his face, replaced by a man who had survived the insane horror of modern warfare, and now feared only the beast within.

There hadn't been a lot of chatter between the few patrons in the bar before, but now there was dead silence as everyone focused intently on the two brothers. Bill slowly slid off his stool and stood close in front of John, prolonging the suspense. He had to look up slightly because of his brother's height advantage. "You got to stop sneaking up on me like that, Johnny. Why, I mighta snapped and killed ya." They both laughed as they clasped hands and pulled each other into a hug.

"How'd you know I was here, you nut?" said Bill as they separated.

"Oh, Pop's been strutting me all over town today, and when I finally decided to walk home from the office, I saw the Franklin parked out front—process of elimination."

Bill motioned John to the barstool next to his and called out to Penny for drinks all around.

When they were settled in, he raised his beer in the space between them and waited for an answering "clink" from John's glass. "First things first. Here's to you and your lovely lady, little brother, I'm impressed. Congratulations!"

John hesitated a moment and then tipped his beer back for a long pull and came face to face with himself in the bar mirror over the top of his glass. An unexpected flood of guilt seized him, and he stopped swallowing for just an instant, but enough to make him choke.

"Whoa there, fella, slow down!" said Bill as he slapped his brother on the back.

John drew the back of his hand across his mouth and swallowed hard before looking around the room for a quiet spot. "Let's go over there," he said with a nod in the direction of an empty table by the pool table.

In the beginning, the conversation centered mostly on Bill's exploits in the merchant marine, mainly because both brothers were avoiding talk of the war. Cold beer arrived at their table from the other patrons with such regularity and at such short intervals that they had fallen hopelessly behind, leaving nearly the entire tabletop covered with schooners brimming with amber liquid. Bill had a substantial head start, and by now an almost imperceptible slur had begun to creep into his words. John's tolerance, never good under the best of conditions, put him on roughly an even par. As time passed, the "Three Sisters" worked their way into Bill's Lake Superior storm stories, and the women he had carnal knowledge of in every Great Lakes port deep enough to float an ore boat got a little prettier. John laughed or acted incredulous in the right places, but the moment when he would have to talk about Matt hung heavy over him. His little brother was everywhere he looked, especially the dance floor and the player piano at the end of the bar. Looking through the blue haze of tobacco smoke and the alcohol fog in his brain, he could see Matt bent over, swaying from side to side as he threaded a music roll on the take-up spool.

"Does Pop still worry all the women in here for a dance on Saturday nights?" he said.

Bill laughed and threw back the last swallow of the beer he was working on. "Yeah, and Mom still gets in a huff and walks home. He hasn't met his match yet. Everyone knows he's the best hoofer on the Marquette Range, but I'll be damned if he doesn't remind me of a dancing bear."

John smiled but was remembering Matt with the French lady in front of the YMCA.

"Uh oh! Looks like Mom sent the cavalry after us. We're in deep shit now," said Bill.

John twisted in his chair to follow his brother's gaze in time to see Jacob threading his way through several tables of first shift miners, looking this way and that. "Jake, over here!" he called out, waving his arm over his head. The noise level had been increasing steadily as workingmen stopped for a drink on their way home, but John's time in the Corps had given him ample decibels to be heard over the crowd.

When Jacob walked up, Bill pulled out a chair and motioned for him to sit. "I'm glad you're here, little brother—we could use help with this," he said, waving his hand over the glasses of beer. Jacob looked a little uneasy, as if expecting to be the butt of a joke, but still took a seat, hoping for the best.

John corralled four schooners between the index finger and thumb of each hand and slid them over in front of his brother. "This ought to get you started, Jake. You're way behind, so drink up."

"Mom is spittin' mad at you two," he replied. He knew Bill wouldn't be fazed by that information, but he was surprised that John didn't seem to care either.

"Speaking of Mom, how in the world did you and Rose survive the shit storm when she found out you two wanted to get hitched?" said John.

Jacob set his half empty glass of beer on the table, tucked in his chin, and gave a mighty belch.

John laughed and said, "Any old horse can burp, but only a true champion can let one like that."

"I'll drink to that," said Bill, holding out his glass.

"Here, here," replied John and Jacob almost in unison as they clinked their glasses with Bill.

"Pop was pretty steamed, but that was nothing compared to Mom's silent treatment. It was dicey for a while, at least until we got the word about ... Matt ... Sorry." He looked over at John with a pained look.

There was a long silence as John stared down at his beer, slowly turning the glass in a pool of condensation with his thumb and middle finger.

"Hey Johnny, just—"

John smiled and cut him off. "It's OK, Jake. He was your brother, too."

"It can wait. Drink up, boys. We're all in the shithouse with Mom anyway; might as well get good and fried before we have to face the music," said Bill.

"You remember that place up on the Dead River by the cabin, that rock outcropping back in the woods that looked like a fort? It was a place just like that only bigger, maybe a square mile and surrounded by fields of waist-high wheat. That's where the Germans were holed up. The underbrush was so thick in there even that old Springer we used to have would've had trouble. When we were about halfway across, it seemed like every German in the world opened up on us with machine guns. Our fellas were dropping everywhere without even firing a shot; it was like shooting fish in a barrel." John paused for a moment and took a long drink of beer. "We were pretty close to the rocks when Matt went down. He was hit in the chest, I don't know how many times, but it was over quick. By the time I got back to him he was pretty far gone; he never said anything."

All three brothers were staring down at the table, unwilling to speak or make eye contact.

Finally John broke the silence. "When I made it across the field...I...well, a sniper got me in the shoulder and gas shells started landing all around." John almost said "I stabbed the German boy behind that machine gun with Matt's bayonet," but when the words spooled out in his mind, he realized the effect would be about the same as if he were sitting there in the blood-spattered uniform he had worn that day. His brothers would never be able to come to grips with the idea that he had killed a man, in fact many men, up close and personal. He knew then and there that he would never confide in anyone about what happened at Belleau Wood.

All three brothers were glad for the distraction when the big dockworker with the loud mouth came up behind John and broke into their conversation. "I got five bucks here says none of you boys knows the difference between your dick and a cue stick." When nobody answered he went on. "How about you, soldier boy?" he said to John's back.

Before John could answer, Bill got a sudden inspiration and replied through a cocky grin that his brothers knew well. "Let's say for the sake of argument, you're lucky enough to beat me in a game of eight-ball, and then beat my brother Johnny here. That means you'd have to face Jake. Beat all three of us, and we'll triple your money. Lose to one of us, and you pay each of us five. That's the deal. Take it or leave it."

The big man threw back his head and bellowed out a laugh. "Oh, stop it! You fellas are scaring me so bad I might shit my pants!"

"Damn it, man, it smells like you already did," said Bill with an equally boisterous laugh that seemed to confuse the big man.

The dockworker snarled and pointed his cue stick at Bill's head. "Better save that for later, boy. Put up or shut up."

"This fella is a pretty fair stick," said Bill.

"Better than Jake?" replied Johnny.

Bill thought about it for a second then said, "You been keeping your hand in?"

Jake finally caught on to where all this was leading and held up his hands palm out. "Wait a damn minute. He's too mean and butt ugly for me. Just count me out."

Oh, come on, Jake, it'll be like old times. Bill and I will set him up and you'll be the ringer."

"Well ladies, it seems it will be just the four of us for supper tonight," said Robert in a light-hearted manner that irked Elizabeth. She looked quickly around the table without making eye contact.

"Rose, will you start the rolls?" she said. Robert reached to his left and placed his hand over hers.

"I'll call Penny after I have my coffee and make sure everything is all right."

Elizabeth looked at him, and even though her tense facial expression hadn't softened, he could see the hurt and sadness in her eyes. The meal finished up as it had begun, in an uneasy silence. Rose excused herself to begin getting ready for work, and Arielle busied herself clearing the dirty dishes from the table. Judging from the look on Rose's face, it was easy to predict that Jacob would catch hell at her earliest opportunity. When Elizabeth stood and started to help with the clean-up, Robert gently took the dirty plates from her hands.

"Johnny is on the kitchen detail tonight with Arielle; I don't mind filling in."

Robert had teamed up with Arielle to wash dishes many times since her arrival, and to relieve the boredom, it was their custom to teach each other simple phrases from their native languages. As with his son, Robert found the melodic feminine qualities her voice lent to the words more compelling than how the phrases might be used in practice. Even when she spoke the simple English expressions Robert taught her, he found the interesting inflections her accent added to the mix very satisfying.

On this night, however, Robert seemed preoccupied, to the point that Arielle found it unsettling. She kept shooting sidelong glances at him for clues when she had the chance, but the only possibility she could put her finger on was the boys not showing up for supper.

Feel like giving a French lesson? It's been a while?"

"Bien entendu," she replied.

Robert nodded and looked down at his hands drying the plate Arielle had just passed him.

"OK, here's the first one...how would you say 'The autumn colors are very beautiful here?'" he said and waited for her translation.

"Les couleurs d'automne sont très belles ici." Robert moved his lips as he turned it over in his mind but didn't respond, so Arielle repeated the phrase, slowly this time. When her pupil looked up with a sheepish expression on his face, it was easy to see in him an older version of John.

"Can we try a different one? Here goes: 'Why would a young woman ever want to leave such a place?'"

Arielle started to frame the translation and then suddenly realized what he had said. She slowly dried her hands on her apron as she gathered her thoughts. "I *must* go Mr. Castor ... I do not belong."

"My son doesn't think he is good enough for you." The puzzled expression on her face encouraged him to press on. "My two cents ... I don't care about what brought you and Johnny together, or how it is that you ended up in our little corner of the world, all the way from France, but I know as sure as we're standing here that you both will be making a big mistake if you leave without sitting down together for a good, old-fashioned, heart-to-heart talk. I'm sure you've spent enough time with him to know that he is a very sincere and caring young man, a young man who happens to care for you very much."

He finished drying a creamer and handed it back for her to put in the cupboard above her head. There was a step stool under the sink that Elizabeth and Anna used to reach the top shelf, but for Arielle tiptoes would do. When she stretched, the edge of the sink pulled her loose-fitting dress and apron tight over her belly. With a sigh she stepped back and dropped into one of the kitchen table chairs. She rested her elbows on the table and pressed her interlocked fingers to her mouth. Robert took the other chair across from her. For a fleeting moment, she toyed with the idea of telling him the real reason she had to leave, and leave soon.

"I think Mrs. Castor would like me to go ... maybe Johnny too."

In a soft voice Robert said, "When is your baby due, Ari?"

Arielle locked eyes with Robert, not sure at first if she had heard correctly. So many nights she had lain awake thinking about how this moment, if it ever came, might unfold, and now that it was here, it didn't seem at all like the tragedy she had imagined. The relief of having nothing left to hide swept through her, leaving peace, perhaps mixed with resignation, in its wake. She didn't move or speak, just closed her eyes to shut out the world for a moment and savor the feeling. After what seemed an eternity, she felt strong hands grip her wrists and gently pull her forearms down to the table.

"Ari, open your eyes." Robert loosened his grip and slid his hands down over hers. "You have to trust me. I'm not going... ."

"The baby is not John's." she said, cutting Robert off. He nodded his understanding but kept his silence.

Arielle lowered her eyes to the table as she continued. "He was a German Major, the enemy. He said his men would keep the other soldiers away from the chateau. Even my village was spared for a time. It seemed like a small price to pay. Like everything else, it wasn't a small price, and it was for nothing; he is dead, all his men are dead, everyone is dead." Arielle paused for a moment to fight back tears. When she was ready to go on, she looked up and held Robert's gaze.

"It does not go well for a collaborator in my country. John saved me from that, even though he had just lost his brother and was in pain from the gas. He saved me, asking nothing in return. I might have been old and ugly, for all he knew. You must not tell him ... I don't want to hurt him."

Just then they heard footsteps crossing the hardwood floor in the parlor. They both stood and quietly resumed working on the dirty dishes.

"Would you like me to walk you down to the phone office?" said Robert as Rosemarie came around the corner from the dining room.

"No thanks. I'll be fine," she replied. She snatched an apple out of the pedestal bowl on the kitchen table without slowing down as she passed by and then pushed through the back door and called back over her shoulder, "23 skidoo!"

"I won't tell him on one condition." Arielle handed a dripping plate to Robert and waited. "I want *you* to tell him." She slowly nodded her head as she stared down into the murky dishwater. She could hear her father speaking to her, speaking those same words.

John slowly circled the pool table, chalking the end of his cue stick as he searched for his best shot, and there were a lot of possibilities since most of the balls left on the table were his. In spite of all the beer he and his brothers had consumed, he was remarkably surefooted and displayed almost no outward signs of inebriation. His aim, though, had certainly suffered. Also beginning to fail was his ability to ignore the verbal barbs from the big ore dockworker that seemed to come just as he was lining up a shot. When he bent over the table this time, he waited for it before taking aim down the shaft of his cue.

"Damn, soldier boy, I wish you'd get some of your shit out of the way so I can get at that eight-ball and then take care of your little pipsqueak of a brother over there."

John took a shot to a corner pocket, too hard, but it still went in after bouncing back and forth across the opening several times. He straightened up and turned around to face his opponent, who was slightly behind and to his left. His voice when he spoke was disarmingly casual. "You can say anything you want about me or to me, but I gotta tell ya, you look more and more like an idiot every time you open your mouth. Oh, and by the way ... if you insult any of my family again, I'll rip your head off and take a shit down your neck." John's catalog of vulgar phrases was rich, thanks to his time in the Marine Corps, and it served him well on this occasion.

The dockworker was not used to anyone talking to him like that, and he just stood there with a blank look on his face as he digested the insult. "You're dead, boy. Now stop jawing and take your goddamn shot," he said.

John gave him a pleasant smile and then turned back to the table and dropped two more balls before missing a shot. The game was over very soon after that, and John took a seat at the table with his brothers.

"It's all yours, Jake. Our friend has a big mouth, so don't let him bait you." Jake picked up John's cue stick and took a final drink, watching the dockworker rack the balls over the top of his glass.

"Show him where the bear shit in the buckwheat," said Bill.

Jake's mind was already completely focused on the task ahead, so without responding, he set his empty glass on the table and walked over to examine the setup before positioning the cue ball.

"House rules, I'd like another rack please, and a tight one this time," he said. The big man repeated Jake's words in a sarcastic falsetto then looked around to see if he had an audience. The only people even remotely interested were a sprinkling of patrons who had seen Jacob shoot pool.

"OK, little man, let's get this over with. I'm getting real thirsty and I need your money to fix that." Jacob studied the rack for another moment and then spotted the cue ball in the kitchen up close to the rail. When he finally made the shot, his body was still and there was only the slightest movement of his right arm; in fact, it looked more like a flick of the wrist. Nevertheless, the rack exploded, balls spreading out in every direction, and several finding pockets. He now had his opponent's undivided attention. The thought that he may be getting hustled was beginning to firm up in the back of his mind. He watched carefully as Jacob chose his first ball and lined up the shot. The implication wasn't lost on him when the young man bent over his stick and glanced around the table to plan his strategy before taking the shot. From that point on, Jacob proceeded to run the table and as a final insult, he sank the eight ball in his called pocket from a three-rail bank shot.

The big dockworker was so furious that for a few seconds he could only make unintelligible guttural noises. When Jacob held out his hand for payment, he swatted it away, grabbed a fistful of the younger man's shirt below his chin and lifted him up on to the balls of his feet.

"When I'm done with you, your own mother won't recognize you, you little asshole!"

Before he could make good on his threat, he felt a hand come down hard on his shoulder at the base of his neck.

"Let him go," said John in a soft voice from right behind the dockworker. To demonstrate his sincerity, he curled his fingers over the man's collarbone and tightened his grip. The dockworker gave a startled howl, pushed Jacob away, and spun around to face the threat behind him. When he saw it was John, he backed up a couple of steps, lifted his cue stick above his head and slammed it down on the edge of the table, breaking it in half. He deftly flipped the broken stick in his hand and brandished the fat end at John like a bat.

The Roosevelt was busy at this hour, mostly with young, unattached miners celebrating the end of another shift, but with the exception of chairs and heavy boots scraping the wood floor as men cleared the area around the combatants, there was silence. No wagers were being made about the outcome, but most were secretly betting against John, especially those who were familiar with the shy kid from before the war.

"Soldier boy, even better yet!" he cried. "You got to learn to mind your own damn business ..." He lunged and brought the broken cue stick around, aiming for the side of the John's head. The young man didn't try to duck or dodge out of the way; he didn't even turn his head to look at the roundhouse swing. Relying solely on his peripheral vision, his left hand shot up lightning fast and caught the handle of the cue in his palm with a loud smack. The sudden premature finish of his swing threw the dockworker off balance, and he stumbled forward until the two men were only a foot or so apart, pushing and pulling the cue stick and trying to wrest control. The man snarled in John's face, baring a mouth full of rotten teeth and unleashing a smell that reminded John of the battlefield, but his attempt at intimidation backfired when he looked into the vacant eyes of a man who had killed before and knew he was about to do so again.

John sensed the slight hesitation and took the opportunity to twist the broken cue stick out of the man's hand and toss it aside. In one fast, fluid movement, before the other man could react, he reached up, grabbed him by the throat with his left hand, and tripped him backwards by hooking his foot around behind the other man's leg. A quiver radiated out across the heavy planked floor when the dockworker landed hard on his back with John on top of him and still clutching his throat. To make matters even worse for the dockworker, John's knee sank into his abdomen right below his ribcage, knocking the wind out of him. As Bill and Jacob looked on with the rest of the stunned miners, the man's hands slowly slipped away from John's wrist, and he began to turn blue. No one watching events unfold that night attached any significance to why the Marine repeatedly reached back and clutched his right hip while still gripping the dockworker's throat. If the holstered .45 he was reaching for had actually been there, he would have drawn it and shot the dockworker in the face without so much as a second thought. The usual scenario in a typical mining town bar fight was bare-knuckle punching, something on the order of boxing, until one or the other of the participants couldn't go on; killing the other person was rarely the intent. What they had just witnessed was something much different. It happened so fast and with such violence that many of the onlookers who had looked away for a moment missed the whole event.

The sound of a familiar voice calling his name began to rise above the roar of battle in John's head, causing him to release his death grip on the man who lay beneath him. It was Matt! He looked around, thinking his dead brother was behind him, but there was only thick smoke; he could taste cordite and it burned his nose. He heard it again ... coming from the smoke. It suddenly occurred to him that if he could hear his dead brother calling to him, he must be dead too, killed by someone or something as he struggled with the enemy soldier. He had seen men simply disappear in the flash of high explosives, vaporized by an artillery shell or perhaps shot in the head by a sniper as they shared a canteen with a chum; they had not the slightest notion of what hit them. More than dying, John feared being cheated out of a last thought or prayer, or even a final resting place. He always hoped he would have at least a few seconds to fix an image of home in his mind, or say goodbye if his brother was with him when it happened. He now knew that the *how* and *why* was only important to the living. He had walked across an open field with other men, all wearing the same uniform, carrying the same weapons, wrestling with the same fears; they had walked into a storm of machine gun fire with friends dropping all around. Against all odds, they kept walking, they kept the faith. He felt himself drifting in limbo between the living and the dead, looking for Matt.

"Johnny! Johnny, let him up, come on!" said Bill. He had his arm across his brother's chest, pulling him back. Jacob was on the other side of John with his hand under his armpit, trying to pull him to his feet. When John turned to look at him, he was stunned. The face of the person looking back at him was not the face of the brother he knew, but it had been transformed by what must have been the darkest primeval instinct of survival.

Chapter 26

Bill rolled on his side and patted around on the surface of his nightstand until his hand landed on a crumpled pack of Camels. He dug around with his index finger, pulled out a bent cigarette, and let it hang from his lips while he felt for matches. Mollified by the smell of sulfur and burning tobacco, he rolled onto his back and drew smoke deep into his lungs. Late-morning sun streamed through his window and made his eyes ache, even behind closed lids. He slid his hand under the extra pillow next to him and touched an unopened flask of Jack Daniels, thinking "hair of the dog," but remembering his resolution, he pulled his hand back and rolled out of bed. He was headed down to Roland's today to buy a car and needed to keep his wits about him. The last thing he wanted was to wake up tomorrow and find he had spent a bundle on a piece of junk. Vic was a pretty good egg and would make him an honest deal, but he didn't want any surprises. His confidence in landing a job with the state in the office of the Mine Inspector was beginning to wane, but if he did get it, he'd need reliable transportation pretty damn quick.

When Bill opened the door to his room and stepped into the hallway, the wonderful aroma of apples cooking down came wafting up the staircase to him. He quietly pulled the door closed and leaned back against it. Memories of long-ago autumns helping his mother make apple butter came back to him. The day before "the big cook" as they had called it, she would send him and his brothers out to old man Pulcifer's orchard to fill wooden bushel baskets with whatever variety was being worked. As they picked, they stuffed windfalls in their pockets for the apple fight that always broke out once their baskets were piled high. He and Matt usually started it, but it would always end up every man for himself. By the time they got home, they all carried a substantial collection of red welts, occasionally even a black eye.

With a smile on his face, he went downstairs and paused in the archway between the dining room and kitchen. A big cast-iron kettle emitting steam and bubbling noises was on the stove, but there was no sign of his mother. Just as he stepped forward on his way to the back door, he heard the clinking of glass coming from the pantry around the corner. Recalling the childhood prank he used to play on his mother when he helped her in the kitchen, he quietly pushed on the door until it was almost closed, then gave it a quick shove so that the noise of its hitting the jamb would let her know that she had been caught. The reaction he got this time, however, bore no resemblance to the ones he remembered. There was a shrill scream followed immediately by the sound of breaking glass. Bill quickly grabbed the doorknob, but it was locked and the skeleton key that was always in the lock was not there.

Fearing there had been a horrible cooking accident, Elizabeth came running in from her husband's office at the same moment that Bill decided he needed to find some help, and quick! In the ensuing collision with her burly merchant marine son, Elizabeth gave out a startled shriek and reeled backward, instinctively throwing out her right foot to keep from crashing to the floor. Bill lunged forward to catch her and succeeded at least enough to break her fall, but as a result he ended up lying on top of her in a very awkward position. Amid curses and wildly flailing arms and legs, Bill extricated himself as quickly and gently as he could without causing further injury to his mother's dignity. Her astonishingly colorful words were strung together with a precision even his old shipmates would have admired. When Elizabeth had herself marginally under control, she reached for Bill's offered hand and let him pull her up.

"What in damnation is going on in here?" she exclaimed, trying to see around her son's bulk. Bill himself was still trying to piece together what had happened, but it suddenly dawned on him that it was not his mother who was locked in the pantry. Just then they heard a muffled cry for help accompanied by a pounding on the door.

"I've locked ... someone ... in the pantry by accident, I'm sorry, Mom, I guess I wasn't thinking."

"Nothing new there," she said as she pushed past him to the pantry door. "Anna, are you all right?"

"Yes, Mrs. Castor, I'm OK, but it's really dark in here," came her weak reply.

"Just hang on a second, I'll get you out. Stay still so you don't cut yourself on the broken glass." Elizabeth reached up on the door trim to a key hanging from a nail, glared at Bill, and then butted him aside with her hip when he didn't take the hint. When the door opened, Anna was standing there with her arms crossed under her bosom and her eyes closed. Elizabeth stepped forward and put her arms around the young lady.

"There now, it's OK, Anna, just a little accident, you're OK," she said. Elizabeth stepped back to arm's length with her hands resting on Anna's shoulders and waited for her to open her eyes. She pulled a cotton handkerchief out of her sleeve and dabbed at her tears, fighting down the impulse to pinch her nose with it as she once did with her children to stay ahead of a runny nose.

Bill just stood there looking on, still incredulous that an innocent little prank had caused such an uproar. "Nice bubs but kind of a plain Jane," he thought to himself. As he wrestled with the problem of how to address this person who must be the housekeeper he had been hearing about, his mother saved him the trouble.

"Dear, this is our oldest son Bill, who I'm sure is very sorry for the distress he has caused you. Bill, this is Anna." Anna quickly dropped her hands and tugged her dress down before speaking.

"It's OK, ma'am," she said, not taking her eyes off Bill. "Papa took me in the mine once when I was a little girl, and I've been afraid of small, dark places ever since."

Bill finally jumped in, anxious to deliver his apology and get away from the house. "I'm sure sorry, Anna. I meant no harm," he said, extending his hand. Anna hesitantly took it and gave him a surprisingly firm shake.

"It's OK," she replied. Bill nodded his head but didn't really look at her. When she finally released his hand, he turned to his mother.

"Gotta go, Mom. Hoofing it over to Roland's to look at a car." Elizabeth thought of making him stay to help clean up the broken jars, but she softened when she remembered his favorite trick to scare her when he was a child. She rolled her eyes and turned to Anna.

"Grab the broom and dustpan, dear, and let's get this mess cleaned up."

Jacob tried hard not to show his irritation with Rosemarie as they walked downhill toward the center of town and the telephone office. It seemed as if every day since Bill had returned she acted more and more distant. At first he thought it was probably his imagination, but not anymore. Before, they always walked close and slow, with her hand in the crook of his elbow. The last few days, as now, she had shifted her carryall to her right side, making it impossible for them to walk arm in arm. He knew Rose well enough to know it was not an accident.

"Something bothering you, Rose?" he said. Without slowing her pace or looking over at him she said, "Why do you ask that, Jake? Don't be silly! Just thinking about my shift, I guess." Just then the heel of her left shoe caught on the edge of a section of sidewalk that had heaved up the previous spring; it would have sent her sprawling had Jake not grabbed her at the last second. Without a word of thanks, she held Jacob's shoulder to steady herself while she checked for damage.

"Damn, damn, double damn! I can't wear these. Mrs. Steiner will have a fit if she catches me in these." She sighed and looked at Jacob for the first time. "Would you be a dear and run back to the house and fetch another pair of shoes for me, the navy ones with the little white flowers on the straps?"

"Sure," he said with a nod, happy to be needed.

"I'll go slow and make the best of it until you catch up; they're under the bed near the foot. Thank you, sweetheart. I don't know what I would do without you." When Jacob was on his way, she continued down the sidewalk, moving slowly, careful to put weight only on the balls of the foot in the broken shoe. Just as she was about to cross Euclid Street, a bright yellow Paige Roadster turned the corner a block over and headed her way. As it drew near she was standing on one foot checking the heel of her stocking for snags.

"Hey, Doll, have a blowout?" said Bill. Rosemarie could feel a blush rise on her fair skin as she looked up and quickly straightened her overexposed leg.

"Damn it, Billy, you scared me!"

"What do you think of her?" he said with a sweep of his arm over the passenger side seat.

"Is it really yours? Oh, Billy, it's the bees' knees!" she replied, taking a closer look.

"Lock, stock, and barrel, Babe." He patted the seat. "Let me give you a lift."

Rosemarie looked back over her shoulder. "Thanks, but I better not. I sent Jacob to fetch me another pair of shoes, and he'll be here any second."

"Oh, come on … once around the block, then. I'll bring you right back here and no one will be the wiser."

Rose took one more look back up the hill. "Oh, all right. Let's get a wiggle on, then."

Rosemarie had failed to see Jacob standing in the early evening shadows cast by the tall, silver maples that lined both sides of the street. When she stepped out of the snappy little roadster, still breathless from the deep rumble of its engine and the reckless abandon of Bill's driving, the first thing she noticed was her navy shoes with the little white flowers lying on the sidewalk. For the first time since she had decided to marry Jacob, she had the unsettling sensation that maybe she had taken too much for granted.

Chapter 27

On the second Saturday of every month, the Roosevelt was transformed into a family-friendly community dance hall. Since the presence of women was crucial, no alcohol was served; in fact, the bottles behind the bar were draped with red-checkered tablecloths. In recent years, the rise of the Prohibition movement had made many of the ladies touchy about public intoxication. The committee in charge of decorating the room had chosen Thanksgiving as this night's theme. Many of the tables and chairs were pushed together in the back corner of the room to clear the floor and long simple benches for the participants, or in some cases their sleeping children, had been placed along the base of the walls. Tall shocks of dried cornstalks adorned the ends of the bar, and bales of straw, each supporting a pumpkin or a picturesque grouping of gourds, were lined up on the floor in between. Against the wall next to the dartboard, stood a scarecrow stuffed with straw that had been left over from the previous month's harvest dance. By adding a threadbare top hat with a cardboard buckle and a black sack coat to the scarecrow's canvas pants and red flannel shirt, it had been more or less transformed into a rather disheveled looking Pilgrim holding a cornucopia full of dried flowers in the crook of its arm. As yet unnoticed by the decorating ladies, darts protruded from its chest in a pincushion effect, along with one stuck in a strategically placed bull's eye that some enterprising patron had drawn on the front of the pants with chalk from the menu board. It seemed to suggest that this Pilgrim's Native American counterparts hadn't been as friendly as popular folklore implied. Paper chains made of orange and brown links were draped around the room between the trophy racks of ancient deer heads that hung side by side on all four walls. The mounts had lost patches of hair here and there, reminiscent of mange, and the dry air from woodstove fires on long winter evenings had left chilling, hollow sockets where their glass eyes had been. On the positive side, the freshly oiled plank floor filled the air with the smell of linseed and soap.

Bill had arrived early to fortify himself before Penny stopped serving drinks and was holding down a long table when the rest of the family came through the door. His mother was in the lead followed by Rose, Arielle, and Anna. A few seconds later, his brothers and father came in. Anna had never attended a dance at the Roosevelt and only dared attend this one at Elizabeth's insistence. Not surprisingly, she was nervous, her eyes darting around the room and then back to the other ladies so she could imitate their comportment and blend in. Everyone, including Bill's father, seemed uncharacteristically somber and intent on avoiding eye contact. Jacob, who was sitting across the table, kept looking past him at something near the bar. Finally curiosity got the better of him, and he turned and glanced over his shoulder. Directly in his line of sight was the player piano stacked high with tattered boxes of music rolls.

A steady stream of people had been coming through the door, grabbing up the few remaining tables and adding to the already substantial din of chattering friends anxious to get a knee up. As the appointed hour for the dance to begin came and went, it started to dawn on people that there was no music. A spontaneous hush rolled through the crowd, and whether it was real or imagined, Robert felt as if every eye in the room was on him. When the boys were little, and again when they went off to college and the merchant marine, he had taken over the job of changing the music rolls and making sure there were eager youngsters on hand to pump the pedals, but it was different now. He knew his youngest boy, who truly shared his love of music and dancing, was never coming home from France, and it made this stark reminder even more painful. He pushed his chair out, placed his hands on the table to push himself up, and hesitated for a moment with his head bowed. When he felt Elizabeth's hand close over his, he flinched involuntarily from the long-forgotten gesture. He opened his eyes and held her sad gaze. Again he started to stand, but as he turned away from Elizabeth, he saw Bill walking away toward the piano.

As was the custom, they started out with several familiar waltzes to get everyone warmed up, and then as the night progressed, more challenging dances were thrown into the mix. Robert was usually among the few diehards still standing at the end of the evening, but oftentimes by then he had worn out his welcome with most of the ladies and was left without a willing partner. It was no secret that everyone in the family except Robert could take or leave the monthly dance, but in truth, they actually did enjoy watching him cut a rug. His glee was infectious and he had a way of making even the worst partner look good. He was a big man who could dance just about any dance with precision and flair. Another custom, this one thought up by Elizabeth, was that once the music started and Robert was away from the table canvasing for partners, she would produce a piece of paper and pencil from her knitting bag and take wagers from the rest of the family as to which women would dance with him and which would not. Everyone put in a nickel and the most correct guesses at the end of the night took the pot. One exception: if anyone guessed correctly on the last dance, they split the pot.

Bill was not a good dancer; in fact, he avoided dancing altogether unless he was a little inebriated or was seeking favors. No chance for the latter here, but he definitely had the former covered. He toyed with the idea of asking Rose, if for no other reason than to needle Jake, but before the idea went any further, a withering look from his mother warned him off. Just as when he was a little boy, she always seemed to be one step ahead of him. Although seated next to each other and outwardly congenial, Johnny and Arielle seemed unusually glum, and uneasiness was beginning to bleed through Arielle's nearly impervious pose. Bill still had a hard time putting the two together, and maybe his instinct was right and one or both were having second thoughts. She was so striking and refined that everything he thought he knew about women was called into question. It was a given that Johnny wouldn't dance, so asking Arielle looked like a safe bet, in fact a highly desirable one, but on the other hand, he was pretty sure French people wouldn't know anything about American dances. A spontaneous vision of her kicking her legs high while holding up the hem of her skirt flashed through his mind. He caught Anna looking his way a couple of times early on, and it now occurred to him that perhaps he could use her to showcase his new, more altruistic self. With that in mind, he went over to the piano, pulled one of the music rolls out of the stack that he knew he could dance to, and handed it to the young man who had taken over piano duties. When he returned to the table, rather than sit back down, he walked around to where

Anna was sitting and leaned over her shoulder from behind to be heard over the music and buzz of conversation.

"Dance?" he said. When she glanced up at him with a look of uncertainty, he got the bad feeling that she might give him the icy mitt and make him look like a fool in front of everyone. In his mind, he was doing her a favor, but clearly he hadn't thought this through very well.

"OK, swell," she finally replied, to his relief. She scooted her chair out and headed for the dance floor ahead of him. Their timing was good, so just as they reached the open area of the floor, the piano struck up Bill's selection that allowed for a very basic version of the Turkey Trot. Anna turned to face him and raised her right hand palm out for him. He pressed his palm into hers, reached around with his other hand, and cupped her shoulder blade, maintaining a decent space between them, and they were off. The one-step they were doing called for the dancers to be slightly offset, so if the couple didn't know each other very well, they could simply look straight ahead over each other's shoulder. That's the way Bill and Anna started out.

"Sorry I scared you the other day," said Bill a little louder than was needed. Anna turned her head in his direction and started to reply but crinkled up her nose instead.

"What?"

"Your breath smells like a brewery." Bill felt a blush rise in his face, some of it from a flash of anger and some from humiliation. He turned away, thinking that his partner was a little too blunt.

"You wanna stop?" he said, looking at her out of the corner of his eye. Anna shook her head "no" but didn't speak. Bill couldn't see it from his angle, but the look on her face said she wished she had kept her mouth shut. When the music stopped, she started for the table and Bill fell in behind her. After a few steps, she suddenly stopped and spun around without warning, causing him to crash into her and nearly knock her down. Bill reached out quickly and grabbed her forearms to steady her.

"Are you OK?" he said, showing real concern but also thinking this really wasn't going very well.

"Don't be mad, Billy. Sometimes I say things without thinking. I liked dancing with you." She looked down after speaking, but Bill couldn't tell if it was shyness or if she was inspecting the black marks his high-top boots had made on her delicate, beige flats.

Perhaps because she called him "Billy," something only his immediate family did, for the first time he took a real look at Anna. She was really quite pretty, in a wholesome sort of way. Her golden hair, pulled straight back into a coil of twisted plaits, and her blue eyes were the perfect complement to the understated color of her Nordic complexion. Bill didn't detect any perfume when they were dancing, but he thought the faint scent of some kind of soap he didn't recognize was quite pleasant. As he stood there holding Anna's arms, her innocence and virtue seemed to radiate. Maybe it was the juxtaposition of his worldliness and her naiveté that opened a conduit for some unlikely connection, but in any case, the way he looked at her was different now. The next song began to play, and Anna looked over Bill's shoulder at the dance floor.

"Do you waltz?" he said. She nodded her head and smiled, revealing a beautiful row of upper teeth. Bill stepped aside and gestured for her to lead the way.

Unlike his older brother, Jacob actually enjoyed dancing, or more to the point, he liked having his arm around Rose. He was a little self-conscious and klutzy, but he was game. His only job was to follow her lead and keep from falling down. Things were still a bit tense between them since the day he caught her getting out of Bill's new car, but he was starting to get cold feet about dragging his indignation out any further. Her brief remorse gave him at least a taste of what it was like to be in control, but all in all, it wasn't a very rewarding experience. He glanced to his right and followed her scowl out to Bill and Anna as they turned on the dance floor. "Damn, I knew that uppity little bitch was up to something!" said Rosemarie under her breath. Jacob pondered her words for a moment and said, "What do you care? Billy can take care of himself. I think she's nice."

Rosemarie shot a contemptuous sideways glance at Jacob and dismissed Billy and Anna with a limp wrist wave. "Good riddance. Come on, Jake, let's shake a leg." She jumped up, and when he didn't react fast enough, she literally pulled him to his feet and headed for the dance floor.

This was the first time John had been in the Roosevelt since the incident with the man from the ore dock, and the surroundings just added to his gloom. He knew in his heart of hearts that he would have killed that man with no more pause than stepping on a June bug if his brothers hadn't intervened. That was the day his fragile mental state began to unravel. Up until then, he was able to keep Belleau Wood at arm's length, but now he knew it was going to take a lot more than crossing the Atlantic Ocean or fantasizing about Arielle to put the war behind him. He realized that killing a man face to face was a deeply personal thing, and there was just no way he could see to atone for sins like that.

As he looked on, a familiar face twirled briefly into view on the periphery of the dancing couples and then disappeared again just as quickly. It was Bessie DeWitt, a girl he had had a crush on in high school. From that brief glance he could see that the intervening years since their school days hadn't been especially kind to her figure, and her lanky partner, stooped and oily looking, could have used a pair of trousers with at least another six inches of inseam. He remembered well the look of incredulous disdain on her face that day when he finally mustered the courage to ask her to go on a hayride. The teenage fantasy that played in his head night after night back then, the one where he died defending his classmates against some long-forgotten invader to win her adoration, rose to the surface and played in his mind's eye. As always, she knelt over him when he looked up at her and drew his last breath, but now her face was deadpan, and her hands glistened red from searching through the pockets of his tattered uniform.

As the hours of being in the midst of people having a good time wore on him, he began to feel more and more isolated. He found it almost intolerable that these people were so blissfully unaware of the human tragedy taking place four thousand miles away in a vast quagmire of putrid smelling mud crisscrossed by countless miles of barbed wire. His shallow smile and sad eyes were a thin cover for the upheaval going on in his mind. Personal failings played over and over in his head, taking on imaginary substance with every cycle. His misery was so dark that it poisoned the air around him. He knew that Arielle would leave soon and that any chance he might have to convince her to do otherwise was slipping away, along with his faith and the person he once was. If he could put the war out of his mind, even for just a few hours, he would be truly grateful, but he knew he had no right to happiness or even to draw his next breath. Looking around the room, he had the thought that most of these people would never know the unimaginable ugliness of warfare. Short of seeing it for themselves, they would have to rely on the survivors to bear witness, and anyone who had survived that insanity knew that to be a fool's errand.

Elizabeth looked up from her knitting, and with an almost imperceptible shake of her head, watched Rosemarie and Jacob wind their way through the crowd to the dance floor. The two seats they vacated separated her from the only remaining family members at the table, so she slid down, pulling her tote of yarn along the tabletop until she was next to Arielle. Earlier in the evening she had danced with her husband a few times, more to "show the flag" than for enjoyment, and now she was content to let him have his fun while she knitted and watched the interactions of people she knew in the crowd, including her own children. She too had noticed Arielle's edginess, but unlike Billy, she knew what was behind it. There was a time not long ago that she would have been outraged over the whole situation, but losing a son and seeing the devastating effect the war had on Johnny and the young woman beside her had put things in perspective. She reached over and touched Arielle's arm to get her attention and gasped in surprise when she jumped.

"I'm sorry, dear. I didn't mean to give you a start." Arielle took a deep breath and turned to Elizabeth.

"No, it's my fault. I'm not sleeping well." Elizabeth looked over her shoulder at the clock above door.

"It won't be much longer; another song or two will probably do it. I was the same way with my first two; it didn't get any easier, but I suppose I just got used to it." She had Arielle's attention now, but the young woman didn't reply in case she had misinterpreted Elizabeth's words. Elizabeth let the silence hang between them for effect as she focused on her knitting. "I don't know what I would have done without the help of my sisters." Elizabeth dropped her hands in her lap and looked up with a sigh. "You're a strong young woman, Arielle, strong enough to make your own decisions and live with the consequences, but ... I don't want you to go it alone."

Arielle was speechless and brought a nervous hand up to her lips as she held the older woman's eyes. Elizabeth leaned forward to see around Arielle and make sure Johnny wasn't listening. "It's not just you that needs help. He needs it too, help I think only you can give. I know that boy better than anyone does. He's trying to make it easy for you to leave because he thinks that's what you want." Elizabeth looked down at her hands and gathered herself. When she looked up and continued, her face and words were filled with emotion. "When I was your age, I put very little stock in anything my mother said, and I know there's a good chance you may feel the same way about me. I think maybe you're too polite to tell me so, but I hope you will take this in the spirit it is intended. You need to tell Johnny the truth and let him make up his own mind. You owe it to him and to yourself."

This time Arielle looked down and then at John out of the corner of her eye. Before she could frame a response, the rest of the family came back from the dance floor, single-file and zigzagging their way around tables and clusters of people. Robert was with them too, bringing up the rear, but rather than taking a seat, he walked around the table and stood behind Elizabeth.

"Just one more dance tonight and it's a Tango," said Robert with a little theatrical dismay.

"So who's the lucky woman, Pop?" said Bill. His wide grin seemed to indicate that he expected to split the pot. Robert waved down his son's smartass question.

"Struck out again this month," he replied. Just as he spoke the last word, the player piano pounded out the opening notes of "Jalousie" to an empty dance floor. Robert scanned the room one last time, just in case, and started to sit down, when a sprinkling of applause from nearby tables rapidly spread across the room, picking up hoots and whistles along the way. He froze and looked again, trying to understand what all the fuss was about, when he felt Elizabeth tug on his shirtsleeve. It was then that he noticed Arielle's offered hand. He was still confused, especially since she was nodding her head at Elizabeth, but when he took her hand, she smiled up at him and arose, ready to be escorted to the dance floor. Robert had no idea how this was going to play out, but he quickly warmed to the formality and presented the crook of his arm. By the time they reached the dance floor arm in arm, aside from the tinny sound of the piano, silence had fallen over the room.

Robert looked over at the young man at the piano and made circles with his hand to let him know he should restart the roll. He felt a little awkward as he reached around Arielle and tentatively placed his hand on her back, careful to keep a substantial amount of daylight between them. Arielle laid her left arm along Robert's right so that their elbows overlapped, tilted her head back and slightly away, then settled into her posture with a sigh. Robert was already impressed and was grinning from ear to ear, despite the intense nature of the dance and the seriousness of Arielle. When the music started, Robert bent his knees slightly, took three steps forward followed by one to the side, all the while repeating "slow, slow, quick, quick" in his head. Arielle's steps backward were more catlike but still perfectly synchronized. When they paused after the side-step, Arielle's head snapped around, and they headed off in a new direction, sending a murmur through the crowd. They kept to the basic steps at first, but Robert had seen enough to know he was in business. As the confidence of the dancers grew, the onlookers became more vocal in their encouragement. At the end of one promenade, Robert stepped back and did a dramatic lean away from Arielle. When she followed him back into a lunge, hoots and whistles erupted from the crowd, including his own family; even Elizabeth was smiling now. She turned and looked over to see what effect this was having on Johnny. He was standing like the others, but rather than watch Arielle and his father dance, he was looking down at his hands as if he was surprised to find them at the ends of his arms.

Robert had rarely seen Arielle smile since that first day when he met her at the train station, and when she did smile, the smile always seemed forced. He was enjoying himself so much on the dance floor that he nearly missed the change, but there was definitely a difference in her step, a sureness that hadn't been there before. The song was nearing its end, and Robert, inspired now, decided to end the dance with the flourish that he always imagined. He spun Arielle out to a flare then spun her back under his arm and held her close. She was just a bit shorter than Robert, so for a moment they were face to face. He half expected her to look uncertain about his next move, but she smiled at him and her eyes were alive! He timed the moment perfectly and twisted her back over his bent knee into a dramatic deep dip just as the last note sounded. He held her there for a moment, and the crowd broke out into wild cheers and applause.

Even though Arielle was exhausted from the late night at the Roosevelt, she lay awake, staring into the darkness above her bed. Most nights, images of her home and the war came to her there, but tonight the apprehension of keeping her promise to Elizabeth was strong enough to prevail. She rolled onto her side and looked across the room once more at John, where he lay on the floor under the window. Faintly luminous and drained of color by the full moon, he could have been the apparition of her older brother, or for that matter, any of the dead men etched in her memory, the dead men who came to her on nights like this. When they came, they came with surprising clarity. In her mind's eye she could see the exact spot where each man had fallen and how he lay in death. She could see if their tunics were missing a button or if their pockets had been turned out, and she could see the patterns of rust-colored bloodstains on their uniforms. Sometimes blood told the story of how her dead men had died, and other times it was the tint of their skin or dirty froth around their mouths if they had been gassed. In this quiet of the small hours, she was startled out of her thoughts by the sound and flare of a kitchen match being struck. The wavering smoke from John's cigarette drifted slowly up and passed through the rays of moonlight as if his spirit too, was stealing away. Arielle lifted the covers and slipped out of bed. As quietly as she could, careful not to make the floor creak, she crossed the room and lay down on her side close to John. Without a word, she took the cigarette from between his fingers and tamped it out in the small glass ashtray on the floor next to him. She rested her head on his chest and thought to herself, no matter what happened next, with the sound of his heart beating beneath her, she would try to always remember this fleeting moment. After several minutes of silence, she felt a soft uncertain touch in her hair.

"Don't go, Ari."

"I'm going to have a child, John."

The hand that was caressing her stopped moving. Finally he said, "Do you love him?"

Arielle lifted her head and looked at him. "He is dead; it wasn't like that with us. He told me my father's chateau would be spared, that my village would not be shelled. I thought I could ... I was very ... naif." She stopped and lay her head back down on John's chest. Neither one moved or spoke for a long time. Finally she propped herself up on her elbow and looked over her shoulder at him. It was too dark to see into his eyes, but she thought she could feel them reaching back. When John still didn't speak, despair began to creep into the back of her mind. She had known all along that rejection was the likely outcome of revealing her secret, but it still came as a surprise. Even a good man like John couldn't be expected to take this new information in stride. Without turning away from him, she closed her eyes, and tears began to run down her cheeks. As she had done so many times over the last four years, she willed herself to go on and started to stand up.

Just then she felt John's powerful hands enfold her face. There was a tremor in his touch. "Don't go, Ari." He pulled her down until her head was nestled under his chin. "Don't go," he said again, this time in a whisper.

Silently Arielle took John's hand and stood up, tugging gently on his arm to let him know he should follow. When he was on his feet, she stepped backward, pulling him along until she felt her legs touch the side of the bed. John closed the distance between them and put his arms around her waist, but before he could kiss her, she pushed him back and shrugged her nightgown off her shoulders, letting it fall to the floor around her feet. She stood there watching him, half of her form bathed in moonlight and half in shadow. He held her eyes for a moment and then slowly let his gaze fall across her beauty. When he looked up again, desire radiated from him, and she closed her eyes, letting it wash over her. He reached down and brought her hand to his lips and kissed the sensitive skin of her palm. It was a simple gesture, but it resonated deeply. She sat down on the edge of the bed, swung her legs up, and held the covers for John. When he started forward, Arielle put her hand against his bare chest to stop him and then dropped it to the top of his pajamas and gave a little tug.

John and Arielle lay facing one another with their heads resting on her pillow. Her warmth and the scent of her perfume on the linen beneath the covers was so intoxicating that all of John's yesterdays faded away, leaving him in the most sublime moment of his life. They both instinctively knew that words would weigh too heavily on the tenderness that flowed between them, so they gazed at each other in silence, their faces so close that the life's breath of one became the life's breath of the other. Even though each had been with someone before, this was very, very different. It carried the magic of two souls flowing into one, the profound feeling of holding nothing back and the inner peace that comes from finding a kindred spirit in the grand disorder of life. They knew the real world awaited them, but for now, the only world that mattered was the one beneath Arielle's eiderdown.

"A penny for your ... thinking, John?" said Arielle, trying to repeat an expression Robert often used at the supper table when trying to draw out Elizabeth. John smiled and kept softly tracing the outline of her lips with his index finger.

"I'm afraid I'm going to wake up and see that this is all just a dream. Before the war, I never would have tried to talk to a woman as beautiful as you. Matt always got the pretty ones. Even the homely girls in school seemed set on someone else. I guess I was just too shy, too afra—" Arielle put her finger up to his lips to stop him.

"You are my beautiful man, Johnny." She reached up and brushed a lock of hair off his forehead. "I hope you can accept me as I am ... and my child," she added.

John propped his head up with his bent arm and looked down at her. He put his hand on her hip, gently turned her on her back, and then softly slid his hand over her belly. "When ...? he said.

Arielle turned her head and looked at him. The setting moon had dropped below the upper edge of the window, and it glimmered in her eyes as if they were lit from within. "In March, maybe early in March," she replied.

John laid his head on the pillow and pressed forward, whispering in her ear. "I love you, Ari, and ... the baby. I will be a good father." She turned her head slightly in his direction, and he could see a slight quiver in her lips and the glistening trace of a tear on her cheek.

"Vous êtes mon Sammy … Je t'aime"

Chapter 28

STRAWBERRY HILL

ISHPEMING, MICHIGAN

DECEMBER 24, 1918

As winter began tightening its grip on Michigan's Upper Peninsula, fierce gales of arctic wind roared out of the north across long fetches of open water on Lake Superior, picking up moisture and spreading lake-effect snow downwind over the land mass. There were several proper winter storms that brought everything to a standstill for a time, but mostly the snow came in small amounts, and it came every day. The people of northern Michigan expect harsh winters, but even *they* were surprised by the tenacity of the near-hurricane-force winds that sculpted the snow into graceful sweeping drifts, burying cars and even houses. With the exception of the telephone office and a few markets, everything was closed, even the mines. Several local farmers managed to stay ahead of the snow on Main Street with teams of draft horses hitched to heavy drags, but there was still no way in or out of town until the train tracks and the main highway were cleared.

On either side of the tall, double window that looked out on High Street from the front parlor, were matching, heavy oak chairs, one with claw feet, the other a rocker. Both had substantial Empire Curls at the top and the ends of the arms. Originally the pair had been upholstered in royal blue fabric, but now they were deep red to coordinate with Elizabeth's latest color scheme. In any case, Robert wasn't complaining. The rocker was his favorite and perhaps the only piece of furniture his wife had ever purchased that was actually comfortable to sit in, especially since she'd had the springs retied. He was pitched back a little with his legs up on a matching rocking footrest, and the radiating heat of the parlor stove across the room warmed the bottoms of his stocking feet. George lay nearby on the hardwood floor of the foyer with just his front paws resting on the nearly wall-to-wall oriental rug in the parlor. It was his small show of defiance against Elizabeth's decree banning him from the room. Robert closed his eyes and let himself sink a little deeper into the plush chair. The wind howling through the bare branches of the trees that lined the street and the thought of being snowed in made him feel snug and content. He thought of his mother as he did every year on Christmas Eve. He could see her kneeling next to him by the tree that he and Peep had cut earlier in the day, helping him decide where to hang his favorite ornament. She wore a high-collared white top, the one with the sleeves that bloused over tight, four-button cuffs and a dark green velvet skirt held close at the waist with a wide belt made of tiny onyx beads that she had bought from an Indian woman. Her hair was pinned high in the Victorian style and adorned on one side with a glittery bow. His mother loved Christmas. Every year she would add a special tree ornament or craft decoration. Until near the end of her life, Christmas Eve night in her parlor was like a fairy wonderland of cherished memories twinkling in candlelight. He was grateful now that they had taken the children to Monroe Center to experience that magic, even though at the time it had seemed like a lot of bother. Now it was a family tradition to share fond memories of her on Christmas Eve. In recent years, Peep had made the trip up north to spend the holiday with them, but this year it was not to be. The railroad men were having trouble keeping the tracks cleared of drifting snow, so Robert had telephoned and told him not to risk it. In light of the blizzard raging outside, he was glad he did, but he felt a twinge of sorrow as a vision came to him of the unmade cot beneath the staircase in the old farmhouse, now dusty and dark.

When Robert opened his eyes, Jacob was kneeling over a box of ornaments on the floor between Elizabeth and Rosemarie, who were standing close by, waiting for him to hand up a selection. Usually Elizabeth was in firm control of Christmas Eve activities, running here and there, supervising the preparation of the meal and decorating the tree, but this year the absence of Matt weighed heavily on her. There was a thread of melancholy running through all their thoughts and deeds this year. He shuddered to think what Elizabeth's state of mind might be if not for the prospect of a new addition to the family. It seemed like almost every day she came through the door to his office bubbling over with some new task that needed to be taken care of before the child could properly enter the world. Robert was excited about having a grandchild too, but he was most thankful that Arielle and Johnny had finally found a path they could walk together amidst the tangle of life's uncertainties. Their young eyes had seen too much, but now there was a twinkle of hope in them. What a remarkable young woman, he thought to himself. She had given so much and come away with so little, and still she possessed a warm and sensitive dignity. Even more importantly, her spirit had triumphed over all, and she was willing to love again.

Now that the war was over, Robert knew that Johnny was relieved to be out from under the threat of being sent back to France. His son was anxious to get a jump on the thousands of discharged soldiers who would soon be coming home and looking for work, and Robert figured a young man who had won the Medal of Honor would have his pick of available jobs. Knowing Johnny, he probably wouldn't mention it when he interviewed; in fact, if General Pershing's headquarters hadn't sent them a letter about the award, they wouldn't even know about it. Anyway, Robert had a good job lined up for him if he still wanted to be a mining engineer when the Marine Corps was done with him. He looked across the room at Arielle and Johnny and smiled. His son was sitting on the floor Indian-style next to the chair Arielle was in. Robert couldn't hear what they were saying to each other, but as he watched them, she reached for Johnny's hand and held it on her belly. He looked over at Elizabeth and she was watching, too.

Just then Billy stepped into his line of sight and reached down to retrieve his empty glass.

"How about it, Pop—ready for another?" he said.

Robert held up his thumb and index finger to indicate a small one and got a nod in return.

John held out his glass as Bill passed by on his way to the kitchen.

Robert worried about Billy's drinking, and it was getting harder and harder to look the other way. He would disappear for a few days at a time without letting anyone know where he was going, and then eventually he would show up and sleep it off up in his room. Robert got up and stood in front of the window to watch the wind-driven snow pass horizontally through the glow of a streetlight. No living thing stirred out there, and even the lights from the neighbor's house across the street were invisible through the moving field of white.

"Here ya go," said Bill as he came up beside his father and touched his arm with a glass of bourbon.

"How's that new car of yours in the snow?" said Robert.

"Vic's going to fix me up with a set of chains; not much ground clearance. That reminds me: The other day when I was over there, I saw a pretty nifty outfit under a tarp in the back of his shop. Looked like a pickup truck with the roof cut off. It had skis on the front and an extra set of wheels in the back with crawler tracks. He said it was called a Snow Flyer, but he was pretty cagey about it for some reason."

Robert, still facing the window, couldn't resist grinning and quickly took a sip of bourbon, hoping to cover it.

"Damn, I knew it!" said Bill with a big smile on his face.

"You keep it to yourself—at least until morning. It's a Christmas present for the family." When it became clear that this winter was going to be one for the record books, the fact that he had the ultimate snow machine tucked away over in Roland's garage began to eat at him. His only stumbling block was how he was going to break it to Elizabeth. One day as he was walking over to the Roosevelt for lunch, he passed a shop that was hanging Christmas decorations in the window, and that's when the perfect solution came to him in a flash of inspiration. Make it a Christmas gift! That way even if Elizabeth saw through his flimsy deception, which in all likelihood she would, how could she be mad at him on Christmas Day? It was perfect.

"Come to think of it, you could help me out by going over there and fetching it back here after everyone goes to bed. Park it down there so everyone can see it from here when they come down to open gifts in the morning," he said, nodding at the window. Robert dug in his pants pocket and produced two keys tied together with string. "One of these is for the truck and the other is the key to Vic's garage door; it's all gassed up."

Bill took the keys and started to turn away. Robert put his hand on Bill's shoulder to stop him. "Pace yourself, Billy. Vic says driving that Ford on skis is not the same as driving a car. I don't want any dents in it before we all get a chance to go for a ride." Bill bristled inwardly but was careful not to show it. He and his father had been taking pains not to fall back into their old ways ... but it wasn't easy.

"Sure, Pop, I'll be careful," he replied. When he turned and headed back to his chair next to Johnny, he was just in time to catch Rose's furtive glance. There were a couple of ways he could have interpreted that glance; as was his custom, he chose the wrong one.

Elizabeth raised her voice to get everyone's attention. "Time for some Christmas carols, everyone. Arielle and Rose, I could use your help in the kitchen with the hot spiced cider. Jacob, please fetch enough stubby candles and holders from last year so everybody gets one, and place a taper in each front window. Remember to save two for the organ. You'll find them in a box on the top shelf in the back of the pantry. Johnny and Billy, if you would be so kind as to get the organ out of the sewing room and bring it in here, perhaps we can get Rose to play for us."

There was considerable confusion and good-natured chiding among the young people for a bit as things got sorted out, but soon warm candlelight replaced the harsh, electric bulbs and with it, an aura of reverence settled over the room. The tiny flames of the candles Jacob had placed on the windowsills wavered with every gust of wind that swept around the corner of the house. Robert didn't have a role to play in setting things up, so he continued to rock and watch his family through heavy eyelids. He had a start and came to his feet to join the others when Rose played a chord and held it to set the stops and test the organ's airworthiness. It hadn't been touched since the previous Christmas, when they discovered a mouse had chewed a small hole in the bellows. The memory of furiously pumping the pedals came back to her as she waited for Elizabeth to take charge of the repertoire.

"OK, let's start with 'Hark the Herald Angels Sing.' Whenever you're ready, dear ... " she said. Rose leaned forward and flipped the pages of *The Christmas Songbook* and then straightened up, arched her back, and launched into the introduction to give everyone the key.

Hark! the herald angels sing
Glory to the new-born King!

Jacob stood behind Rose, waiting for her signal to turn the page. Arielle, Johnny, and Billy stood behind the organ, facing Rose, and Elizabeth and Robert stood behind them.

Peace on earth and mercy mild,
God and sinners reconciled!

Just before the stanza ended, Rose nodded her head, prompting Jacob to reach around her and flip the page.

Hark! the herald angels sing
Glory to the new-born King!

The second verse was less well known, and with the exception of Rose and Elizabeth, everyone had to hum along. Arielle looped her arm around John's arm and leaned into him, singing the words quietly to herself in French and visualizing long-ago Christmases. She gathered strength from the people in the room, especially from John, and she was determined that the past would not diminish their future together, but as long as she bore her lost family in her heart, they lived, and she would always look back.

Bill hadn't planned it that way, but he soon realized it was possible for him to run a somewhat critical eye over Rosemarie while she was concentrating on the notes in the songbook and glancing down at the keyboard. The feisty and freckled adolescent he remembered from his youth had certainly turned into a beautiful young woman. Her fiery red hair was done in a fashionable bob, parted on the left with one big wave sweeping down across her forehead, leaving one thin, penciled eyebrow exposed. Lesser waves cascaded over her ears and ended in tight curls on either cheek. She had a smallish mouth, but her droopy lower lip and perfect cherub-bow upper were highlighted to their best advantage with ruby red lipstick. Bill's gaze dropped lower by force of habit and he noted the satisfying way her arched back pulled her off-white, satin blouse tight over her breasts. A couple of fumbled notes broke into his trance, and he looked up and into perhaps the most severe stink eye he had ever encountered. Bill felt heat rise up his neck and blossom in his cheeks. Only his inherent cockiness saved him from becoming completely nonplused, or at least showing outward signs of it. For the remainder of the hymn, he kept his eyes on George, who was in the foyer, snoring and exhaling through his flapping lips. For the first time, it occurred to him with certainty that he was never going to recapture the essence of that idyllic summer and what Rose had once offered freely. As if to confirm what he was thinking, when the music stopped she tilted her head sideways and nuzzled the hand that Jacob had rested on her shoulder. Bill picked up his glass from the top of the organ, held it out toward Rose and Jake in a silent toast and drained it. Before turning away and heading for the kitchen, he took one more look, and Rose was watching him out of the corner of her eye.

George was still lying down, but now his head was up and his ears pitched forward. Robert's first thought was that George was piqued by the vibrations from the organ, but then if that were true, a mournful howl would have been more likely. The bourbon was beginning to deepen Robert's melancholia, so he picked up his drink and wandered over to the front window. As he stared down into his glass, twirling the amber liquid absentmindedly, he thought of some of the milestones in life that Matt would never know. An image of him sitting on his grandmother's lap, reaching up for one of her long, crystal earrings with a look of fascination on his small face came to him, and a lump rose in his throat.

The sound of George's nails on the hardwood floor of the foyer when he scrambled around to face the door drew Robert's attention. "It's OK, George, just the wind," he said. When he turned back to the window and looked out, he was so astounded by what he saw that he gasped loud enough to grab everyone's attention. Standing not fifteen feet away was a man on snow-shoes! There was no color to him as he looked back at Robert from the shadow beneath the brim of his hat. He was completely white with wind-driven snow; in fact, if not for the measured puffs of warm breath streaming away on the icy wind, he could have been a white marble statue. He wore a knee-length wool coat with the collar turned up and an old-style slouch hat, and he had one strap of a backpack over his right shoulder. Robert couldn't have been more taken aback if the ghost of his Uncle Henry were standing there. By now the rest of the family were gathered around him looking out at the mysterious stranger. As they watched, the man reached up and tipped his hat.

"Peep, it's Peep!" cried Elizabeth. "Johnny, quick, the door, get him in here, he must be frozen!" The words were barely out of her mouth when John turned and made a dash for the front door with his father right behind him.

As soon as Peep was inside, Robert and John helped him out of his wet outer layer and hung the garments on the coat tree by the door. Peep's face was chapped red, and snow had turned to ice in his beard and the hair that hung below his hat.

"I hope you'll forgive me for dropping in on you like this, Elizabeth," he said. There was a moment of silence when no one spoke, and then she surprised everyone by throwing herself at him and wrapping her arms around his neck. Peep held his arms out to either side at first, unsure what he should do and not wanting to damage her fancy outfit with his wet clothes, but in the end he was so touched by her display of affection that he just hugged her tight.

"Sorry to spy on you through the window. Just looked so warm and cozy in here, I couldn't resist. Guess you had me pegged for some kind of scallywag, eh, son?" he said to Robert.

"Damn, Peep, what on earth are you doing out on a night like this? Peep shot him a sideways glance, nodded, and dropped down on the coat tree bench, out of breath.

"Can one of you young'uns give me a hand with these boots? I'm not sure if my fingers will ever thaw out," he said, drawing attention to his right foot that was turned out at an unnatural angle. Everyone seemed to start talking at once about what needed to be done to make Peep more comfortable. John was close, so he knelt down and started pulling at the stiff, rawhide laces. After a moment, he felt a hand on his shoulder and looked up into his grandfather's eyes. The cold had made his old war wound, the scar that ran diagonally across his wrinkled face, purple and livid. If you asked him about it, he'd most likely tell you he fell down running for his life, or maybe there was a piece of shrapnel ... It was different each time.

"Thank God you made it home in one piece, Johnny. I was at Chickamauga back in '63, so just let me know if you want to talk ... I'm just damn glad you're OK ... that's all," he said quietly. John didn't answer but weighed the words against the look in his grandfather's eyes a moment longer, and then he went back to work on the bootlaces.

Once Peep had a chance to catch his breath and don a pair of dry socks, he carefully stood up and went from one person to the next with a hug and a few words. Feeling a little like an outsider, Arielle stood behind Billy and Jacob, looking over their shoulders at the fearsome looking old man with a bad leg. Finally, when he had spoken to everyone else, Peep stepped in front of his two grandsons and parted them to either side of Arielle.

"And this beautiful lady must be Arielle, my newest grandchild," he said as he held out both hands palm up. Arielle hesitated a moment then placed her hands in his; she could still feel the lingering winter chill on his skin.

"Oui, Monsieur … Peep," she replied, her nervousness causing her to lapse into her native language. Peep threw back his head and laughed.

"Monsieur Peep, oui, oui!" he exclaimed. I'm sorry, dear, that's all the French I know. You just call me *Peep*." With that, he pulled her in and hugged her. Arielle looked over his shoulder at John, and he was grinning and shaking his head.

Before they all moved into the parlor, Peep grabbed Robert's arm and eased himself down on his knees. "Come over here, boy, I didn't forget you," he said to George. George was so excited, he just about bowled Peep over before Robert could intervene. Even then, the old man made no attempt to dodge the frantic licks to his face. "I'm glad you're getting some damn meat on those bones," he said as he rubbed behind George's ears. He reached under the pocket flap of his wool shirt and produced a slice of hambone. "Merry Christmas, boy—you remember where you got that come pat season. Help me up, son," he said to Robert.

Peep stood by the parlor stove with his hands clasped behind him, warming his backside and chatting with Robert and the boys until the women could join them.

"OK, Peep, you never did answer me about how you came to be standing in front of my house on Christmas Eve, and in a blizzard, mind you, when I know for a fact the tracks are chest-deep in snow in some places," said Robert.

"Fine fellas, those railroad men! They heard folks were running out of heating coal, so they hitched up three carloads and then put one of those big wedge-plow cars in front of the engine. Damn, what a sight it was! They got up a head of steam and blew right through some mighty drifts, throwing snow every which way—made the whole engine shake. I guess the engineer took pity on an old man and let me ride along with him up front so I could keep warm. Damn neighborly of them boys to go out on a night like this so nobody would run out of coal, especially on Christmas Eve."

Bill got up to fetch another drink. "How about it? Anyone ready for a refill? Peep, something to thaw out your insides?"

"Your mother is fixing me a cup of coffee. That's all for me, thanks," replied Peep.

When Bill had disappeared into the kitchen, Peep looked over and saw Robert frowning at his son's back as he walked away.

Rose and Arielle returned from the kitchen with serving trays of fresh, hot spiced cider followed by Elizabeth with a big silver tray of cleverly arranged Christmas cookies.

"Oh, my word, Elizabeth— you made those little white devils that I look forward to every year! Never can remember what you call 'em," said Peep.

"Divinity. They're called Divinity," she replied with a pleased smile.

"And rightly so!" said Peep. He took one and placed it on his napkin and Elizabeth put another one with it before moving on. When all had been served, Robert gave his chair to Elizabeth and sat on the floor between her and his father.

"Well, I guess now's as good a time as any," said Peep as he stood. Elizabeth's sharp intake of breath alerted Robert to something amiss, and he looked up in time to see his father trying to steady himself. He quickly reached out and grabbed Peep's leg to prevent him from falling. The old man put a hand on Robert's shoulder and looked down with a strange look on his face; as if something from long ago had called out to him across the years.

"Damn, Peep, what do you need? Here, take a load off and let us wait on you," said Robert, nodding to the chair.

Peep sat back down and looked over at Jake. "Will you fetch my knapsack from the foyer?" When he had the bag, he dug around in it for a moment and produced a box that was divided into eight compartments by a cardboard grid. Resting on tissue paper in seven of the sections, just as Emma had left them, were her most cherished clear, blown-glass ornaments. The eighth held Robert's favorite ornament from his childhood. It looked a little worn and seedy next to the others, but it caused his eyes to tear when he hung it on the tree. One by one, the family members chose an ornament and placed it on the tree. It was a solemn moment and Peep struggled with his emotions, a battle he often lost nowadays. Every night at home when the old house was dark and silent, save for the occasional creek or scratching of tiny feet in the walls, he could feel Emma's presence, but never stronger than he felt it now. He glanced over at Robert and met his eyes.

"I have one more gift," said Peep to break the spell. He reached in his knapsack again and pulled out a box wrapped in what appeared to be butcher paper secured with baling twine and adorned with a crushed bow that looked vaguely familiar to Elizabeth.

"I know my wrapping job don't look like much, but this is for you, Robert. I'd be obliged if you'd wait till later to open it."

Elizabeth took that as her cue to collect the trays and empty cups and get back to singing carols. She nodded to Rose for help, and Arielle got to her feet as well.

"Jacob, please hand out the candles and relight the ones on the organ," she said.

When it was time for "Silent Night," one by one, each family member touched a wick to the flame of one of the candles lighting the music and raised a candle overhead. No matter what thoughts were going through each person's mind as they stood there around the organ, all felt the presence of their departed loved ones, and they felt the presence of something much bigger than themselves.

Robert and Peep were the last ones still awake when the grandfather clock in the hallway outside his office chimed the quarter hour at eleven fifteen. The condition his father was in after the trek up from the train station changed his mind about having Billy bring the Snow Flyer headframe up to the house, but despite his best efforts to convince his son to forget about going out on such a blustery night, especially when he'd had so much to drink, he had set out on snowshoes as soon as almost everyone had gone up to bed. Peep and Robert sat across from each other with the clumsily wrapped package between them on the desk.

"So, can I open this now?"

"Sure, go ahead. You never were one for sitting on an unopened present," said Peep with an amused smile. "It's not much of a gift … just something I wanted you to have." Peep dug a pocketknife out of his pants pocket and parted the baling twine with just a slight touch of the blade. The paper fell away, revealing the beautiful wooden box that Robert had first seen in Peep's kitchen.

"It's beautiful, Peep. I don't know what to say. Are you sure you want to part with it?" Robert lifted the lid and was a little disappointed not to find the old army revolver. He reached in and picked up the union case that lay on top. There was a daguerreotype of his mother on one side and one of Peep on the other. Robert guessed they were probably taken back in the seventies, shortly after they were married; they looked so young.

"There's a copy of my will in there and a paper with account numbers you'll need someday. I know you've done real well for yourself and don't need any help from me, but you'll inherit a tidy sum when I'm gone. Use it to help Rose and the boys get a start. In that little velvet bag is your mother's best jewelry. You can divide that up amongst Elizabeth, Rose and Arielle as you see fit."

"You planning on going somewhere?" said Robert. Peep looked back at him in silence for a moment.

"I guess I've done everything I had a mind to do. It's not much of a life without your mother." After a long silence the old man continued. "Don't let me forget to give you that Colt Army before I leave. It's out in the hallway in my coat pocket. After we're gone it'll be just another old relic from my war. Maybe you'll want to share its story with Johnny one day. I expect he'd appreciate it more than anyone. There's a small piece of paper with a few of its facts hidden under the hand grip; might be worth something someday."

Just then they heard the unmistakable sound of a Ford Model T engine go past the house on the dead-end side street. Robert jumped up and looked out the window in time to see the taillights swallowed up by a wall of snow.

"Dammit!" exclaimed Robert. "That boy never does what I tell him." Peep joined him at the window, but he was too late to see anything but blowing snow.

"What kind of rig is he driving, for Pete's sake? I don't know much about automobiles but I know they won't go through snow that deep. Even a horse isn't much good in that stuff. That two-track still end at Henry's old trapping shack?"

"Yeah, it's the only way in or out, so he ought to be back in a few minutes," replied Robert.

Robert and Peep talked a little more about the contents of the box, but when the big clock started chiming the midnight hour, Robert got up and went over to the window again. "Something must have happened. I should have my ass kicked for thinking he would just go over to Roland's and bring that machine back here with no funny business! OK, that's it; I'm going after him," he said. Peep got up and joined him at the window.

"All my gear is by the front door. I'll meet you around back in a few minutes." When Peep's words finally registered, Robert spun around to protest, but his father was already gone.

Uncle Henry's ten-acre woods and the two-track leading to the old trapper's shack began where the side street ended, just beyond the carriage house. By the time Robert had donned his heavy wool hunting pants, coat and snow shoes, Peep was waiting for him in the middle of the road, shifting his weight from one snow shoe to the other to keep his blood circulating.

"Give me a minute to grab a couple of lanterns and a shovel. We won't have any trouble staying on the trail but the light will come in handy if he got the damn thing stuck back there." Peep answered him with a nod as he turned and entered the carriage house through the side door. He returned a few minutes later with both Dietz lanterns going strong and a flat coal shovel over his shoulder. Once they were in the woods, the tall hardwood trees of the virgin forest broke the wind and made the going a little easier. Twenty minutes of snowshoeing brought them to a spot where the Snow Flyer's tracks seemed to crab sideways as it continued to move forward, and a few feet further on, the light from the lanterns reflected off the steel crawler tracks where they had come to rest in the bed of a tiny creek.

Robert carefully sidestepped his snowshoes down the embankment, where he could get a better look. "It's not that bad. I think if I clear some of the snow from underneath, it'll drop down on its tracks and come right out."

"He must have gone on ahead to the shack to get out of the storm. Give me your snow shoes and I'll go fetch him back here; he might as well do some of the digging," said Peep.

The cabin wasn't much farther, but it was clear that Billy had struggled. His tracks wavered from one side of the trail to the other, and in several places there were depressions in the snow where he had fallen down. After Peep walked a few minutes, a gust of wind swept the snow aside, and suddenly the old shack was right in front of him. There was a faint light flickering through the badly out-of-square window on the east-facing wall. Peep stepped out of his snowshoes and propped them against the side of the cabin along with the other pair, and then he slowly pushed the door open just enough for him to slide through sideways. Billy sat at a gray, weathered table in the center of the room, facing the door. He was wearing a watch cap and pea coat with the collar turned up. His head was resting on his crossed arms and he looked up when he heard Peep come through the door. Also on the table was a half empty fifth of Jack Daniels and an oil lamp that sputtered from old, contaminated fuel. They looked at each other across the room, but neither man spoke a greeting. It was clear from the outset that this encounter was not going to be a simple meeting of a grandfather and grandson. Peep walked over, picked up an overturned chair and placed it at the table.

"You shouldn't have come after me. This is none of your business."

Peep sat down at a slight angle to the younger man but gave no sign that he had heard the rebuke. Finally, in way of an answer, he glanced sideways at Bill and nodded before looking away again. Bill's eyes were red slits, and his face glistened where tears had streamed down his cheeks and mixed with runny snot. There were smears on the arm of his coat and the top of his glove. Defiant and angry that his grandfather had barged in and found him like this, he picked up the bottle of Jack by its neck and took a long pull. He eyed Peep for a reaction and was ready to pounce but came away empty-handed.

"So, what's on your mind, Billy?"

"What's on my mind? What's on my mind?" he repeated with incredulity, as if Peep should have known the details of his troubles. "I'll tell you what's on my mind! It's all bullshit, that's what; my life is just a big, steaming pile of bullshit. Everything I touch turns to shit. One of my shipmates on the *Pontiac* drank himself to death with hooch he got out of *my* locker, then I smoked dope and got thrown in jail for something I didn't do; they said I murdered a fella in Cleveland ... Oh, and there's more bullshit; I ran out on Rose without even the decency to say goodbye. She loved *me*, not Jake. We were happy, right here in this cabin." He nodded toward the broken-down bed under the window and fell silent with a faraway look in his eyes. Finally he said, "It's just all shit, but it stops right now. So here's to ya, old man teetotaler." He took another swig and then pushed the bottle across the table at Peep. "Makes the old feel young and the young feel happy."

This time when he looked for a reaction, he got one, but not what he expected; in fact, it made the hair on the back of his neck bristle. His grandfather had turned in his chair so they were face-to-face across the table. Yellow light from the oil lamp illuminated his face from below, casting the deep creases below his cheeks and the wrinkles across his forehead in shadow. The bitter cold had made the long scar across his face so red it had the look of a fresh wound, and just under the brim of his hat, his eyes were concealed in deep, impenetrable pools of darkness. It was a truly frightening countenance that no amount of youthful disdain or bravado could match. The ageless malevolence that rushed up from somewhere deep inside the old man filled the space between them.

"Did you think I came here to save you from freezing to death?"

Bill didn't speak and was unable to look away. Peep reached out and picked up the bottle of whiskey, holding it as if reading the label. "This shit always leads men like you and me to the same place." He retrieved the cap and screwed it down on the neck. "You're right, none of my business; life or death ... it's your choice." Bill was still transfixed, and in the silence they heard the Model T engine crank up in the distance. "They say freezing ain't a bad way to go, but I think you're out of time." Peep reached into his coat pocket, retrieved the old Colt and gently set it on the table. Without taking his eyes off of Bill, he slowly slid it across the table. "Brought that home from the war; I think you'll find there's still one round left in it."

Bill sat there, staring at the gun with his mouth hanging open in disbelief. "First shot killed a damn good artillery horse at Chickamauga, the second killed my Sergeant who was dying from a gut wound, third and fourth, a Georgia farmer and his boy, and the fifth, the son of a bitch who gave me this scar. I killed 'em all."

There was a long silence as Bill tried to digest what Peep was telling him. "Saved that last one for myself. Almost used it, too, back when I was your age; been saving it for fifty years, give or take. Guess you need it more than me now, seeing how I'll be crossing over soon enough. Well, go on, pick it up ... quick pop in the head is the best way." Peep reinforced his advice by putting his index finger to his temple and working his thumb. "Kind of messy, but it's quick and sure, and that's what you want." Peep stood up and turned toward the door. "I'll wait outside so you can have some privacy."

Peep had been standing outside for only a few moments, watching the headlights of the Ford draw near through swirling snow, when he heard the door behind him creak on its hinges. Bill stepped up and stood beside him, facing down the trail, and without a word gently backhanded his grandfather's arm with the butt of the pistol. Peep took it and dropped it in his coat pocket. "No matter what terrible things you've done that you think can't be forgiven, you just remember what happened here tonight. You aren't even close to being in my league, son."

Robert brought the vehicle to a stop and jumped out, fully prepared to deliver the tongue-lashing he had worked on as he lay on his side digging snow out from under the Snow Flyer, but before he could begin, Peep waved him off with a barely perceptible shake of his head. It was a tense moment as Robert struggled to fight down his anger, but in the end, Bill breathed a sigh of relief when he realized what had happened in the cabin would remain between him and Peep. It took some doing to get the Snow Flyer turned around in the narrow space between the trees, but soon they were headed home, Robert and Peep in the front seat and Bill stretched out with his eyes closed on one of the benches in back.

Chapter 29

The people of Ishpeming were pleasantly surprised when they awoke the next day and looked out through frosted windowpanes on a beautiful Christmas morning. The clear skies had ushered in bone-chilling cold but also glorious sunshine and that had been in short supply of late. The Castors stood by the rear of the Snow Flyer, looking stiff and drawn up, their every breath sending tiny clouds floating away on the frigid air as they waited for Elizabeth and Robert. When they heard the back door slam they queued up to climb aboard. Rather than hand Arielle up in the usual way, John held her around the waist with his big hands, picked her up with surprisingly little effort, and set her down on her feet in the back of the truck. He then hopped up behind her, and they took a seat all the way forward on the right side bench. He rested his arm on the back of the bench behind her and pulled her close to share his warmth and to make sure she didn't tumble out if they hit uneven ground.

Peep moved carefully to avoid stepping on someone's feet as he went forward in the narrow space between the benches. He took a seat across from Arielle, their knees overlapping.

"Close quarters," he said to her with a self-conscious smile. A few minutes later when she looked at him again, his eyes were closed, and she took the opportunity to study him. Of the group, he seemed the least affected by the cold; in fact, judging by the faint smile on his face, it seemed to agree with him. He was such a contradiction, she thought. On one hand, he appeared to be as timeless and unshakeable as the limestone promontory in Parc des Buttes-Chaumont where she used to go with her father when she was a little girl, and on the other, he was so unassuming and kind. It was that kindness that she struggled to put with his scarred and weathered face. It was easy to see his reflection in Robert and John. When his eyes opened without warning, he was already looking right back at her as if she had spoken his name. He smiled at her uneasiness for being caught out and patted her knee. "You remind me so much of my Emma," he said, just before closing his eyes again.

Rosemarie and Jacob occupied the bench on the left next to Peep. Bill, somewhat the worse for wear from night before, cranked the Ford engine to life and then reached under the right headlight and tinkered with the choke until it settled into a satisfying idle. When he looked up and saw his mother and father stepping carefully, single-file down the narrow footpath in the deep snow, he smiled in spite of his throbbing head and then jumped up in the back and sat next to John. He nudged his brother with his elbow and nodded over his shoulder. John turned to look behind them toward the house, tickling his nose on Arielle's fur hat in the process and then turned back to nod at Bill and roll his eyes.

Arielle wore a raccoon fur roller hat and a belted, gray wool coat that was trimmed at the cuffs and collar with silver fox fur. She had chosen her warmest and longest gabardine skirt to go with the heavy-knit beige sweater that Elizabeth had insisted she wear. Under the skirt she wore wool knickerbockers, also at Elizabeth's insistence. A little perturbed at first, she now saw the wisdom behind her mother-in-law's rather strong recommendations. She snuggled a little closer to John and felt his arm tighten around her shoulders. When she looked back on the journey that had taken her from utter despair in her own country as it was torn apart by war, to this beautiful place thousands of miles away in Michigan's Upper Peninsula, it seemed that maybe the old priest had been right when he said she must walk the path and keep the faith. Even though she had doubted many times along the way, here she was, seated next to this rugged American man who possessed a goodness and sensitivity that she was still in awe of: a man who was generous and kind even as he grieved, a man who had loved her even when he couldn't see her. A movement overhead caught her eye, and she looked up at a black squirrel scurrying along a snow-covered branch over the road. Its passing sent a curtain of pristine powder floating down, sparkling as it passed through slanting rays of winter sun.

Arielle was so distracted by the beauty of the moment she either didn't hear, or perhaps heard but didn't register, the footfalls in the crunchy snow behind her. Suddenly there was a bellowing growl right by the truck, and the next thing she knew, something big with black fur was wrapping itself around her. Across from her, Rose screamed, "It's a bear!" There was another mighty growl right in her ear this time, and she shrieked in terror. Her legs started pumping, first one and then the other, as if she were trying to run away while still seated. Her heart pounded in her ears and then suddenly everything went dark, making her think she had been completely engulfed by some wild beast. Then, through her panic, she heard Elizabeth say, "OK, Rob, you've had your fun. Now let her go before she has an accident." The darkness melted away, and when she opened her eyes, everyone, even John, was laughing so hard there were tears running down their cheeks. She looked across at Peep and he was holding a hand over his heart, trying to suck in air between fits of laughter.

"It's OK, dear. He does that to someone every time he wears that awful coat," said Elizabeth. When Robert walked around to get behind the wheel, Arielle got a better look at him, and she too began to laugh as she wiped at the corners of her eyes. He was wearing a massive, black bearskin coat and a matching ushanka hat with the ear flaps down in such a way that the fur from the hat and coat's collar blended into one another. The coat and hat on Robert's large frame made him look for all the world like the doctored photos of a Sasquatch she had once seen in a yellow press newspaper in Bordeaux. He helped Elizabeth climb up onto the spring seat Vic had taken off a buckboard wagon and then, with considerable effort, he squeezed in behind the wheel next to her, pushing George over to the far right side. He looked back over his shoulder and said in his best Russian imitation, "We go now."

Much to Robert's delight, the Snow Flyer more than lived up to his expectations. When they crossed open fields of deep, unbroken snow, the Flyer seemed to float and would gently lean from one side to the other like riding the lazy mid-summer swells on Lake Superior in a small boat. The first part of Robert's plan to sell the idea of the Snow Flyer to Elizabeth as a Christmas present for the family had gone so well that there was almost no reason for the second part, but since they were already on the west side of town and everyone was having fun, he decided to keep going. Drawn by the sunshine and the need to shovel snow, the townspeople had begun to venture out. The Snow Flyer captured the attention of old and young alike, almost without exception. Elizabeth seemed to revel in the incredulous looks and began waving and calling out "Merry Christmas" to everyone within earshot. Robert rolled his eyes upward and said a silent "thank you."

The road through the western end of the North Lake District was visible only as a ribbon of white through the trees and under-brush, underbrush so thick in places that only rabbit tracks could be seen going in or out. As they traveled further east, the land gradually opened out into large, clear areas of snow-covered muskeg dotted here and there with low clumps of stunted cedar trees and crystallized tufts of sedge. Robert came to a stop and killed the engine on a slight rise so they could savor the natural beauty around them, as well as the profound silence that was so much a part of the experience. Off to their left, the land sloped gently away from the road, and its smooth white surface was striped with long shadows from a poplar grove bordering the road on the right. When they talked, their voices echoed off the hard, cold tree trunks. Robert had a passing impulse to turn off the road and head out across that expanse of sparkling, windswept snow as fast as the Ford would go, but he knew that beneath that picturesque landscape was icy, dark water.

Robert reached down into the deep side pocket of his bear-skin coat and produced a bottle of wine. When he pulled the cork and held it out to Elizabeth, she hesitated for a moment and then looked up into his eyes, feeling a trace of the romance and the carefree days they shared years ago when they were court-ing. She took the bottle and tipped it up and then wiped her mouth with the back of her hand. "Not very ladylike, Castor," she said. A year ago she would have swatted Robert's hand away and given him a dressing down for even thinking she might drink a beverage, any beverage, directly from the bottle. Her complex code of decorum, previously thought to be carved in stone, was so much chaff on the wind after losing Matt. She turned in the seat and looked behind her at Arielle. Without a word, she handed her the bottle and turned back with a smug smile from the shocked look on the young woman's face. When a confused Arielle looked at Johnny, he returned an amused grin and pantomimed tipping the bottle back. A quick glance around confirmed that with the exception of Robert and Elizabeth, all eyes were on her. With an "I'll show you" thought, she put the neck of bottle to her lips and took such a mighty gulp that the bottle burped, nearly sending wine up her nose. She handed it to John and wiped her mouth with the back of her gloved hand as she had seen Elizabeth do. John was so tickled watching his sophisticated lady drink wine out of the bottle like a lumberjack that he almost choked too before passing it to Bill. When it was Rosemarie's turn, she twisted her gloved hand around the lip to kill any cooties, glanced across at Arielle, and then tipped it back like an old hand before passing it on.

The road eventually angled up to more solid ground, and as they crested the rise, the rusty steel of the Barnes-Hecker headframe came into view above the trees. Robert turned to Elizabeth and said loudly enough to be heard over the Ford's engine, "I'm going to stop for a few minutes and make sure everything is hunky-dory." When they pulled up in front of the mine office, the solitary figure of an old man with one arm stood in front of the door to greet them.

"Merry Christmas, Sol! How'd you get stuck working today?"

"Is that you under all that fur, Mr. Castor? The two men shook hands as everyone except Elizabeth and Peep got out of the Snow Flyer to look around. "Well, I take what I can get ... a lot of mouths to feed, ya know," he said, patting the side of his chest where his arm was missing.

"Tell your son that as soon as his boys turn eighteen to come around and see me. I'll put 'em to work."

"Thank you, Mr. Castor. That's real generous of you." Both men fell silent for a moment as they watched the young people walk away towards the shaft house. "That's quite a contraption you got there!" said Sol.

"Well, I wasn't convinced I needed a gizmo like this at first, but after the winter we've had I gotta agree it's just the thing to get out here in the sticks to check on things." Robert spoke much louder than he needed to, counting on his voice to carry. He leaned toward the old man and in a hushed voice said, "That damned thing is the berries, Sol. Why, you get out there on fresh powder and it's like walking barefoot on an acre of tits." Both men laughed, drawing a look from Elizabeth.

"OK, gotta scoot, Sol. Oh, by the way, how much water we pumping now?"

"Nobody down in the pump room to read the meter yesterday and today, but the log entries from last week show mostly a little under seven hundred gallons a minute. Been dropping a little every month or so."

"That's just what I wanted to hear. Looks like we finally licked that problem. You wish the family a Merry Christmas and Happy New Year, Sol."

Chapter 30

Robert was tilted back in his chair, resting his feet on the corner of his desk and staring up at the tin ceiling tiles, lost in thought. A wet snow, the kind with big lazy flakes, had been coming down hard all morning, and even though it melted as soon as it hit the sidewalk, it made him think of the last time he saw Peep. The image of his father on snowshoes looking back at him through the parlor window, white from head to toe with wind-driven snow, was stamped indelibly on his memory. It had been a hard winter that year, and a blizzard on Christmas Eve had brought everything to a standstill, almost eight years ago now. His mother had always delighted in telling the story about how when he was four years old he *captured* a husband for her one Sunday in front of the little Monroe Center church by grabbing a complete stranger around the leg and refusing to let go. That was how he and his mother, then a young widowed schoolteacher, had crossed paths with Will Castor. The year before, a tree fell on his biological father in the woodlot behind their cabin. The only thing he remembered from that day was the last feeble movements of his father's arm sticking out from under the huge, unmovable trunk.

It was only a matter of a couple of months after that Christmas back in 1918 that he had received a telegram informing him of Peep's death—a heart attack, it said. All the memories of the life they lived together, he and his mother and Peep, the life that set the stage for everything that would come after, lived only in him now. Even though he had his own family, including grandkids in recent years, he still felt deeply the sorrow of being the last keeper of those golden days.

"Hey, Pop, we better get a wiggle on if we're going to meet Rose and the kids over at Barnes-Hecker at 10:30! I talked to Ari on the phone this morning, and she said that riding the hoist is all Willy has talked about since Sunday dinner. Roy's the same way," said Jacob from the outer office. "Oh, I almost forgot, that old battle-axe at the county office said they were sending someone out today to do the monthly inspection. She said he especially wanted to take a look at the third level; seems there's some doubt about its being an adequate escape route to the Lloyd-Morris in case of trouble."

Robert shook off his melancholy and dropped his feet to the floor. "If they send Billy out here to do the inspection, you go underground with him and make sure his numbers are good. Jake, you listening? I don't want any harsh words between you two, you understand? Especially in front of the men." He had a momentary vision of Jacob's stoniness as Anna and Billy came down the steps of the Lutheran church in Marquette the year before, laughing and ducking as they were pelted with rice by well-wishers.

"I get it, Pop," Jacob replied halfheartedly.

There were precious few straight stretches of road on the way out to the mine. Numerous curves around swamps and small lakes made for slow going, but on the positive side, the gravel surface was nicely crowned and free of mud holes and wash-boards. George sat between Robert and Jacob on the Roadster's single bench seat staring straight ahead, alert for anything that might dash across the road from the thick brush on either side. His panting from the anticipation made his breath something of an issue for his traveling companions in the small, enclosed space.

Suddenly Jacob gasped and quickly unsnapped a corner of the side curtain next to his head.

"Damn, George, couldn't you have waited just a few more minutes?" exclaimed Jacob as he sucked fresh air from the small opening.

"Whew!" said Robert, looking over. "I don't know what you been eating, but your asshole is pretty wrong, boy." As he started turning his attention back to the road to steer them through the next bend, he saw George tense up and begin to quiver. Standing in the road, broadside on, was a huge buck. Robert slammed on the brakes and skidded to a stop on the loose gravel, narrowly avoiding a collision. The deer stood perfectly still, not flinching a muscle or turning to see what the sudden danger was. As they looked on in awe, its head swung slowly toward them revealing the most magnificent bleached white rack either man had ever seen. Still the animal showed no fear and made no move to get out of the way. When its head stopped moving, its eyes were locked on Robert, not with the vacant stare of a wild animal but with a deliberate and inexplicably knowing look. The animal was so close they could see its breath on the cold November air as jets of steam from each nostril. Both men were stunned, and the hair on the back of Robert's neck stood on end. Even George seemed to be caught off guard. He neither barked nor lunged at the windshield, as was his normal practice. Time seemed to stop as they held in place, looking at each other. Finally, the deer dipped his head and then continued across the road and silently melted away into the thicket.

"Wow, Pop! I've heard old-timers talk about bucks like that, but I always thought it was hog-wash. That big fella wasn't the least bit afraid of us either. How many points, you figure?" said Jacob.

Robert didn't respond but unsnapped his side curtain, leaned out, and inched the car forward, expecting to find a well-worn deer run through the underbrush that would accommodate a rack that big, but there was nothing, not even a track in the soft shoulder.

Robert turned onto the narrow access road to the Lloyd-Morris mine to drop off Jacob. The plan called for his son to go underground with the county mine inspector, probably Billy, and walk the connecting drift to the third level of the Barnes-Hecker.

Jacob stepped out of the car and then leaned back in before closing the door. "You going back to the office after you take the boys for a ride on the hoist?" asked Jacob.

Robert turned his head and just nodded without making eye contact. There was an awkward moment of silence while Jacob waited for more, but finally he shut the door and walked away with a puzzled look on his face. Robert couldn't put his finger on it, but something Peep had told him once about a deer nagged at the back of his mind.

Robert reached over and scratched behind George's ears in just the right place to make him roll his head and groan. "We'll get an early start tomorrow, boy, and see if we can kick up some birds now that all the leaves are down. Maybe we'll try that spot up along Gold Mine Creek; won't be long before the boys will be old enough to go with us." Robert fell silent as the reality of George's advanced age caught up with his train of thought. He sighed and looked up at the towering head frame of the Barnes-Hecker. Except for the hoist sheaves turning at the top of the structure and the rumble of iron ore as it tumbled out of the skips and into waiting rail cars, it looked as if not much was going on. Robert knew that a thousand feet below the surface, fifty men toiled in damp, dimly lit drifts, some of these extending out from the shaft for half a mile or more. There were men drilling holes in solid rock for sticks of dynamite, men loading the blasted out ore into trams, and there were motormen and brakemen running the electric locomotives that pulled the trams along the rails to the shaft, where skips would lift it to the surface. These men were tired and dirty, working long hours at one of the most dangerous professions on earth to put food on the table and clothes on the backs of their families.

Usually during his normal workday, Robert's attention was so focused on the details that affected the production of the mine and the safety of the men that he scarcely took notice of the big picture—but not today. Today he saw with a clear eye a giant, ugly, man-made structure set against the pristine natural beauty of the Upper Peninsula of Michigan.

The faint ringing of the hoist signal bell calling for the man cage broke into his thoughts and he looked at his watch again. It was a little after 11:00. No surprise that Rose was late, but maybe for once it was a good thing. He was still shaken by what had just happened back on the road and had lost his enthusiasm for taking the boys for a ride on the hoist. In a few more minutes it would be too late to go because they would interfere with the operation of the mine when the men were coming to the surface for lunch. Just when he had decided to call it off, a car horn blared close by, and Rose skidded to an abrupt stop behind him.

He rolled his eyes and stepped out of the roadster with George right behind him.

"Sorry I'm late, Daddy," she said as she stood on tiptoes and kissed his cheek. Under a long, off-white cardigan, she wore a loose-fitting beige midi-blouse over an off-white pleated skirt. A wisp of bobbed dyed black hair lay against each fair cheek beneath a russet and tan striped cloche hat. A long, double strand of pearls, penciled eyebrows, and full bright red lips completed her look. Robert's eyes were drawn to the freckles faintly visible beneath carefully applied foundation, perhaps the last vestiges of the fresh-faced little tomboy she had once been.

Roy teased George with a stick for a few minutes and then ran up to his grandfather and slugged him in the leg with the one-two punch he had learned from Robert after the family dinner the previous Sunday. Robert reached down with an ease and agility perfected on his own boys, snatched Roy up, and held him horizontally against his side in the crook of his arm, all the while ignoring the squeals of delight and flailing limbs.

Rose put one hand on her father's forearm to steady herself as she bent her right leg up at the knee and rubbed at a spatter of mud on her cream-colored hose. "Damn," she said under her breath. Giving up with a sigh, she dropped her foot and smoothed down her dress. "Isn't Jake with you?"

"I dropped him off over at the Lloyd-Morris. The county's sending out an inspector this morning to take a look at the adit that connects to the Barnes-Hecker. I told him to tag along and make notes of anything he finds wrong, especially if they send Billy. They'll walk the third level and come to the surface over here when they're done."

"That should be a merry time," replied Rose with a smirk.

"Where's Willy?" said Robert.

"Ari and Johnny decided to bring him out; they're dropping the baby off with Mother. This must be them," said Rose as she turned and looked back towards the road at the sound of tires crunching on gravel. The instant John's red Buick came to a stop, the rear door flew open, and Willy popped out on the running board to survey the landscape before stepping down. He was seven years old now, lanky and tall for his age. Traces of his mother's features were easy to see in his young face, but not so obvious was his thoughtful and deliberate way that came from John.

When Robert set Roy back on his feet, the little boy ran over to his cousin and put up his dukes. The older boy was excited about riding the hoist too, and on any other occasion would have gladly obliged him, but today he was taking pains to act like a grown-up.

John got out of the car and came around to open the door for Arielle. She was always touched by the courtesy, but it was not a common practice in Northern Michigan, and it made her a little uneasy about calling attention to herself. She walked over to Robert and Rosemarie while John stayed back and lifted the right side of the hood to look at the engine.

"Car trouble?" asked Robert as Arielle walked up. She wore a bulky, forest green fisherman's sweater over tan jodhpurs and scuffed, dark brown riding boots. A vision of her astride the beautiful palomino Arabian mare that John had given her for her thirtieth birthday came to Robert; her posture true and confident, her fair tresses flowing gracefully in harmony with the horse's mane and long tail. The way she controlled the animal with just a quiet word or a gentle touch of rein reminded him of Peep. Even though her attire was more casual than her sister-in-law's, and certainly more masculine, her extraordinary beauty and elegance easily carried the day. She touched Rose's shoulder in greeting and then placed a kiss on each of Robert's cheeks.

"It does not like water—something like that." Robert gave her an amused smile and then walked over to offer his assistance.

"Don't say it, Pop," said John without looking up.

"Don't say what, son, that you should have bought a Ford? OK, I won't say it."

John grinned in spite of himself. "Every time there's a little moisture in the air the damn thing runs rougher than a cobb," he said as he swabbed the inside of the distributor cap with a scrap of dish towel.

"You going to ride the hoist with me and the boys?"

"Naw, I guess not. Better get this put back together while you're gone so we can make it back into town."

"Take it to Vic. He's a good egg and will have a look-see, even though he sells Fords."

"OK, boys, let's get after it," called Robert. He had to say it only once, and they quickly fell in step with him as he started for the shaft house. They were excited, but just a little fear and uncertainty kept them close and silent. Just as they approached the area at the base of the headframe where the man cage and skips containing ore entered and exited the one-thousand-foot vertical shaft, they heard and felt two muffled explosions from deep underground.

"What was that!" cried Roy as he dropped his grandfather's hand and stopped dead in his tracks. Robert laughed and motioned for him to catch up. He looked at his watch to see how much time they had before the men came up for dinner; it was 11:20.

"Come on, I won't let anything bad happen to ya. They're just blasting down some ore. They always do that before they come up for dinner so the smell has a chance to—" Robert stopped and bowed his head to listen. No sooner had the rumble from the two blasts died away than the ground began to tremble and make a noise like distant thunder. Robert started forward and then abruptly stopped, remembering the boys were still with him. He spun around to shout for John, but his son was already running toward them.

"What is that, Pop?" he shouted above the roar.

"Don't know, but I gotta get down there pronto! Here, hang on to the boys."

Robert quickly crossed the last few feet to the shaft collar and motioned for two men who were coming over on the run. The wind-storm coming up the shaft took his hat off and blew open his coat. "I think there's a broken air line, Ed! Close the valve on the main!" he shouted over the din and pointed. "Al, signal for the cage." Before the miner could reach the call switch, the sounds around them abruptly changed as the lights flickered out, and nearby electric motors spooled down. Still gripping the switch arm that sends sig-nals to the hoist operator, Al met the astonished look of his friend Ed and then turned to their boss, who was crouched at the edge of the shaft, looking down.

As they looked on, Robert seemed to come to a decision and suddenly stood up, closed his heavy canvas coat with a couple of buttons and stepped down onto the emergency ladder that followed the shaft into the mine. Just as his head was about to disappear below the edge of the shaft collar, he stopped and locked eyes with Johnny. The roar of water and debris rushing into the mine from somewhere far below was so loud that neither man tried to speak. John mouthed the word "NO" and shook his head slowly, knowing full well that his father would do whatever was humanly possible to save his men, and failing that, he would likely perish with them. He knelt down, pulled Willy and Roy into his arms, and held their heads against his chest. When he looked up, his father was gone.

Arielle was only half paying attention to Rosemarie's ram-blings. Her seemingly endless capacity for talking about herself, her possessions, her talents or the shoes she got on sale at Gately's, had long ago bored Arielle to the point that now she simply tuned her out and made no attempt to interject a thought of her own into the one-sided conversation. Instead, she leaned against the passen-ger side door of Rose's car and watched George as he sat next to her father-in-law's car in front of them. His unwavering attention was focused on the last point in the distance where his master had disappeared.

Rose broke off her chatter for a moment at the sound of the two muffled explosions. "Just routine," she said when Arielle looked over at her. As she began to launch back into whatever she had been talking about, they gradually became aware of a low, continuous rumble that rapidly increased in intensity until they could feel the vibrations through the car seat and hear something rattling under the hood. Rose gripped the steering wheel and strained forward, looking for a reassuring sign that would quell her rising uncertainty, but instead, she saw John running toward the shaft house. "There's trouble," she cried, throwing her door open and jumping out. Without waiting, she took off at a fast trot and had covered almost half the distance before Arielle could catch up.

"Wait! What's the matter?"

Rose didn't slow down, but when she turned to answer, before she could get a word out, the steam whistle high up in the headframe began issuing repeated shrill blasts declaring an emergency and striking fear into the heart of every wife and mother for miles around.

By now, the dayshift men who worked aboveground were gathering around the shaft house, eager to know the fate of their friends and relatives underground and even more eager to go to their aid. When Rose and Arielle arrived, these same men gently but firmly kept them back away from the shaft. From the first sign of trouble, both women were anxious to be reunited with their children, but only now was the scope of the disaster beginning to sink in, especially for Rosemarie. Not only was her biological father killed in a mine accident when she was a little girl, but now Jake and Billy were underground and in harm's way somewhere between here and the Lloyd-Morris mine a half-mile away. Her sharp intake of breath and the stricken look on her face prompted Arielle to reach for her hand. "Jake and Billy are down there," said Rose and she began to sob.

John suddenly became aware of the men pressing in behind him and stood up. With the boys in tow, he pushed his way through the miners and was gratified to find Ari and Rose standing a few feet away.

"Hang on to these two and make sure they stay out of the way. Pop's down there trying to figure out what happened, and I want to stay close in case he needs me," said John. Roy was clearly frightened and would be manageable, but Willy was headstrong and curious. When he turned to go, Arielle grabbed his sleeve.

"Your brothers—" is all she got out before a wrenching crash from deep in the mine drowned out her words. John turned away at the sound but then looked back at her. In that instant before he broke away, she saw crushing despair flood his eyes, the kind of despair they both prayed they would never feel again. Once more the miners parted and let John through. In the few minutes that he was away, Ed Hillman and Al Tippett, unable to stand by and do nothing, began descending the emergency ladder to see what had become of Robert.

John crouched at the top of the ladder and watched the glow of their lights get smaller and smaller until they were completely swallowed up by the infinite darkness. There was a flurry of angry curses behind him, and suddenly George was at his side. He crouched on the edge of the shaft, gave out several sharp barks, and then backed up and charged the edge again. The crazy look in his eyes reminded John of army mules caught in the open during an artillery barrage. After several more runs at the open shaft, he dropped down on his front elbows with his paws dangling over the edge, threw his head back, and gave out a mournful howl. John could have easily reached out and grabbed his collar—but he didn't. He once stood on the edge of his own abyss at Belleau Wood and back then, he had taken the leap into almost certain death to get revenge and to go wherever Matt had gone; he accomplished neither. It wasn't a leap of faith, but a leap that held the promise of sweet oblivion. There were men who didn't take the leap but wished they had; in the moment, they chose life over all else. They came home, but they had already begun to die a little each day until eventually, it just didn't matter anymore.

The hollow echo of shouts coming from the shaft broke the spell for George and pulled John back to the moment. There was another rending crash that shook the ground, and suddenly Al burst out of the shaft and sprawled on the ground gasping for air, followed immediately by Ed and then a man John recognized as Rutherford Wills. Wills collapsed on the cold concrete of the shaft collar after his desperate eight-hundred-foot climb up the mud-caked ladder. He lay there struggling to breathe and writhing in agony from muscle cramps. Ed knew all eyes were on him, but he couldn't speak. He looked at John and shook his head and then rolled on his back and closed his eyes.

When George flew by on a dead run and plunged into the crowd of miners, Willy jerked his hand away from his mother and took off in pursuit. Arielle recovered quickly from her surprise and gave chase, fully expecting the men to once again bar her way, but this time no one dared to challenge her. Perhaps it was the look of icy determination on her face, or her complete lack of fear, but the way forward opened, presenting her with a sight that she would carry with her for the rest of her life. On the far side of the ten-by-fourteen-foot shaft opening, lay three exhausted miners. On the near side of the shaft, kneeling on the very edge looking down, was her husband. Willy stood next to him with one hand on his father's shoulder and the other gripping George's collar. He, too, was leaning forward and looking over the edge. Arielle's first impulse was to rush forward and pull both of them back, but their precarious spot so close to the brink stayed her hand. As she looked on, the rumbling beneath her feet began to subside. Water, quicksand and debris made the final rush into the last untouched places in the mine, forcing out the remaining pockets of air and pushing it up the shaft like the dying breath of some great underground beast. John wrapped his arm around Willy and they pressed forward. Their hair was blown straight back, and their clothes flapped wildly as they squinted into the foul wind. It was 11:43, twenty minutes after the miners on the first level detonated the last two charges before breaking for the noon meal. In just twenty minutes, fifty-one men who had no more on their minds than the food their wives had packed in their dinner pails and a quiet smoke, were lost.

When it was clear to John that no one else would be coming up the ladder, he rose slowly like an old man and took Willy's hand. When they turned away from the shaft, Arielle was right there in front of them with a bewildered look on her face and her arms hanging limp at her side. John wrapped an arm around her shoulder and pulled her into a hug while holding Willy tight to his leg with the other.

"It's over, Pop's gone ... they're all gone," he whispered into her ear. They stood rooted to the spot for several long minutes while John gathered the strength to move on. As soon as they were clear of the rapidly growing throng of people from nearby mines and the town, they saw Rosemarie keeling in the orange mud sobbing and pounding her fists on her thighs. Roy was pressed to her back with his arms around her neck and crying too, though he didn't know why. Arielle squatted down in front of Rose and grabbed her hands, trying to break into her hysteria and get her to stand when suddenly Jacob stepped out of the slowly shifting crowd and trotted over. He looked quickly at John for answers and then knelt beside Rose and with a hand on each of her damp cheeks, gently turned her head toward him. When she realized who it was she collapsed into his arms. John knelt and put a hand on his brother's back.

"Where's Billy?" he said. Jacob turned and looked at him as if he didn't understand the question.

"I don't know. He never showed up this morning. The new fella they sent out, Hillman I think, said Anna phoned to tell them Billy was a little under the weather." The brothers shared a knowing look. Hillman and the Cap set out to do the inspection on the connecting drift about an hour ago. How bad is it?"

John looked down at the ground between his knees. "It's bad. The mine filled with water so fast only one man got out. Pop's down there ..."

Jacob stared at him for a moment and then slowly turned away and closed his eyes as he held Rosemarie tight.

A week passed and efforts were still underway to pump the water out of the Barnes Hecker and recover the bodies of the fifty-one men still unaccounted for. The best guess of the Cleveland Cilffs engineers as to the cause of the sudden inundating rush of water was that the last blasting had opened up a vug or large underground crevasse filled with water. Above ground, over that area on the first level, there had been a large swamp. Immediately following the disaster, the swamp had simply disappeared into a massive sixty-foot-deep hole that quickly backfilled with water, creating a small but deep lake. William Mathers threw every available company resource into the recovery operation as well as into the task of helping the families of the lost miners. They had succeeded in clearing the shaft down to the first level, eight hundred feet below ground, when yet another failure again filled the mine with water. At that time it was determined that recovery efforts were too risky, and Mathers ordered the shaft sealed permanently with concrete.

A pall had fallen over the Castor house on Strawberry Hill, just as it had on many other households in every ethnic neighborhood in Ishpeming and Negaunee; in fact, everyone on the Marquette Range felt the loss and shared the feeling "there but for the grace of God go I." John, Arielle, and their boys came for supper every evening and stayed the night so Elizabeth would not be alone. Willy had been very quiet since his grandfather's death, but still he left no stone unturned as he tirelessly explored every room and every closet in the big house. His favorite place by far, though, was the small out-building they all referred to as the "chicken house." It was built around the same time as the main house by old Uncle Henry, whose fried chicken was legendary and still spoken fondly of at church potlucks by the few parishioners old enough to remember. Back then there were no neighbors on Strawberry Hill to object to a crowing rooster. Somewhere along the line, the "chicken house" had been converted to a storage shed and workshop, even though it had been many years since anyone had done more than store a shovel or rake in it. Willy spent hours puzzling over the rusty tools that hung from the walls or that lay in the rafters overhead. Even at his tender age, they whispered to him across the generations.

Although Willy was constantly on the run during daylight hours, the baby, Paul, was more of a captive audience and was never more than an arm's reach away from his grandmother. Arielle and John were happy to share the boys with Elizabeth and took the opportunity to go on long, slow walks around town, quietly arm in arm.

With the exception of Robert's empty chair, every place at the dining room table was occupied, giving this special gathering the feel of Sunday dinner. Elizabeth was content to dote on Paul and let her three daughters prepare and serve the meal, mostly a job of assembling the latest dishes and baked goods dropped off by neighbors and distant well-wishers alike; Robert had touched many lives with his easy manner and genuine concern for the welfare of the miners. On this night they were expecting someone from the Cleveland Ciffs home office who would go over Robert's will and survivor benefits. It was the final bit of unfinished business.

"What time is the suit from Ciffs' Legal Department supposed to be here?" said Billy between mouthfuls from across the table.

"I told him to get here at 6:00 and we could discuss things over coffee." John looked back down at his plate and resumed picking at his food. The thing he found most troubling about the state of his father's final affairs was the finality.

Jacob had his head down as well but made no pretense of eating. He felt a discreet kick on the side of his foot. "Jake, you eat something before it's stone cold. You're setting a bad example for Roy," exclaimed Rosemarie under her breath. Jacob nodded slowly without looking up, stabbed a couple of string beans, and dragged them through his applesauce before lifting them to his mouth.

Just then John was startled out of his thoughts by the front door buzzer, and a look from his mother sent him to answer it. When he pulled the door open and saw who it was, he was momentarily speechless.

After an awkward silence, the man spoke. "Hello, Johnny, may I come in?" he said.

"Mr. Mathers, of course, please come in!" replied John. "I'm sorry, we were expecting someone from the legal department." Mathers nodded and squatted down to scratch old George behind the ears. After putting the older man's hat and coat on the hall coat-tree, John led the way to the dining room. When they came around the corner from the parlor, Bill jumped to his feet so suddenly it alerted everyone else and prompted Jacob to stand as well. Mr. Mathers bent slightly at the waist, took Elizabeth's offered hand between both of his, and spoke a few quiet words of greeting before continuing on around the table, acknowledging each family member with a friendly nod. Everyone's name, even the children's, came easily to him.

Once the preliminaries were out of the way, everyone seemed to realize at the same time that the only empty place at the table was Robert's. Mr. Mathers took in the empty chair and untouched place setting and for once seemed a little nonplused. As he began to cast about for another option, Elizabeth reached up and took his hand. "It's OK, William, please, sit here," she said. When he was settled in, Elizabeth pushed her chair back, but before she could stand, Arielle and Anna got to their feet and headed to the kitchen to prepare the coffee. At first Rosemarie hung back, afraid she might miss some key exchange, but she quickly changed her mind and joined the other ladies when she realized not doing so would draw unwanted attention.

When everyone was settled back in, Mr. Mathers took a sip of his coffee and slid a stack of papers out of an expensive-looking, dark brown bison valise with brass appointments that lay on the table in front of him. The papers were held in four identical bundles, fastened with a large paper clip in a precise manner so they aligned vertically. For no other reason than to satisfy his own curiosity, he glanced quickly at Rosemarie under his brow while holding his head in such a way that he appeared to be reading the topmost page. He could almost see the wheels turning as she counted the shiny paper clip tongues.

"Before we begin, if I may, there are a couple of things I'd like to say. In the future, if there's anything any of you need, any way I or the Company can help, I hope you won't hesitate to let me know. " Mathers paused for a moment and then went on. "The loss of your father will be a blow to Cleveland Ciffs.

His experience and the way he had with the men just can't be replaced, but much more than that, he was a cherished friend, a best friend, and I will miss him dearly."

There was a long silence as everyone waited for him to gather himself and move on. Finally, he sighed, and one by one, handed out the copies of the will, one to each of the boys and one to Elizabeth. He gave everyone a moment to look over the summary on the first page and then glanced at Rosemarie again to gauge her reaction. What he saw stopped him in his tracks. He had rehearsed in his mind on his way over how he would handle her if there was a bad scene, but to his great surprise there was no anger or indignation. She sat on Jacob's left, leaning into him, their arms intertwined and her head resting on his shoulder. Robert had confided in him about the altered will several times over the years, knowing someday this moment would come and never knowing exactly what to do about it. Mathers smiled to himself, feeling his old friend moving in the room. He looked over at Elizabeth, and she was smiling back at him as she bounced little Paul on her lap.

The somber meeting with Mr. Mathers left John feeling melancholy and in need of solitude. There were no surprises in his father's will, and everyone was relieved, including Mr. Mathers, when they reached the last bequest. The door to his father's home office had been closed since the mine disaster, and up until now he'd been avoiding going in there. When he pushed the door open and switched on the light he was thankful to see that someone had cleaned and straightened things up. The most notable change was the top of the big desk. The stacks of newspapers and overflowing "in" box were gone, leaving just the telephone and the wooden box Peep had given John's father for Christmas back in 1918. Even the ever-present smears from George's nose had been cleaned from the lower panes of the big bay window. Almost as if the old dog was following his train of thought, John heard nails clicking on the hardwood floor behind him. When George lumbered over and settled into his favorite spot by the window, it occurred to John that he probably had been waiting days for someone to open the office door.

"I miss him too, boy," he said under his breath as he dropped into the desk chair. George didn't look up at him but rested his head on the low windowsill and blew a sigh out through his lips. John reached out and slid Peep's wooden box across the desk until it rested in front of him. He ran his hand slowly over the lid to feel its smoothness but didn't open it. Instead, he swiveled in the chair and faced the window as he had seen his father do countless times. Arielle's reflection appeared in the glass as she silently padded up behind him on bare feet. She put her arms around his chest and rested her chin on his shoulder. Sorrow was everywhere in this room, in the worn armrests of the chair, the smell of the books that lined the shelves, in the old photographs, but in their image, reflected back to them from his father's window, was the continuum of life, and hope, and purpose. John put his hands over hers and looked out beyond the glass at the dark columns of trees fading off into the murk of Henry's ancient forest. The moon slipped from behind a cloud and in the middle distance, its rays shone through, making the wisps of rising ground fog luminous with the spirits of those who had gone before.

Acknowledgments

I wish to personally thank the following people for their help in creating this book:

Lloyd Hevelhorst, friend, historian extraordinaire and fellow member of Battery D, First Michigan Light Artillery.
Sue Boback, President of the Ishpeming Area Historical Society.

Thomas G. Friggens, director of the Michigan Iron Ore Industry Museum in Negaunee, Michigan.

Pam Gianola, friend and confidant.

My wife Maurine for her patience and tireless editing.

Author's Note

On the morning of November 3, 1926 at approximately 11:20, the Barnes-Hecker iron mine near Ishpeming in Michigan's Upper Peninsula was suddenly inundated with water, quicksand, and debris following a routine blasting operation. Fifty of the day-shift miners and a Marquette County mine inspector perished in a matter of minutes. The only survivor was twenty-one-year-old Wilfred Wills, who narrowly escaped death by climbing an 800-foot vertical ladder in about fifteen minutes, an amazing feat of physical endurance. Following the disaster, Cleveland Cliffs put together a team of experienced miners and engineers and attempted to pump out the mine and recover the bodies of the missing men. They had just reached the first level, 850 feet below the surface, when the head office of Cleveland Cliffs suddenly called off the effort and ordered the shaft permanently sealed, citing safety concerns. Within hours of that decision, an underground water dam burst without warning, flooding the mine once again. Ten bodies were eventually recovered, but the rest remain entombed to this day. Mining was and is one of the most dangerous jobs on the planet, so accidents back in those days were commonplace; in fact, unless there were multiple fatalities, many times these accidents were not even considered newsworthy enough to appear in the local papers.

For a better understanding of Michigan's mining history, I would encourage the reader to visit the extremely well-done displays at both the Michigan Iron Industry Museum in Negaunee, Michigan, and, located practically next door, The Cliff Shafts Mining Museum in Ishpeming.

Glossary

drift. A horizontal tunnel extending out from the shaft and used to access the ore body.

level. The elevation of the workings below the shaft, ie. 3700 Level is 3700' below the collar.

headframe. The structure sitting over the shaft that holds the cables, pulleys, and sheaves used to raise and lower the skip in the shaft.

tram. A car on narrow gauge rails used to transport ore from the workings to the shaft.

skip. A bucket suspended on the hoist cables used to bring the ore up the shaft to the surface.

cage. The device used to transport the miners up and down the shaft.

hoist. The equipment that lowers and raises everything up and down the shaft.

shaft house. The structure surrounding the shaft collar

shaft collar. The point at which a shaft intersects the surface.

raise. A vertical or inclined excavation that leads from one level, or drift, to another.

dry. A building where the miner changes into and out his working clothes.

over burden. The ground between the upper level and the surface.

vug. Fissures opened by tectonic activity.

chaux. Plaster or quicklime.

camion. French truck.

boche. Derogatory term for Germans.

soogee. A term for cleaning the deck or paintwork.

THE CASTOR FAMILY TRILOGY
by Frank P. Slaughter

The Veteran

Brotherhood of Iron